VMK

D1197270

COFFEE AT 245 B

Daniel Lilie

Publisher, Copyright, and Additional Information

Coffee at 245 B by Daniel Lilie

Copyright © 2020 by Daniel Lilie

All rights reserved. No part of this book may be reproduced or transmitted in any form or by any means, electronic or mechanical, including photocopying, recording, or by any information storage and retrieval system without the written permission of the author, except where permitted by law.
For permissions contact Entrepôt A at: danfleur5@gmail.com

This book is a work of fiction. Names, characters, places, incidents, and dialogue are products of the author's imagination or are used fictitiously and are not to be construed as real. Any resemblance to actual events or locales or persons, living or dead, is entirely coincidental.

ISBN- XXX-X-XXXXXXX-X-X

Editing by Sharon Brinkman
Cover design and interior design by Rafael Andres

For Melissa, my coffee partner

ACKNOWLEDGEMENTS

Coffee at 245 B is about curatorial obsession, strange families and unfocussed mucking about. It is also about the shifting perspective that comes with age. Small compulsions and interests and observations can be a bulwark against oppressive work and routines. For many people, their best moments lie in fantasy or some kind of unobtanium in the form of a dream profession or spouse or idea that does not come to fruition. I am grateful to have a chance to share some observations with anyone who has a chance to read them.

I also want to thank my editor Sharon Brinkman and my layout and cover design team led by Rafael Andres for producing an elegant looking book. Thanks as well to my friend Patrick Hasburgh who provided intuitive and patient encouragement for my writing.

And thanks for my smart and very entertaining family who brook no fools.

PREFACE

Trevor Herald made a cocktail he invented called a "Kumez." His wife, Paige, taught him to make kumquat syrup with a dash of nutmeg. Fresh grapefruit juice, kumquat syrup, mezcal, and soda in roughly equal proportions unless you felt like doubling something. Shake until frothy with frozen pineapple cubes so it did not become diluted. Garnish with mint. He had just moved into a studio in either the Archstone or the Avalon Garden apartments (why couldn't he remember which?), and the view from his tiny balcony was mostly parking lot and dumpster that gave off a wicked sour milk blast the second the wind shifted. Whenever he was sure it was the Avalon, doubt crept in and he heard the Archstone gremlins murmuring, "Archstone... Archstone..." It would be simple to just look at the sign, the branding, but he wouldn't let himself do it. It was forever thus, a life in purgatory between two goliath apartment companies.

It was dead humid in Westchester County summer, and because of COVID, even eighteen months after the county was moved into phase 4, which was allegedly back to normal, the pool was closed. So he chose to sit in a dirty plastic chair on his tiny balcony nursing a Kumez over a walk in the woods with the mosquitos and ticks. A disease called EEE was a thing now, killing you in a very painful way. Overall, he thought having COVID and EEE and being stung by a murder hornet might be better than living at the Arch-Avalon.

His old boss Rick Nugent would have said something like "hey, Herald, I like your drink. Does it come in a men's version?" He took one of the 10 mg Adderall capsules that was prescribed for Cole's ADHD and pulled it apart, releasing the tiny particles into his cocktail, watching as some floated and some slowly sank.

Trevor recalled thrashing Nugent at squash at the weird and venerable Union League Club. Damn, that club was creepy. White members and black help. Some kind of Reconstruction feel- good project that seemed a perverse parody of what was really going on.

After talking about it for months, bloviating about his skill and how in college he had briefly considered joining the semipro racquetball circuit, Nugent booked a court. Arriving at the club, the doorman, an African American in keeping with club tradition, stepped aside and with an obsequious wave said, "Welcome, Mr. Nugent." Trevor trailed behind as his boss power walked to the lockers. It was a sea of mottled white skin. The locker room smelled like camphor and tuna. And as the old men were in half states of dress and undress, the shirttails of their J. Press oxfords dangling around their saggy balls, a lot of them were eating sandwiches. Ham and cheese, tuna, even peanut butter. Trevor, a white man himself, could only marvel at the profound whiteness of it all.

Warming up, Nugent took awkward, looping strokes. Trevor looked where he could exploit the weaknesses in his game, and it was clear Nugent would have trouble dealing with a high lob serve to the backhand that hugged the side wall and a hard serve to his forehand. Trevor started with a lob, one that arced beautifully and feathered the wall, so limiting Nugent's backswing as to obviate a return with any sort of power. Trevor controlled the depth and pace of the rallies as the match went on, getting to the *T* like a shot and concentrating through his swing to hit his cross courts crisply and rail shots deep. Nugent was panting after the first game, Trevor winning it 9–1. The next game was a 9–0 bagel, and the third 9–2. Nugent bent over double, tugging the hem of his shorts, his face crimson, a lather of sweat dripping onto the speckled rubber mat just outside the court. The rubber, chemical odor from the mat was tinged with the old boiled-wool club smell.

"You okay?" Trevor asked.

"Give me a minute," Nugent said, still doubled over, a nutcracker waiting for a little girl to wind the key. "You're in some kind of shape."

The truth was that Trevor was in decent shape but was also a far better shot maker than Nugent. The boss was red and getting redder. When he asked for a "minute," he had raised his hand like Durán "no mas"–style, as if to say, I am not of this world. The words "myocardial infarction" kept broadcasting in Trevor's head. That's how Nugent would want it colored for interdepartmental emails, the medical name lending a corporate gravitas consistent with Nugent's self-preening. It did appear, for about thirty seconds, that an event of the heart might have been occurring.

At last, he raised his torso inch by inch and tiptoed to the water fountain. Trevor took a seat in an oversize tufted leather banquet, listening to the hollow *thwonk* of the squash balls and the occasional metallic clang of the tin from the other courts. The sounds reminded him of graduate school, squash serving as a release valve for the MBA student population—mostly foreigners—between classes and a night of homework. Smelling the players, the old leather, and the must of rubber mats, Trevor realized that his memory of squash was one of the few things he retained from business school.

Nothing was audible from Nugent, and Trevor had to lean in to see if there was any deflection of the chest cavity. It seemed for a moment that a panting Nugent had seized up entirely. At last he reached over and shook Trevor's hand like a sucker: the ol' finger squeeze.

...His time at Pomander Walk was over. Every new kid they hired had better analytical skills than the ones hired the year before. He saw the job specs the firm put out and didn't even recognize half the terms and requirements even for junior employees: Argus, Primavera, GIS, Yardi, SEO, Python, Ruby on Rails, C+++++. My God, what happened to a firm handshake, a pressed suit, and staring an interviewer in the eye? Trevor knew, and it was confirmed by talking to people, listening to WNYC, reading the *Atlantic* and the *Economist* and the *FT*: jobs were remote, outsourced, given to younger workers, and eliminated to whatever extent possible. The Build America Infrastructure revitalization plan that followed COVID and Biden's win was mostly a boon for the construction industry, but not so much finance or commercial real estate as it had been before.

And there was that off-market opportunity—those didn't come around every day, a funky little building on West Eighty-Third Street between Columbus and Amsterdam Avenues. His ticket out. It survived as it was originally built because it had a recondite zoning designation that couldn't be changed without an exhaustive environmental and use-change application to the city council that would not pass for residential use since access to the building was only through an easement in the alley.

Originally the Lester and Levine Sign Painters Building at 245B West Eighty-Third Street—the "B" a mystery. It was the last underdeveloped parcel on the block, everything else demolished and rebuilt or overbuilt with apartments above a commercial base. The building was small, about twelve hundred square feet, spread out among a ground floor, second story, and a small storage room. The ground floor was not entirely on the ground, but sunken a half story, with a dingy brick plaza pigeon toilet. The ghost of the faded ocher and black intertwined-script L&L logo was still there on the side of the building, visible if you positioned yourself just so, and if the sun was out casting enough ambient light so the black maw of the alley contrasted with the faded oil paint.

L&L brought in steady work after the depression from Horn & Hardart, Robert Hall, Gimbels, Hudson automobiles, and Seiberling tires. Lucille Lester studied sculpture at the Pratt Institute and started designing signs for clients. When she met Morton Levine, a scaffolding contractor, they merged to form L&L. The building was built in 1946 to their specifications, the showroom on the second floor and offices and studios on the sunken first floor. The architect convinced Lucille that by sinking the first floor, they could get an additional six feet of ceiling height, ideal for mock-ups and artistic ambience, along with retaining more privacy from curious gawkers and peddlers. One of the more interesting things Trevor saw during the walk-through with the broker was a pamphlet left on top of an old file cabinet. The Bauhaus typography on the cover read "Inzikhistn," which Trevor found out was a modernist, Yiddish literary circle in the 1920s and '30s, founded by the poet Yankev Glatshteyn.

Trevor had sketched a simple floor plan based on Red Hook. An old Probat would fit perfectly in the half-sunk floor and people could watch the roasting from the main floor. It was a neat plan that needed a mere $750k or so to put in motion.

- 1 -

Paige Herald scoured the country for small fruit producers, the last holdouts against the corporate food cartel. It required introspection and nerves, teasing out detail from laconic stone fruit farmers, many of them from Scandinavian stock, reserved and stolid. She probed to get them to reveal their theories about cultivation, marketing, and production arrangements with distributors and farmers markets. Paige liked to say that fruit writing was like forensic reporting, trying to piece together a crime post facto. The way most fruit was grown these days was a crime, a fandango of managed genetics, pesticide application, and marketing. It galled her that a lot of growers glossed over their complicity with corporate America. Delivering a softball-size red blob designed to withstand a week in a big rig and sit in orthogonal attention at a Piggly Wiggly or Grand Union and be labeled a "hothouse" tomato was deception, as pure and prevaricating as pushing a subprime loan on an uninformed borrower. For every heirloom kumquat she crunched, Paige stared into the face of a dozen dirty farms.

As soon as Trevor moved out, Paige lined up extra help to stay with Cole and Nora. Her parents lived upstate and they were willing to do one weekend a month in Tarrytown, and maybe a little more here and there. She told Trevor she was going to her parents' for Thanksgiving but dumped the kids with her folks and flew to spend the weekend in San Francisco with her friend Sondra Taylor. Even before Trevor moved out, she was pestering Paige to leave him and movc in with her in San Rafael. "Just as roommates," Sondra said.

They were at the SFMOMA, staring at Pieter Hugo's photograph "Mallam Mantari Lamal with Mainasara," a Nigerian rough boy kitted out like an extra in *Spartacus*, his two hundred–pound spotted hyena chained and muzzled into strange submission, looking like a spaniel knackered from a hunting trip. Apparently in Nigeria this was a thing, toughs earning a living from parading exotic animals—mostly hyenas—in public places, extorting a few naira, or better yet dollars, for a chance to pet the animals, drugged or beaten into submission.

"Weird and freaky," Paige said, "but I can't take my eyes off these."

Sondra looked at Paige and moved closer, into Paige's personal space. "Yes. I keep looking at them like they're dogs, but they're not. They're huge and feral and their mouths are huge. Aren't hyenas polysexual or ambisexual or bimorphic or, you know, the thing that Jamie Lee Curtis was born with..."

"You mean hermaphrodites? I think so. At least when they're younger. Supposedly you can't tell which is which for a while. Look at that thing. Something so desperate and cruel about it. It reminds me of slavery. You think we're so troubled. You have an article on deadline, or your Brazilian wax stings, or your feeble husband forgot to get you the right kind of gluten-free bread, the one that doesn't taste like rodent shit in the rodent-gray wrapper, but we're just swinging free."

"I love that about you. Really, that's what I love. You sneak off from your family for the weekend to go cross-country, to come see these photographs with me. I mean, no one's spontaneous like that. No one." Sondra turned her face toward Paige. She had slipped a Tic Tac in, so there was no worry there. She thought she saw Paige's upper lip quiver, hover for just a fraction of a second, enough to receive a kiss, but just as quickly Paige sidestepped to the next photo, eyes fixed on the hyena man.

"Damn," Paige said, "one thing's for sure. If you live in Lagos and drag a huge hyena around all day in big chains, you don't need a gym. These guys are ripped. Makes you wonder."

"Doesn't do a thing for me, girlfriend." Maybe sounding like she was on her way in or out of juvie would do the trick. If you were flirting with the idea of taking up with a woman, why would you want her to be like your Dockers-wearing, train-commuting, flatulent, sports-watching husband? "Don't get me wrong. He's hot in a black Spartacus kind of way. I wouldn't kick him out—"

"I wouldn't either," Paige said. Thank God, Sondra thought. She couldn't have finished that thought convincingly, had hung herself out to dry. What did this woman want from her? She had a gift, albeit a strange one, of probing the reproductive exigencies and genetic provenance of the fruits of the world, roaming from Modesto to Kerala to Ankara to Jaffa, knitting modern agronomy with ancient cultivation into ten thousand–word nail-biting articles that left you as breathless as a taut thriller.

"It's a strange thing, being married," Paige said. "You just go along, fitting yourself into a box, and convincing yourself that it's great, your reality. Then you wake up one day and you're clammy and sweaty, and something's gnawing at you and you're looking at your husband and getting twitchy. What's wrong? you're wondering. Like that scene in the movies when Danny DeVito is talking about how every tiny thing Rhea Perlman does is driving him batty. You're thinking life is imitating art, and like Thoreau said, life is an art, and you're not living it because of the guy sitting across from you licking blackberry jam off his pinky."

They left the exhibit and headed down to the café. It was one of those days when San Francisco teemed with couples picking at avo toast and microgreens. It took long enough after COVID-19, but people were back, museums were back. Everyone a tad further away, some still wearing masks against medical advice, but what could you do? Sondra had worked hard on her fit, choosing the buttercup-yellow Hermès scarf with a petunia motif. She put her hair up and plucked her eyebrows into a fetching arch and, frankly, felt about as feminine as ever since she had left Stanford. Paige wore gold cat-eye specs and Lulu yoga pants that worked to full effect, showing the results of her stepped-up Pilates routine. She and Trevor had bantered back and forth about whether there was such a thing as stretching your muscles. He insisted it was a Pilates cult thing, your muscles being your muscles, but she was sure she could feel it, seeming taller and lankier and noticing her butt deflecting more acutely from her waist. "Look at my butt," she told Trevor, who looked and looked but was resolute. "You can't make your muscles longer, and you definitely can't make your butt longer, if that's what you're getting at." She didn't miss Trevor, but she missed moments. His chronic aches and pains, an array of dings, bruises, lesions, sports injuries, and calamitous conditions, born from nothing. He began to resemble a comedy routine, a comedic type of psychotic ranter, rasping and spitting with his mouth on top of the mic: "You know what I hate? Doing jack shit and waking up injured."

- 1 -

"You should do Pilates with me. At least it'll take your mind off your perceived problems. It's hard to ruminate when you're bent like a pretzel and pumping your legs."

"Your husband," Sondra said, "you're thinking about him, aren't you?"

Paige pulled her headband off, shook out her hair, and smoothed everything, petting herself. "Why did you think that?"

"Maybe because he moved out. Maybe because of that barista..."

"Cat Gjertsen?"

"Was that her name? Sexy name."

Sondra was a thoroughbred, her lacrosse-player legs rippling through her skinny jeans, which, if you were getting technical, she shouldn't have been wearing, the knobby bulges from her quadriceps femoris protruding through the denim. She was formidable, taking up extra space, a double major in English and some tech subject that Paige kept forgetting, quadratic or linear something or other, the thought of commingling good literature and complicated math as appealing as anchovy paste on ice cream to Paige. But Sondra kept kissing up to her, telling her how brilliant and analytical her writing was, how she nailed the science part, the biogenetic aspect of things. Paige knew it was a ploy, unwarranted flattery.

In her weaker moments, which was to say when she was having alcohol, not wine, but tequila or something,

Paige convinced herself that she wanted to strip off Sondra's clothes just for the spectacle of it.

"Guilty. What are you going to do about it? He's still my husband for God's sake. For a while, anyway. Poor guy had to move to Elmsford next to the train tracks. Weird—he doesn't know himself if it's the Archstone or the Avalon. And he's a city guy—must be killing him."

"Sounds like everything... and anything is killing him."

"Yeah. He was mumbling something on the phone about hemorrhoids. I guess his dad had Thanksgiving catered by some crazy fancy caterer. Sounds plausible for LA. When I picture LA, I don't see a lot of warm and homey kitchen scenes, families gathering around while the turkey roasts. Then again, it's not such an SF thing either."

"I like what we did. Cocktails and a bistro dinner. Spared me from going to Noe Valley to my aunt's house. Not sure if I can handle that anymore. My uncle's drinking caught up to him, and he just sits around with this nasty BO while they bicker. Gross."

"Oh yeah. You don't see that train coming 'til your married. One day you're picking out cool furniture; the next day you're wondering how he makes those teeny-tiny wheezing noises at night. You are wondering whether they can technically call it homicide if you accidently smother him with a pillow. 'Officer, I was just spooning him and didn't realize he was struggling.' I have the same aunt living in Norwalk. Same split-level with the three little windows on the front door running in a diagonal. She's seventy-eight and smokes in the exact same spot on the sofa where she's been rooted for the last thirty-five years. Gets the mail at precisely one twelve. Opens up the Fetzer Chardonnay—handier now that it comes in a box—at five twelve. My uncle's been checking out for the last twenty years. They could be bowling pins to each other."

"Bowling. I used to love bowling. Remember duck pin bowling? Those little stubby things? Whatever happened to that?"

Paige looked confused. "Can't say I remember duck pin bowling. Maybe it was a Vermont thing."

"Vermont? I thought it was a New York thing."

"Why does everybody assume everything's from New York? Pickles, cheesecake, Caesar salad, duck pin bowling. It's a big country. Fruit's like that too. No one seems to know where stuff originates. Apples? China probably. Oranges? Middle East. Dates? Figs? Middle East, of course, biblical foods. We're good for corn, some blueberries, and that's about it."

"What's your favorite fruit, or three favorites? Your desert island fruits?"

"They're all fantastic at their peak, grown right, with perfect weather. But for a desert island I'd have to pick Golden Russet apples from Samascott Orchards, Fuyu persimmons from the Japanese guy with the tunic and that wabi farmers cap who sets up early in San Luis, and

Meiwa kumquats, which are a lot sweeter than those oval Nagamis, which are little acid bombs. Don't you just love the sensation of swallowing something whole? They're like little balls without the hair. So cute." Paige squinched her face up as she said "cute," which kind of rankled Sondra, who also didn't love the balls analogy. "Oh, and I forgot about the Dekopon mandarins, seedless and spectacular."

"Didn't you write about those having a tendency to split open?"

"Not those, babe, the Gold Nugget mandarins. Those can go pretty easily at the stylar end."

Babe. So that's the way it was. Talk about her husband, then the ball reference, then the gratuitous use of "babe," just for shits and grins. By rights Paige should be gay, purely gay, an opportunity now to split away from stifling Westchester County—there were barely even any farmers markets there, it snowed half the time, and the woman made her living chasing down citrus growers. Sure, she had kids, but they grow up eventually, and what's his name—Trevor, Cal, whatever—seemed like the domestic type.

"You should move out here. Easy pickings for you on the Central Coast."

"Ha! The courts would take a dim view of the kids flying back and forth to California, unescorted. Maybe in my next life."

"Whatever. You're cool either way. I don't click that well with folks out here. SF, for all its charm, is not the convivial paradise, all coffee shops and North Beach bohemian bonhomie, that East Coasters think. I had to take a continuing-ed course on the hill at Golden Gate, and it was July. And the fog rolled in, and I swear it was sleeting—in July! You need your car out here, and Union Square and the piers are colonized by dopey tourists, and there is too much curation, too much focus on the culinary scene, too much introspection and backlash against breeders. I'm not a breeder, but I'm smart enough to know that without kids, who's going to give you an IV or invest your money or take out your trash? The straight women are dikey, and the dikes are chic; I can never figure it out. And everyone thinks I'm straight. I think I'm straight half the time. I want you to think about it. About you and me."

"Ok," Paige said, stripping off the cat eyes and noticing, for the first time that day, that Sondra had put a lot of effort into her grooming that morning.

- 2 -

After settling in Queens in 1946, Hugo Herald (né Hesterwald), Trevor's father and Hakoah Vienna attacking midfielder, trained at the Maspeth Oval with its rock- hard ground and bitter cold swirling wind. When Hugo complained about running in the cold mud, Benny Hesterwald reminded his son about the old country, toughing out encounters with thugs and fans who threw coins and bottles and lit cigarettes at them. Benny taught Hugo how to hold off a defender, made the boy play one-on-one, showed him the art of striking the ball just off center to effect a right or left swerve. He taught him the "dark arts" of where and when to elbow an opponent in the ribs or leave a knee by accident-on-purpose in the balls. Benny himself had flyer speed, in his prime dashing past opposing flank players and whipping the crowd into chanting his number, "Sieben, Sieben," when he cut inside and unleashed his booming shot or raced outside and delivered a cross. Like his father, Hugo was two-footed, something that always kept defenders at bay. With a player who always wanted to get the ball back on his favored foot, a smart defender would start to overplay the strong side. Not with the Hesterwalds. Always clever, always scheming was what they said about Benny. When Benny came up through the youth ranks and took his place in midfield next to Bela Guttman, Hakoah fans knew they had something special.

Hugo joined Hakoah's youth side when he was twelve and made the senior team at sixteen. Benny was still starting for Hakoah in 1920, a star even at thirty-eight, a marvel in a time when most guys were hanging up their boots at thirty. He ascribed the longevity to a vegan diet. After a game in Silesia, Germany, Benny and a couple of other Hakoah players were bored and saw an article in the paper about a man named Rudolf Steiner who was lecturing on something he called "biodynamic farming" at Koberwitz. The lecture was closed to the public, but after learning that the men were from the famous Hakoah squad, the organizers let them in. Steiner spoke about the fragility of the food chain, of the need to keep soil nourished, and started to drift away from the subject matter, talking about the spiritual connection between people and their food sources, something that befuddled the peasant stock farmers in attendance. The theories stuck with Benny, and against the odds he became a vegan in a kosher household at a time when meat was a social barometer of prosperity.

Hugo Herald was born in 1926 in Vienna's Favoriten neighborhood. Benny owned the Drill café in Favoriten. Matthais Sindelar played for Hakoah's rival FK Austria Vienna. All of the city's café culture was obsessed with Sindelar: his hair, his position on the pitch, his balance, and most of all his icy cool demeanor in front of the opposing goal. Benny saved a zeppelin pastry for Sindelar after the local derby matches. Quite the sweet tooth that Sindelar. "At least you don't smoke like some of those guys," Benny told him. Drill was pastry heaven, boats of whipped cream and pots of coffee served in between the broadsheets that traveled from table to table.

By that time Hugo had made the first team for Hakoah as a number 8—an attacking midfielder in the scheme set up by the Scotsman Jimmy Hogan. Hogan came to Central Europe, and Hakoah specifically, to spread the gospel of his newly invented "W-M" system that arranged players in a symmetrical formation that formed the basis for soccer tactics for the next several generations. The W-M was an attack-oriented scheme that relied on the flexibility and endurance of the central players to read the game. Bela Guttman, a Hungarian Jew who fled the White Terror in his home country, was the mastermind at the point of the W, and Hugo was his counterpart in the M.

Hakoah clinched the first professional Austrian League championship in late May of 1925. Hakoah's goalkeeper, Alexander Fabian, broke his arm but continued to play in the game, resuming at forward. Remarkably he scored the winning goal. The players were all at the Drill until late, and Benny closed the shop in the early morning after the last reveler left.

Two Christian Social Party men walked up on either side of him.

"How was your celebration?" one asked.

"Fine—what do you want?" Hugo asked.

"We thought you'd never ask. Business is good at the Drill, no?"

"Why do you ask."

"We don't like it so much. The coffee is bitter and the dishes not so clean. Oh, and there are far too many Hakoah supporters for our taste."

Benny started to walk faster.

"Oh, and we are not keen on Jewish soccer teams. England or maybe America might want your clown act."

* * *

"Dink und Dunk? What is that?" Hugo had asked when they turned on the Cowboys game later on Thanksgiving Day. Trevor was muttering about dinking and dunking becoming common in the NFL.

"It's when you throw a whole bunch of short passes. You try to get a few yards at a time. It gets kind of boring if they try it all game."

"Your grandfather Benny played Dink und Dunk. But with a twist. They used to say he would lull a defender to sleep and then... boom! Change gears like a Ferrari with all that low-end torque, such beautiful machines. He was a goal scorer, your grandfather. A real goal scorer."

The convergence of the two footballs. Trevor loved them both. Hugo played with the senior Prospect Unity team, and then quit, not quite good enough to make money at it. Queens was changing even back in the 1940s, baseball being king, but football and basketball and even hockey gaining, with the Rangers taking up residence in the new Garden in 1927; Tex's Rangers they called the team, for the owner, and the name stuck. Rangers in Manhattan, weird and wonderful to conjure the image of a bunch of Mounties with hockey sticks patrolling lower Midtown, but the dicey neighborhood around the first and second iterations of Madison Square Garden sure could have used it in the late sixties and seventies when you kept looking behind you and in front of you walking from the surface lot to the arena's entrance, which never seemed to come on a cold December night. Hugo took little Trevor to a couple of games a year, driving across that cool bridge, the Queensborough, which sloughed off the Queens dandruff with a regal flourish that yielded the Upper East Side. Hugo would point the nose of his

Coupe de Ville south on Fifth ("Never take Second, too many cabs," he told Trevor), and they would bomb down to Forty-Sixth and head west to Ninth, then south again to the same lot.

"But Dad, the one on Eighth is the same price and a lot closer."

"Yes, but the best chestnuts are on Ninth." Those were a beautiful thing, the chestnuts, roasted in foil on coals and plucked from the steel sliding door as if they were a delicate soufflé, and who could argue? Unlike coffee, where they had to draw deeply on imagination to proffer the flavor notes, the persimmon tang and crème brûlée, the honeysuckle denouement, the chestnuts served by street vendors at Madison Square Garden in the early 1970s had the complex umami structure of the most pedigreed terroir-suckled food on the planet. Sweet and savory, buttery and nutty, they peeled the bitter black-brown skin from the nuts as they walked, noses dripping from the wind, their coats whipped up behind them, Hugo eyeing the crevasses to avoid the punks and dope fiends and pimps lurking for an easy score.

- 3 -

Trevor's trip to LA started with an iPhone cricket chirp at 3:30 a.m. that shook him from the penumbral depths of a cleansing dream that had him at the center of a mandala and armed with a crossbow. For ten fitful minutes, Trevor mounted an aerial assault on a fortress. He had been floating on his white steed, sifting through white sugar clouds toward his destination. JetBlue left at six thirty, and the backward math made a three thirty wakeup essential, especially with the new COVID check-in protocol.

As soon as he got off the plane, Trevor grabbed an Uber to Intelligentsia Coffee in Venice. Pre-COVID, Abbot Kinney thrummed with the leggy, salt-air glamour of the daytime leisure class, yoga-fit moms and film types with round-rimmed shades talking about projects. They spent freely and quickly: lunches, puppies, trainers, rubdowns, nails, hair, teeth, tucks, lipo, kiddy stuff, cars. Indulgence in the teeth of yet another recession.

He could have made a day of it in Venice, popping in and out of the shops, but it was the day before Thanksgiving, and Hugo and his Hungarian wife Eileen were hosting a "day before Thanksgiving dinner." Paige was taking the kids to her parents for Thanksgiving and wouldn't that have been awkward.

He sat alone at a gigantic table at his father's house in Los Feliz Oaks. Beatriz, his father's maid, brought a bunch of platters to the twenty-foot-long salvaged factory table, once used by a millenary to stack and cut bolts of felted wool and rabbit fur. The caterer, Lux and Provenance, furnished little ID tags for each dish. Lux and Provenance referred to this food as "South American locavore-pastoral," with an emphasis on foraged, cultivated, and fair-trade food procured with a conscious and conscientious mind.

Trevor stared down at his shoes, Chromexcel brogues, undyed, tanned using the "pull-up" method, wherein the natural tannins in the skins are left in the leather, "stuffed," as it was called in the trade, imparting a very waxy texture. No one wore shoes anymore. COVID was a sneaker and sweats boom. But he spent a fortune on his Aldens and was going to get his money's worth. The pair he wore today was on the cusp of gray and tan, an indescribable color he found irresistible.

At Pomander Walk, shoes were signifiers of status. Cheap shoes betrayed a niggardly worldview, nearly as bad as brown bagging your lunch. Too much shoe, on the other hand, unless you were a senior managing MD, announced you as an overcompensator. In Tarrytown, he had his longwings and wingtips stacked in cubbies. They were two distinct styles that people always confused: longwings, or "gunboats" as they were known on the style boards, having the broguing carried out for the entire perimeter of the shoe, whereas the wingtips, or "short wings," had two distinct brogue patterns, which in the side view described two arches.

Trevor's toe started to throb. Could gout be psychosomatic? It all could be, apparently, or at least that was the opinion of the savant neurologist who had researched specific sites in the brain that created endorphins and had produced a twenty-year study attempting to prove the inverse relationship between positive thoughts and sickness.

Trevor liked substantial shoes made from heavy, waxy leather and thick rubber soles branded Dainite and Vibram and Lactae Hevea. He loved the idea of perforations, a vestigial detail from the bogs and swamps of Scotland, when the holes were essential for drainage. Not that the holes would have kept your feet warm after your leather brogues were soaked in an icy peat bog on a frigid Scotland morning, but it was a charming idea. He had about nineteen pairs, everything from suede to army grain to waxy leathers in colors that you would be proud to wear to the Pai Gow lounge at the Rio, but brogues nonetheless.

Trevor liked watches too, not for bling, but for the patina, watches that were heavy on the wrist with old Valjoux movements, especially his favorite, the bi-compax 7733. Bulletproof. Urban armor. With its V-shaped cam and manual-wind engine, the 7733 was the wrist equivalent of an old FJ Cruiser or Ford Bronco. Trevor believed an old watch parsed and extruded time in a beautiful way. Hugo gave him a watch when he graduated from Columbia, an orange-dialed Doxa that was given as a promotional gesture when he produced *Barracuda* (1969), with Donal Heffernan as a barkeep who fleeced tourists in Barbados. Heffernan wore the watch in the film, a fact that Trevor was happy to tell anyone who noticed it.

It had been a couple of weeks since he'd seen his shoe collection. He had brought one wheelie and a duffel bag to the sublet, hedging bets about whether Paige would change her mind. The apartment was on the fourth floor, finally closer to a train station, this one being renovated with no end in sight. There was an incessant electrical swoosh and brake squeal that permeated the leaky windows. If he left the windows open, he could smell burnt rubber from the brakes, train barbecue along with the dumpster smell. His bags were against the wall in the room, which was bare except for the futon that he stuffed into the back of the 4Runner and lugged up the elevator even though management was super strict about using the freight for that kind of thing. The day he dragged it up, he was reminded of dumpster diving along Broadway freshman year, about as pre-COVID a memory as you could have. In the nineties, if you got out by 5:30 a.m. the day of trash pickup, you could snag some amazing stuff, especially midcentury finds, before everyone discovered the period. Like in college, he had dinner sitting on the futon, eating bean thread noodles with spicy peanut sauce and watching *Family Feud* or *Sports Center* or *Chopped* on the Food Network in case he had to pick up some tidbits to talk to Paige about.

The new place in Elmsford was sort of on the way from Tarrytown to Red Hook. One thing he wasn't worried about was money for Paige to pay the mortgage. Paige had money. They shared accounts, except for Paige's "royalty" account, which she for some reason had set up herself at some credit union. For the new place, he prepaid one month's rent plus security, so with the bit of severance from Pomander Walk, there was about a six-month cushion before he'd be cash-strapped.

Reduction in force. Trevor had never heard the term before he caught some corporate shrapnel in the ass. "Fired" used to be the word, but that was so old-school, direct and pejorative, like you couldn't *do* a job, and as everyone knew, except for surgery and accounting and science, where you had to use a microscope, most folks could do any job with a modicum of competence, or at the very least bluff their way sideways for a while. Trevor watched Nugent for signs of life as Debbie slid over papers for him to sign to indemnify Pomander Walk and its subsidiaries, successors, affiliates, et alia from adverse publicity, lawsuits, talking dirty about Pomander Walk or any of its officers, performing audacious acts of parkour in the windswept plaza, or giving Nugent the behind-the-back finger on the way out. In his head Trevor was preparing the sanitized version of his ignominious departure from Pomander Walk about how the business model changed and, going forward, Pomander Walk decided to outsource real estate services as an efficiency measure.

Immediately after, as if it was a reflex, Trevor hopped the subway to nowhere and found Red Hook Roasters near the end of Van Brunt. He asked for the owner and said, "I'd like to train to be a barista."

"You're in luck," he said. "See those bags? Stack them behind the roaster and then talk to me." Trevor stared at thirty sacks of Yirgahefe dry processed roast from Ethiopia. They dotted the floor like burlap lilies. He had some Adderall in him and felt strong. Not a problem. He liked the look and feel and of course the aroma of coffee in the sack. Coffee bridged art and science. Coffee cherries needed to be nurtured through sorting and sifting and drying before they were even ready to ship, the preamble to the prelude to the overture that was bringing small sour beans into a state where they were ready to be brewed to life.

If he wanted to ask Hugo to invest, he knew he had to have a convincing story, something more than liking to drink coffee. He needed to be more like that guy Chuck, the volunteer gardening consultant at his kids' school in Tarrytown. Rugged Chuck always had his sleeves rolled up just so for the moms. He built raised vegetable beds from reclaimed Hudson Valley barn wood, varicolored masterpieces that thickened with sunflowers and bean stalks in early September. Chuck would have had schematics, an operating plan, and suppliers lined up.

Hugo's dining table was massive, almost a thousand pounds of weathered six-inch-thick maple top and girded steel underpinnings, and it had to be disassembled and reassembled to fit through the courtyard door. If you were an industry player in LA these days, it wasn't enough just to have a table. The table had to have provenance, a backstory. A team of interior designers, color consultants, architects, furniture makers, and landscape architects saw to it that Hugo' s home was fanatically curated. It was a working house, model fit and photo ready. Hugo's film career had wound down, but at eighty-four, he still had the energy to obsess over a cause, and a specimen Gregory Ain house devoid of clutter was it.

Trevor heard wet feet on tile. Hugo appeared, rewrapping his towel, accidentally flashing his low-riding genitals. Why was he swimming when the food was coming out? Who was to question Hugo Herald? It was his house, and he had every right to stand naked in his Gregory Ain–designed courtyard doing nothing. Oddly, his father paired driving loafers with the bathrobe. Trevor stared at the rubber soles with a hundred little nipples.

"I should only be around for another twenty Thanksgivings," Hugo said as he finally came to the table. His robe had the words "The Venetian" embroidered on the chest. Beatriz came, lickety-split, asking "Mr. Hugo" if he would like a drink. Her gray A-line shift was embroidered "WOLF BRAND—FROM TABLE TO INDUSTRY."

Trevor wondered whether all of America was required to wear clothing with writing on it? Clothing with writing was a signifier, a division of the classes. Anywhere public—rest stops, Vegas, the mall, the airport—eight out of ten people were walking billboards. He had a theory that original thought began to decline with the advent of words on clothing. When did it start? Was it sometime in the seventies when hippies started expressing themselves with silkscreen machines, pressing wet batches of jockey shirts for five bucks a pop at campus concerts? But whereas it was once a novelty to display one's affection for a tribe, it was now so commonplace as to be invisible. And tattoos had started the descent into advertising from what had once been a purely graphic depiction of something relevant. Today you had Disney and Apple and sports teams inked into limbs across America. For three hundred bucks, any schmo could park his Ford Escape at a suburban tattoo joint, entering as a regular person and emerging as an unpaid brand avatar.

Trevor took out his 2.0 readers and saw what first looked like rice was actually farro with caper velouté, Thai basil, and flash-fried lovage. Paige would have loved this food. Next to that was caviar—hackleback, with smoke vapor and sunchoke crème fraîche. Beatriz was unfazed. She plunked down the platters like she still needed social distance. Whoa, sister, that stuff is $250 a plate. Could have been mac 'n' cheese for all she cared. But Trevor did notice she was packing stuff up in the kitchen, making it look like she was serving, but strategically loading up an insulated cooler bag. That was a thing with domestic help: you had to *watch* them according to the Pomander Walk managing directors who referred to the nannies as "the cartel."

Trevor could not help hearing Henry Kissinger every time his father spoke even though he had been in the U.S. for almost two-thirds of a century. Hugo looked every bit the aged Hollywood prince: browned skin that covered him seamlessly from feet to bald noggin, which was splotched with red liver spots. He had taken to collecting terry-cloth clothing, a lot of it stolen from hotels, and mostly wore pastel-colored shorts with black sleeveless undershirts.

Before Trevor's eyes, or rather away from Trevor's eyes, since he lived three thousand miles away, Hugo had changed into a full-blown Angelino. This from a man who came to the U.S. to play soccer, became a union steamfitter, and was a live-in superintendent for a big Art

Deco apartment building on the Grand Concourse in the Bronx in the early fifties. The narrative that Trevor recalled was that Hugo lived in a basement apartment strewn with asbestos-wrapped conduit. He was a self-styled New York hobbit, emerging from his lair only to answer frantic tenant calls to unclog toilets and hunt down rats.

"It would have been nice if your sister could have joined us. I could have helped with the airplane ticket," Hugo said.

"I'll let her know for next time, Pop. She's trying to finish her degree and auditioning at the same time. They work them hard at that place."

"They better work them hard for the tuition they charge. Maybe she should have gone to my film school, the Academy of the Streets of Elmhurst."

"You mean the predecessor to Juilliard?"

"Exactly. Film school? Forty-five grand a year? I was a pipefitter for three years before I could afford a Bolex camera. Maybe pipefitting is the best training. You know when I did that hockey movie back in the seventies, someone asked why so many hockey players come from those godforsaken frozen places in Canada. You know why?"

"Why?"

"Because the choices are hockey... or coal mining. So maybe pipefitting and coal mining should be on the curriculum at these fancy film schools. Let me tell you something about pipefitting."

"Yes, you've told us once or twice before—"

"A pipefitter works high-pressure systems, not like a plumber with only water and drain and so forth. We worked boilers, steam, things that explode on a moment's notice." Trevor had heard so much about pipefitting growing up that he had his own fears about exploding hydraulic systems.

"One time, this job at a nursing home, I get a call at two in the morning. There's fizzing in the pipe, the night super tells me. I wasn't union yet, so when a call came in, you put on your overalls, got your tools, and got on the subway. The subways ran once an hour that time of night, so you were there with the bums and the rats. And you can only imagine the filth. Who, tell me, in this day and age, would do a job like that? Getting to the job was too hard for the bums who call themselves laborers today. It's all about the benefits. Who's taking their precious benefits? The corporations, the Republicans, the Chinese. Everybody is taking, and meantime they're not working." And that was before the virus.

Trevor gripped his four-fingered pour of whiskey—cask-aged Tuthilltown Distillery special-edition rye—and warmed it with his hand before gulping half the tumbler. The liquor sloshed back in his throat with a dyspeptic burn. "Fired." That was the word. You could only soft-pedal the concept so much: RIF, layoff, workforce reduction, seasonal reduction, declining business prospects, shift in senior management. It was all an excuse. In the corporate world there were three classes: winners, survivors, and losers. Except that the losers were sometimes the winners because they were liberated to move on, to escape the tyranny of the pipeline, the review, the expense account, and the internal traumas and indignities of the vagaries of making a profit ramified through the foibles of thousands of tiny minds sifting through the ledger of their own insecurities. After the pandemic, every penny was at risk. One false move.

None of this was relevant. He looked around the great room, a vast modernist canvas where the living and dining areas elided into one fifty-foot expanse. The focal point of the room was a custom, amoeboid Vladimir Kagan sofa, offset by two Hans Wegner Flag Halyard chairs, sprung from steel and hemp cord, swaddled in shag wool throws. The floor was butter-smooth concrete, similar in color and texture to Hugo's head. What did this room cost to furnish? Two hundred thousand? Three hundred? More? What was Trevor's ask—a measly $600K? For a 50 percent share of a whole townhome—a tiny townhome—in Manhattan? How could Hugo pass?

Eyeing the museum quality of Hugo's living room furnishings, Trevor was staggered by the disparity in his and his father's living circumstances. If he was still in the will—who knew what was going on with a fairly new wife in the picture—then someday he might come into some money. But except for a smidgen of prostate cancer—and what old guy didn't have it?—Hugo was healthy as an ox. Health was a big bragging point for Hugo. He still got together once maybe twice a year with the old crowd from Thomson Avenue in Woodside, formerly Newtown, Queens. It was a remarkable group, a group of six, now five, after Eli Pfefferman died in '03, but he was just an optometrist, the least creative and entrepreneurial of the bunch. Of the five remaining guys, three were in show business—Hugo; Al Meltzer, who got rich designing advertising posters for Broadway shows; and Ken Bellard, né Isadore Jacobstein, who was still being cast (albeit as the geezer) in midtier action films.

In the eighties into the late nineties, Hugo was quick to point out how successful they were, punks from Queens, detailing the corporate conquests and Hollywood triumphs. But over time, the news briefs started to resemble medical chart updates. Meltzer had begun to forget things, Bellard had a minor stroke, and Art Pozner had COPD and prostate issues and was one of the few to make it off the COVID-induced ventilator in 2020. Trevor did sense that maybe, just maybe, Hugo was starting to slip mentally. No conclusions, but at his age, it was a thing to watch. Eileen, his wife, in her early sixties, had the ginger locks and bust of a classic Hollywood temptress with a torpedo bra. Her dermatology practice was successful, but Trevor couldn't get a sense of what the financial arrangement was between her and Hugo. If there was a prenup, no one talked. A Beverly Hills dermatologist would be expected to be worth more than a fair bit, but around a bill or a dinner check, Eileen's prehensile alligator arms failed to reach as far as the table, helpless to pick anything up.

"Pardon me," Hugo said in a clipped Kissingerial manner as he got up, his canary yellow terry trunks still dripping from the pool onto the polished terrazzo floor. "I'll be back."

With a moment to think, Trevor flip-flopped about what kind of baked goods to carry in the coffee bar. You could not, in this era of superbly conceived and executed high-concept joints like Intelligentsia, Sightglass, Blue Bottle, Four Barrel, and Stumptown offering supremely well-edited little nibbles for nine bucks a pop, just plop a bunch of OBMs (obligatory bran muffins) on a plate and expect any repeat business. On the other hand, keeping a batch of delicacies sourced from artisanal pastry chefs from all over the city could be difficult. In San Francisco, he gorged himself on chewy little almond cannelés de Bordeaux, ethereal morsels with a velvety texture and an orange liqueur. But before he worked on the pastry selections for the place ('Ography Coffee? Wharf Roasters? Bridle Path Coffee?), he had to settle on the ethos. Was it to be a full-service roaster, selling beans B2B and wholesale? Was he a neighborhood coffee company with different bean vendors? A bakery? Small plates? Breakfast and lunch? Veggie, vegan, macrobiotic, dairy only?

Trevor's stomach was a botched mess. He was still on New York time and, wide-awake in the guest room at 2:00 a.m., he had resorted to taking a Lunesta (or was it an Ambien?). This was on top of the two Advil he popped for the pressure headache he had after getting off the plane. Against his better judgment, but as a salve against the clear-air turbulence, he ordered a ginger ale that he knocked back straight instead of sipping because of having to wear his mask. He avoided drinking water on the plane, because if there was a more challenging thing to do than take a piss on a plane when you were superglued to a window seat with four snarling flight servers popping cans of Diet Coke while the plane bumped its way across the flatlands, he was not aware of it. And that damned middle seat now turned around like if someone sneezes, it would just stay around their face. Dehydration and the meds made his stomach roil. Since he was fired a month ago, he was a sure bet to bolt awake during the night with his pillow soaked through. The sweat was abundant and disconcerting. Sometimes even the cool side of the pillow was clammy.

But coffee bars had sugar everywhere. At least most of them did, except for that one place in LA in the Arts District where the baristas looked at you like your eyes were on top of your head if you asked where the sugar was. Maybe he could do a vegan-style menu, with honey or agave as the only sweetener. Honey wasn't vegan anyway. Agave only, then? Agave-sweetened muffins and savory snacks. But no bran. What kind of display case would the shop have? He needed a name for it first. Briefly he thought he would call it "The Schoenberg," after the composer. But maybe Twelve Tone or 'Ography would be better. Cater to the Upper West Side intelligentsia. Except there was barely any such thing left. It was mommy money now. What kind of coffee place did the mommy money want? Farmhouse chic, like Sonoma County.

What did Beatriz bring next? Squash. An orange puree, so he assumed butternut or acorn. The one time of year the caterers were allowed to do squash. Ordinarily squash was the death knell of a party, but on Thanksgiving it was a rite and a staple. He could have a bit of turkey, move it around, and a healthy mound of squash. If Eileen gave him look he might have to have some turkey. He didn't think she liked him, and Hugo didn't like anyone Eileen didn't like. Delicate. And he had to ask for money. Better to do it in front of her. If he tried to wrangle an audience alone with Hugo, she would find out later anyway and queer the deal. He'd have to spill the whole story, how Rick Nugent at Pomander Walk Capital called him into his office overlooking the old Paramount Building in Times Square, the big clock marking 8:35 with its huge Beaux Arts hands and Frisbee-like dial markers, just hanging there, stuck in time like on 9/11 when everything stopped. Trevor stared straight down Nugent's Alden cordovan tasseled loafers (were they color 8, he wondered, or brown calf that he polished to a high gloss?)

while Nugent delivered the preamble to firing. Unlike all the other times, Trevor didn't listen to the words. Nugent seemed to speak encrypted gibberish. No words, just vocal effects. As Nugent spoke, a worker in a climbing harness lowered himself down the façade with a rope, furiously squeegeeing and smearing the window with a rainbow of soapy water. It was gray and drizzling, and the facilities management team at Pomander Walk was still sending small brown men with specious work documentation down to sway and bob thirty stories up so the managing directors could have squeaky-clean windows. The Aldens tapped a steady beat. No doubt Nugent had been pulled into HR the afternoon before, coached to talk from a script. The paperwork was all ready. Sign here if you want your severance, over here to ensure that neither party impugns the other's reputation.

Trevor was convinced that Hugo would like 245B if he had a chance to see it himself. The photos in the brochure taken by Evan Paschman, the building's agent from Fleischmann Woskauer, were too stagey, trying to put lipstick on a pig. It was the desultory patina, the musty realm of abandoned commerce and light industry, that gave the building allure. What could he be doing with a measly $600K that was better?

Fifteen minutes alone at the table and still no sign of Hugo or Eileen, or even Eileen's little living muff, a Brussels Griffon with a lazy eye named Rufus. Beatriz was in the kitchen, talking in singsong interrogative Portuguese, and packing, always packing. Nothing in that language was declarative. Question everything. Next to the squash was another carb platter, individual pies with nicely crimped edges. These must be empanadas of some sort. Who was supposed to eat all of this? Supposedly Eileen's kids were showing up in between going to see friends.

Hugo came back from the bathroom, a dry pair of terry shorts replacing the wet bathing suit. "So nice to have my family getting together. Look at all this delicious food. It's hard to believe that your mother even thought about cooking all these years."

"That was quite a while ago," Trevor said. "I doubt that if she was here today she would think about cooking. I mean, it's so easy to get amazing food delivered to your door, with all the catering in LA. And to think there would be such a socially conscious South American caterer—"

"Yes! Eileen got their number from the woman who brings the drapes. Did you see the drapes? You can only get modern drapes—the real deal like they had in the Case houses—from a couple of places. Drapes and modern are not friends." Hugo picked up his fork and poked and prodded a couple of the plates. "Fantastic," he said, making a plate. "Trevor, why don't you help yourself. You look skinny."

How Hugo was ever a plumber—a *steamfitter*—was a mystery to Trevor when he saw his father in this setting. Hugo piled food on his plate, not really eating, freely letting different foods touch each other, a big no-

no for Trevor, who methodically separated everything on his plate into their own fiefdoms. That's why the coffee cupping process was so gratifying for him, independent small cups lined up for purity checks, teasing out the distinct flavor notes. Coffee flavors were described every bit like wine now. Who knew where the science ended and the pretense began? Persimmon, walnut, peach, cardamom, kiwi, durian, fava beans, leather, sweat. Some were a little more acidic, lots had chocolate in them. The dry-process coffees were too full of astringent tannins for Trevor's taste, but people paid up for them.

But the way the cofferati parsed flavor profiles was as unctuous and silly as the wine people. Then again, his deviated septum was getting worse, causing fitful night breathing and making him prone to sinus infections. It was conceivable that his sense of smell was failing and that others had keener, more precise noses and palates. True, it was exactly the appreciation of coffee as a commodity with provenance and nuance, to be appreciated as much as its revered cousin the grape, that made the dream of creating his fourth- wave concept 'Ography (still debating whether to use the apostrophe; it was distinctive but maybe pretentious) possible, the premise of the whole thing dependent on his father and lender accepting the assumption that a one and one-quarter ounce ristretto shot of espresso would sell all day and part of the evening long for $3.75.

Hugo pushed a plate of antioxidant-rich Japanese sweet potatoes—the purple ones— toward Trevor. "Your grandfather, he was quite a character. My friends would come over and he would ask them if they wanted some fermented vegetables. He had big stinky containers. He called them pickles, but I knew a pickle, and that stuff wasn't pickle. The other guys laughed, and I got the name garlic boy."

"Tough neighborhood. You managed to survive though. And he made a vegetarian out of you too."

"That was nothing. When I was in the Bronx, I would take my lunch out and you know how it is, everyone looking over and seeing what everybody else has to eat. And these other guys, the Germans and the Irish and the Italian guys, are pulling out their meat sandwiches, and they look at poor me and see my vegetables and fruit. 'What's wrong with you, Jewgo? You not a meat guy? You a fruit, Jewgo?' And so forth."

"Is that why you started eating meat?"

"I started eating meat when I realized that we are really just evolved chimpanzees, and that when vegetarian food is in short supply, a chimpanzee will eat meat to survive. If one eats meat to survive, it is almost the same as vegetarianism." Hugo dug into his plate and looked over at Eileen, who had Rufus on her lap. When Trevor was a kid, they had a dog named Pickles, a mixed-breed Lab that Hugo ruled with an iron fist.

Hugo was in the stage of life when everything revolved around his wife's toy dog and spoiled kids. Eileen's kids were smart but calculating. Will was a hydroponic gardening consultant, and Stella had a boutique on Main Street selling eco products. They were following their muse, Eileen said. And cashing their monthly checks from Eileen and, in Will's case, taking several hundred grand from Hugo to buy into Venice.

"So tell me, how is your sister doing?" Hugo asked. "I know she is enrolled because I get the bills."

"Doing how? Personally?"

"Personally, professionally. I hate to see that business degree wasted, but I suppose she needed a change. I keep telling her come to Los Angeles. The beaches, the sunshine. New York is wonderful for just a part of the year. The gloom and the cold and those crowded subways are not for everyone. Your sister has always loved the sun."

"She's doing fine. I'm the one who has had a little course correction."

Eileen perked up at that. Trevor was fifteen years older than her kids, but he always sensed she was keen on competition, always asking Trevor for details about his compensation package when he was at Pomander Walk. "What happened?" she asked. Trevor looked at Hugo and cleared his throat. "Nothing that isn't happening to a lot of people. In a way, we never recovered from the CMBS collapse thing and now COVID and everyone afraid of their shadow. Tough times. Half the workforce is working from home. Commercial property has been cut in half basically."

"You were fired?" Hugo asked, just like that.

"I suppose you can call it that. Honestly, I couldn't stand another day working for the chump I had for a boss. I came on when there was tons of leasing to do. We were knocking down hundred thousand square foot deals like one a day. But when there's that much market dislocation—"

"Dislocation?" Eileen asked.

"When things crap out. Investment bankers use it. I suppose for you it would be like saying a patient has a spot instead of a melanoma."

"So then, when people ask me how my son is doing, I can say he has a dislocation?"

Something Kissinger would have said, Hugo pronouncing "when" like "ven." As a younger man, he fended off the accent, but it was boomeranging back.

"Tell them what you'd like. I'm a dreadful salesperson, to be honest. It's the tyranny of the pipeline that wears on you. When the economy starts to sputter, everyone starts to micromanage. It gets very mercenary. I don't want to be a guy who's only as good as his last deal. And I have a business plan, something new entirely."

Beatriz came to clear the table. She clanged the plates together and looked like she was pissed that she had this gig. Eileen set Rufus down, and he nipped in behind the maid on a scrap hunt. Hugo failed to ask Trevor what kind of business it was. Hugo was losing his taste to engage anyone about anything serious. He earned the privilege to avoid any kind of tension.

"Let me ask you something, Dad. You're from Vienna, right?"

"It depends how one should consider where they are from; I have no memory of Vienna to speak of. Maybe Freud would say my id was formed there. You know the id? A famous idea I never hear about these days. As I recall, the id is formed at about the age of two. And I am rather fond of my id. So then, fine, I will happily admit to being from Vienna."

"Well, Vienna is a great coffee town, and so is New York. I am going to buy a building and open a coffee bar on Eighty-Third Street."

"Hmm," Hugo said, "sounds very expensive."

"No doubt," Trevor said.

Eileen fiddled with her necklace, a crystal cross wrapped in overlapping braids of silver, hemp cord, and pewter. "Aren't there so many of these new coffee places these days? It seems a new one pops up every day. My girlfriends and I are drinking lots of tea. Are you thinking of tea as well?"

"No. Tea is its own thing, a specialty. I love tea, but the two don't play well together. Coffee has terroir, the same as wine. That's one reason you're seeing so many new places springing up. And finally the growers are getting organized and demanding higher prices for better beans. The industry is smartening up."

Eileen swirled her fork around a bit of couscous. "What is it with all these kids who can spend seven dollars for a cup of coffee? I walked into that Intelligentsia on Abbot Kinney with Stella and Will, and they grabbed a few things for the condo, and when I went to pay I almost fainted—a hundred and seventy-eight dollars for a couple of pounds of coffee and a little kettle and beaker that looked like companions for an Easy-Bake Oven. I told your father that a few trips over there would be like a down payment for another condo."

"See," Trevor said, looking over at Hugo, hoping he was tuning in, "that's the trend now. Coastal elites want to be seen, and they want to be seen consuming things when they go out. They want to be perceived as players."

"Oh, it's a scene all right," Eileen said. "I felt like I was back in college, waiting to see if I could get the nod to sit at the popular kids' table. All those writer types sitting and staring to see if you're somebody."

Trevor was losing Hugo. An old man ready for a nap. Beatriz had changed back into civilian clothes. The table was cleared and dessert was set up buffet-style in the kitchen. "Meester Hugo, everything eez set in the keetchen. S'okay for me borrow thee car like I ask yesterday cuz my boyfriend he got another violation and they took heez car right on Sepul-veeda behind Vons and he walks back to our place and I walk today—okay—and take the bus but it was still a beeg walk. 'S no problem eef I drive some and we can get car back tomorrow?"

Crap. Everyone in Hugo's pocket. The moment was gone. Eileen scooped up Rufus, and Hugo was staring at Beatriz, admiring her balls, but also a little shocked that she would ask to borrow his BMW 650 convertible with the custom metallic bronze oxide paint and parchment leather when she knew that he knew that the story about the boyfriend was a lie and that she was just another LA grifter, squeezing him for a little juice and wanting to make her boyfriend happy by getting the boss's car to joyride on the canyon roads on his day off while she caught the sun and pretended she was Natalie Wood.

On the way to the bathroom, Trevor saw a duffle bag under a side table. The zipper was slightly open, and there was something golden and substantial looking inside that made him pause. Unzipping it just a little, he saw a gold statue a little over a foot long. There were two winged figures holding up a stylized globe. It was heavy. He thought about taking it but snapped a couple of pictures and put it back.

Whose bag was it? And had he really seen the Jules Rimet trophy, maybe even the real trophy that was stolen, found, and restolen in Brazil in the 1980s? That Hugo had somehow acquired it wasn't crazy. His dad's old friend Bela Guttman had a posse of scouts in Brazil, one of them landing him Eusabio for Benefica in the late fifties. And Guttman, who survived Nazi work details and death camps by hiding in closets and traveling in disguise and even going back into the belly of the beast of Central Europe during the war after living in New York, was capable of intrigue and deception. But then again, it was probably just a prop or some joke from back in the day.

- 4 -

In the Adirondack glory of the lobby of the Mohonk Hotel in New Paltz, Cat Gjertsen grabbed Luc Lattimore's hand. Luc was the weekend bartender, senior enough to cherry-pick his shifts. Cat had done early yoga and qigong and had her usual glow, radiant in the morning no matter what had gone on the night before. On Friday she closed down Red Hook Roasters, nudging the last two stragglers out at about ten to eleven, a starry-eyed couple, although she noticed that didn't stop the guy from checking her out, catching him turn toward her a few times with that sneaky way guys have when they pretend to cough or clear their throat and turn sideways. At forty, Cat was still spritely, a mother of three from three separate men. Weather permitting, she wore belly shirts that rode up to show the Green Tara mantra tattoo that rode from her hip bone to the top of her crotch. The Sanskrit symbols jibed with Cat's almond shaped eyes and outlook on life.

On her best days, she wore her black hair pulled back and moved quickly with a dancer's, slightly splayed-foot walk.

Cat pointed to a sign. "Look, it says that there are fishers in the woods, brought in to control the porcupine population. But you know that—you probably come here a lot."

"Not really. I just kind of come to work and go home," Luc said.

"You're a big liar. I'll bet you come up here with all the ladies."

"Uh-uh. You're the first. I swear." Luc didn't see a lot of good-looking single women Cat's age at Mohonk, a resort set up for family reunions. Cat's plan originally was to go for a yoga weekend at the place that used to be Kutsher's, a Borsch Belt mainstay, but at the last minute, the austerity didn't appeal to her, too much of a good thing. She wanted to eat banquet food: oysters and prime rib, and lusty, egg-swaddled French toast with thick syrup and burnt coffee for breakfast. She was being pestered a lot by that guy Trevor, who initially seemed kind of cute in that intellectual way but had lately started taking a harder and harder line with her, going from a deft and occasional flirt to proposing the kind of dates that made her gag: old-fashioned dinners and brunch kind of stuff that she had been through a million times with what seemed like every guy in Manhattan and Brooklyn. Cat liked to dangle herself, a girl who liked to ride a vanity high as a guy was getting interested. Trevor revealed too much, became too invested in her. “I don’t date married guys,” she’d told him Friday. Thank God, because the little bit of cute he first evinced, some angularity in the jaw and an athlete’s gait, started to wear off. She defaulted to the rocker types anyway: skinny jeans, no chest, two-day shadow, leather bracelet instead of a watch. Luc was a rocker type crossed with a mountain man, a guy with potential to see the whole of the Green Tara script.

Trevor did smell like money in the way that a lot of fast-talking neurotic ethnic guys did, and there was always a need for a sponsor here and there, a guy to buy her a casual dinner—not a dinner date—or someone with a cottage in Greenpoint or New Paltz who wouldn’t mind her along with one or two of the kids, just for the chance to see her in a bikini. Lately, he was talking about a big plan, buying a building on the Upper West Side and turning it into a roaster/café with a cupping room, the first roaster in the neighborhood. She had half listened when he droned on about his father, an old Hollywood guy who produced and directed a scuba or hockey movie or some such thing in the seventies that was a big hit mostly because of the violence and then did some TV stuff that brought in some real money—she wasn’t entirely sure because she was juggling the Marzocco and four flat white orders and the food while Trevor was just doing foam, which, granted, needed to be done right, but really just required you to stand there and swirl the pitcher a tiny bit. She had to do the final pour as well, because no matter how much he wanted it, Trevor could barely do a decent fern, let alone the pinecones or Scotties or ravens that she was legendary for, and especially not her superspecialty, a pair of boobs that she did for some of the regulars.

Luc leaned forward to look at the sign. "Fisher. Huh. Never saw one. Never even really heard about one 'til now. Sounds like a nasty little bugger."

"They found one in the Bronx a few years ago. A cop took a picture. Crazy!" Cat said.

"No way. What's next? Wolverines in Central Park?"

Cat ran her hand up the inside of Luc's forearm and gently squeezed his elbow. "Let's go look for one," she said and sprang, very much catlike, ahead on the trail.

Here's a quiz for you: what's the rarest predator in the country? Get it right and there's a surprise for you."

"Dunno. Bobcat?"

"Uh-uh. Two more guesses."

"Fisher?"

"Dumb one."

"Cattle dog? I don't fucking have a clue."

"Jaguar."

"Jaguar? Like those African cats with spots?"

"South American, doofus. And they're rosettes, intricate designs with a center. The center is what makes the pattern different from leopards, which have a slighter build, by the way."

"So that's South America. Not the U.S., last I checked."

"They don't breed here, but every now and then one of them slips into the White Sands national recreation area way south in New Mexico. A rancher had one trapped up in a tree. Asshole shot it. Not even a rancher. Some dentist. It's always a dentist. You got a gun, Luc?"

Luc adjusted his boxers. Was this a date or a hazing? No wonder she was so good-looking and on her own. Always a catch. It was either a fleshy cougar with Merit Ultra Light lingering in her breath, or the ones like Cat with a deep agenda.

"Yeah, I got a gun. This is gun country."

"New Paltz isn't the country. It's a fucking college town. Any place with a Starbucks on Main Street and sixteen boho clothing stores and the same number of jewelry stores and that has goat cheese on the menu all over town isn't the country. Makes you feel big, does it, the gun?"

Luc thumbed his lip side to side Belmondo-style, an affectation he practiced to cool himself down. "You ever shoot—a gun that is, not from your hip?" he asked.

"Yep, one of my exes was a marine. When we lived in Oceanside, we'd drive to the desert and blast away. Kind of fun for a while, but one gun just seems like any other gun pretty quickly."

"Okay. Half credit. At least you're not one of these Brooklyn girls who drive an hour and a half up Eighty-Seven and think they know everything about everything up here. You know, 'cause I've about had it with that nonsense." Luc pulled out a flask, took a sip, and offered it to Cat.

"No thanks," she said. "Not one to drink and hike. Besides, I need to stay sharp for the fishers." She mock attacked him, bearing fangs and claws.

"Holy shit, you're scary when you do that."

"Yeah, that and a lot of other stuff."

Luc was a little less good-looking in the direct light in the Mohonk woods. His pallid rocker looks were flattered by the dim amber glow of the lobby bar, and the graceful shake-and-pour bartender's routine. Outside, he looked a bit feral, his cheeks pocked from adolescent acne, with filmy gray eyes.

"What's up with not knowing about fishers if you're such a big hunter outdoors guy?"

"Who said I was a hunter?"

"Got it. You're just packing then."

"Right on."

"At least you keep manly habits. I know this guy in Brooklyn. What a hypochondriac. His hobby is inventing strange medical conditions. Like every day he's got a new affliction—gout, eczema, rhinitis, celiac, tinnitus. Guy's forty-four and sounds like he's ninety-two."

"Sounds like he should shoot himself to get happy," Luc said. "I'll let him borrow my rod."

"Rod? You're kidding me, right?"

"Rod—it's a legit term for a gun. So you like him?"

"Not exactly. But he does like me. Dude's married. Or recently separated. He can be mildly amusing."

"So you're hanging with a married hypochondriac? And you're hassling me about owning a gun?"

" Just a guy who wants me to run his coffee place. He can buy me lunch. I don't see a problem with that. I'm an entertaining gal."

"What's a coffee place? Shop? Roaster?"

"Coffee operation—a bar with a roaster. Smack on the Upper West Side, which is actually pretty cool. I'd be the front of the house. A barista and all, but also the manager."

"Whose money?"

"Dunno. His father, I suppose. Some old producer type in LA. I kind of know his sister too. She left a big job and went back to film school."

"Alright then. I might want to check it out. I'm sick of the Hudson Valley CC seven-year plan. It's not the theater of dreams it's made out to be in the brochures.

"Try being a Mankato State dropout with three kids."

"Who?"

"Me."

"You have three kids?"

"Yep."

Luc took the flask out again, this time tucking it between his belt and jeans. "You fucking don't look like it. Where's your muffin top? Who pays for the little buggers? The marine?"

"Three dads. And my burlesque troupe, Urban White Females."

Luc stood back, propping himself on a crooked stick he'd been carrying, defense against a fisher, should one strike without warning . "Let's head back. I gotta hear the whole story."

- 5 -

Always drama, Phoebe thought when she heard the first few bars of Bernstein's "Mambo." The mambo was Trevor's ringtone. She was on her third round of Horowitz playing *Vers la Flamme*, creepy and disjointed, but more compelling with every sweet puff of her joint, prerolled Girl Scout Cookie. It was one of those Manhattan nights when the gloaming made you smoke and drink at the same time, the mist seeping through the warped double-hung window facing the courtyard that had been repainted so many times it looked like a white prune. The neighbors bitched and ranted to the super and the manager and the other neighbors in the elevator about the smoke, and it was starting to make her wonder if she was in fact smoking too much. The problem was that West Eighty-Sixth Street was square, too many stroller jockeys and a full sixty-three city blocks from Twenty-Third Street, the unofficial start of downtown.

- 5 -

"Dad said you should have come to Los Angeles," he said right off—no hi or happy Thanksgiving.

"Fuck that. I'm gonna pay two grand round-trip to wear a mask for six hours on JetBlue so I can sit in Dad's house getting figuratively bitch-slapped by that Botoxed beeyatch he calls his wife?"

"She's family now. Almost family. Anyway, she's spending family money. Mine and yours."

"Yeah, we'll she's a spender, a full-on Beverly Hills shopotron. So what else is new?"

"No, not clothes or shoes—an apartment."

"Dad and his girlfriend bought an apartment? Like he needs more real estate at ninety-five?"

"Not for them—for Stella."

"Seriously? They bought it for them?"

"Seriously—the whole down payment."

Phoebe was down to the end of the joint thanks to a roach clip that she saved from her Columbia days, not once thinking when she put it in her jeans pocket on move-out day that she'd be sitting in the lotus position more than fifteen years later about thirty blocks from campus sucking the bejeezus out of the thing talking to her brother on the phone. Horowitz was hammering the shit out of the last chords of the Scriabin. She once read he could span an octave; length was one thing, but power another. But what really mattered was contrast, a true pianissimo making a triple forte sound like a thunderclap. In orchestra, the best conductors were always leaning on the pianissimos, getting more out of a lighter touch with the bow. The way you modulated the response of a cello or a piano or a Marzocco espresso machine or a film was vital to the outcome. Take the Marzocco, her brother waxing poetic about the damn thing, the handmade production process an absolute marvel, a lot like the way the Swiss made watches, he said, old tools and even older workers hunched over magnifying lamps, a machine oil smell in the air, the Futurist Marzocco logo looming over the bits and pieces of semiassembled units.

"Truly horrifying. This is like a bad movie, watching your old dad getting fleeced for love. Stella or Will?"

"Stella."

"Thank God. At least she sort of works, if you call sitting in front of a merchandise case all day working. What does Will do again anyway?"

"At one point he was a hydroponics consultant."

"At one point? Whenever I hear that I confuse it with colonics. I guess they both deal with water. So what did he say about 245B?"

"Not so much. I didn't bring it up."

"What?"

"It's complicated. My hemorrhoids were going crazy, and I ate something funky—not sure what, there was so much strange stuff on the table. Not strange exactly, but a lot of it from this caterer on Sunset, and I was just kind of blocked, not eating and tired from the flight."

"You have hemorrhoids? Inside or outside?"

"Both. Mostly inside. It's stress. I had them banded—"

"Banded?"

"Just what it sounds like. They slap on these dissolvable rubber bands that shrink tissue. The doctor had these really thick fingers. I couldn't believe it, but once you're in, you're, like, committed. You can' t really screen that kind of thing on the phone—'Excuse me, nurse, but can you text me a photo of the doc's hands?' Eat fiber in case it's hereditary."

"Fortune favors the bold. Just 'cause you got fired and your wife booted you out doesn't mean you can bail on your project. But you'll have to go through Eileen to get to Dad—you know that though. My guess? She'd be happy to rat-fuck you if you let her."

"Listen to you. You sound like you're still on the desk. Outside of finance and body shops in the Bronx, no one talks like that. I think I have gout, by the way."

"Isn't that a fat guy problem?"

"I thought so, but the other day my toe was throbbing. I practically had to sit down in the middle of Abbot Kinney. I need a blood test."

"Maybe it's that psycho diet you're on. What's it this week? Gluten? Dairy? Sugar Paleo?"

"All of them. A cocktail. I can't eat out anymore—it's all a conspiracy. Reduction sauces, hitting everything with a third of a stick of butter. You ever wake up sick at two in the morning after eating out? It's the butter."

I can eat anything. Maybe 'cause I'm younger. You're like the princess and the pea."

"Now you're sounding like Paige. She was convinced I needed something to fret over, and that I was jealous her career was starting to move. You can't make up toe pain. You either have it or you don't."

Phoebe was smirking. She was younger, but took on the parental role, dispensing advice. She looked around her apartment, her head gently spinning, the shabby-chic bric-a-brac that she collected from weekly trips to the Chelsea flea market taking on kaleidoscopic intrigue. Her apartment was perfect, she thought, period appliances burnished to a cream color, either white faded to yellow or yellow faded to white, the muntins on the crunchy double-hung windows with their historic layers of paint, and the oak floor, solid and varnished from eighty-five years of footfalls. The hallway emitted a comforting, baked-chicken smell like a lot of New York buildings, bubbies and zadies sitting over Formica tables near their phone, lamenting the infrequency of calls from their grandchildren. She had a stipend from Hugo, $1,500 a week. She preferred the term "stipend" because it sounded academic. Behind her back, her friends called it a trust fund, even though that technically wasn't correct. For a long time she made a point of picking up the check, but then abruptly reversed course; let them prove they liked her and not her cash.

"So what doctor you going to next? The homeopathic guy who asks you what your favorite foods are, or the naturopath who wants you to pop pills made out of intestines?"

"Make fun of that naturopath if you want. Didn't you go for your eczema?"

"Once. Five hundred bucks later I had some pills and a bottle of homemade tonic that smelled like licorice and sardines. Dastardly stuff. I chose the eczema. But hey, back to your financing. What's your plan?"

"The way I see it is we have one shot, and that's to team up. You should think about becoming a partner. I'll buy the building and you'll be the manager, COO, whatever. I'll roast and run the front of the house. You can train, hire, and have the books. He won't turn down both of us."

A simple "let's be partners" might have done it, but there it was, the not-so-subtle play for control. "You can have the books," Trevor said. No one wants the books. Everyone wants the front of the house, the design, the customer interaction, the interviews for the weeklies and buzz from the cognoscenti and design snobs lying in wait to pounce on the next little big thing in the coffee world. The bar was being raised with every new venture, the concept purer, the baristas more arch in terms of their body art and superbly edited work wear, the coffee sourced from ever more equitably and ethically run micro plantations. In fact, the small, well-run growers, particularly those who focused on heirloom trees, were becoming small celebrities, courted and schmoozed by the green buyers.

"When you coming back?" Phoebe asked.

"Tomorrow night. I got a call from the broker. He's wondering what's up. Says there's action on the property."

"Have you met a broker who says there's no action on a property? No developer would want it. It's in that mid-block overlay district and there's no bonus. And after COVID, the banks haven't been so quick to lend on bricks and mortar. Also, you're staring at the ass end of Brandeis High School. You know it's mayhem when school lets out. I mean, at a price, someone would grab it and renovate, but for the number they want, I'm thinking there can't be that much action."

"By the way, something else interesting came up."

"What's that?"

"You remember that old soccer coach friend of Dad's?"

"Yeah. Bela Lugosi or something"

"Guttman. Bela Guttman. Lugosi was the vampire. Anyway, he was kind of mobbed up. At least in the soccer world. And I think he might have gotten a hold of the World Cup trophy after it was stolen in Brazil—they call it the Jules Rimet."

"So?"

"So I saw a World Cup trophy replica, or at least I'm pretty sure it's a replica, in a duffle bag in his house. Not sure who's bag it was. Had to be a prop from some film because if it's the real thing it's worth maybe seven figures.

The real one was stolen, then found, then lost again. A dog in England got it back when it was stolen the first time in England.

"If it's real, you could sell it and buy 245 B."

"That would be something, huh?"

- 6 -

Phoebe's friend Cat Gjertsen wanted better things than just being a barista. She wanted her own shop. Phoebe warned Trevor about cool girls like Cat. "You know, the ones who flirt but would never admit it," she said. Phoebe saw it first hand once or twice, Cat subtly brushing against him during her shift, letting him know she was there, consciously pulling her hair back to reveal the asymmetrical double piercing on her right side, the left lobe deliberately closed, because how quotidian would it be to have both sides pierced once like the stroller moms. Phoebe noticed Cat preened a lot around Trevor, fluffing her hair and air-kissing customers.

Away from the structure and soul-crushing accountability that Pomander Walk imposed on its employees, Trevor loved the casual culture at Red Hook and being able to dress how he damn wanted to.

He had commuted to Pomander in multiple steps: car/walk/train/walk/subway/walk, sometimes with a bus or cab element added. The tiny Tarrytown station parking lot was wait-list only, and nothing opened. You would have thought after COVID everyone would be working from home, but two years on, people were getting sick of their families and returning to the office where they could joke and relax and go out to lunch without having to justify what they were doing every moment of the day. With no space, he had to park outside the no-parking zone in the neighborhood around the station, which meant a mile walk just to get to there. Any hiccup for any leg of the trip made it close to an hour and forty-five minutes.

Commuting was circumscribed by the precise allocation of time: thirty minutes for breakfast, another thirty for grooming, another twenty for the creep down Route 9 to the station, a full day at the office squeezing brokers all over the country for an extra nickel of rent or pass-throughs, chump change in the context of any discrete transaction but millions for Pomander Walk's bottom line when multiplied by the square footage of its prodigious portfolio, and then a reversal of the commute back to Tarrytown.

At Red Hook, he jettisoned the dress attire but felt naked. Compared to the kids, he was square, a protoboomer, no Cyrillic or Aramaic lettering on his body that begged to be decoded by customers. Cat and Jerry and Toni worked the line like puppeteers, shifting their outfits around to reveal just enough skin and art to get people to stare. Toni also had her lip and tongue pierced, and Jerry, a six-foot-four biracial giant with a massive Adam's apple that looked like he'd swallowed a squirrel, shaved one side of his head where he had a small maple leaf inked in red, marked as a Canadian, a proud son of Regina, which Cat of course called "Vagina," reminding him seventeen times a shift that he was a "Vaginian." Watching all of them work was a treat, though, chamber music as coffee making. The herculean Probat manned the engine room, beans swirling, fuel for the no-nonsense Ditting grinders that pulped the beans down to all dimensions of tiny, from fine-grained espresso powder to the coarse brown sand preferred by the delicate porcelain and glass beakers used for the pour-overs.

Cat had a trick that involved setting up four or five drip cones on a rack with five hundred grams of perfectly ground coffee—twenty-five dollars per pound coffee—and pouring the water when it hit 170 degrees without having the pots below. She'd act like she forgot about the dripping coffee, turning to chat, wiping down the frothing arms on the Marzocco or grabbing a cannelé or macaroon from the case, all the while checking out the concern from the people in line, staring aghast at the catastrophe that was sure to happen, the water cascading through the filter cones with the attendant kinetic angst of twelve dollar a cup coffee splashing onto the Carrera marble, the hypercool protocol of expensive bohemian coffee bars precluding even a modest intervention ("Hey, I think the coffee is about to spill all over"), until her inner clock sent her whirling with a fistful of forty-dollar Hario V60 600 mL pitchers, sliding them neatly in orthogonal perfection.

"And how about Cat," Phoebe said, "what are you gonna do about her? You need a barista with star power and who can caress a decent shot out of a John Deere combine."

"Uh- huh. Customers love her, that's for sure. But have you met Cat Gjertsen? Chick rolls her pants down, show you her Venus dimples. I mean it works in Red Hook, but the Upper West Side? All those moms?"

The setup Trevor had envisioned had the three of them running the show, Cat in the role of celebrity coffee spokesperson, the lead grinder out front, fluffing the crowd, men and women, old and young. So many new coffee bars had hit Manhattan, even with a lot of them going under after COVID, that even if you had the edge by roasting on-site, you needed the theater to go with it. As there were very few homely restaurant hostesses in New York, so it was with the coffee trade. In truth, Phoebe wanted the Cat role, but as much as it pained her, she had to admit that being a barista, or more to the point, a great barista, required technical and people skills that were beyond her reach.

- 7 -

"Beatriz, be a dear and warm this up for me," said Eileen, her little Brussels, Rufus, tucked in the crook of her elbow, with only his tufted little elfin head peeping through. She had a billowing pashmina draped over a lavender velour track top, and without making eye contact extended her arm toward Beatriz, who rolled her eyes as she took the cup. Trevor noted that Eileen had polished off her second espresso from that idiot-proof $4,200 Jura machine that Hugo had installed flush with the varicolored Heath tile backsplash, another $2,500 spent on running a dedicated supply line to the machine, and probably another couple of grand for the one tile guy in the Hills who could cut small tile and work minor logistical countertop miracles, like making your $8,000 espresso setup look like it had been there all along. To humor Hugo, Trevor waxed rhapsodic affirmations of the Jura's brew, which in truth did not have the acidity, balance, or bronze crema that he could coax from his $550 semiautomatic machine. When you got into the fully automatic range, the appliance did all the work, leaving nothing to the barista. Just the morning before at Dashing Coffee Works, he had asked the barista (no obvious body art) whether the Dandy roast that was on the counter was what they were pulling. It was, and she took the opportunity to lecture him on stuff he knew: that the flavor depended on the variables—the grind, the tamp, the water temperature, and, Trevor concluded, the funk and style and moxie of the barista. At first it bothered Trevor that she wasn't showing any body art. She was petite, with a crisp bob, wearing a lime American Apparel sleeveless T inside out. Maybe a hire for 245 B down the road.

Eileen stopped at the mirror to fluff her hair. Beatriz handed her the mug, and she took a quick sip. "Phfft. This is scalding!"

"So sorry. The microwave, it's been a bit tricky lately. I will tell Mr. Hugo. So sorry Ms. Eileen."

"Achhh! I could have been badly burned!"

Eileen turned to Trevor and held out a limp hand, shaking it in that floppy way women in their goddess years have, gripping the front part of Trevor's hand so he couldn't grip back. "What a pleasure having you here," she said.

"Same here, Eileen. And the little fellow's name again?"

"Rufus," she said as he thrust his little doe-eyed, mustached visage higher, looking for a nuzzle.

"You know where my father is? All this food has been out here. I think the hot stuff is getting cold and vice versa. You can only watch the Detroit Lions for so long, but I suppose you haven't seen much of the Lions at all over the years."

"I've never been one for baseball. Or football. Either way, frankly."

"Football. American football," Trevor said, remembering that Eileen was originally from somewhere in middle Europe, not exactly an arriviste, but she played dumb about things American to her advantage when required.

"You know your father. Everything in his own time. And I do mean everything."

Eileen's perfume and the clingy knapped violet terry of her sweatpants. The top folded over her waist like a schoolgirl was visual overload. So was Cat Gjertsen in an enticing way, the Earth Mother siren whose revelation of an ankh tattooed at the small of her back had started his downward spiral.

Eileen leaned into Rufus, nuzzling and talking baby talk. "You are such a little puppy... aren't you such a little lovey puppy. Yes, you are such a puppy."

Trevor was flanked by Eileen, who did not credibly seem like the Bel Air dermatologist that she in fact was, with her pedigreed microdog on the one side and twenty-six plates of untouched catering on a twenty-foot table on the other side. The enormous farmhouse doors were slid to the side on both ends of the dining room, opening the room up entirely to the outdoors, revealing the courtyard pool and undulating peanut butter and chocolate chip hills of Mulholland Canyon. In the morning, Trevor heard on NPR about a mountain lion spotted in Griffith Park, a wanderer that had crossed I-10 and the 405 in pursuit of a good trail and perhaps the chance to snatch a purebred from someone's backyard. Even in a city with more pavement than dirt, big predators like coyotes and mountain lions defied the odds. Every five years or so, a coyote would appear in Central Park, probably starting her trip at the Croton reservoir, traversing the patches of remaining county parks in Westchester, then down through Van Cortland Park, and finally flanking the Saw Mill and West Side Highway into Manhattan. Plausible enough, but how did they make it for the last leg? The closest western Central Park entrance, at Frederick Douglass Circle, was at Central Park West and 125th Street, which would require a fully grown coyote to trek across on one of the busiest cross streets in Manhattan. Even in the penumbral light of dawn or dusk, a large coyote would be sure to draw attention. The wacky thing was that for some reason, when a coyote was discovered, it was tranquilized and relocated, somehow violating some unspoken urban law of tolerable fauna. The raccoon was the magic line. Bigger than a raccoon and folks were spooked. And the news out of the Bronx was that a policeman on dawn patrol saw a fisher, an arboreal predator whose range had been mostly confined to heavily forested and remote parts of the county. They were reportedly recolonizing their historic territory, sometimes settling in suburban neighborhoods and freely dining on pets. Trevor had heard from Cat Gjertsen that there were some in the woods near Mohonk in New Paltz. One of them got up one day and decided to head to the Bronx.

"Eileen, did you hear about the big cat in Griffith Park? You might want to think twice about taking Rufus there."

"A million guns in Los Angeles and now they're letting a pet killer roam the hills. We should organize a hunting party. It would be a grand thing. Shall we get the main course started by the way? I have no idea what your father's up to. Oh, and I invited Stella for dessert. Hope that's ok with you."

"Not at all. It's the holidays. They're in the Valley, right?"

"Not for long," Eileen said, smooching Rufus machine-gun style. "Your father and I helped them get a little place in Venice. It's just a one-bedroom, but the developer really has an eye."

Maybe Hugo was starting to loosen up with the checkbook a little bit. He had brought up moving to Palm Desert or Rancho Mirage. But buying a condo for Eileen's kid? She wasn't bashful about spending other people's money apparently. Venice prices started at $1000 a square foot, placing even an eight hundred square foot loft in the $800,000 range, translating to a down payment of $150,000, and that's if Eileen's kid had enough W-2 income to get a loan, not a simple thing these days.

Eileen was attractive in that Eastern European yogurt and Pilates and impeccable posture way. She channeled Zsa Zsa Gabor, or maybe it was more Eva Gabor, the smarter one. Good carriage, Trevor's deceased mother would have said. Lots of grooming going on, bits and nibbles of Botox and premium mani-pedis. Her hair was somewhat out of control. As a dermatologist, she probably had plenty of professional courtesy credits from her plastic surgeon friends. LA put a premium on smooth. Everyone looked smooth in LA, tanner and browner than in New York. On a gray day, all white New Yorkers looked half-dead.

But then there was the "Red Lobster." A retail broker in New York who was deeply tanned even in midwinter. The tan complemented his equine-themed ties: bits, horseshoes, saddles, and blankets. The Red Lobster could always be spotted throwing off his Biarritz glow, even in the dim corner of a Sheraton ballroom during a dismal broker's luncheon. In LA, nut-brown skin was required.

"How wonderful. Is it a condo? One of those conversions off Lincoln?"

"How did you know?"

"Just from driving around. And in New York, checking out new projects is a sport, so it's kind of second nature by now. I've actually been looking to buy a little building myself. Or with other investors obviously."

"Is that so? That's wonderful. I'm sure a lot of your friends in the business would love to back you."

"Not so sure. It's more of an operating idea, a coffee roasting business. I mean it's real estate too, but it's going to be a pretty big project to get off the ground. When are they closing?"

"Oh, just last week. They just closed, but it's a ten-day escrow. All cash so it's quick. The kids are so excited. It's sooo nice down there at the beach. I wish your father would move down there, but he's fixated on the swimming pool. Like he's the male Esther Williams. And it's ten degrees hotter here. You can feel it getting cooler on the 10 as soon as you go over the hill."

Eileen put the side of the back of her hand next to her mouth, hiding what she said next. "But he'll never sell this place. It's all ego, you know."

She bent down and released Rufus, a reluctant tawny ball of fluff. As her cup moved across the air, Trevor smelled something— a bit of liquor, brandy or rum, or more likely one of the strange eaux-de-vie she collected from the home country that tasted like gasoline—lacing Eileen's coffee.

Phoebe said she thought she was starting to detect some incipient Alzheimer's during Hugo's last visit to New York. But maybe it was just too much drinking. At the Rangers game, he was telling her about how in the forties Edgar Laprade could stickhandle end to end to score, but he could not remember the score of the game in front of them. Now Trevor was starting to think that Hugo and Eileen were simply running on scotch and pills. Phoebe said he kept telling her how great the weather was in LA and how wonderful Eileen was—she was a doctor, did you know?—and how she should move to the West Coast. If he was in New York, he told her, there would be nothing left except to tally up his friends dying off, probably suffocating alone from COVID.

Phoebe really couldn't complain a whole lot. Hugo was paying for her second round of grad school. She had her MBA, but she realized that finance was brutal and mind- numbing, and she'd have to bail out anyway if she had a kid or two, but that was moot, at least for the moment, since at thirty-eight she was between relationships. It was a no-brainer to go to film school with her father's connections; just a couple of references on the application seemed to do the trick, making up for the lacunae in her creative CV. Although with digital production now, anyone could write, shoot, edit, and have a completed project for hundreds of dollars in days, versus the thousands and months it took just ten years ago. It seemed to her that her brother was taking the easy way out and that coffee had already had its moment, and with all the new social distancing rules, cafés just didn't have the vibe they used to. His "burger analogy" seemed too rehearsed, too defensive: "If competition was the barometer of success, then you'd never see another burger place opened, but a new place opens, what, every six hours in America." Yeah, but anyone will pay $3.49 for a rubber puck of meat on a squishy bun with some goo on top. And on the other end of the spectrum there were endless riffs on meat—organic, turkey, ostrich, beefalo, heritage, farm raised, anti-antibiotic, sustainable, meatless, etc.—but wasn't coffee just an agricultural commodity that most people except for the entitled digerati and bohematards who lived in Williamsburg and Wicker Park and Silver Lake paid exorbitant markups for, while the Dunkin' Donuts did the same thing for a buck a cup?

But at least he had a semblance of an actual business plan. Just like any bozo with a decent Nikon can make a film, anyone can plug some numbers into a spreadsheet and get professional-looking output. At Columbia, she barely passed accounting but took note of the artful dodging involved in teasing out the cash flow from income, monkeying around with the special-sauce items like depreciation, goodwill, and special charges. If Trevor plied her with a couple of drinks, especially that mezcal she liked at Zo, a taqueria fresca in Dumbo that brought or smuggled it in from TJ, she would soften a little and tell him that with a perfect roasting setup, impeccable barista training, the right brewing and espresso equipment, and having enough operating capital to get one of the hot-shit bean buyers with the right connections to the small co-op farmers who were increasingly essential to the lifeblood of the third-wave roaster, he might have a fighting chance. Oh, and a kickass location wouldn't hurt. On paper, West Eighty-Third Street between Columbus and Amsterdam sounded perfect, not only because of the numerology—eight plus three equaling eleven, the same as the month and day of Trevor's birthday added together—but also from the standard retail metrics, pedestrian and car counts, and the one- and three-mile radius tests for income. These were always silly for Manhattan—you didn't need to spend $15,000 for a consultant to tell you that there were a lot of rich folks there, no matter where you dropped the pin on the map. The thing about L&L was that it was in one of those cursed locations. Manhattan retail was—pre-COVID, anyway—a runaway locomotive, rents, prices, and sales increasing arithmetically, and sometimes geometrically, from year to year. But every avenue and street had spots that never made it out of the station. Some had too little sun at key times of the day, especially in winter when the azimuth and skyline brought daylight to an end around 2:00 p.m. On very cold sunny days right at Broadway in the orbit of Zabar's, it was interesting to see how congested the sunny side of the avenue was compared to the east side. L&L was, the brokers said, a cursed location after the firm itself dissolved. The building, with its awkward interstitial spaces, was neither fish nor fowl—no residential zoning and not good for retail or office space either. It could have possibly worked for a graphic design firm or photography studio but had not attracted any takers.

Phoebe knew Trevor was a sucker for the trappings of old New York. She saw it in his eyes when on one of the last showings, he spent a half hour poring through the relics of the sign business: beveled engineer's rulers, paperweights from the '64 World's Fair, ledger books, levels, and calendars from the Bowery and Dime savings banks that had somehow eluded the sticky fingers of the last janitorial staff to have cleaned the downstairs office next to the boiler room.

But what was she? A student. A thirty-eight -year- old student, and a perpetual one at that. She had spent all this time realizing that she didn't want a job. She liked what Paige did, food writing. What a gig. But it also had turned her brother into a freak. Always a bit of a hypochondriac, he was getting wiggy about what he put in his mouth. He told her that going out to eat was getting terrifying. He had borderline-high cholesterol, mitral valve prolapse, fibromyalgia, itching in his balls, dry mouth, tinnitus, eczema, and, worst of all, incipient gout, a blinding and maniacally rampaging pain in his left toe that ambushed him from time to time. Every time they got together, he would count and calculate, cross-reference purine content with calories, study the menu interminably, and settle on something plain. "Can you do an arugula salad for me—no meat or cheese, dressing on the side," he would say after wasting her time. The few vegetarian and vegan spots that she could tolerate were being worn out by Trevor. If she saw that sign on East Second Street, CHAKRA, VEGAN AND LOCAL, one more time, she would have to commit him.

Paige specialized in fruit. Fruit was damn interesting, caught between big growers flaunting seasonality with the faster/more/cheaper angle versus the farmers market provisioners. Paige made a few trips to California every year, and Phoebe wondered whether she had something going on out there. A fter Paige started covering coffee and did a big South American trip, leaving Trevor with the kids for three weeks, Phoebe was more convinced that she was planning something. And then Trevor moved into an Archstone or Avalon apartment.

- 8 -

"Crap, Dad. You can't do that in LA. People are packing out here."

"What? Since ven can't you flip someone off? It's vat they call defense driving."

"You mean defensive driving. No, they call it road rage today. Did you see the billboard back there? Captors versus Convicts?" A big billboard showed two wrestling teams, a disciplinary force of thick-necked warden types in military wraparound sunglasses, trunk-like forearms at the ready to administer a beating; Team Convict had tribal neck markings, weapons-grade facial hair, and a look of feral enmity that had Trevor crapping his pants from the creamy, gemütlichkeit interior of the Beemer.

"No. I don't read when I drive. No coffee, no food, no phone. I have the Bluetooth, but who wants to get head cancer. I made it this far without cancer, except for a tiny bit in the prostate. That doesn't count. Every man alive my age has prostate cancer."

"I know. But trust me, flipping off two guys with neck tattoos in a low rider isn't a great strategy. I think you should be happy you can still drive. Ninety-five is a very advanced age to still be behind the wheel."

"He cut me off. In the Bronx back in the day, I'd have run him off the road."

A giant SUV, a new Nissan Armada, three times as high as the 650, swerved in front of Hugo on Lincoln.

"Goddamn mother!" Hugo said. "Why'd you let me take Lincoln? I hate Lincoln. Joyriders and assholes on Lincoln. And Culver's just as bad now with those furniture stores. I liked it better when it was just the back lots—no people, no cars."

"Jeez, I thought you were mellower now. Eileen says you're mellow compared to a few years ago. You should have let me drive."

"Now you want my car too? Bad enough the maid takes it. She was with her boyfriend back there. I wasn't fooled. You smell the perfume? They were all over the leather. I should charge her for the detailing. That's LA for you. Exciting LA. Everyone wants to be out in a convertible. Not like New York. New York, they get excited about the money. Here they take the money for granted. They want the action like the celebrities—the achoo-lation."

"I thought you still miss New York. You've been out here, what, since 1976?"

"The friends are falling fast and furious. COVID put it in overdrive. We have our reunion next month. Five of us—me, Al Meltzer, Ken Bellard, Eli Pfefferman, and Art Pozner. I'm the oldest by ten years. Today, sad to say, everyone is known by what they have: COPD, et cetera, et cetera. We're going to do that walk around the old neighborhood. I want to go to that football stadium in Jersey. What's the outfit that plays there? The Red Balls or something?"

"Red Bulls, Dad. Bulls."

"Okay. I thought Red Balls was strange. But who names a team Red Bulls? What's football have to do with bulls?"

"It's a drink. The company that makes the drink owns the team. They can name it whatever they want. And they mostly call it soccer now. In fact it's soccer in the U.S. Football is—well, you know what football is."

"I know what football is. And *fútbol*. I know them all, Trevor. You know what I have in the trunk?"

"What. The ball? You still have it?"

"The ball. Your grandfather's ball, the one I brought over. Every Hakoah player was told to pack a ball. They weren't sure what was going on over here. Even in New York."

"That thing has to be, what, about your age."

"You got it. The guy who sold me the car couldn't believe it when I told him. He played for UCLA. Nice fellow."

Hugo was planning to take the ball to New York, show it around to the guys. In the long arc of material desire that spanned his days in the Bronx, scrapping and scrimping, he was in the divestiture phase. Parsimony reigned as you aged. If there was no symbolism, no link to family or ideas, he didn't want it anymore. Daily, he'd pack a box with stuff, no logic behind it. One day it would have a couple of ties, a power tool, and a book, the next day shoes, a watch, and a plant. He'd carefully place it on the floor of the tiny back seat of the 650 and drive down to Fourth Street, into the belly where the stench of the soiled and disenfranchised Angelenos queued and genuflected before the welfare-dispensing agencies, unchanged through three generations of Republican and Democratic administrations, brown brick monoliths with the smog of ages crusted permanently on their façades, surly and beaten-down administrators inside, desperate to quell the anxieties of the hundreds waiting for something—anything.

"The sphincter of LA," Hugo said.

"What, Dad?" Hugo was still sharp, very sharp, but here and there the way he engaged you was getting strange, Trevor thought. His transitions were abrupt, eliding the space between topics when once there would have been a soupçon of information to bridge topics, bring the Henry K inflection sharply into focus. "What are you talking about?"

"Fourth Street. I am ashamed to say how it hasn't changed from the day I moved to Los Angeles until today. All of us—I mean people in Hollywood with money—should be ashamed. I always thought that little bridge, Fourth Street, as the gateway to the city. But how can you have a gateway when you are driving and you see an encampment of homeless people as far as the eye can see. What is the use of all these films, all the money? Every day I pack a box. Eileen stands and says, 'Hugo, put that stuff back. What's a homeless guy going to do with a Charvet tie?' And I tell her it's none of her goddamn business. I am old enough to do what makes me feel good and I don't care if they use it to wipe their ass; that's their business."

"But if you feel that way, why not put something in the box they can really use?"

"Sure. Sure. I do. I give them something anybody can use."

"What?"

"Cash." Trevor looked at his father, a portrait of equipoise, gray tufts of Brillo eyebrows pointed toward LAX as they whooshed through the browned marshland past LMU. Seabirds stood in the glory of perfect November LA, surf weather, one of those days when Southern California raises the endless-summer banner, soft breezes and gossamer sundresses laughing at Des Moines, Dubuque, Scranton, and all points east and north. Trevor resisted his New Yorker's instinct to be blunt, to strike at the heart of the matter and ask why his father would be giving away cash in boxes to strange homeless people in LA. It was tautological in a way: man becomes successful; man consumes everything he can possibly consume; man reflects on life as he enters God's waiting room; man acts selflessly and purges himself of worldly possessions.

"A lot?"

"Depends what you mean?"

"A hundred?"

"Maybe more."

"Two?"

"A nice wad. In a clip. With cash, you need to have some dignity."

"No doubt. That's a wonderful gesture, Dad. One thing I saw by accident was some kind of statue in the house. It was peeking out of a bag on the floor near the bureau in the hall. Do you know what that is?"

"On the floor? I don't remember putting that on the floor. That is a World Cup statue that Bela gave me. Don't get excited; it's a fake. But I don't know why it was on the floor."

"Not your bag then?"

"It may or may not be my bag. I have to see it."

"Please look right away when you get home. I have a feeling that may not be a fake. And if it's not, you need to keep it close by."

In a couple of hours, Trevor would be heading back to New York, groping his way back to the Archstone/Avalon from JFK, taking some shuttle and snaking through sterile bits of lower Westchester, dropping moms and dads back at split-levels, colonials, bungalows, capes, and Tudors that reminded him of his nice house that he still partly owned but wasn't allowed to live in. Trevor liked to say his house was a craftsman-Colonial, but Paige was quick to shush him. "For God's sake, it's just a Colonial," and she'd roll her eyes, implying that he was always trying to make a bigger deal, or as she also said, "a big deal," out of everything.

Trevor thought about those boxes, neatly packed, dropped off in front of the Social Services building or maybe randomly and the shock and delight that some delirious souls, itchy in their lice-ridden underclothes got from finding something so utterly alien.

"How did you come up with the idea of random boxes?"

"I call it manna," Hugo said.

"And you? Does that make you—"

"God. Yes. But in the most humble fashion. In a modern way. Modernism broke from formalism, from the old ways. I was young when I left Vienna, but what was happening there before I left had a big effect. Music, design, film, therapy, what have you. The modern world exposed mankind in its two basic forms: people with imagination and people afraid of their imagination."

Trevor fumbled with his carry-on, a Filson briefcase that had so many pockets he could never remember what he stored where. After rifling through just about every one, he found his boarding pass. "It's a theory, Dad. I'm happy to chew on this more. But if you're so committed, why don't you do something a bit more structured. Start a foundation, or bring in some of your friends in the industry?"

"Yes. This is the same thing Eileen says. 'You're not helping a damn thing by flinging boxes at people. Start a charity'—and so forth. But my feeling is that this has to be a movement of consciousness, a velvet revolution. People have to see for themselves first, and then the big guns follow. So tell me, Trevor, what charities is Pomander Walk Capital involved with?"

Never use a preposition to end a sentence with. Trevor had heard that somewhere. Didn't hurt Hugo. He made millions in film speaking English with Mittel European bastard fractured syntax. Trevor, even with his Columbia diploma, couldn't hold down his corporate hot seat. Who was warming that spot now? He missed his view, looking south from 1 Penn Plaza, the bulbous Paramount Building clock never quite reading the correct time, but jazzy, and a Times Square avatar that announced, "You are here." In New York. At Times Square. The building was part of the connective tissue of old Times Square, the stringy fat hanging by a thread like the glimpse of sheet music you could still get at Colony Records, or the few remaining neon signs inviting you for a cocktail or a veal chop. Just a matter of time before the digital and pedestrian-only Times Square cannibalized the old Times Square—tickers for sports and stocks and the national debt, numbers and stats whirring by for the fanny packers and teeny throngers among the few remaining pickpockets and grifters trying to make a dishonest living. Trevor could go there now, unfettered by deadlines and projects, free of Rick Nugent and hearing about his kid, a junior at Collegiate, the sixth man on varsity hoops, better than the starters, but consigned to the sixth-man role by a certain Coach Schmidt. Bizarre how Trevor knew the details about the basketball program at Collegiate, another by-product of Nugent's unrelenting narcissism. To hear Nugent senior talk, Nugent junior had the whole package, a scorer with Magic's court sense and selflessness, Bird's positioning and ice water demeanor, and Jordan's pure scoring. "And he's still growing, six-six already."

"Wow. That's something. Sounds like he should be starting. What's wrong with Schmidt?"

"Beached," that was what the traders called getting fired. He wanted to mash everything into one jumbled plea before he hopped out at the JetBlue gate: "See ya, Dad. Thanks for the lift. Got fired and need six hundred K to buy a building for a start-up that I need permits for and don't have any track record or staff or working capital, but hell people love coffee, right? You love coffee, right? Can't miss on West Eighty-Third, even though it's maybe on the dimly lit side of the street—oh, and there's no actual street level, you can't really walk in a front door, so to speak, but easily remedied with signage and taking down the masonry half wall where the pigeons crap, not to worry, if you're a destination in Manhattan folks will seek you out—they don't need to be drawn in like you're at some godforsaken mall." The commercial property market was in a rare down cycle, still in COVID recovery. Trevor was the only person he knew of who had lost money in the Manhattan condo market, buying his loft studio in '98 and selling it in '07, not quite getting back to even. He needed to make up for that. The market had been sloshing around post–Internet crash, the Japanese had pulled out, and the Internet bubble had yet to buoy the market. Paige had forced his hand then, wanting a Tudor in Tarrytown with original cabinets and updated appliances and a garden window framing a yard with mature rhododendrons and yellow roses. Trevor was always the one bitching about the city, the contempt for real estate and finance that grew over time, and that was brought even more sharply into focus when Lehman expired and the entire real estate finance infrastructure was about to collapse. Thank God he didn't bite at that AIG job; that would have been even worse. Paige wore him down eventually. There was no private school in the Heralds' future. They drove to Tarrytown on the first decent Saturday in March and put an offer in on the first place they saw.

"The chairman sends around a memo every year for some crazy charity, the Simian Relief Fund or something with orangutans and gorillas in Rwanda and Indonesia. The brochure has old people snuggling with apes. Very weird. It's like an invoice before you get your bonus. They send around a list of who donated in the newsletter. It's not good form to not be on the list."

"That's good. Everyone needs to do something. You'll see as you get older. Your legacy becomes an obsession. No one wants to go softly into the night."

Hugo wove the 650 through a brocade of rental shuttles, black cars, cabs, and private cars jostling for optimal drop-off points, reflexes still sharp, better than his own, Trevor thought. Amazing for ninety-five. Almost as soon as the car was stopped, a thickly muscled LAX cop in a crisp white button-down, buttons almost popping at the chest, started approaching. Hugo saw the cop peripherally and said, "Okay, Trevor, it was wonderful you were here—love you. Better get moving before this SOB writes me up." Trevor brushed his cheek next to Hugo's and smacked a kiss skyward, LA-style. Hugo's cologne was musky (did they kill the civet or just harvest the scent—Trevor had made a mental note to find this out someday, the civet being a midsize predator that fell through the cracks, neither cat nor dog, not on anyone's cuddle-toy list, but likely on its way out, CITES class four or five probably), with a seventies patchouli note. Heck, the cologne probably *was* from the seventies.

He leapt out of the 650, eyes averted from the looming bulk of the parking cop—why didn't they just put up those signs they have in Manhattan: "Don't even think about parking here," a legacy of either the Koch or

Dinkins regime—no, definitely Koch, he was the strident one, Dinkins the bumbling mathematician, appeasing everyone, leading the city into a chaotic ball of flaming shit, notable for crack vials crunching underfoot as you walked through the west side blocks and the fearsome Squeegee Men, rags at the ready, pouncing on your windshield, ostensibly to clean, but really to befoul a perfectly clear piece of glass only to extort a buck or two to reverse the process.

Trevor was happy to see the departures board, two days in LA being the perfect amount. Not that there was anything to get back to, but he was looking forward to going to Red Hook Roasters just to get a better sense of how it all came together. That Cat Gjertsen was too much, playing him like a pawnshop zither, pulling strings and making him half crazy. He walked by a store in the terminal called "LA Magic," which seemed like an infringement of sorts, unless Magic himself owned the place. But if not, could Magic really have co-opted a whole name for himself? Well, there it was, maybe enjoying a brief run before the lawyers clamped down. He thought about bringing shirts back for Paige and for Cat. The one he liked was Dodger blue, with bold sans serif lettering that read "LA, So Gangsta It Hurts." They also had it in reverse, blue letters on white. Maybe blue for Cat and white for Paige.

At least the airport retail was occupied, not like the malls and even some of the streets and avenues in

Manhattan and Brooklyn, knock-on casualties of Lehman and Bear Stearns and AIG and Morgan and S&P and Moody's and that whole Gold Coast finance and real estate mafia, the kings of casual Fridays and bonus hawking, guys whose shingle-style mansion lifestyle barely took a hit while the lesser economic lights suffered. But Trevor felt a pit in his stomach whenever he saw a vacancy, especially when he went to Central Avenue or the malls in White Plains and Stamford and Nyack and saw a big fat gaping hole where there used to be a Circuit City or Linens 'n' Things or CompUSA, not that he shopped at any of them, but there was something comforting in all that commercial discourse, the dim fluorescent gloom of the stores and the bold signage. Where did the clerks go? Trevor wondered on his site visits for Pomander. Shuffled and redealt to the next airless big box, if they were lucky? On to Amazon and Walmart and logistics centers that were taking over entire towns. What was their health care plan, their retirement? Retail vacancy gnawed at him, jobless now himself, thinking about taking on even more risk with a new business, doubling down on his own luck—what would his kids think if he failed at being both a corporate tool and an entrepreneur (what were you then?).

He felt strongly about New York. If you delivered the goods, the bodies were there. The suburbs were a bigger risk, the little villages always in mortal combat with the malls. Sure, there was some mom-and-pop space in

Tarrytown and Nyack, the latter with a rare bookshop that would have been at home on Waverly Place, but it was more of a novelty. The malls were the pulse, homogeneous to be sure, always tinkering with the mix. Pomander Walk had a mixed-use portfolio, with very little pure retail. Most of Trevor's retail deals were for the lobby levels of office buildings. Urban retail was a different animal, the retail brokers in Manhattan all cultivating a shtick. Hank Levine wore Hermès ties, never the same one, bragged about his conquests, always had an intern in tow, a fresh-faced guy or gal from NYU, looking like they just got bar or bat mitzvahed while he dictated commands to follow up on this or that. Leslie Unterman had the brass balls, all her competitors underpricing or overpricing locations. She had done all the deals, the queen of upper Madison—Prada, Pucci, Breitling, RRL, Weston, Miu Miu, all of them, worked with all the best interior architects. The best of the best. Her boobs were high, at an impossible angle, her knees polished, attenuated, alluring. Cross and uncross. Sign here. A killer.

Unterman wouldn't have known a mall if it fell on her. Trevor was drawn to malls like people are to car wrecks. The worst malls were roiling pools of angry fringe people, clammy in cheap cotton separates with writing on them, poorly tattooed, and very angry. One guy Trevor saw in Nanuet had on a T-shirt that was plain in front and adorned with crossed pistols in the back with bold, very elegant sans serif (could it possibly have been Gill

Sans?) lettering that read "For My Fucking Enemies." In the terminal, Trevor felt himself devolving in real time, his face getting stubblier, his clothes more ill- fitting, his mood unbalancing. He needed to eat something, but it was all airport food and chock-full of gluten, his new perceived enemy. Maybe a Caesar salad would do, separate out the romaine from the gluteny crouton bomblets, avoid the Parmesan, salty and tasty, but maybe it moved the needle on his LDL, and why risk that? He hadn't worked out in LA except for some push-ups and a little Pilates in Hugo's guest bedroom. He thought about using the elliptical, but Hugo had it in his bedroom and Eileen was always around, Rufus snuffling along behind her. Jogging was out ever since he got the MRI back showing how there was a quarter-size chunk of cartilage missing from his knee. He went in whistling, sure that it would be arthroscopy and a quick return to CrossFit and basketball, but his stern Korean orthopedist had his pointer out, circling over and over the offending part of the scan, looking like a bird had pecked it. Microfracture surgery, piercing the interior of the kneecap and allowing the healthy cells to flow through the membrane and hoping for them to take root, like sod, was the recommendation. Fine if you were, say, Amare Stoudemire, entourage at the ready, car service whenever and wherever, but for an ordinary schmo, navigating Manhattan on crutches for three months plus another five months of rehab was untenable.

What happened to the days of take an aspirin and call me in the morning? It was all so interlinked now: diet, exercise, battling the inexorable tendencies of your cells to shrink, fomenting the cancers and degenerative conditions that were there, watching how it was all going, how many antioxidants and nutrients you took in, when and if they were going to bust their move. Digging around the Internet, he found something called the Stress Scorecard. His total was at the high end of the top bracket. No amount of wheatgrass or kava or resveratrol could handle that. But eating his Caesar, or at least the romaine part of the Caesar, he caught a glimpse of himself in the reflection of the Lacoste shop, and it wasn't half bad, despite the nonsense, despite the devolution. Nonsense, what a great way to frame it, Trevor thought. Nonsense conveyed that your hardships were a mutation, something deviant and illogical that would fade as quickly as they came on. My nonsense, he told himself, and was reassured. His stubble could be viewed in a different way, reading in another article how women preferred a shadow on men, not clean and not hirsute, but stubble. Pomander Walk was a smoothly shaved shop, Rick Nugent still sporting the prep school–bred hairdo—a side part and a hank of droopy blond-brown hair arcing over his smooth forehead. Nugent lived in Greenwich, and it was possible to pick out its commuters even before they boarded the 6:03 on track 26, women wearing Hermès and Chanel, men in

Paul Stuart. The Hudson train commuters were earthier, much more of a backpack and sensible shoe crowd.

Trevor dumped the rest of his salad, most of it, into the trash bin, the one most likely to be trash, not recycling or composting or upcycling. "JetBlue flight one seventy-six to JFK will be boarding. Passengers with special needs, please approach the gate with your boarding passes." In the new order of things, Trevor's boarding pass was barely above cargo. It was just a matter of time before the cheapest fare class had to ride outside the plane. Trevor licked the inside of his lip, felt a bump, and wondered if it might be oral cancer.

- 9 -

It always helped Trevor to get a ride from a disenfranchised Eastern European refugee. It was only in the back of a ride share that you could talk to someone from Georgia or Uzbekistan. The pulse and diversity of New York was expressed by array of drivers' nationalities on the Van Wyck service road as much as any place else: Salvadoreans, Somalis, Bangladeshis. He noticed he was riding in a Lincoln Town Car. "How many miles on this?" he asked Grigor, his driver.

"Eight hundred thousand, but this is the second engine."

Sad thing, though, the Lincoln Town Car was phased out by Ford. The Town Car was the ultimate workhorse, not unusual to have a million miles on them. They were the dark beads of the necklace outside the shiny towers of finance, including Pomander Walk, at 1370 Eighth Avenue. It was a new skyscraper but in the arriviste part of Midtown, where there were still development sites left into the nineties. If you were the facilities director at an investment bank and you wanted a headquarters, you convinced yourself that since the managing directors took black cars to work anyway, you could pick anywhere in Manhattan—even Jersey City—as long as the tower had enough stone in the lobby. Besides, the brokers always touted that there was more fashion and music and media on the west side, which in broker-/banker-speak meant better-looking women. That's what all the brokers would say after scanning the room to make sure there weren't any, well, women lurking about. Jimmy Heffler from CBRE loved to talk about the sculpture in front of Crédit Lyonnais on Sixth Avenue, a woman without arms, feet, and head, as having just the "good parts" left. Jimmy and his team represented Pomander Walk in the acquisition of the site, earning a 5 percent commission for his team on a land sale that equated to $400/FAR (buildable) foot, which, based on a 465,000 gross square foot tower, was $9.3 million. After giving 40 percent to the house, that left $5.58 million for Jimmy. He probably gave his partner a million and the analysts a couple of hundred thousand, leaving poor Jimmy $4 million or so for playing one round of golf at Winged Foot with Sam Alterman and Buzz Piatkowski. Trevor had a ringside seat at some of the biggest real estate deals in the city. Even though he worked for a merchant bank, he was basically an owner's rep and was on salary and bonus. Decent, but he was a bit player in the high-stakes game.

It was hardly Trevor's first recession rodeo. It was slack in 2000, after the Internet crash, and again after 9/11. On his way to a Pomander Walk–owned building in the Garment District, Trevor saw people sprinting out of Macy's a couple of weeks later, spooked by a bomb scare. It was like a video game, a wide-angle shot of Manhattan, closing in on a tranquil scene, and then a little pinprick, a clipped car mirror, a ripple in the sidewalk, and blammo! Buildings coming down, aliens decamping from spaceships, marauding air fleets.

At the Monday pipeline meetings, Nugent would look at the list of prospects. "Abelman, Trotz, and Simon. Been on here for weeks. Anything new?" Nugent snapped his head to the side, like the preppy kids did in high school to get their hair out of their eyes. "Or are they shouting 'fire in the hole'?"

"Not a lot new, Rick. It's hairy out there, too soon for anyone to focus on leasing. They like the floorplate, and the work letter is decent, but they're pushing for a hundred dollars a square foot. Lots of landlords are getting nervous in this environment."

The tyranny of the pipeline went away from Tuesday through Sunday but came back with a vengeance each Monday morning when the alarm went off. Thoughts of a deficient pipeline plagued Trevor during 3:00 a.m. night sweats, bolting awake and lying there, fidgeting and rolling, thinking about how to flesh out the meager pickings from the new week's updates, how he would need all his powers of embellishment to weave a promising tale. It was 2007 redux. To compensate for the lack of activity in the market, the partners pushed the leasing meetings earlier and earlier. For them, it meant having their cars come an hour earlier, in the winter black and airless streets of the Upper East Side. For Trevor, that meant catching the 5:26 from Tarrytown, which, working backward, meant a wakeup call at 4:15, Trevor needing to have a real breakfast, with some cholesterol-free protein and gluten-free bread or muffin. He could not, like the other MDs, grab a coffee and a bun and jam it down at the meeting. For one, it was his show. He had to be on, giving the updates, injecting pace and energy and enthusiasm into the proceedings to keep his job alive, and make them think he was the man, the catalyst. The pipeline was the devil and Sisyphus combined; you pushed and pushed and got results, and they wanted it faster and harder. No pipeline and you were doomed, a minister without portfolio. But then the pipeline was not something you could control, especially in a tanking economy, or worse, a skittish economy when indecision was the coin of the realm.

"Patch me into your thinking here, Trevor. We"—the imperial *we* was something Nugent used to burnish his power seat—"need clarity on this one, Trevor. *Someone* is leasing space in this town, are they not?"

"Umm. There have been a couple signed. One forty K, one a hundred, but those were legacy deals, well in motion before Lehman. I can't think of a major deal that was in the incubation stages before then that is progressing well. I mean, I don't have *all* the research in town, but close." Nugent squinted at Trevor, and sneaked a peek at Alterman and Piatkowski, reading cues to see how much heat he should put on the little man.

"Right." Nugent rolled through the word, staring at the comps harder, a quant in prep's clothing, the big man, the guy from Greenwich who could wear the blue suede chukka boots without feeling like he stole them from a clown, the crepe soles all stealth on the fine wool rugs the MDs splurged on, making it easy to creep up on people. The Pomander Walk offices were muffled except for the sotto voce clicking of keyboards providing the swap and CMBS market quotes. The only real colors that weren't neutral were the RGB Technicolor graphics of the Bloomberg terminals—charts that mapped success and failure by the minute or even moment. The superthick oriental carpets were, according to Filip Bennet, the Gensler interiors lead, supposed to "ground" the staff in turbulent times.

In his office, Nugent laid it on thick with family photos on the credenza: Bermuda, Winged Foot, Nantucket, his '67 XKE. MDs could furnish their offices as they liked, and Nugent brought in his Greenwich decorator, Missy or Mitzy, Trevor remembered, who gave the office, at Nugent's direction, the club look. On the right day, walking by Nugent's office could be fantastically entertaining, a glimpse into the chintz and mothball world of one of the private boat and tennis clubs that dotted the sound.

Outside the office, in the weak submarket of Midtown known as Midtown West, the built environment was dreary, the people generally beaten down by life, or worse. "Other borough" riffraff converged on the discount sneaker chains and quick-serve restaurants near Times Square, which sometimes seemed to be the last bastion of everyman's space in Manhattan. Trevor wondered what Nugent thought the time they were walking back from lunch, outside the back entrance to the Garden, where there was a deli/Korean salad bar that served the grunts their daily slop. A lurching and angry black man was surrounded by little Hispanic busboys—it looked like the attack of the Smurfs. It was clear the bigger man had pissed them off royally. He charged one of the little men and connected with a right cross, knocking the poor guy down and sending the busboys scurrying as the offender sprinted into the flow of cars on Forty-Fourth Street. Trevor looked over at Nugent, who was trying to look cool, but to Trevor he looked like a little boy in need of his mommy. Then there was the time when a couple of thugs were stomping a guy in the gutter right outside the entrance to the Port Authority. "Christ," Nugent said. "Where the fuck are the cops?"

Trevor, unaffected by his uninspiring triple-shot Starbucks mocha, the coffee eliding into the sugary chocolate milk part, looked around the conference room and started noting the residences of the Pomander Walk team around the table. Nugent: Greenwich. Alterman: Manhattan during the week, Southport on the weekends. Piatkowsi: Rye. They all were players in some version of when the Manursing and Greenwich Beach clubs finally closed down the bars at 9:00 p.m. on Sunday night and the members bobbed and weaved back to their A8s and 500s and Range Rovers and convinced themselves that they were just a little tipsy, that's all, and what's the big deal driving the back roads to your house when no one was really out anyway. Cops did not set speed traps to bite the hand that fed them, same as in all his time in Cali. Trevor never saw a single jacked-up pickup truck pulled over by the cops, even though they were the ones going ninety and not giving a rat's ass who was in their way or how many lanes they jumped without signaling. It seemed, based on an entirely unscientific assessment, that the cars pulled over by Southern California sheriffs were midsize European and Japanese sedans and older pickups and vans driven by Hispanic drivers. A Semper Fi sticker seemed to grant you immunity, and a Semper Fi sticker on an aggro truck conveyed double-triple-fingers-crossed immunity. While New Yorkers took to actual combat in the street and subway, Californians, resigned to high-speed travel on I-5 and the interlaced network of freeways from Chula Vista to Pasadena, had to express their innate toughness and "kill the-bastards threatening the sanctity of our avaricious, freedom-loving, Second Amendment–revering" impulses through bumper stickers glorifying the military, Brazilian martial arts, gun rights advocacy, football, tattoo emporia, the iconography of death and peril, motor sports, and adherence to the sanctity of protecting something called "freedom," the meaning of which, if it was to be adduced by the bumper stickers on I-5, could be broadly determined to be protecting a scruffy patch of land while poised on your Kawasaki all-terrain vehicle, an assault rifle slung at the ready across your camouflaged chest, your pit bull/Rottweiler crosses foaming and at the ready, keeping a group of scruffy foreign hostages at bay while the authorities came to kick their asses back over the border. And of course, there would be copies of the Constitution and Bible in the Kawasaki for quick reference.

After listening to Trevor's desultory wrap-up of the desultory tenant market in Manhattan, the MDs' attention drifted toward where they would be having lunch. Alterman was too clever to have gotten clobbered by the Internet sell-off in 2000, getting into Indian and Chinese equities with superb timing. But fast-forward to the Great Recession and it was a different story. Nine/eleven hit the market hard; 2008 hit the partners hard. Trevor managed to shuck and jive through the lean years.

He hardly did any leasing, but no one else was doing it either, so the pile moved sideways, and he kept his job.

"I lost forty percent of my net worth in the last nine months," Alterman said. "Lease me some goddamn fucking office space so I can tell that pin dick from CALPERS to stop calling me on my motherfucking weekends. They got the big piece, but we got the little piece. It ain't like we're trying to *give* it back to Deutsche Bank." Nugent loved to hear Sam Alterman curse in his Bronx-inflected New Yorkese; it made him feel like he was one of them, a street fighter, not the pansy with the blue blazer and umbrella in his drink.

"Could be we are holding our rents a little too aggressively," Nugent said, winking at Trevor, getting his back in front of the partners. No getting shot in the back by Rick Nugent, no sir, not in front of management. Rick Nugent was throwing down for the sake of his boy.

"Forty percent," Alterman said. "You, Buzz? What's your number?"

"Let's call it forty too. And guess what? Dartmouth did not lower its tuition. And Stanwich did not lower its dues or its minimum. My wife's hairdresser seems to be doing just fine, and last I checked, none of us stopped eating. Any more vacancy at 350, 1700, and here, and we're going to be feeling the heat. Not the little heat, the big heat." Piatkowski was an outsized man in terms of bulk if not height, a crazed weightlifter who drank weird shakes for lunch that had powders and solvents and ingredients ending in -oxylase and -osinate. His chest must have been fifty-four inches, all muscle, his biceps the size of a petite woman's waist. He did have a hint of a gut, though, which made Trevor wonder what was the point. You elevated parts of your physique to superhuman status and left others flaccid, unattended. It was like those antiaging doctor gurus, with their gray and bald heads engaged in conceptual jiujitsu with their massive pecs and rippling abs. Business up top, party down below. Back in the day, Trevor went through his own bench press phase, jacking up 245 pounds four times at his peak, preening for the girls at Equinox, while they in turn were fixated on getting looks from sweaty celebrities like Marcus Schenkenberg and Michael Olajide. Trevor and his buddy Shep Rosen thought they were all that, sliding the forty-five pound disks from the racks, trying to make them seem as light as a Frisbee, and going through anguished and stagey preparation before a set, each spotting for the other as if they could stop 245 pounds from an awkward erect stance before it crushed a trachea.

With the downturn in the economy came a flurry of activity from HR, stepping into the business void when the money stopped flowing. Urgent memos noting new standards of dress, office decorum, training requirements, travel restrictions, cutbacks in coffee and water service, attendance requirements, and restructured health care benefits came through email daily. No more corduroy trousers or denim shirts. No more reimbursement for intracompany lunches, even if you were talking about a deal. PTO was now something to be accrued with carry-back and carry-forward rules so complicated it reminded Trevor of his intermediate financial accounting quiz in grad school. Pomander Walk used to be a *hamishe* place, full of bonhomie and big bonuses. The admin staff was in-house, run by an avuncular guy who looked like Dom DeLuise and a bunch of tiny Asian women who were from the "ask me how high to jump" school. After six consecutive down quarters, Sam Alterman, having read an article in *Wired* about outsourcing, decided to cut his admin costs and hired a Bangalore firm to run the connective-tissue part of Pomander Walk. "Sixteen cents on the dollar. And no one needs car service home if they work late," he bragged.

One day "the guy" showed up. Trevor was prepping his pipeline report, burnishing the bullshit, making the columns color-coded on the Excel spreadsheet to evince feeling, a connection with the brokerage community. The same names, threadbare prospects, cried out week after week. Alves Murchison, a hotshot digital advertising firm on Park Avenue South, had no intention of moving, but Trevor had kept a scintilla of hope alive after having two shots of Patrón Silver next to one of the junior partners once at Dos Caminos. "We're bursting at the seams," he said. "I'd look at a double-wide floating in the middle of the Gowanus Canal at this point." He gave Trevor his card—Dax Bernstein, Accounts. Trevor wondered how you got the Dax with the Bernstein. Must have been a hipster identity shift, jettisoning his given name, probably a David or Daniel or Douglas after a grandfather, so he could run with Dax, way better for slinging your Pabst Blue Ribbon at the Downward Dog between sets with the tatted chicks.

Check, Trevor thought at the time, addled a bit by the tequila, but copacetic enough to register a note-to-self for the pipeline. At the time it seemed fishy, the whole of New York in defensive mode and this wily dude, small and neat with a goatee and a pick-stitch suit and killer brogues on one side of gray and one side of brown, saying that not only weren't they running; they were expanding. Trevor, simply lubing up a bit before meeting Paige and their Tarrytown friends Judith and Ken for dinner—you had to lube up before having dinner with a lawyer and a stay-at-home Westchester mom—could not believe his fortune meeting a guy who wanted to lease new office space, prime space that even with the work letter allowance factored in would equate to a net price per square foot in the ninety-dollar range, not quite as much as the pro formas that underwrote the project promised but enough to let Pomander Walk, as the managing partner, pay its debt service under the interim servicing agreement.

After two tequilas, Trevor became the extrovert he needed to be to get deals done. Lubricated, he could work a room, even the New York real estate brokers' annual dinner at the Waldorf, two thousand barracudas in an undersized tank, if need be. The problem was he had to hit his inflection point exactly right, feeling the surge of alcohol but still having the energy to articulate his thoughts clearly. Trevor's tolerance was low for a guy, between three and four ounces of liquor max. He had an hour or so when he was loquacious and charming; by the third drink, he veered toward being a ranter. The night of the day that Paige walked into Red Hook, catching him with his arm around Cat Gjertsen's waspy little waist, his hand (and this was a matter of debate between them) grabbing her butt, she started to clam up around Trevor. It wasn't anger, but a sense of her breath becoming truncated, the exact opposite of the deep, diaphragmatic tantric breathing that she craved. That's what she told him, that being around him was making it hard for her to breathe. That night he had a double shot of mezcal, and then another, and in the morning found himself sitting upright on the sofa, fully clothed, like the rootstock of a Japanese maple that had been relocated to another part of the yard. "Actinidia," Paige said, finding him on the couch that morning. "I'll never grow an Actinidia bush."

"Huh?"

"Gooseberry. I like gooseberries, love the jam. You do too. But growing them is a whole different thing, wouldn't you agree?"

"Paige. I spent the whole night sitting up on the sofa. Had some of that mezcal the Rolfes brought over—get rid of it prontissimo, by the way—I can't think and need to barf. Why are you talking about gooseberries?"

"That's a good question. I could have said I'll never sail the Mediterranean or start a women's pro lacrosse league or manufacture dickies from sustainably harvested hemp grown by a fair- trade cooperative in East Timor, but since I write about produce, I made a gooseberry reference. The idea, Trevor, the cheap metaphor I was going after, is that there is a vast universe of things that you can think about that are elusive. Conjuring them is as close as you'll ever get to reality. Even things that are right there in front of you—fruit, in my case—I can talk about and write about but never experience."

"Christ, can you at least make me a cup of coffee? What time is it anyway? The kids asleep?"

"Yep. It's five thirty."

"Ouch."

"I'll make the coffee. Oh, and I think it would be a good idea if you moved out for a while."

- 10 -

The guy came in with a good suit, but no tie.

"Allan Miller." He held out his hand for Trevor, a fish's handshake, low and wormy with a hint of sweat on the palm, enough to make Trevor want to slough it off immediately. Miller was maybe a redhead twenty years ago. He was sixty to sixty-five in Trevor's estimation but had probably been acting sixty-two when he was twelve. An architect and an MBA apparently, but strictly a numbers guy now. Those guys were the worst, their creative impulse snuffed out somewhere in the real estate wars. Out of Cornell or Pratt or Syracuse thinking about becoming Gehry or Jahn or Johnson and instead getting assigned mullion detail for a rental high rise on Second Avenue. Watching the developers and their suits talking rents, equity, waterfalls, and debating the merits of different stone in the lobby. Always diminished by the money guys. Disrespecting the architects, the creators of the project. Even the partners of architecture firms didn't make real money—broker and banker and developer money—off a Manhattan skyscraper. And aside from the design partner, the only guy in the office who could draw, the others having forsaken their scales and Rapidographs and 8F pencils for CAD/CAM, no one gave a crap about the architect. So Miller veered into finance, lording the details of construction and HVAC over the finance guys and the money part over the design team. In gambling terms, he middled it. He was there to probe, Alterman's executioner. For all his barking, Sam Alterman was a softy when it came to putting people on the beach.

"How did you underwrite 1370?" Miller asked Trevor, who took it to mean at what rents.

"Eighty-five dollar average. Higher obviously in the tower, but the base floors are desirable because of the size of the floorplate," Trevor told him.

"I didn't ask about rents. I asked about process. Tools. Knowledge. KTSP—knowledge, tools, skills, and process. Capisce? Here's what I'd like from you. For starters, can you get me some history? The acquisition deal for the land. The brokerage team, the pro forma. Put something together for me like you were starting the process over and submitting a go/no-go. Can you do that for me, Trev? And then we can start to talk."

"Trevor. It's Trevor."

Miller wheeled around, showing the tails of his English suit. Trevor thought that he might as well have had a little placard made up with the saying "Dress British, Think Yiddish" sewn to the back of the jacket. Miller was a physical nonentity, but that's what a good tailor was for, pumping up the flaccid parts, the shoulders and chest and the crotch for that matter, engorging the little man. With a suit on, the peccadilloes and ravages of time were swaddled in worsteds and flannels and hairy tweeds. That was what was such a shock at the squash clubs, watching the white men strip down, unveiling blotchy pink skin, moled and warted and brimming with precancerous lesions and fissures. Blecch, thought Trevor when he undressed Miller from behind, seeing the flatlands of his old man's buttocks and the stick-straight legs. No doubt his scrotum dangled like a marionette. All tough guys when they were suited up, these little men, but put them anywhere real, on a construction site with the union men descended straight from the infernal violence of the Five Points or Boyle Heights or in any medium-security facility anywhere in the U.S., with its profligate incarceration policies (five times that of England, Trevor read), and what would you get? A simpering mess. No architecture degree or ability to break down a balance sheet right to the cash flow could give you the survival skills of a warrior, a Ranger or SEAL, where you could emerge from the Congo River with a combat knife between your teeth and spit roast a tigerfish for breakfast. But it was CASH FLOW that got you big-man status in finance and real estate. The cash flowed was everything, the entirety of the deal, the single barometer of success for everyone. The game was to convey that you and you alone were privy to the genius of the timing of when the cash landed, when the "waterfall" would drench the stakeholders in fresh reams of cash. The analysts sweated. Crunched and recrunched the numbers. Were probed like a seventy-year-old with suspicious polyps. Trevor understood that was the main problem with the unraveling in '08, that it was not the math that was wrong for any discrete pool of CMBS but that no one priced the risk of simultaneous default, the knock-on effect of the entire system being undermined.

"Then we can talk." Astounding arrogance, Trevor thought. Talk on his terms. You build up years of goodwill with a company, swapping family stories, fawning over your coworkers' kids' dopey sports stories like they were working through DNA-sequencing algorithms, going to picnics deep into the stretch-pantsed belly of New Jersey for softball and corn dogs, and then one day a small angry man comes ghosting onto the thirty-second floor and starts dictating what you do and when to speak.

* * *

"Ninety-two fifty," said the driver. Trevor added a twenty and rounded up, making it $120 total. He thought briefly about what it would be like to be a cabbie, a hack. Can't keep all your pride intact. Half the foreigners driving had college degrees, some advanced degrees. He was not living on fumes, but the rent for the studio at the Avalon/

Archstone was $1,250, and although Paige didn't ask him for money (and didn't need it apparently), he shelled out for the kids, the lessons and shoes and incidentals that for some reason Paige was happy to let him buy. Unemployment helped a lot. No wonder Spaniards look so happy and so well dressed. The dole as a lifestyle could be manageable. Seeing Barcelona at the Camp Nou, the whole crowd looked dressed by a personal shopper. And Barcelona was costing him extra for Gol TV and the sports package from Cablevision, which was lining pockets that were already gilded. Barcelona was nonnegotiable, his church. Through watching the Blau y Grana, he began to understand meditation, the flow of things. Tiki Taka they called it, the passes short and tidy. Barca's games were nuanced and choreographed. They won a lot, but in the rare instances when they didn't, Trevor was just as fulfilled, because the patterns were there, affirming his sense of order. Their players were small, tiny even, five-six and -seven against six-footers. Who were these men?

The Avalon/Archstone (shit! Trevor was almost at the entrance and damned if he forgot which it was!) looked good when he moved in, an Indian summer day in early November with sharp sun and the doorwoman turned out nicely in a black pants suit and pumps. I can live with this, Trevor thought at the time. But gray New York was there, and he came back with nothing from Hugo, who was sponsoring half of LA, but not his own kid.

- 11 -

"Aw, jeejee little jeejee baybee. Mwwwwwaaaa! Mama loves her little jeejee baybee." Eileen had her hand under her first-class American seat, groping for little Rufus, the plane somewhere over Scranton, starting its long approach to Kennedy. "Mwwwaaaaa. Almost there, baybee. A couple of minutes, my little jeejee baybee." Hugo was reading *Essays before a Sonata*, by Charles Ives. He had a film project in mind that would link the concurrent threads of new music emerging in Europe and the U.S. at the advent of modernism. Not that he'd do it himself at this stage, but he would still executive produce. Schoenberg, Ives, Cowell, Sessions, Babbitt, Ruggles, Stockhausen, Morton Feldman from the 'hood in Woodside. Feldman was a Peter Lorre lookalike with that greased-up beaver-pelt hair and Coke-bottle glasses. A nerd's nerd. It would be a period film, centered on an émigré's boat ride from Vienna to New York. Ives was a polymath, a jock and founder of the insurance brokerage Ives & Myrick who mastered four distinct subgenres of music. Hugo was obsessing over how Ives, a football player with what must have been electrifying speed—his coach suggested that he become a sprinter—could have been incubating a piano sonata paying homage to the "men of Concord," including Emerson, Thoreau, Hawthorne, and the Alcotts (sic). But then he felt his arm jostled and saw Eileen in the aisle, pawing under the seat for the opening to Rufus's little in-air cage. She was bent over so far that her cocoa-colored sweatpants had slipped down her hips, revealing the spaghetti straps of her thong to the guy across the aisle in 3C. She kept bending over, reaching for Rufus, who was yelping. Hugo gave her a little elbow and she turned to him. "What is it?" she hissed. The guy was still looking, first at them, then at the thong. Hugo wondered if it was the first thong the poor guy ever saw. And then it dawned on him: it was the oldest woman he'd ever seen wearing a thong. Stood to reason he was gawking. Once in San Francisco, waiting to get into Lepidoptary, a vegan cider bar in Hayes Valley, the maître d'affaires approached Hugo and Eileen from behind and asked whether he and his daughter were ready to be seated. "My wife and I, you mean?" Hugo replied.

"So sorry, sir."

Rufus pacified, Hugo got back to his book and saw a photo of Ives with his wife Harmony rowing on Elk Lake in the Adirondacks in 1909. Harmony—what a fantastic name for a composer's wife!—sat at the edge of the canoe in a long cloak, an umbrella shielding her from the sun. Ives is in the middle of the boat, with a smart porkpie hat and a wool suit. No planes in 1909, no Lululemon or Vuori that you bought to give you the illusion that you were still a long ways away from God's waiting room in Palm Springs. Good place to hunt a bargain at the outlets that were built on nativen land now used for maximum cash extraction from the buffet-grazing, bargain-chasing crowd on I-10. Hugo was ninety-five years old, but a child of modernism. Ives was from Danbury and a Republican, but Hugo was convinced he was part Viennese, taking his coffee in Favoriten with Matthias Sindelar and Karl Weigl and Schoenberg in Leopold Drill's old place just off the Favoritenstrasse. The old crowd, the Hakoah crowd, were regulars at Drill's place during the championship run in 1925 when Ives was still going strong. Benny said they went there before and after the games. Sindelar bought the place at a fair price from its Jewish owner and kept the Brown shirts at bay until they may or may not have pumped his flat with carbon monoxide.

By that point, the Hesterwalds were starting to look overseas, to the States, the lucky ones making it to England by the skin of their ass, a few hanging on in middle Europe, hiding under floorboards and under hay beds in freezing barns. A few Hakoah players had hung back from the 1926 tour. "We're fine here. In America no one understands our football," they said. And Hugo did think they had a point. He had cousins in New York who kept the news feed coming. It was all about Babe Ruth and the Yankees. Baseball and boxing and horse racing. The cousins said that soccer was something you did if you couldn't leave the old country behind.

Some transition. You wind up in the Hollywood Hills with a younger wife. Your prostate is swelling with cells that are tired, that don't want to replicate properly, and you feel the need to make a movie that will synthesize the cross-continental strands of classical modernism in the early twentieth century and that will be entertaining enough to attract, if not the masses, then at least a fraction of the art house crowd that would go to a Coen brothers or Wes Anderson or Woody Allen film. Meanwhile, you are glaring at the guy in 3C who is leering at your wife even though he could be her son, but you get it, the trend in society of younger men and older women getting together making everyone fair game, the world no longer sanctioning only older men eyeing younger women but actually favoring the inverse formulation, what with women being a strong majority at four-year colleges and in the workforce. Who could you tell your secrets to? Your dermatologist wife? She liked things simple. His ideas—his hypothecations and speculations—made her squirm. Like his new thing, giving away money and objects. He had taken up yoga and meditation and the deep breathing, and he believed that the flow was allowing him to jettison his stuff and his money while he was still alive.

He was feeling real nonagenarian flow, sensing that at last he could start to make sense of the disparate parts of his life. Like Ives, he was traveling for context. He kept thinking about the word "coda," a musical ending for his life. When he was younger, he thought in Tin Pan Alley terms, a feast of popular song, but now it was purely in the realm of classical music, contemplative, in the grip of other realms, distant sounds. Ives took to the mountains of New York State, the calming peaks and glacial ponds of the Adirondacks in Keene Valley, to channel his southern Connecticut past.

Hugo struggled with the same paradox, LA somehow conjuring his youth in Queens and the Bronx, the odd jobs and the ethnic factions and the Sunday soccer in Maspeth. When Maccabee Los Angeles stormed to a bunch of amateur titles in the seventies, they invited him out to kick around and take photos. He told that one kid—Mickey something whose dad founded the Mattel Toy Company— that it would be a crying shame if he didn't play for Israel at the World Cup in Mexico. And could you believe it in hindsight that he said he had a steady job as a sales rep with his dad's toy company and spending a month in Mexico didn't make sense especially since he could play on weekends with Maccabee. Forty-four years earlier, Hugo came to the US with Hakoah, and he told the kid that. There was a legacy there, Jews playing good soccer, even great soccer, and the chance to play a game with the whole world watching and to be even in the same orbit as those Brazilians was something that he would regret not being a part of.

LA always had a little too much "me" in it. As soon as one of the actors in his films made it big, he saw the changes: break up with the girlfriend or boyfriend, get a flashier car, treat the crew shabbier. Not all of them, certainly not Newman, who was cut differently, but most of them. Like those bags that he kept seeing around the house from that yoga store—was it Lili or Lulu or something alliterative but eminently forgettable— LA implored you to do something every day that scares you. The car crashes and earthquakes and unstable residents oozed danger, a mosh pit lorded over by MMA fighters, the homeless, shiftless film executives, sycophantic real estate brokers, and feral gang members massing at the border.

Hugo sensed 2021 was a lot like '36 when he was still a kid but was made aware of the Bund right in downtown LA for god's sakes and everyone union man in the city (or so it seemed) was in the Silver Shirts. Leon Lewis asked Benny to play for Gotschee F.C. in LA that was also a social club and an extension of Deutsch House that incubated multiple plots against Louis Mayer and—Lewis learned—himself. Benny was thirty-five or so but came out of retirement Hugo recalled, to play for a strange team that only spoke the scary kind of German. The German that had a hard alliterative cadence and sounded like everyone was shouting at each other all the time. Benny brought Hugo along to some of the practice and games, and he just knew the other kids thought something was up. And it was.

"Sweetheart," Eileen murmured, "be a dear and hold this," as she shoved her massive Louis Vuitton satchel, which could have doubled for a hassock, onto Hugo's lap. With that she did a full-on dive under the seat, her rear end now pointing virtually straight up in the air.

"Ma'am! Please sit back and fasten your seat belt. We're landing shortly."

"Pffffft. The nerve of these people. He's suffering under there, poor thing. Hasn't even had a nibble the whole flight. I swear I'll sue if he has any kind of trauma."

"Your tray table. All the way back, please. Sir, your electronic device? Is it completely shut off?"

No, it was not. Hugo's e-reader, a gift from Stella and Will for the holidays—Christmas and Hanukah being elided in the Hesterwald-Conroy household into one multiweek gift exchange that took place not before December 15 and not after New Year's Day—was on his lap, open to the Ives essays. The photograph of Elk Lake was there, in black and white, but he could see the sepia through the grays. When Apple products started to take off, in the mid-1990s, he was among the frumpy, Luddite throngs. "Never for me. I need to feel a book," he told Trevor. But now that he had them, phones and music players and iPads and notebooks, each with its own charger that he shoved into the utility drawer, he had to admit they were brilliant.

As you got older, time needed to be extruded and highly valued. You had to tease out the seconds. An e-reader could keep all your stuff at hand. You didn't have to gather piles of papers and books and worry about overstuffing your carry-on bag. And you could toggle quickly between subjects. He was still, as Eileen said, a little ADD, now with a couple of tablespoons of senility mixed in. Forgetting and remembering at the same time. Elk Lake on a tablet. Swipe and it's gone. Guy over there checking out your wife and you're ninety-five, long dead by actuarial standards. Take her, why not. I'm sick of that saw palmetto/Vita-Man/pumpkin seed regime anyway. Let me read and get that film made. Could Ives and Poulenc and Schoenberg be funny, a buddy film set in Favoriten, the guys shooting the breeze over lebkuchen and coffee? Could that be a film that people wanted to see?

Int. Drill's Café, Favoriten, Vienna, 1923

Arnold Schoenberg, just in from Berlin, is reading the *Ostericher Sports Gazette*. The yellow pages billow over his chocolate croissant and café with splash of milchen. He is intently reading an account of the previous afternoon's match between Hakoah Wien and F.C. Salzburg, which was apparently marred by a fight outside the stadium, when F.C. Salzburg supporters pulled the wooden crates out from under Hakoah fans who were peeping through cracks in the concrete. Charles Ives, the New World arriviste from Yale, walks in, blending in with his beret and French peasant jacket. Ives sidles up to the counter just behind Arnie and pokes him sharply in the ribs from behind.

Ives: Stick 'em up, Schoeny!

Arnie: Ach, bastard! You could have stoppen mein heart!

Ives: Not so fast, my friend. But after you look at this score for contralto, string nonet, and Celeste, with remote eunuchs' chorus, it will be a different story

The plane overshot the runway and came in the reverse way, the Jamaica Bay wind always a bit of a trick. Landing at JFK, Hugo always thought it would be nice to spend time exploring the tendrils and inlets that ringed the remotest part of the five boroughs, the collection of islands and estuaries that was Gateway National Recreation Area. On a nice day, there were cyclists and kayakers and inline skaters, and this part of Queens seemed to defy its reputation, what with the projects in Far Rockaway, some of the roughest in the city, dominating the headlines. But even there, within the boundaries of New York City proper, people were surfing and opening cafés and reinventing the place until the pandemic slowed it down for a while. There was no more New York to make from scratch, so it had to be pulled inside out, from the kishkas, every so often.

Every trip to New York these days was maybe his last. Tomorrow he was going to meet Ken Bellard at the Martin Lande House, at 137-47 Forty-Fifth Avenue in Flushing. He wanted to stay near the airport, but Eileen would have none of it, so they booked the Standard Hotel—the Standard!—the one that arched over the old West Side tracks like a Martian invader in *War of the Worlds*. "How am I going to get to Flushing from the Meatpacking District ?" he asked.

"Cab, my darling. Uber. They have these things in New York with little signs on top that take you anywhere you want to go."

Bellard's father was 103 and had lived at the Martin Lande House for so long that Hugo remembered being a young guy when he first visited him, in apartment 13Q, an auspicious number and letter combination, the hallways redolent of the familiar onion-chicken smell in New York buildings with lots of Jews. It was like they piped that smell in, the brisket and derma and flanken and kasha varnishkes part of the rent deal. Bellard's dad was pretty old way back then—seventy-five in 1982—and the building was almost all European. Hugo was sixty-seven, still playing handball in Venice twice a week and even going for occasional pickup soccer near Santa Monica airport with the crazy Israelis who stood around and bickered for an hour before they kicked a ball.

Hugo could gazotsky around all those geezers if he wanted to as they creeped toward the elevator doors, panicked that their geriatric detritus, their canes and walkers and orthotic devices would fail them. A tribe of dewlapped alta kakas in their comfort shoes. Now that he was where most of them were then, Hugo got it. Every trip might be your last. That was it. Sure, there were outliers like Bellard's dad, Hyman Jacobstein, but it was a booby prize. He was *healthy* for 103, and it was still an abject disaster. He was so old, his grandchildren were old, Ken having fathered a kid with that sexy game show hostess Mindy (or was it Candy?) Moore way back when. The grandkid was fifty-three Trevor told him!

Bombing into the city, Hugo and Eileen's Uber picked up pace as the chokepoint on the Van Wyck magically vanished, the big V-8 roaring toward the steel lattice fortress of the Queensborough Bridge, which for Hugo was an urban mirage: an ungainly bulwark up close, but well knitted and beckoning from farther away. They were pretty close to Al Meltzer's forty-fourth floor pied-â-terre on Third Avenue, from which you could see the ant colony flow of traffic, the bridging and tunneling and boring into Manhattan. He loved Meltzer's place, a sterile beacon in a well-curated building. The kind of building where the doormen had assistants and they all smiled. So big deal if the second you were gone, they started gossiping about you. It was the window dressing that counted, the supplication and artifice and sycophantic pandering that made you who you were, a consumer of real estate a quarter mile into the air.

- 11 -

Hugo slumped into the crevasse of the Crown Vic's vinyl, worn to a trough by thousands of bottoms crisscrossing the city. Rufus was in his carrier in between him and Eileen, who was chirping into her phone and texting at the same time. Boom. The cab lurched to a stop outside the Standard, and both doors were opened instantly by doormen in tight polo shirts and black jeans. "Welcome to the Standard," they said together, very chipper, one black and one white. Ah, New York, the palms were upturned the second you hit the pavement. Little did they realize who they were dealing with: Hugo Herald *gave* his money away; all you had to do was *not* ask. And by not asking, that meant not being overly solicitous with those puppy dog eyes and not saying "Mr. Herald" all unctuous and beseeching and not, if you were a panhandler, reciting, for the umpteenth time, the sad and meretricious facts of your life on the street involving your children, dogs, and checkered employment history. Hugo Herald himself identified the beneficiaries of his largesse, one of the big moves he had left in his dwindling arsenal. He had, he hoped, one big project left in him.

"Be a dear and get these," Eileen said to the black guard, the handsomer of the two. Marrying younger seemed like a great idea to Hugo when he was, well, younger himself. Old now, he had to admit to a certain exhaustion being married to someone younger. At home, there wasn't a lot to think about in familiar trappings, moving from the bedroom to the kitchen and the pool, settling in for a light lunch, tomato soup and an arugula salad, while Eileen kept some office hours and shopped a little bit. Traveling was different. You had to get in the fray and talk to strangers, put yourself about. It was the last thing, exposing yourself, your manners and dress and ideas, to the public at large that Hugo was finding harder to take. He had passed the inflection point where needing to care about other people's opinions and ideas mattered. The good thing was that everything seemed cinematic, as if it was happening for his benefit. Eileen's outfit, the mauve nap of the twisted cotton fiber, the interlaced gold necklaces and array of Bakelite and metal bracelets on her tawny forearm, seemed selected by a wardrobe department. It was not Hugo's wife Eileen; it was the character playing Eileen, the camera recording their visit—perhaps their final visit—to New York.

Outside the cab, he got a good view of the Standard, which straddled the butt end of the West Side Yards. Hugo dug into his travel pants for some cash. The pants were called "joggers" according to the gender- neutral clerk at Fred Segal. He picked them for the flight because he hated the feel of a cinched belt on a long plane trip. Buying pants in a store in LA sure had changed over the years, Hugo told Eileen. A straight man buying stretchy pants was not something that was done in the seventies or eighties .

Digging in, he found a wadded twenty and seven hundreds in his pocket. It was New York, and the standard unit of basic currency was a twenty, anything less an impostor, quotidian singles and fives and tens, and horror of horrors change, something to buy a giant soda at McDonald's or an all-day MetroCard or an MSG-laden lunch at a Korean deli. The creative and consumer classes carried twenties like they were Mentos, fungible and good for a quick fix. "Can you guys split this between you?" he asked as they plopped the bags near reception and hustled back outside. He had forgotten how cold it could be in New York during the holidays, pretending that his Danish fisherman's sweater and linen shirt jacket, bought at a different time at Fred Segal, when one of those astonishingly attractive LA salesgirls who existed to extract money from people like him, old and rich and influential, sidled up to him and got close enough so he could smell the civet musk from her $460/ounce perfume, could keep him warm during a city winter. He learned about the civet from the makeup artist (Dianne or Denise or Delilah?) on *Night Flag*, '71, about a campus raid gone haywire. It was a small catlike predator whose anal glands were expressed for perfume. Note to self, Hugo thought, as the wind corkscrewed in and up through him: do not buy winter clothing in Los Angeles. Finally settling his account with the driver, Hugo saw the erection of the Standard, lit in the night sky, the light and dark rooms flowing into a boogie-woogie rhythm. The hotel stuck up like the finger he gave the driver on his way to drop Trevor at LAX.

The white doorman slipped the twenty into his pocket, and Hugo wondered whether that requested split was forthcoming. Eileen found her way into the lobby and was sitting at the bar. So this was the way it was. Wife starts to get antsy, wants action. Hubby is baggage. Old, withered, needing chemical assistance for everything. "Keep going buddy, keep moving," he told himself. She was on her phone, scanning, reading, here and there texting or typing, looking away only to coo at Rufus, who, against house rules and the sanitary laws of New York City, was on her lap as she sipped her Ramos fizz through a straw.

"Baby," she said to Hugo without even angling her neck away from the iPhone as he straggled into the bar, his poor ninety-five-year-old gonads still feeling the sting of the Hudson River wind, "come here and try this drink. It's a revelation! There's egg in it!"

"You don't say. Egg?" Hugo inched over to the glass and peered in, nose first, close enough that when he stood up, he had a bit of Ramos fizz foam on his nose.

"That's maybe a tad too close, baby. Here, this one's yours now." Eileen turned to the bartender. "Another fizz, please, handsome." It occurred to Hugo that Eileen operated in her own sphere when they were in public. At home—because she was at home—her introspection and self-absorption seemed to fit the context. She had a medical practice, doted on her scruffy dog, arranged ladies' nights, rummaged through the detritus of cable to record shows that Hugo regarded with increasing enmity: housewives of every color and vulgar accent, with bosoms that were downright architectural; competitions for building multitiered cakes and eating insects; morons jousting in what looked like amusement parks with swimming pools; rangers and marshals and cops and sheriffs herding and cuffing miscreants, vagrants, felons; even Amish people with tattoos threatening each other for what seemed to Hugo to be the tiniest slights. But the nadir was the time he came into the den and heard Eileen cackling. On the screen was a chimpanzee in overalls and a red polo shirt, pointing a handgun at an animal control guy, who was dangling a vat of some kind of crunchy cheese snack at the primate. "What? What is he doing? And why is there a monkey with a gun?" Eileen heard it as: "Vit un gun?"

The fact that Hugo still had that accent bothered her, made him seem his age. In LA, no one was allowed to be their age. Lately she was showing him ads with a doctor, a guy in his seventies, who rechanneled his amino acid sequence to remake himself into a sculpted, virile Adonis. "Look at this guy," she said, flinging the issue of *Men's Health* over the nightstand that separated their his-and-hers queen beds, low-slung modern numbers from Design Within Reach, which, when kitted out with the requisite duvets and linens and throw pillows and ergonomic accessories, totaled $14,506, an amount that made even Eileen look twice at the invoice before signing. It did include Gold Glove in home setup, she later rationalized to Hugo over kaffir lime martinis.

The chimp caught a whiff of the cheese puffs, lowered the gun, and helped himself to a handful. "Just watch. They're trying to get him in the cage. He drank three bottles of cough medicine. That's why he was so agitated. Look at this—genius."

Hugo stood in the lobby of the Standard and pirouetted around, all of it again seeming cinematic to him. The trappings were clearly of the aughts—rustic modern stone, undulating surfaces à la Frank Gehry (weren't all these modern architects riffing off Gehry somehow?), geometric patterning layered like a psychedelic Sacher torte. The guest agents were in black, sylphs and Adonises, and they were oh so busy, staring intently downward, averting everyone's gaze in a perversion of what Hugo thought the service industry should be all about, except that this was downtown—no, lower Manhattan— where the equation was reversed: you paid extra for the bitch-slapping, the comeuppance, the beat-down. Eileen put back her new gin fizz and went back to the original one that Hugo had abandoned. He waved to her and pointed outside and flashed the wagging hand signal for "I'll call you," which struck him as ludicrous for a man his age, but the fact was there was no substitute for it.

How crazy was it to be staying at this hotel when the main purpose of the trip was to see his friends and visit Hyman Jacobstein, the only centenarian he knew personally and avatar for him and his cohorts, all rapidly advancing up the ladder of God's waiting room. You kept creeping up, marking the birthdays, and it becomes ice-cold actuarial reality that you have *x* number of years, a very small number, suited for marking in days or for that matter hours—you had mere hours left, and incalculable unread books and countless hours of music to pore through, whole catalogues that you somehow ignored, like Webern and Stockhausen and Babbitt, and even more conventional pieces like Bartók's viola concerto, left unfinished at his death but completed by one of his students. Hugo fretted that drinking Ramos fizzes and canoodling with bar backs was a waste of his precious, vanishing hours. It was all he could do to channel those Sardinians who attributed their longevity to the particulates and flavonoids imparted by the volcanic soil of the region to their wine, with a nod to daily activity, tending gardens and preparing food. Hugo recalled how Trevor's wife Paige was doing a big piece on resveratrol and flavonoids and kept insisting that Sardinian wine was the way to go. He kept asking at the wine store, and they kept saying they had all kinds of Italian wine, but not from Sardinia. Tuscany, Umbria, Piedmont, yes. Sardinia, no. "We sure don't," said the clerk, a surfer type, giving an answer you could get only in Southern California, a preposterous inflectional inversion, a chipper affirmative-negative, which could be flipped any which way, "Sure, we don't," or "We don't, sure," making as much or more sense.

But he was out of LA, back home, or that's the way he felt, if only for a half day every time he came to New

York, the dimmer, slow-baked light and interstitial stretches of weirdness more to his liking than the branded showmanship of ever-preening LA. He shuffled along the pavers of the port cochère, over to an uplit landscaped area away from the hurly-burly of the drop-off area. He could see a flat low ship, barely chugging, maybe a freighter of some sort from the Baltics, a passel of desultory shipmates idling their days away, trudging some weird stuff, tinned fish or nail polish, across the continents.

Glancing up, the half tones of the curtain wall of the Standard shone varicolored hues off the last light reflecting off the Hudson. Hugo could make out some of the interior furnishings in the rooms with the lights on, white duvets tucked to military perfection, headboards that looked like they were woven from raffia or some type of rough grass and sleek silver lamps. Edging closer—at ninety-five it was always about edging closer—he made out forms. He realized anyone on the street could take a pair of cheap binoculars and spy into the Standard's tiny rooms. These boutique hotels put the money in the lobbies while shrinking the actual room sizes to nearly what Hugo had seen in a Japanese airport hotel where they slid you in, coffin-style, to a sleeping bunker.

- 12 -

"Your coffee, ma'am." Ma'am. Ma'am? Drove Phoebe nuts. She was thirty-six, lithe and glossy, her body sculpted by a class called Ka'anuba Tempo, described on the tear sheet as "Zumba meets P90X meets boot camp, an expression of thought, dance, and kinetic power that will leave you breathless and invigorated. Lengthen, strengthen, and flex. Mondays, Wednesdays, and Fridays 10–11:30. Kit Suarez-Fraser and Michael Prince Oonjade, Instructors."

Red Hook had a shipment of Coffee Lua in, harvested from the droppings of the civet or ocelot or red panda or some animal, a delicacy that translated into $12.95 for a 400 mL pour-over serving. She reverse-engineered the profit on the cup. Thirty grams of coffee per 400 mL yielded roughly fourteen servings of pour-over, assuming the barista was reasonably skilled and parsimonious. At retail, this was about $182, and with the coffee costing fifteen to seventeen dollars a pound wholesale, more than a thousand percent markup. Not bad, but this was specialty stuff, an exotic, not consistently available throughout the year or even the growing season. But she did see how the trend toward small-batch growers, with a fair-trade pedigree and liaisons with influential buyers, was shaping the market.

Refinement was coming to the coffee business, and maybe Trevor was on to something. He found a spot on the Upper West Side of Manhattan where there was a historical zoning blip and maybe with the right attorney you could get a roasting operation, even without a scrubber for the effluent, past the Community Board and City Planning and the Board of Estimates and God knows maybe the tribal council of aboriginal bean pickers and actually roast in the middle of Manhattan. That building was a misfit, too weird for a house, too expensive for a teardown, and with the funky way the sunken, setback plaza hit it midbelly, it put most retailers off. And besides, coffee was mother's milk. It was an onslaught: Blue Bottle, Worm Wood, Buffalo, Intelligentsia, Port and Cove, Ninth Street, Red Hook. Starbucks colonized Manhattan in the nineties, retrenched a bit in the aughts, and was back again and now post-COVID shrinking again. Hugo had the money—he told her he had more than $12 million liquid ("Not so much that they call me high net worth," he had said. "Twenty million is what they need. I'm a peon"). But Trevor was just so, well, desperate. The word "flailing" came to mind. He had a good job and fucked it up. Everyone hates their boss, but you don't cut and run. She endured five bad years at JP Morgan, working eighty-hour weeks and sometimes sleeping at her cube, head slumped over, waking up to the security staff coming in at 5:00 a.m., her hair a rat's nest and her pantyhose clammy and stretched every which way. It was her time, she reasoned, and if her dad was willing to spring for tuition, why not? She also had the smarts not to have kids, or even be married for God's sake. It was not a rejection of the institution, but she was out–Peter Panning the Peter Pans, what with the statistics favoring Manhattan bachelors by lots—the figure she heard varied between 2 and 12 percent. Trevor was all over her to commit to opening a coffee business, and why not? She was single, not even working part time, taking two classes a semester and making student films. He wanted her for her street smarts and innate financial ability. Cat Gjertsen was for prowling the front of the house. When Trevor talked about his "vision," and to be clear, it was his vision when he talked, but it was their sweat equity, she sensed that he wanted Cat to be the face of the business and her to be mired in accounts payable. "You've got such a good business brain. I can't do this without you." Her sense was that while he created menus, picked art, and fluffed pillows, she would stare at the books up in a sweaty loft or a cramped corner of the basement.

Phoebe watched the last droplets of Coffee Lua fall into the 500 mL Hario beaker, marked on the outside with the coding "02" like it was from Japanese central intelligence. What was wrong with just "2"? But the Japanese were always on to something, especially when it related to America. They lost the war, but in doing so they were cleverly usurping iconography and products and stylistic cues that were fundamentally American. The best denim in the world? Japan. Best "nel" drip coffee coaxed through porous flannel mesh suspended from a verdigris wire hoop? Japan. Best classic sack-style clothing and Ivy League–legacy accessories? Japan. Best sweatshirts for God's sake? Japan, a country with the foresight not to send its ancient loop wheeler looms to the scrapyard so that now hipsters from Silver Lake to Williamsburg could wear $280 gym sweatshirts that back in the day were standard issue for every kid in America. It was the Americans who went cheap, who outsourced everything, including their debt, which created the imperative that we not meddle in the affairs of our Chinese debt masters, keeping the yuan low, imports cheap, and factories humming along—"Jjjyna," as Trump used to say. So what if there was a fire here, an explosion there. Keep it cheap, baby, keep those floppy tees and giant cargo shorts, designed for the ever-expanding vastness of the American gut and behind, stocked to the brim on the $4.99 table.

And while we're at it, bring on the death and skull iconography, and make sure the slogans get on the T-shirts. Phoebe saw a guy getting off the 2 express at Seventy-Second and Broadway wearing a black T-shirt emblazoned with crossed pistols that read, in huge sans serif letters: "FOR MY FUCKING ENEMIES." Disagree with me and BOOYA, this one's for you. That's the kind of Second Amendment way I roll.

In a disembodied way, she reckoned that cheap goods engendered anger. Everything a volume play, the bigger the box, the more cutthroat the wholesale buy, the happier the consumer. But cheap brought cheap manufacturing into play, which took the jobs, which made people dependent on cheap products and started the cycle over again. Why have a twelve-ounce jar of mayonnaise when you could buy a two-pack of thirty-six-ounce jars for a couple of dollars more?

Coffee incubated in a civet's ass was of course the complete opposite of this. She had Paige to thank, or blame, as the case might be, for dragging her into the slurry soup of coffee and for setting her straight about how monoculture crops were destroying America. Paige was sitting at one of the small two-tops, reclaimed from vast industrial pallets and anchored to the striated concrete wall.

"Did you know," Paige said, "that in Japan, they have a brand of grinder called Royal Fuji, which separates the motor from the grinding burrs so that the heat of the motor won't inadvertently heat the coffee?"

"No shit? Can't say I'm surprised. You think anyone sitting here, right now, could tell if you made two Coffee

Luas, one ground with a Fuji, and one with a Ditting or Baratza? I mean, where does the madness stop?"

"You say madness; I say growth. Growth and change. Coffee is becoming women's business for the first time ever. At least they are clawing their way out of obscurity, getting in on the business end instead of just picking and pulping the cherries."

"And?"

"And?"

"Speaking of coffee, how is it going in the Trevor sense of the world?"

"Yeah. Trevor. Ungh. A mess. A real dog's dinner, this whole thing. He's pressing you to become a partner—still?"

"Yep. I mean I love him, he's my brother, but I'm not feeling it."

"Well, he's gone now. Or at least out of the house, so I can be semi—no, check that, a fraction—objective. Coffee is good business now. You can roast, you can distribute, you can go corporate, with those sterile Bunn machines and tiny packets of whatnot, fructose and creamer and sugar, or you can do a café, but you better be good, and have an angle, purity of design and execution. But to put the whole enterprise together, sourcing and roasting and retail, plus the real estate, is daunting. And Trevor doesn't do daunting. Bet you he's surfing WebMD right now looking at the symptoms of fibromyalgia or chronic fatigue or Lyme disease and how 'rona could kill you if you have any of them. God-awful situation it is. God-awful."

"So sorry. I've never been married, but a breakup is bad enough, let alone a separation. How are the kids dealing?"

"So-so. We're doing a fantastic job avoiding it. 'Daddy's on a biz trip' kind of thing. He flits in and out, pulling crap out of the garage. He took his squash racket the other day. Weird."

Paige picked up her Coffee Lua and blew across the top of the cup. "Think I need some foam with this. Is that sacrilege?"

"Not hardly," Paige said. "One thing you learn traveling to these countries is that there's nothing hard-and-fast about coffee. Jeez, the roasters don't even eat their own cooking. You think these small-batch producers can have their own stuff? No way. They're drinking from the reject pile. They even like robusta coffee, which is shit of course. Some of them laugh about the prices they're getting now for the good beans—"

"Until they see the retail prices and they're pissed they're not getting more."

"Yeah, a bit of that going on too. It's a dance. First they're flattered. You've got a buyer roughing it in hundred and ninety-five–dollar Olukai sandals, kitted out in Patagonia from head to toe, affecting the hardscrabble man- or woman-of-the-land look, and they're fawning all over you, telling you how the market's changed, consumer perception has changed, and that their traditional cultivation resulting in lower yield will ultimately realize higher prices and significantly more revenue over time. Yada yada yada. They're hooked, feeling money for the first time in their lives. The buyer's telling them they can get two-fifty a pound, triple or quadruple what they were getting for blends and higher-yield stuff, and they almost can't believe it; it's like winning the lottery. So they cut an exclusive deal, and then buyer's remorse sets in the second they lock price and don't hedge. And who hedges? Starbucks hedges, Nestlé hedges, maybe Intelligentsia and Green Mountain. But Consuela Flores D'Souza does not hedge. At least not yet. And if she can't move her product at the right time, guess what? That's right, the mold starts to set in."

"Well, if Trevor has his way, that's what I'd be doing, formulating hedging strategies in the basement while Cat slinks up against the customers."

"That slut. Don't get me started."

"Okay, right. Bad example. I do want to defend her for one second. She's hot, I'll grant you that. God knows I wish I had that certain something, but she's a hardworking girl, and, you're not going to believe this, but about the last girl who would shag another woman's husband."

"Wow. So not the way it looked to me when I saw her all over him —"

"I am not defending my brother. He deserves his, whatever—banishment. You're a champ for hanging in there for as long as you did."

"Give me time. I'm just so swamped. The timing is just so strange. I mean, I'm getting asked to do anything and everything. It's all converging: sustainability, locavorism, if that's a word, slow food, anti-GMO movement, exotics like mangosteen and kona and acai going mainstream, backyard and rooftop agriculture, hydroponics, viticulture, canning, poultry farming, you name it. There's even a start-up magazine—have you seen it?—devoted to backyard farming. During 'rona everyone became a farmer. It's like Martha Stewart meets Farmer Bob. I am in demand, sister, and as callous as it sounds, since he's your brother and my kids are your niece and nephew, I'm not really thinking about my family that much—at least not in the compulsive way an outsider would think if they looked at my situation."

Phoebe looked outside, and in fifteen minutes it had gone from sunny to what the weather folks call "unsettled," which was apt for what she was thinking about her sister-in-law, or estranged sister-in-law, if that was a technical thing, who was in such a hyper state that she suspected pills were involved. She knew Paige liked the occasional medicinal supplement, hearing once how she bragged how much she got done with a pill first thing in the morning. Coffee and uppers. If you were sufficiently wired, good times coursing through your veins, what was so bad about having your husband out of the house? You had a schedule: the coffee and uppers for breakfast, a hot bath with eucalyptus oil, white wine, lots of personal time. Probably nice for a change for Paige, even though, reflecting on it, Phoebe realized she was describing her *own* routine. But it was getting scary, more permanent than what used to be just a hiatus between relationships. The demographics for single women started to go severely south as you headed into your late thirties, especially the prospects for getting married, which jumped off the actuarial cliff. So her life was converging with Paige's just as her brother's marriage was unraveling.

Two tables down, there was a big communal table, something that Red Hook Roasters must have resurrected from one of the factories nearby. Six women had colonized the table, a knitting club. Each one had a stroller, mostly $1,400 Bugaboos, kitted out with educational add-ons and lofty baby blankets from those tiny shops in the Village and Park Slope that ordinary people did not patronize. Red Hook—even Red Hook, land of no subways and ghostly industrial expanses—had been colonized by the distaff side of the fund management industry. Smack-dab with COVID rampant, everyone needing an infusion of federal largesse, and the women whose decorating aspirations and unrelenting consumption were fueled by Wall Street bonuses were acting as if NOT A FUCKING THING HAD HAPPENED. Everyone Phoebe knew was in transition: students, middle managers, shop owners, researchers, waiters, personal trainers. Everyone was cutting their cable and grocery shopping with cash and saying good-bye to the babysitter and date night, but the Bugaboo gals did not miss a beat.

Michael Prince, who made Ka'anuba Tempo look like a stroll in the park, had the longest, leanest muscles in existence, and wore an eye patch from an injury he sustained while training to become an MMA fighter in Reno just after he made the long journey from Lagos when he was nineteen, had taken to talking about some very strange eating habits. "I don't eat for taste before six," he told Phoebe one day, as if this confession of austerity conveyed some kind of exalted status, or maybe he was trying to bring her into a cult of deprivation as a means to get in her pants. Not that she hadn't thought about that on her own, always suspecting she was a skinny margarita and a shot away from trekking back with him to one of the resurgent corners of Brooklyn like Bushwick or Bed-Stuy that used to be rough. But it was the money, she knew. Michael Prince was losing clients at a good clip. Dumping your personal trainer was about the first thing that you did when your income got cut in half or altogether. He still held himself regally, the bearing of a junior prince—in fact his brother's name was Prince—and she noticed that he kept himself in tattoos, adding to the menagerie and tribal iconography that crisscrossed his torso and lithe biceps, the ink and the coal brown of his skin eliding into a purply netherworld. The tattoos came before food.

Rather get marked and feel the long dull ache of the inking machine and its toxic deposit, foreign matter invading and punishing you for thinking bad thoughts. Make this sing for me. Make me cry. Remind me who I am. Jews did not get tattoos, Phoebe reasoned, because they were living tattoos, remorse and recrimination at the heart of their daily digest.

"Look at those bee-yatches," Paige said, shaking her head. "Bee-yatches. Betcha they've got fourteen graduate degrees between 'em, and the consistency of their brain is like the goop they put in those jars of gefilte fish. You had that as a kid, right?"

"I have seen it. Had a bite once at my grandmother's. I charfed—"

"Huh?"

"Choke and barf. I have to say they look pretty happy to me. Nothing like whistling Dixie when the *Titanic* is sinking."

Paige pulled her hair back, smoothing and patting, and seemed to fret over a stray that just wouldn't sit right in her headband. "Shit, I need my hair done. Anyway, you think—no, I couldn't ask you."

"What? To watch the kids? I could do that. We could go to the park. No problem. I can do maternal. I can be that aunt in the sitcoms." Phoebe pulled a long sip from her Coffee Lua. It really did have a *je ne sais quoi* factor about it, musk, if musk could be added to the pantheon of culinary pastoral, one of those adjectives like "butterscotch" and "cherry" and "rosemary" that were evocative and hinted at superficial erudition and something that was not there but that everyone wanted. The recondite civet somehow had ingratiated itself to the consumer class, its glands secreting the musk used for high-end perfumes and its alimentary tract for a hotly pursued coffee. Paige had a lot of balls, really, moms with jobs thinking that if you were a single woman you had nothing better to do than to escort their precious spawn around while they had a half spa day. It didn't help that it was a hot topic, every blog and magazine staring you in the face with the dilemma of the new millennium: what to do with all these educated women? How do they raise their precious crotch fruit without diluting and derailing their dreams? The iconic shot, the one with the mom in the snug J. Crew suit and a $1,000 Coach carryall, her swaddled and drooling infant in the crook of her arm, was almost as ubiquitous as the weather-beaten dad at home, helpless in the kitchen.

The murmuring from the knitting table was buzzier now, punctured by a loud cackle here and there. Sex talk probably. What else got that kind of laughing at 11:00 a.m. on a drizzly morning near a bunch of white elephant warehouses, awaiting the fate of the City Planning Commission and the Board of Estimates and the Community Board to be converted into whatever was white-hot at the moment, which nothing was, because in effect the entire planet could not be underwritten because, well partly the fall out from COVID, but more from the slew of bad choices and imperfect algorithms that breached the previously sacrosanct world of mortgage finance. Phoebe had seen it at Bear Stearns, in the impossibly rosy estimates that flowed from the research department, even though they tamped down the rent and growth estimates from 5 percent adjustments every year to 3 percent, and eventually to 5 percent every five years, but nonetheless all the pro formas were geared around continuous and ever-upward—excelsior?—growth projections. It started feeling ludicrous, putting out those reports and having offerings sold out in moments, only to have her counterparts at the other shops calling her in a panic to find out what was really in those CMBS offerings? Where were the shopping centers and were they even built yet?

"Phoebe. Phoebe?" Paige was putting on some lip gloss, barking.

"Sorry. I was just staring at those women—"

"Bee-yatches."

"C'mon. They can't all be that bad. That one, the one with the retroussé nose, the Waspy one, I kind of like her jacket. And she looks a little more engaged, actually listening instead of preening. I think I might like her."

"Not in the mood for charity, sister. I got three mouths to feed, a house to organize, and three big deadlines. Somehow I have to figure out a way to steal away to Sonoma for three days without a travel budget. How do you do an article on biodynamic wine producers without traveling to the source? I'm getting a whopping thirty-five hundred for the piece and they'll reimburse about half the flight, no car, no hotel, no meals. And of course, I've got the babysitting to pick up."

"I can do a day with the kids. Maybe two," Phoebe said.

- 13 -

"Tits to the wind," Hugo said to himself as he clambered outside a yellow cab, the wind once again whipping up under his linen overshirt from Fred Segal's on Melrose. But Fred and his team of West Coast clothing buyers, alas, were not privy to the ferocity of the December wind in New York, and the jacket that felt substantial in the warm glow of a Hollywood afternoon felt like an undergarment now. Eileen sat in the back, waiting for Hugo to fumble with his money clip. Realizing that he hadn't loaded it, he had to dig into the back pocket of his selvage jeans—Eileen insisted that he buy $220 jeans from Japan that felt stiff and hardly moved when he bent, unlike his favorite soft Levi's, which were like butter. Digging and prodding and harvesting some vestigial strength in his forearms—that was what your muscles were, memories, at this age—he yanked the wallet up and pulled out a wad of hundreds, slipping it loosely into the patch pocket of his LA transfunctional blazer/shirt-jac/overshirt/whatever.

"Do you have something smaller? I need smaller," the driver said, cracking the window just a tiny bit, enough to mouth something in English, which was somehow a lot clearer now when the conversation turned to money than when Hugo was explaining where the Martin Lande House was in relation to the Standard Hotel.

"Darling," Hugo said, trying to get Eileen's attention through the window. He had to wipe his nose with his expensive Fred Segal sleeve, having forgotten to grab a handkerchief on the way out. At least he didn't have to wear a mask anymore.

"What?" Eileen said, mouthing it, looking at Hugo through the window, annoyed he took her away from nuzzling Rufus.

Hugo held up the hundreds, stretching them between his hands and making a "small" sign with his thumb and forefinger. "TOO BIG. NEED SOMETHING SMALLER." Eileen shook her head no and held up her hands.

Hugo looked at Eileen and looked at the driver. The hundreds flapped in his hands, a fraction of what he had and an immense sum, probably, to the driver. He saw the driver's dense gray stubble, more like facial foliage, and, standing in the cold, Hugo got a whiff of the rank aroma of the cab, curry and sloughed skin and sweet pine. He motioned to Eileen to get out already, let's go, grab the little mongrel. He folded two bills in half and handed them to the driver, A. Singh, a $98.50 tip. "Be gut," Hugo said, "be gut."

Trevor was late, a trait he had grown into later in life. Once punctual, beating people to a meeting point by five or ten minutes, he had taken to lingering, going over details of his kit and appearance—"preening," Paige would say, making repetitive gestures and doubling back to attend to things that had been done a half hour earlier. Was it incipient OCD? He suspected as much, partly to assuage the guilt of thousands of hours, a career of time theft, of malingering on the job, turning sinecure to outright graft. He drifted for long hours, entering an equation into a spreadsheet, redoing a formula and researching the finer points of a pivot table—what exactly was a pivot table?—before letting his gaze drift to the west, to the cruise ships and working McAllister tugs on the West Side, the ziggurats and Beaux Arts detailing of the Theater District and Times Square bleeding into the new developments, forty-story towers of luxury and ultra-luxury housing, whose interior layouts had been planned down to a gnat's ass, every square inch serving a dual-purpose live/work/play/storage/sleep/sex/dream/craft/create imperative, no pursuit or craft or vice or vision too small to accommodate, and everyone gets to share the modernist lobby and green roof and Bauhaus party room. You were in good hands these days if you moved into a new Manhattan building, and Trevor looked at the new towers going up and wished he didn't have to suffer at the Avalon in Elmsford, Manhattan being out of the question for him, too much too soon, like you had it planned out that way. And then it was lunchtime, and there was always time for a walk, which became a stroll, which morphed into a tour, all justified by needing to see the competition, the psychogeography of Manhattan and how the intricacies of place and form and materials dictated price and prestige. He had to see how an entrance looked at different times of the day, how the elevators were programmed and whether they were efficient, how the staff greeted faces familiar and not, how the lobby stone and furniture suited the building exterior, and how happy the people looked. He remembered reading how a girl chose a college based on observing that the students walking around campus were looking up, in contrast to her second-choice school, where a downcast gaze prevailed. So it was with the sun, more important in winter, when it was a scarce resource. Walking—it was the walking that got you in trouble in New York and at the same time pushed you forward, every block and accomplishment and full of prospects. And it was the walking that Trevor missed when he went to LA, naked, bereft without it. Whizzing by all the good stuff all the time, the Gregory Ain homes on Mulholland, the volleyball in Venice, the upmarket design stores at the Beverly Center, and everything in between. LA life was in large part defined by getting in and out of garages and negotiating the sometimes byzantine arrangement of tickets, vouchers, validations, and gratuities (pre- and postparking) that determined your happiness and fate.

Trevor's walks at Pomander Walk, first done under the guise of market and competitive research, started to become extended, and began to define his day. If there were no meetings in the office, they began to actually replace his day. The culture at Pomander Walk was success based, leaving its employees to sink or swim. If you hit numbers, you were safe. Otherwise, you had a target on your back. Unvarnished capitalism. Personality played a factor only in determining your relative share of the pie and whether you were MD material. You needed to golf or hunt, even in a New York firm. The partners had bought a quarter share in a Jackson Hole lodge and had their yearly retreat the third week of January, right after bonuses were announced. That way they got out of Dodge for the "LBs," or Leave Behinds, the admins and interns and strivers. Trevor was an LB, as was pretty much the rest of the real estate group, considered by senior management to be a necessary evil, running a brick-and-mortar operation only to make sure that the stuff wasn't run into the ground before the assets were sold off and the partnerships unwound, hopefully distributing double-digit returns to the investors. "Leasing," Nugent told Trevor once, "is shit business, a kiss-ass bunch of nonsense for guys who flunked corporate finance. You work for an investment bank, but not in an investment bank."

- 13 -

So out of habit, he walked the mile and a half from the downtown Flushing station to the Martin Lande House. It was at least twenty years since he had been to Jacobstein's apartment. Hugo dragged him there not long after the guy moved there in the mid-eighties, the tenant roster looking like someone had lifted an Ellis Island logbook and translated it into white letters not so orthogonally arranged on a black directory. Each tenant had a code that you punched in, and then, if the coast was clear and the hearing aid properly tuned, you'd get buzzed into the building. There was a decent solarium that in the early days almost buzzed with activity, cards and foreign newspapers crinkled and coaxed into position on the dun-colored card tables, an undertow of German and Russian accents and the baked-chicken smell, always baked chicken. Walking in the cold, the twenty-five minutes or so taking him from the penumbral to darkness, three out of four faces Trevor saw were Asian. The restaurants were Korean and Mandarin and Szechuan, few signs in English, and, had he not been sure that he rode from Times Square on the 7 express train, whooshing up the tunnel into winter light from Lexington, he could have sworn that Flushing, in the twenty years that old man Jacobstein had moved there, had become annexed by Asia. Jacobstein was not quite young then, but a youthful eighty, which Trevor now saw as not elderly, at least if you kept yourself up. Shit, those Cenegenics ads showed guys in their seventies with ripped abs and massive torsos, and in California, guys were surfing and biking into their golden years. In a generation, the world had changed, seventy the new fifty, fifty the new thirty. Jacobstein, though, was ancient now, hollow-boned, a centenarian. A whiff of death came over Trevor when the door crept back, the old man inching it with the timidity of someone who knew that a push-in robbery would send him to certain death, either from the impact of the door slamming into him or from a heart attack, the latter a vastly preferable option, based on empirical data from polling the three or four other surviving Europeans about their embolisms, catarrhs, and health-related shibboleths.

"Jesus, Hyman," Hugo said, "you look like shit."

"Forgive me," Hyman said, in English even more Yiddish inflected than Hugo's. Trevor looked to see if Hyman's fevered lips moved when he spoke. The words came with slow, dull breaths. "Well... vat should I look like? Should I look like this young man?" Hyman said, slowly raising his hand, first the elbow, and very gradually the forearm, followed by an index finger. "He is the picture of health. Of youth. Enjoy it, son. It moves fast. Everything moves fast. Except me." Hyman tried to laugh, but was only good for a weak, raspy chortle.

Fuck. The curse, Trevor thought. He was careful never to address aging fully frontal, like looking right at the sun. Better to sublimate, let it stew. Hyman tilted his mottled face toward Trevor, his rheumy eyes leaking, nose snuffling, the breaths coming in discrete pulses, labored, counting down to a denouement before the respirator would take control. Trevor rubbed his temple with his palm, kneading life into it. He was healthy, he possessed health. But the fog was hitting him, his adrenals deflating from the nightly spike of cortisol that coursed through his system and gave him a sense of dread that hung over him like a cartoon balloon. This shriveled little man, Trevor thought, thinking about the state of his own health, what was left? He's the one who's made it to the endgame, still able to take the lumbering Martin Lande elevator down one floor at a time, the cab shaking the wobbly innards of its passengers, who surely felt every thrust and parry like it was a violent kick to the ribs. "Shtarker," Hymen said. "A real shtarker you got there, Hugo."

It was Hugo, in fact, who mentored Dougie Bellard, Hyman's grandkid, who took after his dad Ken, getting the attention of a wizened little Broadway agent with Lew Wasserman glasses who made it clear right away that he should not revert to the family name Jacobstein but instead keep his dad's stage name. Two generations of actors in the Jacobstein clan. Trevor was between Ken and Dougie's age. Hugo never pushed him toward the business. Trevor always thought it was for poseurs and narcissists, less a career than a calling. Hollywood, and LA for that matter, was where opportunities and front-runners went to flaunt their skills.

What you got with a Hollywood career was a lifetime hall pass. "Ken couldn't be here; he's shooting in Vancouver. Ken had to meet his agent. Ken's at an audition." A cubicle jockey did not get that space. Once in a cube, always in a cube, Trevor thought. And there he was, dutifully arranging his schedule to tap the coordinates of Hugo and Eileen and tiny little Hyman Jacobstein, whose own son did not care to preempt a single thing to see his failing father. "Where is Ken, by the way?" Trevor asked.

Hyman started to speak, choked down some phlegm, started again, choked a bit more, and rasped, "He's—he had an important meeting in the city. He's always running around. Hard to pin down, but a good boy."

Trevor looked around at the yellow photos. Hyman in his war uniform, although apparently he was never in a war, just liked to model the uni, according to Hugo, wearing it to family picnics and for Sunday drives. Kenny's publicity still from his early days, all blue eyes and dark blond ringlets framing mouton sideburns as fuzzy as a Rambouillet sheep, was front and center, the rest of the photos in a circle around the celebrity. The story was that Kenny was on Manson's list and that he was in the McQueen party orbit, but Kenny just kind of shrugged and acted goofy if someone asked him about it. It was like if you acted, even though the pinnacle of your achievement was a tepid two-season run of a cop-doc drama called *Titusville*, you could plead selective amnesia about any question. From a mensch like Trevor, folks expected a straight answer, an MBA-tinged analytical response with a firm grip and good eye contact. Kenny acted just like his photo stills, puppy dog dumb, the playboy legacy always there, his hair and skin eliding into one big lobster-colored tableau, age spots crowning his shiny dome. Like Hugo, he wore a lot of white. What was it with white in Los Angeles? It was a hard color to pull off, should be allowed on starlets only. No man could wear more than a white pocket square and pull it off.

That Trevor was thinking of Ken Bellard even when the guy wasn't around spoke to the culture of celebutard fucking that permeated both coasts.

"Hyman. There's something I've been meaning to ask you all these years," Trevor said.

Hyman did not react.

"Hyman—a question," Trevor said louder.

"Yes—vat is that?"

"Did it upset you when Ken changed his name? You know, for show biz?"

"Vat?"

"KEN'S NAME. WHEN HE CHANGED IT. DID IT UPSET YOU?"

"Ant vy should it haf made me upset?"

"No worries. I mean, don't worry. It's not a big deal." Trevor gulped at his own West Coast gaffe—using the phrase "no worries" in an actual sentence. Like greeting someone with the words "hey you," "no worries" was the ultimate brain cramp, an unctuous apology, a tooth-grinding banality, a cryptic and hollow and shallow way of deflecting culpability. In every exchange or transgression or breach of trust or miscommunication, someone needed to be assigned the task for worrying.

When Hyman's head slumped, Hugo looked at Trevor and furrowed his brow. One minute a shtarker, next minute a schmuck. Would Ken Bellard, even before his stroke, have asked Hugo a question about Trevor? Did Ken Bellard know that Trevor even existed?

Hugo tugged a small shoulder bag up onto his lap, a European-style flight bag made from red vinyl that he kept from the sixties. It had an oval, tricolored logo on it with the name of a defunct petrochemical company, Unoil. The bag was so old that it had done the style boomerang, hip again a generation later.

"Hyman, I know you like these," Hugo said, unwrapping some old-time baker's wax paper and revealing some homemade lebkuchen. The scents of ginger and cardamom filled the room, briefly intruding on the baked-chicken smell. Hyman pulled his glasses tight and moved his head down, a chicken about to peck. Hyman peered at the cookies, sniffing a bit and studying. Older people were suspicious, but ancient people reverted to the feral state, sniffing and appraising like dogs. One false bite and it was curtains.

"Have some," Hugo said, "while you're still kicking."

At last Hyman picked up a lebkuchen, inching the large cookie toward his mouth. He pushed it in, gummed it, crumbs being forced out either side, then the whole cookie kind of self-destructing in a way that made Trevor think of the World Trade Center imploding, a victim of its own structural efficiency and design. Hyman chewed a bit with a feeble effort and revealed in his moist black maw the partially digested treat . Eileen had her phone out, Rufus in the crook of one arm as she scanned her email and Facebook page , surely one of her friends posting something of prurient relevance.

"Yes. *Gut*. Yes. *Gut*," Hyman said, nutating like a bobblehead in slow motion. Trevor watched him eating the cookie as if it were a nature show, hyenas methodically shredding an ibex, nibble by nibble. Surely this was the only, perhaps the last, lebkuchen that would make its way into the Martin Lande House, which had seen a complete ethnographic transformation in the generation that Hyman had lived there. The foods being prepared and consumed in the building mirrored the neighborhood, kimchee and noodles and steaming bowls of soon du bo with the tendrils and squiggles of tertiary sea creatures replacing the kreplach and chicken and kugels that warmed the bones of the building in the 1980s. During his brisk walk down Thirty-Seventh Avenue to the Martin Lande House, Trevor remembered that joke about Chinese civilization being old and Jewish civilization being even older, begging the question of what the Jews ate for all those thousands of years.

"I can't taste so much. I don't know..." Hyman trailed off, crumblets falling from the crevasses at the corners of his lips, the hollow bones on his face receding from the rum and peach tracing paper of his skin.

"What?" Hugo asked. "What is it you cannot taste. Not COVID God forbid. You got the vaccine, I know."

It was quiet. Rufus stopped his energetic exploration of the interstitial spaces of the apartment, hidden dust bunnies and hard candies finding permanent homes under chairs and behind credenzas. Eileen heard the silence and looked up from her phone.

"Apples. Where are the apples?" Hyman hung his head. Hugo looked at Eileen and nodded toward the door—maybe it was time to get out while his friend was still intact. They had a seven thirty reservation at the Post House. Art Pozner was bitching about how he couldn't eat steak, something about how his prostate meds made it hard to digest meat. Or maybe it was his dental work, a bridge that had to be redone. Hugo made it clear to Art and Al Meltzer and Trevor that if they didn't all make an effort to get out and go to a restaurant, it would be written on their tombstones that they were devoured by a famished old man.

Trevor was going to go to dinner but had no plans to eat there. He knew the drill at these steakhouses: huge portions, iceberg lettuce with an ocean of blue cheese just for starters, five-finger scotches, and ramekins with cheesy potatoes and bacon bits flanking the brontausauran slabs of beef. Bringing America to its knees, that shit. No wonder these guys were a Baedeker of medical horrors: COPD, stroke, prostate cancer. The cloud, the health cloud was over him, thinking about the meal. But he was hungry, had worked up an appetite walking miles in the city today with the whipping wind, and inhaling the farrago burst of garlic and aromatic sesame oil coming from the noodle shops. Why couldn't they just stay in the neighborhood, step out of their comfort zone for once, and eat ethnic?

Hugo stood up, flushing the crumbs off his Fred Segal linen. Trevor looked at him and wondered whether his old man was really starting to come undone, sporting summer fabrics in New York City in the late fall. "Hyman," Hugo said, "I would love to ask you to dinner. We're meeting Kenny at the restaurant, you know."

"Kenny? My son Kenny?"

"That's the one. The famous actor Kenny Bellard. We can take you there and back."

Trevor and Eileen and Rufus and Hugo waited for two half-notes. Hyman finally looked at them and smiled, an adrenaline rush of cognition. "No. You young folks enjoy. I'm quite happy here. Tell Kenny I watched one of his old films, the one with all the girls and the car."

The car was a 507. The greatest BMW ever that at one point was so out of favor it was consigned to the scrap pile. The 507 that brought BMW to the brink of financial ruin, a German sports car conceived by Benny Hesterwald's friend Max Hoffman. Hoffman was a half-Jew born in 1904 a block away from the Hesterwalds. The Hesterwalds let Benny play with Max but were careful.

"You never know" was the mantra at the dinner table, always wondering what Hoffman's Catholic mother was telling her son about Benny. Hoffman loved soccer and followed Hakoah but wasn't public about it, couldn't be branded as a supporter, which could have had some heavy consequences. That didn't stop him from lining up at the peepholes outside the stadium to watch for free. When Hoffman came to New York, Benny got him tickets to the big ASL matches at the Polo Grounds and brought him along with the players to dinner after the games. Hoffman never forgot this, and one day in 1959, Hugo saw a semi pulling up in front of his house. Turns out Hoffman had a 507 that he saved from being melted down, the cars having more value as scrap in some cases. It was dinged a bit, but still had good bones, wearing matte ivory paint and glossy Michelins. The movers wheeled it off the truck and handed Hugo a clipboard. "Sign here and it's yours, Mr. Hesterwald."

The 507 was a strange beast, Hoffman's inspiration, reified and brought to life by Albrecht von Goetz, the aristocratic automotive designer Hoffman enlisted as his chargé d'affaires for enticing the pragmatic and recovering firm of BMW into producing a sports car for the U.S. market. It was filmic, to be sure, Hugo thought, but he could never bring himself to breathe life into the thing, preferring it as sculpture. As jejune of him as it was to think it, he could not help but see the car as a starlet, not the new breed—"lusty and busty" like Mansfield or

Russell, as they joked at the Friars Club—but European, small-busted and well proportioned. The 507 drew his eye to the uppermost curve of the car—that was really the only thing that Goetz would have had to do, that one line, a precursor of the Japanese reductionist philosophy of design—from the small round headlamps through the bonnet and the petite A-pillars, the small swell of the passenger door and finally to the 507's rear end, which Goetz privately joked about. Even back as the brief saga of the 507 was unfolding, with its meager production run of 251 cars plus three prototypes, Hugo saw the pancontinental elements and Hoffman's involvement as something that haunted him, a legacy of European involvement and failure. As spectacular as the car was and the fortuitous way it literally landed in his driveway, he was uneasy around it. He had made his way westward, finally realizing that the Bronx wouldn't cut it for a filmmaker, and the farther west you got, the more the Europeans had assimilated, especially in LA. The car made him think of Hoffman and his father, scrambling to make a living from soccer, and then of Vienna, which existed only in his infant consciousness.

After a bit, the car needed a cylinder, and it became a driveway ornament, eventually going up on cinder blocks. In LA, though, cars got noticed, and one day Hugo got a knock on the door from a production assistant who wanted to rent the car for a *Beach Blanket Bingo*–type film, *Bits 'n' Pieces*, starring an up-and-coming matinée idol named

Ken Bellard. The contract Hugo signed gave the studio an option to buy the car after filming. They were going to invest some money, and the car was stylish enough that the production assistant thought it might come in handy on the Warner lot. Hugo, scrambling for financing for his own films, and far from a car buff, decided to sell for what he thought was pretty good money. Two years later, Hugo was reading the *Times*, and there it was, the 507. And who should be standing next to it but the beaming owner, Kenny—little Kenny—right out of central casting, his wife in the background in a white bikini with a torpedo bra, next to the kidney-shaped pool, the terraced landscape of the Hollywood Hills cascading gently down to the playful cylinder of the Capitol Records Building, all the boxes of the actor's fantasy neatly checked off in one brilliant Shulman photo. Ken Bellard. Ken, the ne'er-do-well, according to Benny Hesterwald, trouble in a bottle, just for shits and grins liked to send Hugo the 507's annual insurance appraisal from Hagerty, which in 2008 was $1,307,000.

"On that note, Hyman, that very painful note, we are going to bid you a good evening. Darling, can we manage to corral our little friend Rufus? Trevor, are you joining us tonight?" Eileen scooped Rufus up and wrapped herself with her long goddess scarf, layers and layers of gossamer blue fabric. "As always, my friend," Hugo said, "be well, and be good to yourself."

- 13 -

Hyman stood behind the door, a tiny gnome, Trevor sensing that the conversion to fungible dust had already started inside the old man. He pushed the door shut. "Don't forget to put your sign out," Hugo said, referring to the little hangtag that signified you were alive before turning in. "Ach, I'm fine," Hyman said.

They rumbled down the elevator, stopping twice, once for a surprisingly spry and preternaturally smiling Asian woman who looked like she might have been flirting with being underage for the place, and once for a tiny sprite of a man, Asian of course, but with a dark-skinned female aide who guided him in the cab by the elbow. "It's sleeting out, I think," she said to no one in particular, just a shout-out, some general reportage, talking to the elevator panel and the forlorn array of plastic buttons, the thirteenth floor superstitiously elided. The three of them politely stood aside, deferring to the residents and their aide. For some reason, Rufus snapped suddenly at the aide. Eileen used her tough-love voice: "Rufus! Stop that nonsense. What's gotten into you? You're a sweet little baby. None of that now, you hear?"

Trevor was trailing everyone, buttoning his jacket, wondering why he'd taken his messenger bag, filled with coffee detritus, pencils, ephemera, business forms, nutraceuticals, and medications. He was like an overgrown, balding Eagle Scout, a New York City Transit buccaneer, an avatar of crafty (literally) Williamsburg heritage branding. His jacket was wax wear, a fabric called

British Millerain with high tensile strength and resistance against briars and insect bites. His boots were overbuilt for the urban environment, really designed for heavy-duty hiking, soled with two inch thick Vibram rubber. It became clear to Trevor, in accumulating what he called his "fortress" wardrobe, that his stuff would start to outlast him. In his REM sleep, interstitial moments that preceded consciousness, he had started seeing his stuff resurfacing fifty years later at thrift shops and swap meets. Another inflection point, he thought, your belongings, your shoes and coats and accessories moving on to your kids or even strangers who wondered who the codger was with the bad taste, theirs being spot-on for its ironic subtext. Trevor never thought in his twenties or thirties about things outlasting him. Same with how television and commercials geared toward seniors became less funny over time. In your forties, you might not need a pelvic mesh, but the thought of there being something called a "pelvic mesh" grabbed your attention.

"Trevor. Please. We've got a reservation." Hugo had turned to look at Trevor, who had barely left the vestibule. The wind was swirling, and the aide was right, it was sleeting, slicking the blacktop, especially where the grease spots had formed in the parking lot. The vapor lamps illuminated the tufts of white hair at Hugo's temples, normally smoothed by the application of a bit of what he called "pomade" that Eileen bought at D'Artagnan, the men's apothecary on Rodeo, for $67. Like a gnomic

Batman, the flimsy linen of his shirt-jac flapping in the breeze, Hugo waved his wing in exaggerated fashion for Trevor to hurry up and get into the black car, which was named Jazeera Express, like the Arab network. Eileen, sitting in the Lincoln, let out a shriek and lunged forward: Rufus had scampered off her lap, chasing a squirrel that had darted across Elder Avenue and was climbing a telephone pole. A pampered little Los Angeles lapdog was finally having his day, squirrel hunting in New York. "Ahhhhhhhh!" Eileen yelled.

Hugo turned and saw Rufus running across the street. He lurched forward, knowing that Rufus did not respond to commands like "Come!" or "Here, boy!" having been raised in west LA within five feet of his owner at all times, which obviated the need to respond to anything. Eileen might as well have picked up the pooch in a Baby Björn, the infant prince dog suckling at her teat.

Like a kid on skates for the first time, Hugo's legs in a flash shot skyward, sending his heart into a spasm, although his heart was strong and his arteries were unsclerotic, a source of wonder to his cardiologist. What was a problem was the clown-like fall onto his coccyx and the attendant pain, which took him back to the time he tore his Achilles playing the Greek Americans in the final of the Cosmopolitan Cup in 1950. Then, he had been backing up slowly, watching the Greek goalkeeper, thinking about making a run into the channel between the left fullback and the center fullback, when he felt like he had been shot in the foot, only to find that there wasn't a soul within twenty yards of where he was standing.

Fifty-eight years later, Hugo's synapses retraced that pain, and there he was, lying still on his back in the grease-slicked cold of the gutter of Elder Avenue. Trevor ran over, and Eileen gathered her Hermes Birkin, wrapping her goddess scarf tight before going to see what happened. She was a doctor and had done well at USC med school—you had to do really well to get into a coveted specialty like dermatology—and she still could feel her way around a general medical problem. Trevor stood there in his protective gear, sheltered from the elements, the sleet deflecting off the armor of his jacket, the button-in wool liner providing just the right amount of toast to keep his core warm. It hadn't occurred to him to take off the coat and lay it over his ninety-five- year-old father, supine and shivering and motionless in the middle of a street in Queens, lit by the phosphorous of the cobra-head streetlamps now that it was dark.

Hugo stared straight up, seeing Eileen and the goddess scarf as a big black blur in the glare of the lamp, a bulwark. Her breath was minty and pleasant, but mixed with the effluent from the car, which was idling, unafraid of burning four-dollar-a-gallon gas, waiting for resolution, already getting heat from the dispatcher about a pickup at LaGuardia at eight thirty (big shot, regular customer, better not be late). "Hey, mister," the livery driver asked Trevor, "do you want I should wait, or you call ambulance?"

"Trevor, your coat!" Eileen yelled.

"What? What's wrong with my coat?"

"Give me your coat! Look at him! He's freezing to death!"

"No!"

"What do you mean, no? Give me your goddamn coat!"

"I was talking to the driver, Eileen— No, sir, please stay a minute."

"Have important call from dispatcher—I cannot wait on this customer."

"Wait—here, Eileen." Trevor turned to the driver. "We'll pay, we'll pay our fare and the next fare, just arrange it please. Can't you see we have a crisis here? A real problem?"

Rufus had disappeared, a fact that occurred only to Hugo, who was not sure if he had feeling below his waist, the endorphins kicking with such a surge it amazed him that he had that much juice left of any kind. Wasn't that really what aging was, evanescing fluids and amino by-products, the lubricants and life force drying up, denying the glands and organs of vital fluids and nutrients, the body seeking ever more creative methods for transporting nutrients and forestalling oxidation? Reverting back to his atavistic accent, he mumbled to Eileen, "Ver is he? Your little dog?"

A flash of glee came over Hugo. The cycle of injury and recovery was familiar to him from a long soccer career, and he was happy to have it back, at least for the moment, thinking about how you felt the instant you went down on the pitch, the fans looking on, wondering if you'd be able to get up, a wounded warrior. He could see the concern, Eileen for a moment at least diverted from the obsessive connection with her dog and her friends and her grooming, worried about him, or at least faking it well. His son Trevor was flustered, his downfall. Flustered, but earnest, trying to make good. Never producer material, that kid, could concentrate on only one thing at a time, too linear. That's why he could never take to soccer, good on the ball and fast, but you need that sense of what's going on around you. Hugo still thought he could make it in for steak at the Post House. Wouldn't all that protein help with the healing?

"Don't move, don't try to get up," Eileen said to Hugo. To Trevor: "Ohmigod. Where's the dog?" Trevor moved down the hill, toward the ball field and the edge of something called the "Queens Botanic Garden," which, unlike its venerable Bronx counterpart, was less an attraction than a chimera, an aspirational patchwork of plant life demarcated by chain link. The driver got out and closed the back door, gurgled something into his speakerphone, and gunned the Town Car toward the Van Wyck.

Trevor glanced back toward the scene and, with a bit of effort, pulled back the cuff of his waxed cloth coat to glance at his watch, a first-generation Heuer Monaco, a gray model with black sub dials that was rarer still than the iconic classic blue with off-white sub dials that McQueen himself let drape from his wrist for every still taken during the film *Le Mans*. The Heuer was a graduation gift from Hugo, who said he got it from a production manager who was involved with filming *Le Mans*, although the watch itself was not connected with McQueen personally. It was a stunner, practically genuflected over at Pomander Walk, even though the MDs were deep into wrist candy that they bought after all the other bonus money—the down payments and kitchen remodels and apology diamonds—had been accounted for, the least they could do for themselves was to drop $15K on a half- way decent Panerai. But vintage was its own thing, and the Monaco's charisma made even the traders stop and have a looksie-dooksie. Trevor, aware of the sleet and the potential for even a bit of moisture to compromise the delicate balance of the inner workings of the fragile Caliber 11 Chronomatic movement, jerry-rigged by Heuer with a stop-start module sandwiched on top of a Buren watch movement to become the first automatic chronograph watch in 1969, quickly tugged down the edge of his coat to protect it from the elements. He knew this was frivolous, awful to be caught up in material concerns when the very well-being of his father was being questioned.

An ambulance was there, red beams flashing, and two EMTs had started to load his mummified father into the ambulance. Rufus was still unaccounted for. Eileen started shouting and waving. Was she waving for him to come or to get a status report on Rufus? All he could hear was "Yoo hoo! Hello! Trevor! Trevor!" If he headed back up Elder to the ambulance, he would lose Rufus's trail for sure, but heading toward the Botanic Garden would look like he didn't care about Hugo.

This was the calculus of panic, Trevor reasoned. This was why, he also knew, it was a blessing that he was born between wars, lacking the capacity for action. He had marveled at the Pomander Walk traders, who stared at multiple screens with varicolored trend-line analyses, doji patterns, and intraday price consolidations and breakout moves that triggered a fight-or-flight response. They moved a lot of money quickly with confidence, while Trevor, in leasing, as a supplicant and accessory to real business, cajoled people to inchworm their way toward a decision. The doors to the back of the ambulance closed. Trevor fished in his back pocket for a bandana to wipe his nose and his brow. He was sweating beneath all that hunting fabric. He knew what was next: he had to find a $2,800 Brussels griffon, whose range was normally from the pool patio to the master bedroom to Eileen's lap while she eased her Mercedes convertible through the wilds of Beverly Glen and Santa Monica, the little sniffer looking around like he owned the whole goddamn doggy universe. “Rufus—here, boy. Rufus!” Trevor yelled, trying to command the floor, the scene, like a trader.

- 14 -

Yeah, she was forty-something years old and had three kids, but so what. If you had the figure and the sass, and the ass for that matter, why couldn't you do urban burlesque in a costume that consisted of a thong edged in feathers, sequined pasties, and stacked-heel sling backs that just about let you shuffle from one side of the stage to the other? Cat was the queen bee, the one with the body and the looks, tits and tats nicely peeking through the feathers, making the small crowds wonder just what the significance of the markings was, the three circles of declining circumference—bubbles that traced the line of the inside of her hip bone. The tattoos were good for the figure; you wanted the hollow to show, not the fat, and you kept your habits accordingly, smoking if you needed to (on the sly, of course) to keep away from junk food and booze, but heaven forbid not from the occasional spliff. Luc was in the audience, coming down on his off day from Mohonk, a semiregular now in her rotation. She told him he had to come down to check out the bar scene and the new mixology that was part of the locavore and herbalist revival taking place in the community gardens and rooftops of Brooklyn.

Tonight, Urban White Females moved away from the center, not another Brecht meets the Brownshirts routine, all Liza vamping and campy cabaret, but a Glass and Stockhausen and Boulez soundtrack, edgy and annoying. The seminudity was of course the major attraction, but Cat saw no reason why, once you pulled the crowd in, you couldn't raise the bar a bit, force-feeding them something they hadn't heard. She told Luc it was the same thing with the aromatics and shrubs and exotic bitters that her friend Rance was whipping up on his Williamsburg rooftop, cascarilla and cinchona bark, and something medieval sounding called zedoary root. Rance had a two hundred square foot space outfitted with tubing and chemistry beakers and sixty-four-ounce growlers lined up like soldiers with handmade labels stuck on them for all the flavors. Before the show, they had done a tasting, first the shrubs by themselves, and then mixed with a little Grey Goose vodka to see how the flavors combined. Luc came to the show with about four or five shots of vodka in him, and funny thing for a bartender, he didn't take too well to all that liquor.

He watched Cat shimmy onstage, doing a little drag-and-drop routine with a feather boa. The music was horrible—what the fuck was she thinking?—a brutal arrangement of a soprano who sounded like a cat being mangled with violin and piano accompaniment of shattered glass. Luc scanned the program notes:

A Weltschmerz of hope greets guests as they descend into the second phase of harmonic interplay as realized by the New Serialists. Vestigial patterns of light from the setting sun are seen through a clerestory, candles are lit, and the guests are arranged in a semicircle, facing a fresco of biblical iconography and Romantic figures drawn from Strauss's *Don Juan*.

This was exactly why he lived upstate, to be away from this clutter, to not have to fake liking things to get laid, to focus on the A-to-B aspects of life and have the outdoors close by for a refuge. This was what happened when you got sucked in by these urban bee-yatches; you had to endure going to art things and paying triple for basic restaurant food, and shelling out for cabs all over the place. Luc pulled a butter rum Life Saver that had been stuck to the pocket lining of his 501s, a relic from some sleazy upstate date, playing darts or pool at the Jinx or Top Hat in New Paltz. Must have bought the Life Savers—thinking they were mints, not a kid flavor—to cover up the stink of unfiltered Camels. Christ, he didn't like that either, being upstate with the dropouts and homophobes and small-town flunkies with their local contracting businesses and salon jobs and tats that got ever nastier, revealing desperation and sad aspirational messages that interwove dead relatives and abandoned kids and exes serving time like it was some kind of badge of honor to have yourself reminded of your failings every fucking second of your life, at least when you were naked. For some strange reason, Cat's body art hit him just right, probably because it was juxtaposed with an upscale affectation of speech, the cadence and polish of her words carefully edited, not too smart, but far from dumb. She was a lot smarter than her decisions. Three kids with three dads, and she was barely over forty. He was old enough to play out the endgame before he got involved with someone these days. Part-time custody of three kids, maybe full time once they got to high school, who knew? He never felt paternal, but he was thirty-eight, and it was seeming like now or never with kids, and if he was honest with himself, he knew that someone else's spawn would never feel absolutely right to him in the way that he knew his own children could, hypothetically dreaming. He knew where Cat was pushing this, for him to move to Williamsburg, which would be a stretch for him, but in fact she didn't even live in Williamsburg, but in Bushwick, which was like a neglected colonial outpost. "It's so close, it might as well be annexed," Cat had told him, but he didn't see it. The difference for Luc was the percentage of urban desperados. His politics leaned right, but his sensibilities leaned left. Too much of one thing or too many of one kind of people made him squirm.

"Whadja think?" Cat asked, breathless, a thin sheen of sweat on her brow beneath a crown of purple and ochre feathers.

"Awesome. You show a lot up there, that's for sure."

"Uh-huh. That's the idea. Give 'em their money's worth. But whadja think besides that? Too edgy?"

"Baby, I live in a town where there are two types of music: classic rock and oldies. Three if you count crooners from the Stone Age. Anything with a violin in it is too edgy."

"Yeah, I tried to tell them—Beth especially—that Stockhausen is a stretch, even for Bushwick Ave. You can't have someone screeching and ten minutes of silence. I only have two tits to show."

The room smelled like cloves and pot and malt. Beth and the two other women from Urban White Females wrestled their jeans and sweaters on over their boas and rhinestone bras and pretty little underthings. Wendy, the tallest of the four, took her shirt completely off in front of the dozen or so remaining patrons. Her breasts were vast, interplanetary, and she had namaste marks on her sternum.

"So you think you could handle this kind of thing on a regular basis? You'd miss working your special magic at the Mohonk." Cat looked at him, whirled ninety degrees, thrust her butt out, and spanked herself. "I'd make it worth your time," she said.

"Yep. I can see that. Plenty of spots to tend bar, I'll give you that."

"For a while. I think if we start bottling those shrubs, we can get the distribution going pretty quickly."

"Uh-huh. And how much does your friend want for a partnership?"

"Fifteen grand gets you thirty percent."

"I'll think about it. That's a lot of tips. Don't have it now, but I'll think about it. He have any kind of plan, something I can look at?"

"We can ask."

Cat and Luc slipped outside. It could have been colder, the air just kind of hung there, slow moving like before it snowed. She felt good onstage, jumpy almost from the Adderall, which she upped to twenty milligrams before performing, making her less self-conscious, which was a relative thing since her friends, if they had a problem with her, got snarky about all the gratuitous ass-shaking and flirting she did, just short of coming on overtly, but a sexual carpet bomber.

"Let's go to Red Hook."

"It's not closed?"

"I have the keys, dummy. I open and close the place."

"I could use a shot or two. How long does it take to fire up the Slayer?"

"I'm not making coffee. We can do it behind the counter—right where the money goes."

Cat's words were extruded, processed like an aluminum industrial part. To the words "do it," Luc ascribed the word "widget." I want to widget behind the counter. The prospective encounter was fraught with small perils, like, for example, the three babies who apparently had been conceived in not such responsible fashion by his companion. She was bounded and trussed with remnants of her burlesque gear overlayered with a fur-trimmed gilet and white cashmere beanie. Her dreadlocked hair poked out at odd ends, and her rouge was thick and rough and catalyzed the light from the sodium streetlamps, making her high cheekbones seem as pronounced as a tribal elder in a Walker Evans photo.

"What would—what's his name? Hank—"

"Trevor."

"Yeah, what would Trevor have to say about that?"

"Trevor would say you're the luckiest motherfucker in Brooklyn. I could have his first born in exchange for just letting him watch me bend over."

"Like you need someone else's firstborn. Where are all your kids tonight, anyway?"

"Farmed out. One with the dad, one with the aunt, one at home with a sitter."

Luc buttoned his denim jacket to the top. The wind was picking up after the calm. Where were they going? They were just stumbling down Bushwick Avenue. Cat was leading; she always led, tension and power in her stride, extracting a lot more pace conceivable than breaking down the physics would lead you to believe. She was five-four, maybe and a half, but leggy, with long muscles—Pilates muscles that bowed out slightly and gave her knees just the right amount of attenuation, the muscles set at the right length and angle to do the job they were supposed to. For Luc, it was about balance and supple strength. Some women were attractive and curvy but lacked physical poise. He was just a bartender, but he was proud of being picky, and good-looking enough to be able to be picky, that was the cool thing. He could barely keep up with her, a half-step behind. Every time he said something, Cat had to wheel around and say "what?" his words eliding into the Bushwickian vapor.

"Jeez, can you slow down. I can barely keep up with you."

"If you didn't smoke so much, and maybe got to the gym or something—"

"Sorry. Didn't know you were such a gym rat."

"I'm not—I don't need a gym. You ever dance and vamp onstage for two and a half hours? I can eat anything I want. Plus, I have a wicked-fast metabolism. Come on, slowpoke, I got plans for you."

"Listen, I'm not sure I'm down with this thing. They probably have cameras on and shit. Last thing I need is some kind of rap sheet."

"They do have a camera. Any business where you have employees taking cash has a camera, dope. I'm the one with the key and the code. You have nothing to worry about. Just don't take any money."

"All righty, then. So they're going to go through the security film and see us, and..."

"Yeah—so what are they going to do, fire me? I can walk in anywhere and take over the whole coffee operation. It's like a joke. I got to fire those guys up, give 'em a little goose now and then. So Cat Gjertsen screwed some guy after-hours. It's called PR, man. Put it on Tik Tok for all I care. I got the whole town ready to hire me. Let 'em fire me if they want. C'mon, dude, you're, like, a total buzz kill right now."

"Yep, but I've got exactly eighteen dollars, and it's what, twenty-five for a cab to Red Hook?"

"I've got money and an Uber account like we have here in the big city. Bigger problem is finding a cab. Hey, there's a Fifty-Eight bus. We can connect downtown. C'mon!" Cat took off, a dead sprint from almost nothing, boa flying, heels clicking, the strings of her thong riding up past the low waist of her jeans and, Luc could swear, kicking up dust off the concrete. He chugged behind her, woozy from the wormwood concoction that they kept pouring from some kind of funky decanter into his rocks glass, which had muddled mint and some kind of smashed-up little sour berries. The drink tasted like strong anise, like that green stuff Chartreuse someone made him try, but then it got bitter and smoky. Apparently it was a small- batch liqueur called Besk. Now it was almost killing him. He wanted a pillow and a futon. Anywhere would do.

Cat flagged down the bus, which opened its doors midstop, a big no-no in the MTA handbook. She dangled backward off the landing, the bus driver snarling at her. "Ma'am, I am closing the door."

"Shit—er, please, hold on. He's coming. He's a little sick. Please."

"Watch the door, ma'am. You need to step in or step out."

"Puleeze. One more second. C'mon, you fool!" she yelled down the block to Luc. "Move it!"

The driver activated the door and it flapped and smashed, or half flapped and half smashed all 105 pounds of Cat Gjertsen, smushing her bag and smacking her in the nose so she saw stars. The doors flew open and again smashed into her, this time knocking one of her heels off into the street.

"Fuck you!" she screamed at the driver, a portly African American man in standard-issue MTA grays and dark shades. The sunglasses were strange for the nighttime, but he thought they helped project authority. By his demeanor and glazed look, he was nearing retirement, not pleased at all with getting graveyard duty in central Brooklyn for exactly this reason; you were dealing with punk-ass white kids who emerged at crazy hours from these industrial buildings where they were doing God knows what—screwing on trapeze and dressing up like hookers and she-men and whatnot, or you got your fare-beaters and punks. The punks he could deal with, usually going all Bill Cosby on their ass: "Get off my bus, or there's going to be a problem, son," but these dopey white people drove him nuts, like they hired some kind of limo service and he was getting paid to kiss their ass. His bus, his rules. Still, he liked to look at the girls, and this one was cute enough to stop for, but now she was a royal pain, fucking up his route and maybe getting him into some kind of disciplinary hurly-burly if she ever got sober enough to look at his badge number and follow up with a complaint.

Cat hopped off, back on the street, defeated. Luc, huffing, finally broke into a jog.

"Thanks," Cat said. "You broke my heel."

"Sorry—I'll take it to a shoe guy."

"You could have trotted at least. Shown some spunk. Where's your energy, dude?"

"Pretty low, truth be told. It's a funny thing—" He looked down in the street and shuffled his left foot in front of his right like a dog clearing some brush. "New York takes a lot out of me. Doesn't anyone get a chance to relax down here, kick back and have a beer without thinking about the next gig or investing in some kind of half-assed business deal? You can't even talk to anyone without them looking over your shoulder. Maybe the next guy or next chick is hotter or richer or has cash falling out of their pocket."

"I can see that," Cat said. "I can see it takes a lot out of you."

Even with her extraordinary reserves of energy, the catalytic bounce that made her famous, her lithe yoga body and spunky gray-blue eyes were starting to feel fatigued. She was propping this guy up to what end? He was a scraggly interloper, a parlor trick, a flailing house cat in an above-ground swimming pool. Luc seemed pixilated, not a person, but tiny fragmented Luc nucleotides that blobbed together to form something larger. It could still grow, she thought, consuming more, but not learning more. She knew that in some sense she was a failure, both a serial and parallel failure, multitasking into oblivion, knowing that it was bad for your brain, trying to do too much and not realizing any pure enlightenment of process. Her kids were her life, at least that was the party line, but some days they were a speed bump to her carpe diem modality, and they had to subordinate their needs to hers. So she was a bad mom, cavorting after midnight in a dodgy part of Brooklyn with a guy she dragged, almost literally, from behind a bar in a fancy upstate hotel. It was something women with poor self-esteem used to do, a stepping-stone to a house in Larchmont, parking your crazy wild-hair days neatly behind you and eventually bartering your assets for your husband's paper assets. Some of her girlfriends, the conventional ones, or the ones who were able to switch gears, were hiring decorators, selecting the appropriate gloss levels of kitchen paint, and studying the architectural roots of beadboard, an essential interior detail for a shingled home.

"Where do we go now?" Luc asked but did not direct the question to Cat.

- 15 -

If there was one thing Trevor mastered at Pomander Walk, it was spreadsheets. Pivot tables, three-variable graphs, inverting and reverting data. Showing the analytics, the juice, where the money was made. Buzz Piatkowski would thumb an investment memo with his pinecone-thick digits, dark springs of hair popping up from his knuckles, skip through the "boring word parts," and get straight to the graphs. "Where are the fucking numbers?" he would say. With spreadsheets, you had to get to the point where they were second nature. Trevor thought it was like playing the piano: thinking bogged you down. As soon as you had to get into the "help" module, you were screwed. Things had to flow, or the numbers wouldn't cooperate, and your sheet would go all circular argument on you, not divulging a thing except your own illogical thinking. When he was a kid, Trevor had a brief go at the piano, taking lessons from a guy who played in studio gigs and as a backup in Doc Severinsen's *Tonight Show* orchestra, but he quickly found out that the piano was his enemy, unable to get how anyone could get parallel motion down. His hands wanted to go the same way, left/right/left, like a military drill. Two hands doing two different things was something to marvel at. Trevor had read about Leon Fleisher's bout with focal dystonia, a cramping condition, and became fascinated with the repertoire for one-handed pianists. Trevor sometimes was afflicted with pins and needles in his hands and forearm when he woke up and started to think that his pinky was reflexively moving into a position that could not be technically considered cramped, but kind of curled. FD had apparently not been diagnosed until 1995. Trevor kept a notebook with reference points for what he thought of as the mystery conditions: FD, Lyme, fibromyalgia. The medical world continually flexed back and forth on these. These ailments were divisive, not for casual conversation anymore, neither camp brooking fools. The naysayers were, of course, "healthy," although with time Trevor began to question the meaning of the word. Could you be healthy if you had a gut, even a small one? A minor drinking problem? Skin cancer, even if it was removed to what Eileen referred to as the "zone of comfort," past where the epithelium could be contaminated? Tinnitus? Getting an ailment and obsessing about it was just being vigilant, protecting your loved ones. It was all a delaying tactic. God gave you fifty, and then you roll the dice. You could roll sooner too. Look at Keith Richards, the bastard's face showing creases in the creases, but his arm candy getting lovelier and lovelier.

So Fleisher first embraced being one-handed and then fought it off, redemption as it were. Charles Ives, Trevor heard from Hugo, just walked down the stairs and shut his musical self off—poof! Done at fifty-two.

Hugo was analytical and he loved soccer, so Trevor was preparing a spreadsheet that he thought his father would approve of, cross-referencing Italian classification of midfield positions with responsibilities of employees in a coffee bar. Trevor was congratulating himself on two counts: one, providing for entertainment while Hugo rehabbed himself from his bruised coccyx, and two, providing the subtext and context to get the nerve up to ask for a loan, or better yet a grant, or perhaps a combination, that would give him the cash to make Evan Paschman, the broker for 245B, take him seriously. Paschman was at the end of his rope—you only got so much runway in the New York real estate trenches, and lately Trevor was getting put-up-or-shut-up vibes from him. There was only so much tire kicking you could do—hell, there were legions of commercial investors who flung around millions without even looking at a property, knowing beforehand based on location whether it was a rehab or a tear down and exactly how much it needed based on location. Paschman made it clear that some Orthodox guys were interested and that it could go any second.

A Korean guy found Rufus, and Eileen paid him a $500 finder's fee—the offer of a reward having been written on the tag. After an overnight for Hugo at Booth Memorial, Eileen refusing to stay in Queens and overnighting it herself at the St. Regis rack rate of $1160 for a tiny room next to the elevator shaft, they were able to change their ticket and head back to LA, Trevor following to "help" but in reality just wanting to get away from winter in New York. The kids were in school anyway, and Paige told him to go, since it was getting weirder when he would come around, sitting in the kitchen with a cup of cold coffee and putting on a happy dad act that no one was buying.

The Italian names burst off the page: mediano, trequartista, mezzapunta, regista: fantastic, alliterative things, so artful and suggestive that they could only have emanated from the vivid peach newsprint of the Italian sports paper *Gazzetta dello Sport*, which Rizzoli on Prince Street carried for years when he roamed SoHo on a regular basis. He wished he had enough Italian to buy that beautiful broadsheet, which was quite a sight when it was unfolded at one of the coffee shops, the colorful paper draping softly on white marble and flanking the chrome and bright white ceramic of the tableware. He kept asking himself whether he wanted to be in the coffee business because he loved coffee, bled it like these crazy tattooed and bejeweled guys who rose up from the barista ranks to buyers and spun off to open their own places, wildcat types with a gut for good beans and the kind of disarming approach to doing business that sat well with the locals in Guinea and Peru and Eritrea, or whether he just liked the trappings, the bourgeois aspects of the business—how the final product looked as opposed to the painful and exacting steps needed to get it there. He had read recently about the "Stanford duck," the Stanford student who had an unflappable and calm outward appearance but was paddling furiously beneath the surface, juggling to make everything come together. So it was, he knew deep down, with a coffee bar, so pretty and pristine and elementary looking on the surface but needing massive coordination to bring it to life. He was a dilettante, a flâneur, tattoo-less in a sea of hard men and women. He needed the Cat Gjertsens of the world—forget how hot she was, that he had no chance with her—she knew how to get things done. He knew how he wanted things to look, an editor, not a producer.

Trevor called it research, time spent in other people's coffee bars and roasters. He made his way down from Hugo's in the Hills to the Arts District, east of Alameda Street and Union Station, a thin strip of neighborhood rebranded practically the second there was a new apartment building and one hipster business, in this case a place that sold sausage for twenty dollars a pound. Trevor liked to drift over to the LA River, which in this part of town was of course just a massive concrete trough used for filming chase scenes and bad car commercials but, when viewed in a different light, with the latticework of Art Deco and Art

Moderne bridges linking the neighborhoods east of the 101 to downtown, could be considered the true gateway to Los Angeles. He noted this on the Amtrak, while he sketched with a Viking Verso 150 double- sided pencil. The train slowed and creaked and switch-backed its way into downtown past the bridges, masonry WPA efforts with scrolls and ziggurats and Beaux Arts detailing that went unnoticed by the traffic. The Fourth Street Bridge was the flagship, the avenue into the Arts District, a dun-colored Deco beauty with two entrances that led to a narrow walkway.

Trevor holed up in a new roaster/café, Orangutan Coffee, whose logo was a burnt orange stylized eponymous creature, balancing an espresso in each gigantic mitt, a cartoon glyph that suggested opening a $5 million roaster in the heart of the Arts District was a walk in the park, when Trevor knew full well the machinations and anxiety and supplication involved in courting the brokers and building owners and attorneys who made the deal happen. And that secured only the real estate, the precondition to making it happen. For a roaster of this complexity, there was an army of consultants to coordinate, engineers and artisans who brought the project to life, repurposing Probat roasters and salvaging beams and millwork that gave the illusion of being there for the past hundred years. And then there was the sourcing, the deals with the microlot roasters and small family farms that were easy to cut ten or twenty years ago, but now that they were all allied with advocacy groups and fair-trade programs, there was no mystery, no ability to cut a deal anymore, all the growers having instant access to pricing from the auctions. A lot of them were also locked up with exclusives, with the savvy buyers entering into multiyear contracts that provided for the beans to get marked to market.

Cross-pollinating soccer and coffee was not his idea. Every Italian café in New York had soccer jerseys—especially for some reason the sylphlike Pippo Inzaghi—and Italian cable droning on and on with some Serie B game between provincial towns no one had heard of. It was enough to put him off soccer, realizing that what was exotic to him, interesting for not being football or baseball or basketball, was prosaic to the average Italian. Where, as a kid, Trevor hung on to every soccer broadcast, snippets from the BBC and big events like the World Cup fussed over by U.S. announcers new to the sport, on Italian TV it sounded like droning, the announcers projecting apathy. Trevor spoke no Italian, but liked to hear the language, alliterative and singsong, unlike Spanish, which he understood more of but which sounded harder and more inflected with slang. But the idea of getting into the nuance of position, indeed parsing the differences in playing the *same* position, seemed novel and bright, and, in what he thought was a stroke of brilliance, Trevor had the notion of organizing his shop around the positions and roles defined by the taxonomy of Italian midfield play.

As progenitor and manager of the operation, he would be the centrale, the box-to-box guy, indefatigable, fulminating, domineering when need be. Cat, all coiled energy, would be the mezzapunta, the advanced role at the front of the house. Phoebe, the thinker, would be the obvious regista, the deep-lying distributor and organizer. He did not have an obvious choice for a trequarista, an artist to fulfill the roasting role, and he knew that in the incestuous world of artisan coffee roasting, this would be a tough one to fill.

That Trevor had a blank document open on his Mac, about to pen his thoughts about the differences between the trequartista and regista—the former an attacking midfielder exemplifying the role of the number 10 shirt, the latter more of a traditional number 5 in South American soccer, a midfielder who sits in front of his defenders, providing a focal point for distributing the ball from the center of the pitch—was a provocation, a flanking strategy. More than that, it was a strange detour, especially in the back-alley sun that flooded through the roll-up-style doors that had become so fashionable in California, blurring the space between the inside and the outside. These doors were becoming common up and down the coast in cafés, bars, and restaurants. Could they play in New York or was it too cold and rainy? Or maybe they'd be a wild success, a fancy-free import from the left coast. But he was getting ahead of himself. He checked his voice mail, and sure enough there was one from Evan Paschman.

"Hey, pal, Evan here. The deal is hot, my friend. Hot hot hot. The Hasids are all over it, but want a thirty-day look, so the seller is waffling. He doesn't want the thing off the market while someone's kicking the tires. But let me know if you want to move on it. The clock's definitely ticking. Ciao."

Trevor had the detritus of uncertainty spread out before him: four Blackwing pencils, same as the ones Thomas Wolfe wrote *Look Homeward, Angel* with longhand on legal pads, two sharpened and two unsharpened, three small Postalco notebooks filled in with sketches and to-do lists, most of which were not completed, a half of a Cortado in which Trevor reluctantly breeched the profile of a pirate rendered precisely in rivulets of 2 percent milk foam dappling the burnt brown surface of the drink, a Timbuk2 special-edition messenger bag with alternating panels of biscuit-colored hemp and black wool, purchased from the flagship shop on Hayes Street in San Francisco, a digital camera that had some kind of fuzz in the lens but was not quite worth replacing, an iPhone with a data plan that was seeming like an increasing financial burden now that he was unshackled from the misery and regular infusion of pay into his Chase checking account, and a bag of almonds, every third one tasting rancid. In the blogosphere, this stuff was known by the acronym "EDC," or Every day Carry, grown-up Boy Scout paraphernalia, stuff that if you were eleven would be tethered to a metal clip hanging from the outside of your floppy cargo shorts or to a D-ring on your backpack. As Trevor's corporate fortunes and aspirations dwindled, he curated his EDC with increasing intensity: better and more stuff, the penknives and flashlights and pencils imbued with hyper-mechanical powers of protection. Like his fortress wardrobe, his stuff was armor, a bulwark against the Rick Nugents of the world. In an apocalyptic pinch, you could, in theory, whip out your Emerson A-100 folding knife or your tactical pen, made from extruded and knurled steel, and deploy it as a deadly weapon. In fact, even a tiny metal or plastic implement called a Kubota could be used with deadly force.

Orangutan Coffee's reclaimed benches and integrated tables proved to be the perfect context for the display of Trevor's EDC. He was on his third Cortado, the first two made perfectly by Pat/Jean/Terry/Chris, the last by a guy—THE guy, by the looks of the looks the women in the line were giving him, another one of those andro guys in skinny jeans and tiny beanie with bed head hair. He had two stars, one six-pointed, one five-pointed, inked on his left forearm. One star for art, the other for science. The science was the roasting, the mix between the gas and the air and the beans, getting the roast profiles dialed in by trial and error, learning the quirks of your machine, whether it absorbed heat quickly or did funky things mid-cycle. The art was dressing the room. Cat, even if he paid her eighty grand, would be worth every penny at 245B. He could even pay her a bonus. He needed Cat, more than he needed Phoebe, but Phoebe was maybe the key to Hugo, though he was becoming less convinced about that. Two Star didn't decorate his latte, even though he did decorate the girl's in front of him and the girl's behind him.

He deleted Evan's message and stared at the spreadsheet he was preparing to show his father. God, he hoped the old man would be sufficiently medicated when he glanced at it. What would he be getting? Vicodin? OxyContin? Demerol? Some kind of diluted morphine? Something that would remind Hugo of his old teammates, attacking mezzapuntas and defensive medianos. But Trevor was checking his sanity too. This plan, this idea of opening up a coffee roaster, was becoming as tortuous as his intestine, with diversions and twists and pitfalls, a business analogue of diverticulitis, a nascent explosion, rather than something logical and linear.

Trevor watched another barista—gender neutral, with a Bhodi-tree chest tattoo and another one on their neck that was in sepia sans serif block text in a small perfect rectangle too small to read from a distance. They were grinding espresso in a gleaming brass machine. The machine's burrs whirred with power, designed to create a mix of "fines" and larger particles, the fines acting as mortar to create the right mix to resist the water and pressure, coaxing a perfect layer of umber and gold crema. A home grinder, even a good one, would churn the particles evenly and make a more simplistic, occasionally insipid drink. You had to curate, be on top of it, source the right stuff. Trevor knew that espresso required perfection. Marzocco made a paltry 3,500 machines a year in its factory about twenty miles from Florence. Slayer probably still made fewer than a hundred or two a year. There were wait lists for the good machines. You had to have a dual-boiler machine that was capable of pulling shots from dawn to dusk, ensuring that the transfer from espresso to steam didn't rob heating capacity from the process. You had to suck up to the reps who kept the deals for their buddies, refurb units going for half price and demo units coming out of that superfunky showroom–cum–operations center in the Ballard neighborhood in Seattle. What was that place? It was kind of like a free-form hipster espresso machine geek fest, folks just standing around offering you espresso with machines sitting around in various states of assembly.

The barista started frothing, tracing lazy ovals with their wrist, getting the steam nozzle all down in there. They had a distant hipster gender-conflicted expression that complemented their ensemble of white oxford shirt, brown herringbone vest, and Mies van der Rohe specs, tiny acetate ovals that expressed detachment and a connection with coffee. Badinage was discouraged. Not even the celebrities got a rise out them, simply the same humorless service. But damned if that strange creature didn't absolutely nail their frond, the basic leaf form of course being the starter art for good baristas, but the fineness of the leaves and overall shape was vastly beyond a beginner's range. They were so antipathetic, these kids. Dazzlingly turgid. Divining something else— the screenplay, the club drama—got them through their shift. Petulance was at a premium these days.

Pomander Walk made you feel bad, that was part of the corporate calculus. Rick Nugent had an arsenal of slurs, insults thinly veiled with a coating of corporate bullshit. But for the coffee bars, it was a trickle-down, soft hazing, haute and unapproachable baristas foaming and grinding and decanting drips and droplets of coffee and various milks into cups. Trevor knew this was the special sauce, the ability to hover just above the fray, testing another level of coffee consciousness, which set the great apart from the quotidian. He knew he didn't have it himself, but he saw it in others—Cat of course being one of them.

Hugo was at home, with an attendant, a woman Eileen found through her anesthesiologist friend at Cedars. Trevor stayed in Hollywood for a day, and if it was weird with just Hugo and Eileen, the addition of Agatha, the Romanian aide, plus Eileen, plus Beatriz, who somehow kept her job even though Hugo mumbled something about her "taking liberties, but she cleans a good house." Even though he was running on financial fumes, the severance and the liquidated 401(k) from Pomander Walk sifting through his account like the last grains of colored sand through a cheap hourglass, Trevor put himself up at the Days Inn on Venice Boulevard, next to the Hopper House—Dennis, not Edward, of course, and spitting distance from Abbot Kinney. He was renting a white Ford Escape, considered "full size," one of the few cars that provided comprehensive protection against getting a date. Cheap was expensive and expensive was cheap. For a couple of extra bucks he could have gotten the Mustang, or even that red Malibu, but he didn't want to seem profligate when he pulled up to his father's house, even though the Teslas and Eileen's electric Panamera would have humbled almost any rental.

Agatha was kind of a shadowy character, literally in the shadows, running and hiding when Trevor came to the house. Strewn around were little pamphlets in some strange language with little squiggles and accents over the letters. There was a lot of a word Trevor recognized as Jesus, but no overt Catholic words or symbols. The pamphlets seemed like the ones the Mormons held up to the door in a beseeching way, a kinder and gentler form of proselytizing than, say, the Hasids in lower Manhattan, who took to ambushing Semitic-looking folks on the street, getting in your grill and asking without a hint of self-effacement whether you were Jewish. "You Jewish?" they would ask (to Trevor it sounded a lot like "You a fish?"), and when they approached him this way, his unease, he realized, was not so much that they were asking whether he was, in fact, a Jew, but that the unvarnished manner in which they did so seemed brutish, like a captor interrogating a prisoner.

Eileen finally opened the door, on her way out to Bikram and Whole Foods and maybe a mani-pedi. Agatha ran to the dining room, flouncing the drapes behind her, hissing something about "another one." "She's shy," Eileen said. "Your father's resting." Trevor was on to Eileen being on to Trevor about wondering about where she was going. She didn't want the unctuous little bastard to be all eyes and ears when she wanted to leave the house. A girl had to get out; it was as simple as that. What was Trevor, a grown man with two kids and a failing marriage, doing hanging around his old father's house with nothing to do? She was no Hilda, her friend in Bel-Air married to the rhinoplastician who raised two kids and then found herself rudderless and trying to twin herself with her husband who was quite keen to keep her bored and housebound. Eileen was close to getting up the nerve to tell Hugo that he had to get Trevor to leave them alone, that it was their time to kick back and delight in the abundance of the God's waiting room ambience of Southern California without being reminded daily of the failure of his oldest child to amount to something. What was the kid after? Had to be money. No one dotes on an old man creeping toward incoherence for nothing. No job, no girl, no plan—that was her take on him. If not quite the black sheep, then a very dark brown. Her kids were getting a little nudge, that's all. They were working, and you had to reward that. They were on a path, a trajectory. This kid Trevor evinced failure and suffering. It creeped her out. Warren Buffett said it best: give them enough but not so much. The funny thing was that at this point, her practice was worth almost what Hugo was worth. She didn't keep on it like she should have, but in 2007, in the fiscal year that ran July through June, her practice grossed $2.65 million, with two and a half doctors, one and a half nurses, one tech, and an admin. Her take-home was about $750,000, which even in LA was decent. The practice, she was told, would trade for about a multiple of two, maybe two and a half, which meant that it was worth about $5–6 million or so, her share being 70 percent. Not too shabby for the daughter of an RV salesman from San Jacinto. She could have easily given her kids the money for the Venice place, but Hugo, whose poor synapses had started to shrink and distort, had become militantly generous, and needed the affirmation that came with giving money away. She had things on autopilot until Trevor got separated and boomeranged back "home," hanging around Hugo, seeking some kind of unobtainium from an elderly guy who, truth be told, was not seeking attention.

Looking at his spreadsheet, Trevor kept adding line items. That's the way it was with budgets. They only grew, and then the rule of thumb in the real estate business was that once you finished a pro forma and accounted for every conceivable cost and added a contingency, and then a contingency on a contingency, the actual project itself would run at least 20 percent more than what you projected. At least this was the case in New York, perhaps not in Tulsa or Dayton, or Fargo, where a more pragmatic and prudent sensibility reigned, an approach born of austerity and parsimony that was inculcated in the churches and schools and community groups of a small city. In New York, the swell of competing interests and speculative exuberance about real estate and the prospect of making money made inflation a stark inevitability. No projection was conservative enough. The money let you know this. Sam Alterman, faced with a cash call or quizzed about an element of risk that one of his analysts had not properly underwritten, got a rush of blood that flooded his dappled temples and turned them beet red. The money got to him bad. It was his firm, his money, his reputation, and his liver spots sprouting on his bald, umber, burnished Hampton pate. The analysts would recast the numbers based on more granular assumptions, teasing out new data relating to supply and demand, functional obsolescence of competing properties, the shape of the long-term treasury curve, swap rates, anticipated changes in appraisal law, SOX legislation, and behavioral transformation relating to the workplace germane to Pomander Walk's—and by extension its equity investors'—investment in the deal. Do it again, the money wants to know. "Now," Sam would say, settling in with a sheaf of freshly printed pro formas, "let's see where we are with the new assumptions."

Trevor faced new assumptions each day, wondering why he was waking up in a Hilton Garden—or was it a Hampton Express or Red Lion Quick Check—he actually forgot this morning, rubbing penumbral particulates from his eyes, peeling back the double curtains just enough to let some light in but not enough to let the early risers hustling with their wheelies to get to LAX for the 7:55 to Dallas see him in his undies. Breakfast was oatmeal from the vat, settled and clumpy, with too much brown sugar and gummy raisins. The cheery clerks at check-in chirped at each new checkout victim, "Was everything all right? Would you like to leave that all on your card? All righty! Have a great day!" At five thirty, their bowels in knots and facing a morning hustling to LAX to face the masked indignity of queuing for forty minutes to get scanned and patted and boarded near the end with only middle seats near the lav left, there was not a lot of chirping back at the perky concierge crew. Trevor took a Styrofoam cup, acutely aware that some poor sea mammal, a doglike seal or frumpy walrus or chattering dolphin, might wind up with the residue of the cup, an indestructible evil by-product of product engineering, adhering to the digestive entrails of the animal, sickening it and consigning it to its deathbed. The coffee was poetically bad, three or four separate rancid notes: rags, earth, cat pee, and something that flashed across Trevor's mind as nothing other than monkey ass, although once he thought about it, he reckoned it was unfair to criticize monkeys like that unless you had the chance to get close enough to discern something that led you to conclude that in fact a monkey's ass could offend as badly as the coffee. Snob he was.

He stared down the offender—a Bunn machine—a big suitcase of a container that spelled out "Coffee," as if it were defending itself. "You are an impostor, just an empty vessel, a symbol of a lot of what is wrong with America, something purporting to be what it is not." Coffee done right was not far away, Intelligentsia in Silver Lake a mere five miles or so from where he was staying, but the product was conceptually a billion miles away. Was it that the fanny-packers and software salesmen and tea-loving Asians who passed through the Holiday Inn just wanted the runny eggs and pork products to get their day going, the coffee just a hot brown broth, its quality of no consequence to them? Every point of indifference about coffee removed Trevor from the space he needed to occupy, that of coffee evangelist, as confident as Tony Robbins speaking at the San Diego Sports Arena to his acolytes. Make Hugo believe, make him understand how nuanced and bright coffee was becoming. How big it was on the global scene. That there was still room in the market for five-dollar espressos and thirty-six dollar a pound beans.

He was feeling robust: those new pills, ostensibly for prostate support but having an overall stimulating effect just like they promised in the infomercials. Orangutan was it, the place, Trevor decided. It was downright cinematic. It was LA after all, and it was literally in the shadow of the Fourth Street Bridge. There was something seamless about the way the space flowed and the staff's breezy insouciance. One minute a barista glided over, the next one of the managers—only discernable by a very nuanced formality of dress, a lack of ostentation relating to accessories and visible and provocative tattoos—would step in and quickly tally the bill on an iPad for electronic signature. The tattoos were dazzling. When they started getting common, Trevor just kind of looked at everyone who had a tattoo and lumped them together, like animal lovers or tree huggers or embroidery ladies. But he had spent so much time in and around the coffee business that he was able to start to see subgroups and stylistic differences. And there was a huge gulf between having a tattoo and inking as a lifestyle. One thing they could all do was sling the iPad around and take money in. And wow, were these some big-ass totals. Thirty-three fifty for two espresso drinks and a pound—no, check that, twelve ounces!—of Nicaraguan dry process. Twenty-two dollars for a ricotta cookie and two iced coffees. Trevor did the math, trying to extrapolate the average number of transactions per hour, adjusting for peak and slow hours and, because Hugo would insist, including a conservative contingency.

There were distractions in every direction, the female customers, taken in aggregate, that is to say, if he did a big mash-up of every woman working in Orangutan or coming in to the shop, would be an approximation of Cat Gjertsen. He loved and hated her. Big deal, she sort of ruined his life. Did this make him special? Every day there were what, tens of thousands of marriages unraveling at some rate, the catalyzing factor being just about anything. Paige was basically right, but a lot of it was just the way that you related to fellow workers in a sexy, hipster workplace. You worked retail, and it was all out there. Like, you could walk past a hot girl who had a scent that was a trigger for you like eighty times a day and not succumb the slightest bit to flirting. Pomander Walk was exactly the opposite, everyone all belted up in corporate armor, thick leather shoes with broguing and tailoring that were supposed to be signifiers of class and affluence, and most importantly an attempt to sublimate overt sexuality in the workplace. But that didn't work either.

Seeing the endless parade of tattoos, it pained Trevor that he had none. Not one. Not even an arrow or spike or horseshoe or four-leaf clover or something from the Sailor Jerry canon picked after having one shot of tequila too many with a fraternity brother, were it the case that he had any fraternity brothers, or even a posse that was a simulacrum of such. Trevor raised the Green Shit Mountain or Chuck Full o' Balls or whatever the hell it was that they brewed at the Harriott Milton Double Extended Best Comfort Suites or whatever soul-crushing stuccostrosity he was staying at. It smelled like a dishrag. There had to be room for more good coffee.

- 16 -

Phoebe was looking at color wheels and De Stijl typography and combinations of colors. Paige was doing chaturangas to exhaustion on the burnished parquet of Phoebe's studio on West Eighty-Sixth Street. "It's—been—a—struggle," Paige said.

What struggle? Paige and her brother were effectively, if not officially, separated. They were both acting single. The kids were becoming outsourced, shuffled, and dished around like tapas in a crowded bar.

"You know, without a husband around. Bitch of it is, I can't date, and can't plan anything. Freaking purgatory." Phoebe noticed that Paige was getting super fit. She had on persimmon-colored yoga tights that she folded over so that the waist was an inch or so below her belly, which was impressively devoid of stretch or puffery for a woman who had just crested forty. There had to be a word for that, the fold-over look that showed abs. Something with a little onomatopoeia, like "twerking" for abs.

"You're looking hot. You know that. I haven't seen you look this good since you guys got married. I need to get married and separated just to get that gleaming lioness look."

"You know it. It's work after forty, though. I can see my ligaments in Technicolor. But you gotta half starve yourself, which for a food writer isn't such a hot thing. What's with the color wheels? You getting the landlord to paint?"

Phoebe just flipped through the wheels without a plan. She just liked the monotony, the plenary assortment of tones so close in hue that they needed to have numbers assigned to them. They were like sparrows, whose taxonomic provenance was fussed over by ornithologists, like the neutral grays and beiges and faint red-pinks that could barely be discerned with the naked eye but could be matched at the paint counter with startling precision. Phoebe collected tiny paint samples, storing them in her tiny coat closet, thinking that she was going to use them one day for a Dia-worthy installation, stacking maybe fifty thousand of them with a Lucite substructure and needing a crane and an oversize flatbed to creep up 9A to Beacon.

Paige unfolded and refolded the band of her hot yoga pants, smoothing her tummy as she went. Her face had a slight sweat sheen and she glowed.

"So, what's next for you?" Phoebe asked.

"Dunno. Kids are the first priority, of course. I want to move back to the city, or maybe SF. Not sure if that can be arranged, you know, legally. And on top of that, I'm slammed. I've got a feature due on kumquats. There are a bunch of varieties, can you believe it?"

Phoebe pointed to a thin slat of a red-yellow-beige color called "tartar sauce."

"What do you think?"

"Of what?"

"This color, tartar sauce."

"My opinion? It's gross. Gross color and even grosser name."

Phoebe shuffled the wheel and gently pinched her abdomen, which yielded to about an inch, maybe an inch and a half of fat at most. She was pretty fit herself, but seeing Paige's rock-hard almost six-pack was a revelation. Girlfriend looked like she was banging moves next to Sean P. or P. Sean or one of those sleek trainers like her beloved Ka'anuba Tempo guy, who liked his profession because of the girls. What a gig, that personal training stuff, if you were a guy. Parade of women.

"Whatcha gonna renovate? Isn't this a rental?"

"Since when can't you renovate a rental? I'm always thinking about renovating, but you know, I'm like a half step ahead of getting evicted. And then there are those assholes upstairs clomping around at three in the morning. Sounds like a meeting of the Dutch wooden clog society."

"Maybe they need a dose of Liquid Ass?"

"What? Liquid what?"

"Liquid Ass. Look at the Amazon reviews. It's a neighbor-revenge thing. Compared to having your face shoved up an elephant's heinie."

"Shit, I needed some of that when I was on the desk. I can't believe the traders didn't know about it. I wouldn't mind testing it on that cranky bitch Hanna Orlovsky in 8A."

Paige was doing some breathing, tossing her hair back and talking on the exhales. "Can I give you a little sisterly advice?" She didn't look at Phoebe, who, in truth, wanted to shake her head no. No, she did not want to hear what her estranged sister-in-law, who was honing and toning her body to great effect on both genders, had to say about her own slacker tendencies. It was okay to hang out with her, do some 420, talk shit about their girlfriends, but candid, proactive, life-affirming advice? No thanks.

Paige, not looking, went on: "You need to be more expansive in your outlook. I know your background is numbers and an MBA and learning how to be just the right kind of bitch in a sea of swollen dicks, and that has colored your worldview, which is certainly understandable. But at some point you must subordinate the vituperative and petty aspects of your daily Sturm und Drang—yes, I am invoking a clumsy German expression because it is evocative and explanatory here—and it is kosher even by Orwell's standards of never using a foreign phrase if an English one will do—and embrace flow."

Phoebe went back to the color wheel. Impressive leap from the primary colors and the chromatic rainbow. Why did they wait to introduce it in school? Would all those colors, so close in shade, be confusing for the little tots? And it was weird how some people co-opted color. Color was just there, not a learned thing. There were no bad outcomes with color. Maybe some good ones, like pacifying inmates and opposing football teams with Pepto-Bismol pink and squeezing a teensy bit out of office workers with what industrial designers deemed to be productive colors, but color was a resource, an element of sorts. And who was to say that everyone experienced color the same—the color-blind did not, of course, but there was some kind of basic trust in assuming everyone's experience perceiving color to be the same. The six million or so cone receptors in the eye probably afforded enough variation to make one girl's burgundy another girl's mahogany, enough wiggle room to render the eighty or so related shades on the wheel to be virtually the same, given a little variance in light, time of day, the underlying primer used (in the event of a painted wall), or whether the perceiver was using eye drops or suffering from a stye. Shit, she needed to be high.

"You got weed?" Paige asked.

"As a matter of fact..."

Phoebe went over to the corner of the studio where her bed was tucked behind a freestanding mission-style bookcase, the intended effect to create the illusion of a bedroom. Square footage–deprived New Yorkers resorted to desperate tricks and trompe l'oeil effects to squeeze the most out of their undernourished apartments. Sometimes it worked and sometimes, as was the case with Phoebe's craftsman-era bookcase, it just looked awkward. She fumbled around in a nightstand and produced the bag.

"Bong, vape, or paper?"

"Bong? You have a bong?"

"Someone left it after a party. It looks gross, but it works."

"Paper, if you don't mind."

Phoebe took out some rolling paper, an elegant little packet, and worked the grass deftly with several precise rolls and a supple lick of her lips. She had a vintage Zippo lighter at the ready, and the sour-smelling flame licked to life, igniting the joint. She passed it to Paige first.

"Why, thank you. I take back everything I've said about you. You know, those color wheels, they're a lot like fruit. That's what I see at the farmers markets, what I see in Torrance and Fresno and San Luis Obispo, remarkable little cultivated boxes of produce. In SLO, there's a Japanese farmer who only does lettuces. He sells out of weathered boxes that look like Martha herself picked each and every one. Mâche, frisée, varicolored arugulas and purply kales and spinach that would make your heart ache. Seriously, my heart starts to beat faster when I see lettuce like that. You can look up and see the fields and mountains behind it—okay, so there's an ugly bunch of big-box stores on the other side—but when you get that late-summer light and the sweetness of the produce lingering, I am ready to move there every time."

"And you don't, or haven't yet."

"I've been married. Tied to New York. But now, who knows? You can't make your ex leave a state, but if you both want to go—"

"He's trying to get the thing going—here, right on the Upper West Side. What makes you think he's bailing on New York?"

"He's a pussy, that's why. It's a test. Does Hugo love me enough to part with some cash before he's pushing up daisies? And don't kid yourself, he likes the game with Eileen. And he is fucking pissed about that whole buying-her-kids-a-condo thing. Not saying he's not into coffee—or at least that skank—sorry, I know you think she's sorta cool—but whatever the deal is, he's rootless now, practically homeless, unless you consider that soul-crushing, airless piece of desolate suburban blight the Archstone a home."

The joint sizzled and the small, sweet embers flared a bright gold-gray, warming against the dun backdrop of the Upper West Side skyline. Phoebe grabbed it and put it down. "If I haven't said it before, I'm gonna say it now. I wish *I* was a food writer. A specialist like you, doing good, all that muckraking about locavorism and the Plate Project, and ensuring the organic and local provenance of the growers at all these markets. Paige, you are doing good for people. You know my theory, that all our problems come back to food, and to take it one step further, back to congressional subsidies for the duopoly of corn and soybeans."

"Ka-ching! Girl, you are so money with that. Couldn't have said it better. Fat people—obese people, morbidly obese people, they are victims. Yeah, some of 'em are stupid and wouldn't turn down a soggy Hot Pocket under any circumstances, but folks are busy, they can't do what the Brooklyn wives sitting at the coffee bar on Fifth in Park Slope do while their I-banker hubbies are racking up the bonuses do. Shit, this four-twenty is making me loooopeeeeyy."

"Yeah. And you'd think the whole Bloomberg thing, banning those god-awful big gulps—as if anyone needs more than an eight-ounce soda, come to think of it, does anyone ever need any soda?—would've knocked some sense into everyone, but it weirdly had the opposite effect, mobilizing the factions and making it a class thing. Who'da thought a half gallon of Mountain Dew could be a political rallying cry?"

"Ah... the class problem. That's our town. You got a problem with that?"

"No, you've got the problem. I read your *Slate* piece."

"I got a death threat from that one. 'Fattie' is a fighting word, I learned. And that reference I made to the titular SOOS, Sudden Onset Obesity Syndrome. That set a couple of folks off. I don't give a shit, makes me snicker—

phhhhhttt! Sudden-onset obesity! Can you imagine? Your ass and thighs explode overnight! Ha!! And I probed a lot for that piece. Took the recorder to the street and interviewed the common woman. Boots on the ground. Does my ass look fat in these tights, by the way?"

"Fat? Seriously? Are you going all body dysmorphic on me? Orthorexic, it's called? Even a fancy food writer like yourself doesn't know what that one is. It's like being *too* healthy, analyzing every morsel that goes in your mouth. What's my food doing for me? One freak in the family is enough. What's Trevor's latest, anyway? Last time I talked to him, he was having numbness somewhere—"

"Ha! Numbness! I thought he was having double vision."

"It was connected, he thought. Dull ache in the shoulder and fuzzy vision. Better than his last thing that needed rubber bands up his ass."

"Achy-breaky-shoulder-fuzzy-syndrome. He's staying in LA for a while, he told me."

"Hmm. Surprised at that. That broker started calling me. Keeps talking about 'performing,' which I think means putting money up, a series of deposits and such. It'll be a blow if he loses that deal. And he'll have to sell that machine."

"What machine?"

"The Slayer. He paid thirty K for that thing."

"What? What the fuck?"

- 16 -

"You didn't know? Oh God, I hate being in the middle of all this marital bullshit. Now I'm on everyone's shit list."

"Well, boo-hoo for you. He's broke one minute, buying espresso machines the price of a car the next. The wheels are coming off, and guess who's picking up the pieces. And working full time. And trying to have some kind of life." Paige snickered. "Don't give me that look. What, am I on some kind of lockdown?"

"Only if it's self-imposed."

"No. No no no. Almost two years of the 'rona virus and I need to get out."

"Yes. Out to Sonoma to find fruit. Tell me about the sexiest fruit. Not the obvious like a fig or ripe persimmon. Something that grabbed you."

"Ohhhh. Fruit is sexy now. I see. I never knew. Raaaaar!" Paige got closer, in Phoebe's space, her flailing cougar hands grazing Phoebe's nose and lips and hair.

"What are you doing?" Phoebe laughed.

"I'm on you like a cat. You're sexy yourself. A fruity-bitch. A bitchy-fruit. A bitchy fruity bitch fruit." Paige kept flailing and kept getting closer, even though Phoebe put her hands up as if to say, "Okay, game's over," but Paige was a juggernaut, a Caterpillar earthmover on a mission. She grabbed Phoebe's cheeks in her hands and placed her lips flush on her still technically sister-in-law's cheek for a big wet kiss."

"Holy balls," Phoebe said. "Did you just do that?"

"Yes. Fuck. Whew. Did I say this stuff was making me loopy?"

- 17 -

Trevor reasoned that everything was in perpetual decay, a Wabi-Sabi reinvention, eliding to dust. Embracing imperfection and flaws was imperative. He was unfocused as usual, but after taking two Adderalls found in deep storage in the medicine chest in Tarrytown, a long-expired prescription intended for, well, he forgot which kid, but thank God Paige sucked at housekeeping and record keeping, and for that matter just about any form of keeping, he felt like money.

He made his way down the coast towards San Diego, a city that looked like paradise in the guidebooks but seeded with too many retirees and soldiers or people who were both. Their views about guns and money were a lot different from his own, so he planned to stop before he reached the city proper.

A loosey-goosey spot, this North County. He had rented a car from one of those discount places near

Dodger Stadium and bombed down the 5. The place was called Dodger Rentals or something like that, a shop that leased out older models, but Trevor was never one for that new car smell, the plastic fug that probably came from a spray can and leeched into your pores or made you grow tracheal lesions (mental note to screen for oral cancer, assuming the test itself was fairly benign). But you get what you pay for, and in this case he had a weird machine called a Dodge Avatar in a strange shade of bile blue, more blue than gray but with kind of jaundiced undertones. The Avatar was a charlatan of a car, billed as a hybrid but still a gas guzzler.

He got out at a fish taco place in Encinitas, thinking that was something of a local specialty, nothing of its kind available in New York, at least none that didn't come from a food truck on one of those dodgy Brooklyn side streets. "Ensenada style," the sign said. The menu had pictures, photos of the dishes all ganged together, like you were a total moron and didn't know what you were ordering. Why was it that the restaurants that insisted on showing you photos—the Cuban-Chinese joints, the pupuserías, the Ensenada fish taco emporia, the lard-loving urban fried-chicken places—had menu items that were almost indistinguishable from each other? It was all a DayGlo dog's dinner, a mash-up of lard and batter and bits of cheap proteins lashed with sauce. It was gross really. The salt and fat content alone in a single meal was mind-numbing. If you ate it all, the calorie count was equal to what a large person needed in a day. Small wonder, he thought, that pants had become "vanity" sized, a thirty-four pant having a waist that measured thirty-seven. What the fuck was that about—so you could have some kind of psychic lift slipping into pants that didn't reflect your true fatness? He was getting fat on this trip. Too many quick-serve meals left him reaching for the sweatpants first.

He maneuvered the taco towards his mouth with a side-to-side motion, the overmoist innards, green and white and red with extra guac—why stint when you were where they actually grew avocados—into the corners of his mouth, a brothy tan sluice. Even at the healthy places, the vegan joints in LA, there was an invitation to binge—big muffins and cakes that were vegan but packed with fats, albeit the natural kind, but stuff yourself with enough cashews and coconut and almond milk, and you're still packing in the calories. The Adderall helped, tamping back the appetite, but what about that blood pressure? He once took a small dose, five or ten milligrams, and had a routine thing—something with the sinuses—and the nurse was all weird when she pulled the cuff off—"You drink a lot of coffee today?" she asked, looking like she was expecting a stroke to happen right then and there. And he had to squirm and mumble something about mixing pills up, it being so early, he had them spread on the counter, and you know how it goes when you're trying to get the kids out the door and everyone's in such a goddamn rush. Rushing. Everywhere. And did he exercise and how many times per week was that? As if? He was feeling good at the time, still near his high school weight, and who was she to judge? How 'bout you, girlfriend, how many times? Not a lot, judging from the amplitude of her lower half, Trevor expertly assessing her backside even through the cheap sheen of her scrubs. And then he was thinking, why did she care, as if she was invested in his health? He was his own health manager, the leading edge, the one who had to take it home and manage the actuarial nuances of cobbling together his meager 401(k) from Pomander Walk with Social Security, assuming the program's solvency, and the imperative of socking enough away in one of those E-Trade or TD Ameritrade deals where you cheerily invested your (abundant) free cash and managed your portfolio like a pro, all your hair there—practically nailed in even as your life allocation was in the rapidly evanescing part of the curve—high-fiving the barista as you checked your big wins before you put your order in. Yeah, baby, just rolled my Costco profits into crypto.

Didja know the first fifty trades are free and they will never recommend a stock? That's for me. TD Schwab Trade gives me all the analytical tools to move the market like a pro and beat the little guy to the trading punch by implementing program trading buy and sell signals seconds before the information goes public. It's an edge. Ethical? Maybe not, but it gives me the trading tools I need. A double-tall extra-dry Cap'll do it for me today, Ross.

And what a place, this Encinitas! Half-dressed women, one foot in the sand, snaking in and out of their cars, a smile at the ready, it was California after all, ambiguity-strained aloha for everyone (look at me, I don't care!). Library to the left, up a hill, a span of the beaches to the right: Moonlight, Stone Steps, Beacon's, Grandview, Ponto, and more, endless summer in real time for Trevor, who had always made the dumb mistake of lumping all of SoCal into one big metroplex.

He parked the Avatar on the scruffy knoll that abutted the train tracks. Seemed legal, or maybe not, he'd find out if there was a big fat ticket, probably one of those $300 jobs for violating all kinds of rights-of-way and public orderliness edicts. Cali was more laid-back than New York but also more of a rules state at the same time. Cops here were sheriffs, like it was outlaws and Injuns gunning it out in front of the saloons. What was that about? Trevor wondered, used to the constabulary convention of "police," hearing in his head the snickering of any self-respecting NYPD beat cop upon hearing the word "sheriff." But the freeway types did look like a young Erik Estrada lifting his leg off his big hog, looking like he needed to pee real bad, all mirror shades and Camp Pendleton bad-assedness, tan twill from head to toe except for those egregiously round helmets, bulbous as a fly's eye. You could go eighty here, passing even quicker, but it was orderly, no weaving or sneaky passing and deliberate cutting off, gonzo-style, like you got on the West Side Highway, the club kids and bored teenagers in their Geo Prizms and Corollas and especially those ancient little Hondas—hell hath no fury like a nineteen-year-old from Washington Heights in a twenty-five-year-old Civic.

Shit, it felt different though, even different from LA, which was ostensibly the same climate but a different flavor of urban, a Stracciatella gelato next to the Nocciola. It was maybe part the ubiquity of the litter-spewing eucalyptuses, planted a century before as railroad tie stock, but proving too soft, and now just giant pieces of kindling waiting for the next epic wildfire. Maybe it was part the ubiquity of flesh, a riptide of board shorts and bosom and abs, profoundly inked, begging for close inspection. New York women kept you away with invisible force, a glare or a sotto voce sneer.

He was on borrowed time, frittering away valuable hours when he should have been at Hugo's side, locking in some of those distant memories, especially from the Bronx days that only he knew about, way before Eileen and her arriviste step- kids who pretended that Hugo didn't have a life that predated California.

He was jumpy, the timed release of the Adderall kicking in. Nice oomph, good burst of concentration, feeling good about pulling out some last-minute, game-saving heroics, wiring Evan Paschman the $750,000 for the down payment on 245B just before some Orthodox flipper from Crown Heights with his black fedora and curlicue payos came with all cash. Have balls, Trevor told himself. Pretend you were the one who got the night train out of Kiev, somehow contriving to get a series of trains, some freight, some passenger, with the forged credentials your father's brother's old estate agent and church organist got you. Pretend you made your way to Italy, where you hosed down a ruddy farmer's swine pen for weeks while you saved enough to take a ferry from Bari to Nice and then take the train second-class north through Paris and to London and then work again sweeping or shuttling sides of beef or being a barman before sailing for Ellis Island. If you were that guy, then it was simply a case of eat or be eaten, and if you profoundly did not give a shit, it was far easier to walk away and in turn prevail. Evan Paschman, a flashy guy, small, big-beaked, had that gall, even though he was a young guy. Always in pinstripes, a broker's broker, looked sharp even at late meetings when everyone else's tie was loosened. Paschman had his brogues shined up—Prada or maybe even Cucinelli, the lord of Italo-country wear whose shoes ran four figures (!), but why even go there when he was imitating Aldens, a real American product that you could get for half or even less. Paschman got the Cucinellis because he knew that you knew that getting them got him noticed in that peculiarly unctuous way that those dealmakers—"players"—had in New York.

Whew. In San Diego you were dressed up if you had flip-flops *and* a Padres hat. Guys wore big ol' T-shirts saying stuff about "Big Dogs" and "Old Guys." Blond guys going silver, hair still with the shag, party mostly out back or the sides now, the top all thinned or gone, to tell the truth, but they were legends in their minds, toes-to-the-nose, still in the lineup, doing the biz off Beacon's or Stone Steps or Grandview—locals only, but the stickers read "Aloha." Mahalo, unless you snake my wave, douchebag.

LA and New York were kindred spirits in the sense that money drove the bus, albeit with a slightly different spin. Down here, in North County—you had better not call it San Diego to the locals— the fish taco was king. And there were plenty of those, of course, and an astounding amount of beer, brewed in tiny batches with labels that vied for esoteric supremacy, devils and frogs and devil-frogs, the idea being that to get beer cred you had to distance yourself from the industrial brewers, the Buds and Coors and so forth. Every store, it seemed, had sixty or seventy kinds of local brews, porters and ales infused with roots and grains and umami things like seaweed and one that dared to bring fungus into the equation.

The only way to see the place was to slow down, so Trevor decided to dump the Avatar and rent a bicycle at one of the local shops, which had dozens of beach cruisers lined up. In a playground like Encinitas, the toys were always on display. He settled on the most common brand, Elektra, and chose a café au lait design with a basket and horn. The tires were cream colored, offsetting the darker brown of the frame and the white basket. If the Duke (Ellington, not Kahanomoku, the surf legend—need to be careful to stray from references that did not involve surf culture) himself had designed a bike to be chained outside the Cotton Club, it would have been this Elektra model, shades of caramel and mocha yummy enough to eat. Trevor loved bicycles that subverted the notion of spandex wearing: transit-oriented, proletarian movers of cargo. Hugo's cousins, butchers in Woodside, had a fleet of Worksman cycles, massive, heavy-gauge steel-framed beasts that were designed to move quarter sides of beef from the shop to the diners that dotted Queens and Northern Boulevards. That was a workout, steadying a forty-five-pound bike into a brisk headwind, keeping it from tipping over with a giant carcass splayed across the front. The better setups had a cart in back. The Elektra was a froufrou little thing, and almost as soon as he pulled off onto a street called Vulcan, kind of a service road to the old Coast Highway, he regretted not going for a black one. In his haste, he had even grabbed a model with a step-through frame, which was really, technically, a girl's bike (why, he wondered, did that stupid convention persist, with few girls or women riding with a skirt on anyway and a men's bike having the horizontal frame to catch you in the balls if the step-over height was a teensy bit too high). In fact he had been experiencing a pain—not a pain, but a tightness, really, a gentle but persisting tugging feeling—in his left testicle. "It's your imagination, Trevor," Paige had said last night when he called to check on the kids, but he was unconvinced, as if you could make up a feeling of discomfort in your ball. He wanted a scan, an MRI or something (what exactly did they do for ball pain?), to put him at ease.

And the thought of an early demise brought him to thoughts about George Gershwin. Voluble Gershwin, prolific Gershwin, prematurely dead Gershwin, would have made it a lot longer with the scanning techniques they had today. Hell, Trevor had seriously considered those preemptive total-body scans, but then figured to what end, what if you got every major system assessed, saw every little fissure and lesion and irregularity—the drusen, for example, that the ophthalmologist told him were lurking in the back of his retina, harmless but rare, and you were forced to be your own health manager? He had driven by 1019 North Roxbury Drive in Beverly Hills, the old Gershwin residence, reconstructed now into a postmodern monstrosity, and thought about the great man with a thousand tunes in his head that was simultaneously reproducing cells at an abnormal rate. Maybe the glioblastoma wasn't a tumor, just another state of being, what came along with the thousand tunes. And then there was tennis with little Schoenberg—realistically, what kind of a tennis player could a protean modernist composer with a Boris Karloff accent have been, as if he even had a second serve, probably lobbed it underhand or some kind of nonsense, with GG sneaking feet—no, yards—inside the baseline, absolutely hammering the forehand, Sampras-like, down the line for winners time and time again. Poor little man, first almost snuffed out by the "affair" and then getting trounced in tennis. Would there have been a starlet or two, who took to a fascination with an erudite and strange looking little classical musician? Trevor hoped that had been the case. Schoenberg and an ingénue pouring out of a bathing suit. Trevor hoped the sad man had the chance.

You could kill yourself here in an instant, whirling to look at girls from the bike lane, that changed into a real lane and back to a dedicated bike lane capriciously, like they gave the job to a meth head, and there were plenty of those too. In fact, Trevor noticed a certain pattern of commerce: nails, booze, yoga, tacos, repeat, and maybe three coffee bars worth a look. He didn't look so much these days, finally realizing that there was an inflection point when you did your research, when you had absorbed as much as you could handle, like the moment when you're in a big museum and you hit that wall when another collage/oil/sculpture/multimedia piece would drive you to the brink of going postal. He learned or read that talent learns from others and genius learns from itself, and he resolved to be a genius. Never once having made payroll, or cleaned a restroom, or disarmed a freaked-out customer, he had nevertheless played out these scenarios in gratifying and exacting detail. What would he do if a server dropped an extra hot chai almond latte on a woman's silk dress right on her thighs? Would he pat? No, can't pat a customer's thighs. You offer towels and dry cleaning and a replacement if need be. What would the blend of equity and debt look like? Would he, could he, syndicate shares like a lot of folks in the restaurant and bar business, paying back at least double-digit returns on investment to your friends and family who got hot and heavy for cash flow even before you had a chance to open the doors? (How, Trevor often wondered, was this a whole lot different from loan sharking, except for the leg-breaking part?) If Hugo punted or if he was too addled or distracted by his new family to come through with what was a reasonable investment—not even a gift, there would be a market return for God's sake, midteens at the least with an opportunity to double your money, and that was assuming a paltry 3 percent annual appreciation on the building—then Trevor would be forced into syndicating shares, prying a hundred grand from ten friends. And he knew how that went, with whoever made noise about investing growing alligator arms when it came time to reach for their checkbook.

By rights he deserved to be an heir. His dad made films that were campy, for sure, but always with a little substance: a character who taught literature at a community college or a waitress who wrote poetry. Trevor had a front-row seat for filmmaking as a career but couldn't brook the crazies, the effeminate stylists and angry lighting guys and the yappy agent types, hyping, constantly hyping. Hugo, in his one or two shots at being a director, was good, his accent tempering the frenzy, aural Dramamine in a tempest. "It's only for zo long," he would say to a star fed up with doing another take. "It's for the last time, a promise. I'll buy ze steaks," just enough Yiddish or German, or some Mittel European–inflected English coming through at the right time, announcing that this was a man of importance, an auteur.

That way of disarming people was a skill, a director's skill mostly, but when Hugo fell back to producing, his comfort zone, he used it too. Producers used to actually work, coordinating everything from the financing to sets to casting; not like today, when everyone and their golf buddy gets some kind of credit, one of the big reasons the credits roll for twenty minutes, the other of course being to hype the soundtrack. Trevor thought that San Diego was more filmic in a way than LA, which was rich in icons, but its interstitial spaces were prosaic and blighted in a dim and dun way. This stretch of North County could still pass for a Beach Boys cover when they had hair and abs. The light didn't come and go but scorched the horizon, so intense that he felt his forearm hairs being singed, even through the tinted glass of the Avatar. On the bike now, he felt sun-ravaged, parched as the stranded man crawling toward the oasis.

There was a headwind, and he was losing steam, wagging side to side a bit. An older SUV gained on him, and he heard yelling—kids, no doubt—and then he felt something hit him hard. Something big and sharp and painful—a palm frond! The little fuckers had leaned out the window and smacked him with a palm frond. They laughed and swerved, bopping and high-fiving. So much SoCal mahalo. You can do that here, he reasoned. It's the cars that make it anonymous, hitting and running. Funny thing was he wasn't angry, not even the slightest bit pissed, his testosterone dipping, mind and body connected after all. As he got older he understood that thinking bad *was* in effect feeling bad, that you could will yourself one way or the other. But he seriously flirted with treatment for low T , only confused a bit about what he was getting it for, what he would do if suddenly his libido got supercharged. But then maybe it wasn't low T, but more like that thing he saw advertised, relating to the amino chain or vasodilation or something even more molecular. If you want a solution you had to get down to the cellular level or recode your DNA. It was coming.

His ideas about a roasting operation, about Cat and Paige and his kids and Hugo, was a bowl of cottage cheese lingering in the back of the fridge, reminding you every goddamn time you opened the door to do something about it. You can't eat it and you can't toss it. Cat, he was sure, was as agile as could be, her energy absorbing him to the point where he was exhausted some days at Red Hook just watching her pull shots and coaxing foam into ferns and dog snouts and snowflakes.

He was at the edge of the continent. It was cinematic, all right, a high bluff, just above where Trevor imagined the tsunami line to be—those poor bastards in Indonesia, bathing in vitamin D one second, the next moment eclipsed by a wall of water, enough to panic, a bad thing for Buddhists if there were any among them, and certainly there were some Japanese tourists at least. From his perch above D Street he was high enough to see the sets rolling in, inky-dot surfers sitting, splayed on their boards, shark meat, if you will, getting up here and there for a French-curve ride and dismounting cavalierly, falling backward into the sea foam. The Elektra fell to the ground, and Trevor abandoned it next to the remnants of a picket fence on the cliff's edge. He leaned into the breeze and sucked in the vertigo, commingling with the surge of the timed-release Adderall—what great stuff, same chemical constituency as meth apparently, and he looked down and thought about cliff diving in Acapulco and how ABC on *Wide World of Sports* showed it every week like it was a real live American sport. Come to think of it, that show, nominally about the "world" of sport, showed everything except the only real global sport, soccer, or *futbal* as Hugo called it, his old man turning on the same show every week hoping against hope that they'd show a glimpse of the Old World, Partizan or Rapid or even one of the Italian giants like Juventus or Milan doing something on the pitch. Hugo, poor guy, relocated from the Bronx to Los Angeles, having saved a chunk of change to get a movie done, and after that it was like his whole early existence was expunged: no boat over from Vienna, no recollection of his semifamous father Benny Hesterwald running the wing with grace and power, no chewy dense bagels coming from Grossman's on the Grand Concourse, no Dodge Power Wagon with the custom storage bins welded just so that stored his tools, no holiday gathering at his cousins' with kugel and "nuss" cake and Grimmelkuchen (a low flat cake cooked barely north of batter with buttery balls of goodness crumbled on top) and wurst and newcomers still filing in from Europe, talking survival. Not we-have-to-eat-potatoes-for-a-month survival, but Walter Benjamin–type attempted survival, getting on a boat to nowhere, being turned back by the authorities in Spain, and cramming a deadly dose of morphine into your mouth to avoid getting repatriated to your "home" country and shot like an animal. But there he was, his old man now truly old, his wife Eileen, bosomy and loquacious and a drinker on the cusp of a problem, more familiar to Hugo than either Trevor or his sister Phoebe, and with his memory being squeezed it was hard to say whether he cared who or what Trevor was or what he wanted.

Trevor let the salt air lap at him. There was a low-speed insistent wind, and it was breaking him down. California was colder than advertised. Not coat cold, but the "it's cold and it's damp" cold like the Rogers lyric. Trevor hummed the song a bit, "Gets too hungry for dinner at eight," drawing out "hungry" in little trill, playing with his voice, even though he had no projectable voice. Phoebe had the music skill, playing show tunes at will, a little like how he imagined Gershwin did at Merrick's on West Forth-Eighth Street, the walk-in trade peppering him for new arrangements and scores. By the time the composer got to 1019 Roxbury with his entourage, in 1935 or 1936, the glioblastoma had become irreversible. Primitive surgical conditions, still basically cutting and slashing. No digital imaging, no pinpoint laser stuff. Made Trevor cringe. They scrapped the house in 2008—with all the surviving Spanish houses in LA, you'd think one of the important ones would have survived the wrecking ball, but uh-uh. At least 33 Riverside Drive was still standing. No way you could in a lifetime amass enough capital, political and financial, to unwind the cooperative and demolish that one. So too with 110th Street, a middling Deco building but stylish and jazzy in a way.

Gershwin (was it crazy of Trevor to have started thinking about a long-gone Jazz Age legend as a friend?) had a taste for luxury but, like Groucho, was an outsider. Hugo knew of him, but he was not a show tune guy, preferring Lehár and Herbert, Old World guys. Gershwin, Trevor reasoned, was an early fusion pioneer, mixing beats before they were called beats. Tin Pan Alley, Catfish Row, boogie-woogie, stride, jazz, that "blue" note. All there in a gumbo. George himself would have loved that crazy reimagined CGI spectacular Gatsby party in that new film. Weird how Gershwin was always defending himself, insecure at the heart of it, trying desperately to learn the technical aspects of music, finally getting Cowell to teach him some proper theory. Did he score the first rhapsody himself or let Herbert do it? Even the glissando was a last-minute add-on, Whiteman's clarinetist riffing on the scale. Gersh looked confident in photos, the splayed nose giving his face the gravitas of a boxer—Trevor had read that it was broken when he was a kid in a roller-skating accident—but the eyes were nervous. He was never where he was supposed to be. The club doors were always a block away, the entrance unmarked, a speakeasy. He was the guy grabbing the card in the taxi, chasing down the girl who he thought could be Mrs. Right. But he was caught in the middle, too Jewish for the Gentiles, too ethereal for his own people. Had to exhaust your intellectual capital at that point, live the tiger's life. The tumor was a gift. It was that way with the hookers too. He had a problem there. No one good enough, or maybe he wasn't good enough. Paulette Goddard was good enough, but only because Chaplin was there, blocking. Maybe had an inkling he wouldn't make it to forty. You have to know these things deep down. Trevor's thing was death by a thousand cuts—his adrenals were spent, utterly drained, his head heavy, spinning after getting off the bike, too much goddamn freshness here.

The beauty of it in California was plain as sand. New York weather had you waiting for summer and then it was an onslaught of pulchritude and just as quickly it was gone again. You never quite got a handle on it. It was a big transient hot gooey mess. Trevor was conscious of his posture out here, pulling himself, as his great aunt—Hugo's sister Esther—had advised, toward the sky as if being tugged by a string attached to the cloud. Yoga and Pilates and meditation were all based on correct posture and breathing and consciousness, a tonic, if he was inclined, to combat his thwarted and defensive baseline. Even the air was helping, supplementing the speed. He sensed that there was more chi in his lymphatic system, a better flush. Spend enough time out here, he thought, and he'd have his own studio, with the obligatory photo of him in pigeon pose, a bare-chested silhouette on the beach at dusk.

He had outlasted Gershwin already, at forty-four, by what, five years? Ives stopped composing at fifty-two, a diabetic, so much for being a jock at Yale. You had to take care of yourself, watch the diet, be aware, keep learning, keep the myelin supple, the synapses taut and electric. He was doing that now, wasn't he? Memorizing the pathways leading to the ocean, noting the pocket mobile home parks and the quirky little dead ends with gnarled fig trees and bulbous avocados still peeking out here and there.

He soothed himself—*self-soothing* was the term he once heard. Agitation was infectious, led to panic, like the attack he had on the subway once, the car sitting at Thirty-Third and Lex, too crowded (he told himself he should have never gotten on), hot, silent, the compressors kicking off. The air was leaking, absorbed by the CO_2 of the riders, the windows inoperable. The conductor came on to say there was a train stuck in the tunnel. That was all. Hope to be moving shortly. Sure, you prick, don't we all. There was sighing, a belch, sour perfume. The train lurched forward and stopped again. Trevor felt his booming heart—how could that little muscle play like a timpani against his chest cavity? He thought about 9/11 and the blackout in '06 and everyone trapped in elevator cabs and subways. Don't connect thoughts like that, he reminded himself. So unproductive.

Wood smoke filled the air. And exhaust. It was clear, but he was a bit queasy. Queasy and clear. His thinking was muddled, the West Coast asses and tits doing it, even if a lot of them were fixed, rigged and trussed and situated just so, the whole fruit department done in wax.

- 18 -

"Yowzer. What the eff is that?" Luc asked Cat as she pulled out her EpiPen and jabbed it into her thigh.

"Sulfites. They can kill me. You didn't hear me choking during lunch?"

"What was it? This place is clean."

"Must have been that emulsion or foam on the long beans. I thought I tasted shrimp. Could have been the balsamic though. That's a trigger too."

"Damn. I can eat anything. Or used to. Never thought about it until a couple of months ago when I put on a couple of pounds. First time ever."

"I'll bet. There's probably a T-shirt for that." Cat rummaged through her bag, a Guatemalan carryall. "Fuck me—that's my last pen. Remind me to pick some of those bad boys up, otherwise next time we dine could be the last."

They were in a prep kitchen, or test kitchen as some people called it, not far up the Hudson in Beacon, which in the early 2000s got a new modern art museum called Dia, located in a former cookie factory with a ziggurat roof that in a lot of ways was more interesting than the massively scaled art exhibited in its white box galleries and expansive grounds. Cat bought them a half-day of demonstration classes for producing small-batch shrubs sponsored by the Vaux Culinary Institute in Newburgh just across the river, and the growers showed up with batches of elderberries and loquats and capers and juniper and dozens of fragrant leaves and local black currants, a special Hudson River Valley success story out of Dutchess County, that perfumed the space in a butler building behind Dia.

Luc, a bartender, couldn't believe the abundance and variety of ingredients, and even more, couldn't believe that there was actually an industry that had grown up around making cocktails. It helped his bar business at the Mohonk. No one settled anymore for some crap rum and Coke, or a generic gimlet or martini. Everyone had an opinion: muddle this, shake that, squeeze a billion Meyer lemons for my margarita. In college he worked at one of the last "authentic" bars on Ninth Avenue, a time-warp closet of a bar with what looked like the Earth's entire remaining supply of brown Naugahyde. The "Muldroon" also had a great four-colored neon sign showing a dapper gent with a big red lipstick mark limning his cheek. Luc thought it looked like a hickey every time he showed up for work, underaged at nineteen, but slick enough to make it seem like he was pouring the house stuff when in fact he pumped from the rank stash of diesel under the bar trucked in from Bushwick by the Muldroon's Satmar owners.

There was a long table done up like a science experiment, ten or twelve stations each with a beaker, three small sterile sampling trays, a miniature mortar and pestle, and small stainless-steel serving bins that had a bunch of pre-prepared ingredients, in the traditional style of mise-en-scène The stone and brick hearth, a remnant of the days when it was used to supply real energy for some industrial process, was kept to a small roar. It was December in upstate New York, but it was mild, in the high forties.

"Global warning," Luc said. "It will put the fireplace out of business."

"Never. It's atmospheric. Even in California they love their fireplaces."

Cat was looking pale, but still taut. Clothed, she looked unclothed. Sheathed. She had been on the phone all morning, working out a complex bunch of childcare moves. Brooklyn, fortunately, had a big supply of immigrant nannies. None of them lasted long, but they were a mercenary crew, and for the right price could be brought in on short notice.

"What?" Cat said after she got off her phone. Luc had overheard a big part of the conversation, and even to a guy in his late thirties who never had kids it seemed strange, this outsourcing. "What's that look for?"

"Dunno. Kids. It's a look about kids. You don't seem to miss 'em a whole lot."

"They're perfectly fine. And you are really, really, dead fucking wrong about that. Everyone misses in their own way. What are you, some kind of technical parenting authority?"

"Course not. Just sayin', you can go long stretches and come off like someone who's single, traveling and scamping around. I think it's cool, just different from other, um, situations that I've seen."

"Yep. I'm not one of these cry-me-a-river moms hanging on every belch and fart coming out of their precious spawn. And even they are wearing yoga pants to pick up from school, checking out of their rearview mirrors who's checking them out. It's a game, Luc. It's only a matter of how you choose to play it. I had three kids—and then it's like, they're going to be okay, maybe better if I'm not constantly in their shit. Already it's paying dividends. I look at some of these other brats whose folks are like an extension of their electronic devices—chauffeurs with a checkbook—and still they're catering and doting and being all kissy-ass every waking moment of the day. And then it's off to college and holy fuck, talk about draining every last penny. And for what? To study psychology or

- 18 -

anthropology and wind up right back where they started, sucking at the teat of Mommy and Daddy?"

Luc was distracted by the scent of lavender. Or was it bayberry or, no, rum and root beer? It was an olfactory free-for-all, new smells catching a microtide and competing for attention. "Luc—hello! You listening?"

"Ya. Ya. Yoga pants. Yep."

"You didn't process a thing. We haven't known each other long enough for that."

"But long enough for you to be staring at your phone constantly. At dinner even."

"That's malarkey and you know it. I barely use my phone. I know women who can't even move their eyes straight ahead anymore."

"You stare at the phone, I'm telling you, a lot."

A couple of hefty guys, culinary school students in silly paper hats, one with a cleaver inked on his neck, almost at his ear, like he was a preparing to be field dressed himself, moved a couple of crates of foraged herbs to the top of the vast stainless steel prep table. The crates had top notes of clove or bergamot or nutmeg. "Today, we will experience the magic mind meld of vinegar and fruit and aromatics. We might get shit-faced, so I hope you all made other arrangements to get back besides driving," he said.

Luc and Cat walked slowly over to the herbs and clasped hands. "Sorry," he said. "I'm tired and angry today."

“Maybe, but you have a point. I’m a helicopter mom, all right, but a helicopter that’s fleeing from the aliens. I need a cigarette and then I can talk about it.”

“Cigarette? You serious? Arghhh. What are you thinking when you’re in chaturanga or downward dog or the dancing lotus or whatever and your lungs are squeezed and you start to feel the lactate building up? Are you inhaling and thinking how sweet it would be to smoke? Isn’t the whole idea of yoga to purge yourself of toxins? I can do two and a half minutes of plank now, and you know why? I can see through the pain. I literally look at it, like tiny fissures or gray globules, and I ignore it, like another *BuzzFeed* or *Huffington Post* blog entry. You can do that, you know, with smoking. Hate it. Fuck it up in your mind.”

Cat rolled her eyes. A few weeks ago, Luc thought yoga came in a cup with fruit at the bottom. She had to drag the guy to class, and now he was bloviating about it. “Wow, you’ve come far pretty fast. Two-plus minutes? Bitchin’ plank time.”

“’Cept I ain’t all, like, competitive with it like all the ladies.”

“Sorry, man, it’s a sport. And an industry. Ask Lulu and Yolo and Crew and Prana and Vuori. Kind of like surfing. Folks act like it’s a big thing with nature, but you ever try to snake someone’s wave?”

“Huh?”

"Snake a wave, like paddle in just in front of someone when a good wave is coming. That's a serious violation of bro-will."

"Never surfed. You live in Bushwick with three kids. What the hell do you know about surfing?"

"For real? You don't get around much, baby. It's cold for sure, but the Rockaways—which is actually part of New York City itself—has some pretty damn good waves sometimes. They even have an event there. I started taking my nephew Ben there when he was six. He wants to be a pro now."

"Sounds like a long shot: kid from Brooklyn becoming a surf pro."

"Not so much. His dad lives in SoCal, a little surf village. Three beaches in a two-mile stretch. He goes in the summer. Out here he's a legend, out there, above average. Those kids have been at it since they were in diapers."

There was a whirring and grinding sound as the instructor started macerating some kind of combo, a purply liquid titrated into beakers by the two graduate assistants, Harv and Lem. Cat and Luc were vague about it, not sure why they were there, just a pit stop to someplace else, someplace better, sexier, jazzier. Harv and Lem had V Culinary Institute scrubs on, white with a badge made up of a crest divided into four quadrants, depicting a boar (distinctly not a pig, based on tusk size and facial gristle), a cleaver, a sheaf of wheat, and a sprig of something, berries most likely. The crest was done in a bold design with wit and a retro feel, but not retro per se. Luc remembered the phrase "retrofuturism" that Jack Telnack of Ford design fame used to describe the original Taurus. Funny, now the look was more important than the thing. Kids—and by kids, Luc reckoned that at thirty-seven, he was closer to middle age than to being a kid—were visual, impetuous, unremorseful about their need to parse a situation, be it prospective mate or acquisition, quickly, a Gladwellian thin slice. You had seconds—no, fractions of a second—to get over on someone.

He felt like he was a beat behind, an incomplete grade. He had started studying physics, took two years of it at City College and did well, but couldn't pay tuition his first semester of junior year, began bartending in Manhattan and Woodstock, and never went back. Then he took up composing, just picked up some books on notation and basic theory, read some Henry Cowell, and started doodling. Upstate was a good place to compose, gloomy half the year, lots of archives and history and modernist sponsors like Botstein at Bard. He was especially taken with Cowell, a Californian, and others from that era like Ives and Lou Harrison. If anyone would have asked Luc what his dream was—not that they did—he would have told them he wanted to rekindle the idea of the Exquisite Corpse, a serial composing game hosted by Virgil Thomson in the dissipation and bohemian fug of 1930s Chelsea, wherein a circle of composers would write a bar and pass the score to the next person. Luc had managed only two completed works, a viola sonata (he liked the alto clef for some reason) and a string quartet for violin, viola, cello, and double bass. He was also through two movements of a sonata for viola and saxophone, the first of its kind for that combination ever, as far as he knew. The middle registers always just sounded right to him, and, bucking tradition, he gave the melodic parts to the wallflower viola and consigned the violin to the "oompah" role typically reserved for its big brother. The inclusion of the double bass was, in Luc's view, a more natural and logical form of quartet than two violins.

Cat hadn't heard a word of this. He looked at the last three weeks like it was a sonata movement—exposition, development, recapitulation. Alternatively, he could see it as a wave. Any metaphor would do with a beginning, middle, and end. He was close a bunch of times to heading back to Woodstock, just bailing, but there was always a fillip, an artful dodge whereby she piqued his interest just a bit more. She was an activist. No, a provocateur. That word kept popping up, even though it was a word he would not have come up with himself, a word that he normally would have associated with the preening hipster types, not his type of hipster—the upstate version, more hippie than hipster—but the downstate variety. She had that ankh too, which snaked around her hip bone, and my, did she have that lovely attenuated waist. And she worked it too, even now, the way she floated across the room toward Harv and Lem, who were both leering like the wolf in an old Hanna-Barbera cartoon, liver-colored tongue drooling and fangs bared, in her direction. Could he blame them?

The $245-per-person course fee included a VCI-catered lunch that consisted of small plates and amuse-bouche that spawned from Il Bulli in Barcelona and WD-40 in New York. Luc, thankfully, saw precious little of that at the Mohonk, whose restaurant was more like a glorified chop house with some spa cuisine thrown in, but here it was all emulsions, sous-vide, and what he called bait-and-switch cuisine, stuff that looked like one thing and was actually something else. Post-COVID, hand food was popular. Grab and go. Tapas, tacos, sushi, pizza. Caloric intensity. Mouth-feel. Not that it staunched the burger and fat culture. It wasn't, it seemed to him, like folks were substituting new foods for the old but that they were adding them. He wasn't averse to shitty food until recently, thirty-seven seeming to be the inflection point when he noticed some incipient wiggling around his waist. His jeans started riding a little lower, like they wanted to crawl away from something, and he added a half mile to his jog around the lake, and then another. He ate cleaner and tried to mimic the line he heard from a personal trainer about not eating "for taste" until dinner. What was that about, didn't everything have a taste, or was it protodeprivation, a precursor to all these boot camps and numbered P90X-type systems that worked great, assuming you could sustain intense aerobic and anaerobic exercise for ninety minutes? Shit, he could take folks out to the forest and make 'em chop wood and run up and down hillocks thick with crabgrass and do pull-ups from uneven maple branches and that would make them scream for mercy. But Luc began to see it was his diet, the evil axis of wheat-sugar-soy-dairy, and of course alcohol, which probably metabolized into all of those, that was starting to thicken him, like his dad. Abdicating the midsection was the beginning of the end. You let your abdominal cavity succumb to the belly, and that was it, you might as get the walker and the taupe bunion shoes and the Medicare Part B or C or D that his mom was always talking about—something esoteric relating to her pharma bill, which ran something like $350 a month even with all the subsidies.

Cat was right about starting a business: a big wave doesn't care if you grew up paddling out a mile and a half into big surf or took the A train with the folks who lived in the Mitchell-Lamas and projects that limned the Rockaways and the only passable surf spots in the New York City limits. Luc looked over at Harv and Lem, who were arranging yet another platter of stuff, this time stuffed eggs marked with terra-cotta streaks and purply roe. They reminded him of the plumbers to be admitted from the apprenticeship at the local, guys trailing tool belts and gear and a heavy dose of the boroughs from job to job. The city was different now, fewer jobs in construction, the union jobs drying up. He knew this from his uncle Rick, a big finance guy at Pomander Walk, the money behind a lot of real estate projects. His uncle was always saying he should finish up his degree and get some finance under his belt and he could get him into the firm. Luc heard about how the deals came together, first the equity, the riskiest money, and then they shopped for a lender. Sometimes there was another layer called mezzanine, kind of a hybrid. It was like a puzzle, his uncle said; you had to keep trying pieces until they fit. The developers all wanted to get rich, but sometimes the deals chased the money and sometimes the money chased the deals. Luc remembered that phrase.

Besides, real estate was just about the vessel, the enclosure. What mattered was what went on with the four walls, right? He had ideas, lots of them, way too many to explain to Cat, who thought that she was doing him some giant favor by introducing him to the world of curated aromatics and artisanal cocktail making. He bartended to live, not the other way around, and knew about the bar business, the crap hours and the vomit and the security you needed every second. Booze was ultimately booze, no matter how you dressed it up. He practically stopped drinking himself, mostly stuck with red wine for the congeners and the polyphenols. Otherwise, he felt like shit, sometimes after only a single drink. He was getting antsy here, sick of being indoors, still tetchy after the 'rona. He was about to grab Cat and tell her he needed some air, when he caught her at the other end of the big steel countertop, where she picked up an egg and threw it at Lem. He picked something up and threw it back at her and then there was a flurry—a food fight! Cat was picking stuff up and hurling it like she played triple-A ball somewhere, a 105-pound fury in skinny jeans. Lem and Harv were laughing, mostly taking the punishment, their culinary scrubs soaking up a varicolored mess of tapas. Cat looked electrified, hyper like a child on Mountain Dew and birthday cake.

Luc stepped back and watched as the deviled eggs and handfuls of jewel-like black currants were flung around, a dreadful waste of good foodstuffs, but a colorful spectacle. He saw it as a mash-up of lots of old television: Three Stooges versus Batman versus Lucy and Ricky at the winery. These dustups were funny affairs: how serious did you get? It was like intramural touch football: everyone had a different idea of how to block, and sometimes the other guy blocked a little too hard and you blocked back harder and pretty soon it was an all-out affair. The social contract. Cat had none of that, preferring autarky over any kind of treaty or arrangement.

Closely related colors: mottled purple and maroon spatters slicked over all the surfaces, the other paying customers standing at the periphery, marveling at Cat, her angular and taut figure expertly heaving stuff and bobbing and weaving like a middleweight.

He grabbed his man bag and dashed out the service entrance, vowing to double down and start composing more.

- 19 -

Hugo was wearing a T-shirt from that new boutique in the Arts District named after a Greek island, something like Adonis or Pellucid, he couldn't quite pinpoint it, but he remembered it was a revelation seeing such a nice shop so close to Skid Row. He always loved the LA River bridges. Fourth Street was the most famous, of course, filmed the most for its "gingerbread," what the contractors in New York used to call ornamentation on buildings that did not serve a functional purpose. The bridge had those filigreed Beaux Arts lamps and exterior railings, and it was close to the parts of the LA River that they used for chase scenes and apocalyptic moments when bad guys would hold the planet hostage because they had buried weapons-grade plutonium under a SoCal Edison substation and had a remote trigger device. Hugo knew this because during the filming of *Get One, Give One* in 1983, when he couldn't get Bronson because he was already too expensive and had to settle for that one-'n'-done douchebag Ricky Peretz (né Perlman, but his agent thought Peretz was more like a tough Sabra, and why not capitalize on Israeli military might, still basking in the Entebbe halo?). They did a scene on the river where Peretz reaches out the window of his Olds 442—gorgeous orange-red, that thing was—and literally scoops Vivian Cecily into the car in one smooth motion. Hugo still winced remembering how hard he tried not to look up her skirt on every take. Even though it was the eighties and you were the director, there had to be some propriety, unless you had massive celebrity and a reputation for lunacy like Polanski, and then everyone on the set just kind of cowered and responded on command. He never got to that point, not the summit or nadir of celebrity, and was more of a technician in the classic European sense. He was not unafraid to think of himself as a filmmaker as opposed to a director/manager type. The craft was important, getting the patina just right. You could tell almost immediately if the gestalt of a film was right or wrong, or at least he could. Took something like twenty-three takes, that scene; that was before CGI of course when you had to stage things with stunt people who were amazing, but still prone to human error. Peretz had to be shooed away from the catering tables, Hugo recalled, eating so much during the film that his nascent paunch was starting to interfere with his credibility as a badass.

Today, his goal was to walk each of the landmark bridges from north to south. In the pocket of his handsome new military coat, a twill beauty that he bought for cash at that new shop—the devil if he couldn't remember the name, he just dropped six hundred bucks there—he placed a small notebook with sepia-colored paper and handsome red dots. He paired the notebooks with a Blackwing 602 pencil, part of a stash of original production units that he hoarded just before Eberhard Faber shut down after the crimping machines failed. Glancing at his notes, he saw a table he had prepared:

Bridge	Date of Construction
East Washington Boulevard	1931
East Ninth Street (Railroad)	1925
I-10	1959
East 7th Street	1927
East 6th Street	1932
East 4th Street	1930
East 1st Street	1929
US Rte. 101	1944
Macy St. Bridge	1926
North Main Street	1910
North Spring Street	1928
Buena Vista	1909
Figueroa Avenue	1937
LA River Bridge	1943

In the other breast pocket of his new coat, which was a shade of oxidized green that was just unmilitary enough to look like civilian wear, Hugo folded twenty $100 bills and placed them in a large paper clip. His mission was to walk each bridge, find a crevasse—a gap in the base of a lamp, a piece of crumbling mortar where there would be a gap, à la the Wailing Wall, or some other semiconspicuous spot—roll up a bill, and stash it, or in some other nook or cranny. He would put up a bunch of flyers that he printed up around Skid Row, notifying people to look around and see if they could find the money.

His coccyx hurt, but the more he walked, the better he felt. He told himself how great he felt for a man of seventy-two. But was he that young? He felt a lot older. Hadn't he had a birthday not long ago, or was that Ken Bellard's birthday at that old people's place in Toluca Lake? God, that guy looked like shit for someone who was once such a handsome bastard.

He was pretty sure he was alone but sensed that someone was trailing behind him, kind of like a spy. Eileen did that sometimes, sprung on him like a spook in a cemetery. "You scared the crap out of me!" he would tell her. "What are you talking about?" she would answer. Like she didn't know. But there was something behind him, a malingerer, someone up to no good. He was immune, though, wanting to give away money anyway. He had a roll of cash bulging at the pocket of his khaki pants. Benny had that after a while, a big roll of cash in his pocket, always at the ready. That was a sure sign that you had made it, not some shitty immigrant anymore mooching off the cousins in Rego Park or Sunnyside with a shiksa girlfriend, but a mensch with a job and a family.

All those bridges in Deco and Beaux Arts—really a stylistic catch basin, Hugo recalling they used that term a lot in New York when a building had no discernable style, but lots of ornamentation. In the rest of the country's mind, LA was an arriviste, everything happening yesterday or just now, but the reality was its history was just as rich, albeit younger, with Hollywood having compressed three hundred years into one hundred. Film bridged the gap. You had Prokofiev and other serious classical composers coming out to make a quick strike so they could sustain their craft—their real craft, getting into the good graces of purists like Virgil Thomson. Hugo mostly made popular films that limned scuba divers and detectives and race car drivers, but he made sure to put in a reference to something esoteric—Bartok or a museum or event that he knew a viewer would have to look up.

Hugo knew he looked like he just came out of the spin cycle, even with his new coat on. Your true coat at ninety-five was the liver-spotted skin and gray bristle that poked through even an hour after shaving. Way closer to death than birth, he was keenly aware that his pores emitted a stale musk. But he resisted. He smiled, pulled his shoulders back, did some ujjayi breathing—yes, he still did a bit of yoga, made him more flexible, freer, able to keep exercising the way he had been doing for the last sixty years or so.

He felt light, smart, capable of true charity, that is to say, charity without identification of its source. This was a concept he learned from Benny the Flyer, when one day years and years back he handed over several twenty-dollar bills to the proprietor of Edelman's Delicatessen at 168th and Haven in Little Frankfurt to buy a week's dinner for the guy with the suit jacket who sat forlornly out front, one of the sleeves having separated from the body of the coat, a cat purring urgently next to an empty saucer.

Eileen—damn, why was she following so close? He was having second thoughts about this marriage. Yeah, the younger ones were great at first, that clear, pure sound to their voice, but she was becoming a smotherer, a fun-buster, as he liked to say. Smothering and mothering, but for his taste she was around when he didn't want her to be and vice versa. Like now, trailing behind in her Jaguar. That was her car, wasn't it? But hers was metallic gray. No, she wanted the metallic gray, but the Indian guy—why was an Indian guy selling Jaguars in Brentwood? Oh, an Indian company—Tata or some name like that—bought Jaguar. Maybe they brought an Indian guy over from Bangalore, make things more authentic. Jaguar was English, though. Why didn't they bring an English guy over? He talked her out of the gray one. Hers was blue. Definitely blue. And matte, not all shiny like the one that was darting in and out of Broadway, following him now, like he was Peter Lorre in *M* with such a dark secret.

He tried to snap out of it, did those eye exercises Dr. Sandler recommended, side to side, up and down, then closing them and taking a sunbath. Could the light defer the inevitable degradation? It's just a theory. He wanted a chance to redo the score to *West and East* (1976) that horrible, treacly violin piece practically ruining the entire film, especially the denouement when Parker and his gang roll through Sonora with the bootlegged liquor. I mean, who scored that shit? The problem wasn't the music itself, part of the pyrotechnic canon, the Vieuxtemps, the Korngolds, the Paganinis, the Busonis, show-off stuff, perfect if you were in the mood, solo vehicles for careers. Those were the early rock stars, that's the thing. But in a film, with a quasi-serious theme: gangsters, Federales, G-men, all entangled with the same three women—almost got Lee Remick for one of the roles—what a finely featured woman—but like always had to settle for the up-and-comers. Big deal. B-list back then. No A-list without the Bs, and who's to say you're stuck there for posterity? Fuck 'em all, critical appraisal is just a commodity, and an ever-changing one at that. Anyone laugh at Jonathan Winters or Milton Berle or Joey Bishop now? Uh-uh. Anyone under the age of deceased, that is. Am I seventy-two? Hugo wondered, feeling older; must be older the way his back hurt so much. Could he be over ninety? They're mapping DNA so easily now. Take some of that spinal fluid, store it, take your code, and is there any question, even a scintilla of doubt, that they'll be tweaking everybody a century from now? Too late for that for me.

His knuckles felt heavy, like he had brass on them. It was getting hot, and he was sick of trying to shake her, his own wife. She was so intrusive lately, asking him how he was doing every five seconds. Couldn't she just leave him alone with his money? It was his to give away. He gave away most of it to her ingrate kids. What were they to him anyway? His own brood, if he was honest, wasn't that hot, but it was different, you had that history, seeing them trundle around, the heavy responsibility, the archive of faded snapshots and thousands of photos stored on your hard drive.

It was an essential part of his narrative, that's what it was. From the Bronx to LA, the Grand Concourse to Hancock Park, and from Vienna before that. He was on the boat, practically pickled in the brine air. Benny wanted to stay topside the whole time, either he was unbelievably excited or got seasick, or hated his wife, probably a combination of all three. But even though he was, what, two, maybe close to three? He could swear he remembered the constellations on that trip. The stars never seemed to be out in Austria, but they were brilliant at sea.

And then on the ship, there was some story about Walter Benjamin, the critic, who, despairing for his life after being turned away at San Sebastián, decided to end it himself. He heard that story somewhere, but it couldn't have been on the boat with Benny, he wasn't even three yet, and that was way before the incident happened. Source? Please, the source? "Eileen, that story, you've heard it a million times." Damn it, he thought, she's so close, but she doesn't answer. But this bridge, Macy Street—and he looked down again at his notebook, which showed the date of completion to be 1926. He was up on it, and it was a blustery afternoon in February, the dead of winter even in LA, and he was close enough to the concrete handrail to experience some vertigo, or old-man light-headedness at the very least. He dangled his head over, let it sway in the breeze, listening to the chthonic echo coming from the "river" below, really some kind of patchwork of rail bed, sluice gate, and weedy embankment where he could swear he shot a film or a commercial some years before. He picked his head up and nearly spilled backward. No! he thought, just coming around from that coccyx fall, nasty thing. Don't need another nine weeks holed up in bed, even with the iPad, which he had to admit converted him from physical books, something he vowed would never happen. And for some reason, he was forgetting whether the Sontag or the Arendt essays about Benjamin made a bigger impression on him, but he did recall being impressed with Benjamin's shifting interest, something most people would regard with suspicion, but Hugo regarded as a necessity, the point being that your life consisted of fragments, episodes really, and there was no purposeful trajectory, and that if you wanted even a fleeting shot at happiness, you had to resolve things one way or the other, even if they had an unhappy ending. One or the other—Arendt, he thought—noted that despite his posthumous success and his polymathic prowess, there was a bit of the dilettante about Benjamin. He, like Benjamin, venerated the small thing, the tiny gesture, the fact that Benjamin had delighted in seeing the entire "Shema Yisrael" written on two grains of wheat in the Musée de Cluny. Hugo needed to make things smaller as he grew older, even as his eyesight degraded. It was a race against time, getting it all out. Okay, Hugo thought, it's okay to have been a B guy in a town that venerates the A-list. It had given him a fine living, a substantial series of houses, each in its own way trading on the virtues of the one that came before, yet better and more keenly in tune with contemporary aesthetic preconditions and standards.

Death suddenly struck him as comedic, just the hamster jumping off the wheel, suddenly emboldened. Flimflamming and flip-flopping through fifty iterations—no, make that flavors—of Judaism, Hugo had settled on the most benign, the cultural form, adhering to the principle of Judaism as a touchstone for thinking about ideas, problems, in a certain way, inverted if you will, knowing the answer and hypothecating the question, but eschewing the rituals and the blind adherence to laws. This gave license to browsing in the megamall of options: Buddhism was one, of course, but that was the default position for the Hollywood and Manhattan elites,

"Jewboos" practically slotted in between the Reform and Reconstructionist movements of Judaism itself. He became a mini acolyte of self-realization, going so far as to spend a weekend lolling about in the sleepy seaside coastal town of Encinitas, where there was a temple of ecumenical self-discovery, originally endowed in large part by one of the Beatles after their India trip. Despite the trappings—the ersatz-guru look denoted by stringing plumes of salt-and-pepper hair, harem pants, and lingering swales of patchouli in a pansexual processional of mildly thwarted carnal adventurism—the self-realization gig appealed to him in the sense that the name "Buddhism" itself was so tepid and fluid that almost anything would work.

Hugo dug through his pants pockets, exploring the crevasses of all four in order—five, including the change pocket—and repeating the sequence. When he finished, he had no idea what he was looking for. "Crap. Must not be that important," he said, looking toward the LA skyline, as if there was a dialogue to be extracted from the Union Bank tower. He felt okay about it, enough to know there was a problem, but not like it was any big deal. The cells, the synapses, had "tails" that grew shorter, that was all, a natural function of aging. He could pay for the extra attention; lord knows Eileen would not be around to help, freed at last. Who was going to oversee this business, the last chapter? Phoebe? Lovely girl, smart girl, but absorbed in her work and her studies. He wouldn't have the heart to drag her from New York. Trevor? Seemed to have lots of time on his hands, but not a caretaker, which was normal for a man. Something about the kid was off lately, turning into a real drifter or God forbid having some kind of problem with pills or booze. Kid seemed jittery the last time he saw him. Too alert, if that was possible.

Strong sun appeared, too strong for the kind of day that it had been up to that point, a gray haze, clouds shaped like nautilus shells, the continents drifting by in nimbus. Beatriz was tugging on his jacket. What was she doing out here, on the bridge? Was she following him too?

"Mr. Hugo, Mr. Hugo. What would you like me to do with the dog food? Garage or kitchen?"

It was definitely Beatriz, and he was at home. He felt unusually focused and optimistic. "How long have I been home, do you know? I was out this morning, touring the bridges downtown."

"You came home, I think, about an hour ago. Someone dropped you off in a big Bentley, blue like the sky. Verrrry fancy, Mr. Hugo. Verrrry fancy."

"Who was driving? Man or woman?"

"Could not say who. The windows were dark. A beautiful car, Mr. Hugo."

Hugo did a reckoning of his friends. Lots of high-end autos in the group. Lester Stacey had a Rolls, but an older one, affecting that old-timey Beverly Hills feel, rolling it up and down the hill, never venturing on the freeways, maxing out at forty mph. Dave Spitz had a Lamborghini, so low that you couldn't park it anywhere since the nose was below the curb bumps at the mall and if you even scraped it you'd be in for a $5,000 repair, so you just valeted it all over the place, that being the idea in the first place. Hundred dollars extra to have it preening in front of the valet. God bless America, Hugo thought. A hundred bucks paid two months' rent on the Grand Concourse back then. Today it was a tip. But even back then there was excess, the casino in Central Park for example that Walker, the mayor of New York, built with his bootlegger's money, basically a dance hall for his cronies to bring their floozies. Not fair that word, though; lots of them were just nice girls working their way up, trying to figure it out, so what if they met a guy in an unhappy marriage? The Packards and Lincolns and Hudsons and even the occasional Duesenberg could pull right into a parking spot in the middle of the park, if you could imagine. No sense getting all bent out of shape today. Excess is what makes the world go 'round in a perverse way, he thought.

"Oh well," Hugo said to Beatriz, "if you need a ride, might as well be in a Bentley."

- 20 -

"Yum," Paige said, licking the last bits of juice from a softball-size Greening apple off her lips. Greenings were okay, but kind of stuck in neutral for her taste, lacking the piney or citrus or vanilla and spice notes of the best heirloom varieties. For Paige, mid-November was as good as it got from a pomological standpoint. She had become one of the stalkers, along with the chefs who ambushed the upstate purveyors who viewed the intrusion of so many heavily pierced and tatted-up chefs as an impediment to their desire to sell the best apples to a variety of customers. Paige was writing about the link between apples and democracy, how the fruit did not grow true from the seed, but rather depended on grafts to reproduce specific varieties. Colonizing the lanes and boulevards and lonely ramparts of the country in lock step with the settlers, apples mirrored the diversity of the nation and of course were featured at Mount Vernon and Monticello, Jefferson raising specific varieties for cider and for eating. She had to keep herself from wandering too far off track, finding herself theorizing about the apple and religion, the apple and sexuality, the apple and repression, the apple and witchcraft, and the apple and the Masonic Temple in America. The fruit had a central role in American history, from the Hudson River Valley into the Piedmont region, bringing farmers and seed peddlers and equipment vendors together to debate the differences and advantages of different varieties. It was impossible to imagine the orange or the blueberry doing this, as charming as they were. And then there was the primal connection between the apple and harvest season, Paige recalling the cider-cold blast from her father's cheek when he kissed her after coming home with a fat bushel of Macouns and a gallon or two of rich cider, already starting to ferment a bit in its vast glass flagon.

Like a lot of heirloom chasers—this was a thing apparently, the phrase coined by Rickard Wilhelm, the *Observe*r columnist—Paige had a soft spot for Pippins, Cox's Orange being her favorite. She also liked the Newtown, named for the eponymous part of Queens, and a favorite of Jefferson's, who extolled its virtue even when he traveled to France. Paige's piece for the *New Farmer* magazine titled "The New Heirlooms" started with the Newtown Pippin, which was a capsule story for all the great apples, starting from a chance genetic recombination on a Newtown Creek swamp bed. Trevor was always talking about some friend of his dad, a rich German guy who lived on Mansion Place near Thomson Avenue who was obsessed with Jefferson and Monticello and, like Jefferson, cultivated two apples for cider, the Hewes Crab and the Taliaferro, and two for eating, the Pippin and the Esopus Spitzenburg. The Pippin diverged into two, a larger yellow apple that stored better and a smaller greener one. Monticello's Pippin became the Albemarle Pippin. Trevor used to get into the cellar with the man's grandson who was a couple of years younger, but without supervision he did things like crack open the big glass gallons of homemade cider that the boys would sip in the lazy hot summer sun. Paige recalled that Trevor sometimes thought he was being raised in upstate New York because he spent so much time kicking around the Olmsted-designed gardens of that vestigial estate, even though it was less than a mile from the stacked, sooty mess of the double-level train tracks at Sixty-First Street in Woodside.

Paige was fascinated by the apple's ability to become dormant, fruiting when it was propitious. More than other trees and fruits, the apple had anthropomorphic traits, its branches becoming arthritic and gray, its skins leathery and callused. The arrangement of parts on an apple was not as obvious as in other fruit. Lacking the dramatic attenuation of the banana or the epistolary defenses of the pineapple, the apple was a hand fruit first and foremost. But it was interesting how different species of apple had their own arrangement of stem, shoulders, and the vestiges of the calyx.

The apple was an enigma shrouded in mystery and as unpredictable as human behavior. She was also flummoxed by America's fixation with beer, which was a perfectly fine drink but was overplayed almost to the point of disbelief. What to make of the scores of IPAs, Belgians, wheats, Pilsners, lagers, and seasonal specialties, all small-batch crafted by guys with long stringy beards in overgrown college towns? Weren't they cannibalizing one another? Even if you liked one IPA, what was keeping you from jumping ship next week and getting the one with the cooler nautical-themed logo or better supermarket pastoral prose that delineated the purity of the hops and aromatics and flavors that went into creating that purple-gold-bronze fizz?

Russeting was the apple's downfall, when those god-awful Delicious and insipid Granny Smiths became the darling of the supermarket discount operators, taste and provenance having yielded to whether an apple could be waxed to maintain its titular good looks for weeks on end. The whole idea of the apple struck Paige as the reason why she wanted to write about food in the first place. Restoring the heirloom varieties was about social justice as much as epicurean delight. In Paige's view, the whole dreary patch of the twentieth century, roughly from after the oil crisis in the early seventies until the Internet stock bubble got the economy going again, kind of paralleled the demise of the American apple. She could almost trace the nadir to one particularly cold and rainy day in 1996 when she was living in a tiny studio apartment in Phoebe's building and still single. It was mid-November and the icy sheets of horizontal rain were almost too much for her to drag out the Wellies and the Patagonia rain jacket to make the trip twenty blocks south—just short of the twenty-two blocks that constituted the mythical Manhattan mile—to Fairway, maybe catching Zabar's on the way back even though it took the inner strength needed to attack the face of El Cap or brave the surf of Mavericks to conquer the cheese counter there on a rainy Saturday. But fueled by a half cup of cold coffee (Zabar's, in fact), she yanked on the rain gear and, passing Ivan, the doorman who always leered at her a little too long, left her terra cotta eleven-story midblock building on West Ninetieth Street into sheets of frigid November rain.

Paige recalled this while she sat in the green room of WNYC. She had been contacted by Maureen Loudery to do a segment on apple stalking, and the frenzy surrounding the Union Square farmers market, which had eclipsed all the other metropolitan-area markets for sales volume and was the darling of chefs and foodies from all over Manhattan and, increasingly, Brooklyn. It had been a dry spring and summer, which extended the apple season deep into November, a real rarity, and her favorite orchard, Marchands, was open in Klettenberg, which was accessible from all the Route 9s, depending on which of the bridges you wanted to cross and whether you preferred looking at the west or east bank of the Hudson as you drove up. Each bank had its advocates, people obsessing over individual formations and groupings of schist. Even Paige, who for her trade was required to extract detail and in fact use scientific nomenclature for the produce she described, was put off by the fact that people had actually deconstructed the drive up the Hudson River into discussable components, as if they could be disassembled for a gallery. On her drives upstate she always packed her tools, which included a leather-wrapped wool blanket from Faribault and a large folding knife designed by a charismatic Brazilian guy, Mario Gomes, who built that magnificent yoga retreat on Route 22 in Bedford, which was a great spot for a staycation. The knife blade was made from upcycled disk plows, and the handle from black-and-white bone and horn. Paige had been accumulating picnic accoutrements from an ever-growing number of perfectly curated little Internet shops. It was fascinating to see all these exotic products coming together—brass coffee urns, pressed cotton and leather document holders, knives with exotic inlays, natural-bristle brushes, and apothecary products with emollients and oils sourced from botanicals all over the globe. Two or three clicks and you were equipped.

With Trevor gone to God knows where (she sometimes wondered how the kids were getting to school and to soccer and piano and play dates), she had started buying lots of things, focusing on Japanese pottery, fruit knives, and barware. It was odd, because as a fractured couple, there was less of a need for entertaining. Dispirited at first, Paige was liberated now, unburdened from reciprocating for anything at any time: Hey, I'm separated, you got a problem with that? But the little trinkets and knickknacks gave her comfort, her pleasure palpable when the packages came, so many that she was able to detect the diesel belching of the UPS truck from two or three blocks away.

Sondra was in from the Bay Area on business, and Paige had invited her to listen in on the interview. They were herded into the windowless green room, with a sofa, an armchair in green velvet, and a side table with energy bars; a pitcher of ice water; and a coffee urn, an inexpensive one like you see at budget motor inns. Sondra was in a Bay Area tuxedo—Patagonia rain slicker over mom jeans and Danner hiking boots. This last choice made Paige recoil, the vast, duck-like appearance of the Danners having a neutering effect on women. Sondra was one of those women whose attractiveness depended on grooming and the artful selection of her kit, and Danner was not a good choice. She made it worse by shimmying up onto the sofa and tucking her feet underneath lotus-style. Paige had given up on a lot of things at home, the kids proving destructive at every waking moment, but one thing she had managed was to keep dirty feet off the sofas.

Sondra peeled off the Patagonia and revealed a long-sleeve sports top that read "Santa Clara Women's Soccer" and had a badly rendered horse logo beneath it. It was scarlet, jarring, and vulgar. Trevor was into that shit. She was forced to make a rule: no more than one article of clothing, including hats, that had writing of any kind on it. You could wear that old-school Canadiens cap with that funny "CH" logo—what the hell did that mean anyway?—but then the Jets thermal would have to stay in the closet. When men were the offenders, it was bad enough, but when women wore logo or branded or lettered clothing, it was somehow more offensive to Paige. Yeah, it was a gender thing, and why should it be worse for women, but it was one of those dicey political things that everyone had to internalize and work out, like wearing a Native American logo. Was it an honorific, or a patronizing slap?

"What position did you play, anyway?"

"Huh?"

"Soccer. You *were* on the team, weren't you?"

"Goalkeeper. Backup keeper, technically, but I did play a few games. Started against Stanford once. That was scary."

"Stanford? Wow. Among other things, it seems like a sports factory."

"Place *is* sports crazy. Folks think it's some kind of nerd academy like MIT, but athletics are huge. It's like MIT grafted onto Michigan or something."

"Crazy. So you like it? Getting shot at and kicked and all?"

"It was a living, as they say. You play stuff as a kid, and you grow, and you are okay, and the coaches need to fill spots, and the parents need to kill time, and they think the sport keeps you away from drugs, which it doesn't—like athletes are all immune from drugs and crap and all, as you can tell from pro football and baseball players. That's what's so wild about it; it's like sports is the only thing people can do with their time, to the point if you want don't want to do a sport, it's like you're a freak. And you've got these parents with thwarted ambition standing around with their fake tits and bad ideas and anger all staring at their kid running after a ball. Blecchh!"

"Paige—you're up," said the assistant for the *Mel Harris* show. She looked about seventeen, with a tubular gray wool dress and thick black knit leggings, what the fashion people would probably allude to as "editor's style," monochromatic and lean. The glasses were also just so, slightly oversize cat-eye frames made from thick black acetate. "Here are your headphones. You can hear everything that's going on, even when we're off air. Just speak normally."

Paige had been interviewed a lot but had never made it to broadcast media. The *Harris* show was old-fashioned radio, a host and three guests spread over a ninety-minute show. People clung to Mel Harris because of the onslaught of digital media and the dilution of talent, everyone and anyone becoming a pundit. Harris was erudite and genial but also had rapier instincts drawn from his days as an investment banker. He was almost eighty now and had calmed down a lot, into his twenty-ninth year of doing the show. He was a legendary polymath and was known to make his guests squirm by taking them on long tangents completely unrelated to their field of expertise.

"I'm sorry, Miss..."

"Sondra."

"Sondra, you'll have to hang out in here, if that's okay." Sondra zipped up her windcheater and shuffled over to the upholstered chair, looking like a rather mopey basset hound.

When Paige walked around the corner to Studio 37, she saw the Mel that she had imagined from listening to countless programs: two Parisian leather club chairs with a dusty kilim in the center. Between the chairs, there was a small Eileen Gray Bauhaus table with a large amber cigar ashtray sitting on top, an unlit Cohiba poised for lighting. Mel was a health nut with the exception of caffeine, and there were two mugs on the table, one a ceramic Tim Horton mug purloined from one of the restaurants in Toronto, the other also ceramic, a facsimile of the famous Greek diner blue-and-white number. The cigar was a prop. Paige picked up on these details and started profiling Mel, who was much taller in person, but stooped. He looked like a cross between Leonard Bernstein and that famous quarterback from the nineties—what's his name—

Montana, Joe Montana. Leather in the face; energy in the blue eyes. A dynamic-looking older man who nonetheless looked defeated.

Paige looked at Mel and tried to do the math. She was forty-four and remembered Mel Harris from when he was on the talk show circuit, even in the waning days of the circle of erudition and mock erudition—Cavett, Buckley, Carson, Douglas, Allen—that engulfed guests and led them out onstage like slaves being released in the catacombs of the Colosseum. Even when she was tiny, Paige evinced a preternatural ability to understand what the guests were actually saying, empathizing with them as one or another bombastic host talked over them or bluntly made them do an about-face when the topic veered into territory that made a sponsor squirm. Even as a little girl, her hair in ringlets and her legs encased in thick dance tights, she could sense when talk show guests were talking too much about ladies' chests and behinds, the audience murmuring and the host turning red and smiling all goofy.

Harris was a survivor, if not quite actually a survivor himself. His mother made it out of Czechoslovakia just ahead of the bad guys, only a quarter Jewish herself, but, as she liked to say, "enough to not be invited to the Christmas parties," and lived in Newcastle before deciding it was too dark and cold and emigrating to New York, which she realized was nearly as dark and as cold. Mel grafted a survivor's mentality onto his early stand-up routines in a few of the places on Fifty-Second Street that liked to mix in a bit of vaudeville and cabaret and burlesque (how quaint those words sounded to Paige as she mouthed them to herself watching Mel—as velvet toned as his namesake Mel Tormé—deliver a request to the listeners to donate their unwanted vehicles to WNYC) before the real business of jazz came on.

Harris was antipodal by nature, believing that the best way to derive a candid performance from a stranger was to adopt a contrasting, if not oppositional, persona. Therefore, to a liberal New York Jew, he played the scion of European burghers, not quite establishment Frankfurters, but from a class of stolid burghers with free-enterprise leanings. To the conservatives, he was an acolyte of Bruce and Kovacs, unpredictable with a bohemian flair, Neal Cassady's understudy. He would set two or three props on the set to unnerve someone—an original *Bitches Brew* for a New York City doyenne serving on the Municipal Arts Committee or a Milton Friedman text for a liberal professor. It was public radio, but to Mel Harris it was still shtick, if not quite stand-up shtick, with its overt pandering and innuendo. On radio, you could not be the assassin that you could be at a stand-up club, but there was more art in being an intellectual assassin.

Paige drew in a sip of tea, minty with a bracing surge of eucalyptus. Someone at WNYC had a bigger tea budget than one would expect from a station that had to continually prolong its fundraising drive to meet payroll.

"My next guest is Paige Herald, author, pomologist, and local produce advocate whose previous works include *Soursop Days*, chronicling the origins of esoteric tropical and citrus fruits, and is finishing a work on apples entitled *The Return of the Pippin: Hunting Heirloom Apples in America*, to be published by Bloomsbury Press in April. Ms. Herald has recently served on the advisory panel for the Plating Project, a foray into identifying new pathways into civilized and nutritional eating on a limited budget, and is a freelance writer for many leading publications, including the *New York Times*, the *LA Times*, the *San Francisco Chronicle*, the *Atlantic*, and many others. I am delighted to have you on the show."

"Thanks very much, Mel."

"So, Paige, the Pippin is an old apple, kind of lumpy and inclined to having scaly brown spots. What drew you to this ungainly fruit?"

"Oh, Mel, the Pippin is a survivor, a great apple that has been through the wringer. Down but not out. It was in Queens three centuries ago, and it has a wonderful piney-citrus flavor and crispness. Real crispness, as opposed to the genetically perfect structure of the Honeycrisp."

"In a sense, you could call the Pippin the opposite of the dreaded Red Delicious."

"Don't get me started, Mel. That is the story—good and bad—of the American apple. What we're seeing today is an apple renaissance, people getting back to first principles. It's like the country suddenly woke up after forty years of wandering in a pomological desert—and COVID—and shouted, 'We want to taste apples again!' It is basically an insurgency against big food—the grocery chains who wanted looks over flavor."

"But the grocers weren't in it alone, were they? I mean, the consumer had to be complicit at some point. Wasn't it the homemaker who started rejecting the ugly fruit and buying the shinier, perfect red and perfect green apples?"

"In a sense, yes. But the history of American food production shows a gradual shift away from valuing seasonal variation, flavor, and nutrition, and towards convenience. It is a familiar story of expansion, commerce, and trans-shipping, one that a lot of your listeners will already be familiar with. What happens, though, is that once consumers let big food get its foot in the door, they abdicate any more say in the matter. The dictum of supply crushes vestigial demand. Once the little apples got the boot, it took almost forty years for them to make a comeback."

"It sounds like you have almost a personal interest in this story. To me, it sounds like you are talking about your children, and may I ask if you have any children?"

Paige fidgeted, pulling her hair back in a long, smoothing motion. With his experience watching his guests' body language dealing with uncomfortable questions, Mel sensed Paige was not at ease discussing her children. Perhaps there was a fissure, even a fracture in her family situation.

"I do, Mel. Two. A boy and a girl."

"And are they still in school?"

"Yes. In a very nice public school in Westchester."

"Wonderful. My children attended Westchester public schools, and I can highly recommend them."

" Well, certainly the teachers are well paid. Some say over—well... let's just say splendidly paid compared to some of their peers."

Mel picked up his coffee mug and wiped the surface below, even though it was bone dry. Paige noticed he had several tropes that involved patting down already sterile surfaces: his brow, his desk, his pants. Mel was a rubber, and she started to believe he had OCD, the kind of owlish old man inclined to saving his fingernail clippings for twenty years. But she tried to do her ujjayi breathing, calmly explain to herself that this was her pattern: vilifying men for their peccadilloes, nothing truly harmful, simply the species adapting to stress. Mel was nothing more than a guy on his third marriage, working through his demons. His profile was, on the surface, standard-issue Holocaust near miss: parents in the belly of the beast, he himself a tot when his mother left the north of England. There it was, in fact, the sepia photo with scalloped corners, little Mel bundled in what looked like a Harris Tweed romper, the earflaps all but obscuring his tiny cheeks. And the shoes! My, how they made kids wear the darnedest impractical lace-up shoes, in this case saddle shoes. Paige surmised, in a fleeting instant, that a collateral benefit of living near

Northampton was having access to good shoes. In a cold climate where you walked constantly, this was no small thing, a well-crafted pair of shoes with a midsole and a stitched-down sole a necessity, not a luxury. The image of Sam Beckett came to her, his haunted cheeks bearing secrets in the shadowed creases, his soles worn down to the absolute bone, not replacing them until the membrane was as thin and elastic as a pig's intestine. In that photo Mel was a beaming toddler, and quite rightly considering the depth and quality of the soles of his saddle shoes.

Paige's thoughts were drifting. Mel himself was mid thought. She was pissed, thinking he was about to ask more about her children, and she would have to dredge up a lot of crap about how she could teeter-totter between her writing and spawn patrol. She had shut down, blasting herself on her own petard, a brutal career move, bombing on the Harris show. Shit, shit, shit. She had to climb back, be twice as quick-witted—rapier, that's what it was called. Rapier wit. But what if he was going elsewhere, asking her why Christmas started after Halloween and didn't end until the Super Bowl. She'd have to go back to where she started, dispatching feuilletons from upstate New York and the Central Coast on farmers markets and the oddball Second Amendment–freak farmers who kept loaded guns on the front seat, but somehow coaxed thirty varieties of lettuce into biodynamic perfection. She could get back to first principles, if that's what it took. Fuck it, Harris, bring it on.

"Spontaneous, correct?" she heard Mel say, and had to ask him to repeat the first part of the question.

"The Pippin was the result of a seed spontaneously dropped in Newtown, Long Island, sometime in the 1600s, isn't that so?"

"Yes—at the estate of one Gershom Moore. The tree finally died in 1805. Fortunately, an arborist and farmer, Robert Pell, had planted about twenty thousand Pippins in Ulster County by then. Also, as many people know, both Washington and Jefferson grew the Pippin at Mount Vernon and Monticello. I believe there are trees you can see on the tours."

"And I take it you've brought your kids along to see this. Are they budding pomologists as well?"

"No, no. They are regular kids, sadly—I mean, not sadly, but regular in the way that kids are sadly becoming these days, tethered to their electronic devices." Damn! Trapped. Lured into providing too much information. Trevor always warned her about this, providing too much too soon. Harris didn't need to know about her kids being obsessed with their phones and tablets. The public didn't need to either. It was a breach. She was so on track and then suddenly off. Harris looked like a tenor sax player, puffing notes to see what would stick. He took his Blackwing 602 pencil (not one of the reissues, but actual old stock from the sixties) and scribbled some notes in a long orange Rhodia notebook. She couldn't make out the words, but noticed his cursive had an old-school style like her grandmother's—sharply clipped tops, like there was a thought ascending that had to be chopped off.

"No harm in trying."

"Excuse me, Mel?"

"Reading my notes. You're not the first. I could show you, but even then, you couldn't crack the code. It would be like trying to decipher the genetic history of a random roadside apple tree in Vermont." His hoary rolling laugh, dark and phlegmy, nipped her comment. She wanted to say that she loved Rhodia notebooks and was planning to shimmy away from the topic by asking him who his local supplier was.

Back to your work. You've been quoted as saying the axis of evil in America is 'eat crap, feel sick, be mean.' Does this sentiment indeed reflect your view of the food world, and the United States for that matter?"

Paige loosened one of the small pearled buttons of her sweater. In the morning she had sweated the choice: lambswool, merino, or cashmere, settling on cashmere for the elegance, but realizing that the season demanded a more substantial yarn. In the studio, it was way cooler than she had expected. It wasn't TV after all, no hot lights adding ten pounds. The expression "having a face made for radio" kept popping up once she got into the studio. No truth here: the cast could easily switch over to the screen, with the exception of Mel, but Mel was Dean/Douglas/Mel Brooks/Albert Brooks/Caine/Sellers/Lorre/McQueen. Bits and pieces. A star.

"Oops, Mel, did I actually write that in something I published? I recall a comment I made at a panel at a conference—Sustainable Systems or Organic Freemantle, one of those in San Francisco that seem to be popping up every ten minutes—about how food choice transcends issues relating to health but extend to one's mental and spiritual well-being. It was something that was directed toward that specific audience, which was obviously uber health conscious, some would say preciously so. It was intended to provoke discussion."

"But don't those words sound inflammatory, almost disdainful of people who can't afford fresh produce or who don't have access to the types of farmers markets that a lot of folks in more affluent communities do?"

"Certainly, Mel."

"Certainly you think that your comments were inflammatory or that some people have better access to healthy food?" The bastard. She was just riffing. Wanted to be breezy in her cashmere. Harris, you're a fuckwad.

"Mel! The latter, of course. As I mentioned, when you're speaking at a conference to a bunch of skinny locavores in the Bay Area, there is a shared mentality, call it a collective consciousness or dare I say zeitgeist surrounding the culture of contemporary food. Having said that, research has demonstrated the link between certain nutritional deficiencies and anger, in addition to deficits in performance in academic settings."

"And that, of course, speaks to the greater disparity in resources between advantaged and disadvantaged kids, I would think."

"Yes, food as a proxy for many things, you could say."

"Are there specific things one can do as a parent to advance the cause of healthy food options for children in poorer school districts?"

"Perhaps, Mel, but this is a sticky wicket. It's a process of evolution, unfortunately, not revolution. You cannot simply introduce healthy food into the system by fiat. There are many entrenched countervailing interests, big food—corporate food, if you will—being the most pernicious."

"Yes, but change can be incremental. There are groups out there—mostly parents, I would assume—who have taken the bull by the horns and started to petition the districts to serve better food. And of course, there is Alice Waters."

"Berkeley is a rare place and Alice is a rare bird. But your point is very well taken, Mel. In our 'Reinterpreting the Plate' project, which is of course linked to this very station, we have a special task force on child nutrition. We're looking closely at the model of other countries around the world where kids basically eat the same thing as their parents, not reconstituted blocks of corn and soy by-products with breading."

"Nuggets?"

"Nuggets! The scourge of America. You can posit a connection between childhood eating habits and the type-two diabetes epidemic in America. Do you know what Medicare spends on dialysis care in America every year?"

"I do not."

"Try twenty-five billion. Twenty-five billion dollars on one disease! We are fat, we are sick, and increasingly we are mean!"

The imperial we. He trapped her again! You can't have your photos splattered all over social media showing the real you, svelte and bright-eyed, and impugn people of size. She deeply felt their pain in a fashion, but was also disdainful, and Mel was teasing this out, really extracting this from her in a masterful way. His assistant stood up—she was bustier, Paige noticed, than it first seemed, not as prim—and Mel rolled his Cohiba around in the ashtray a couple of times, picking it up to inspect it like a jewel.

"If, by some form of presidential edict," he began, "you were appointed America's food czar, how would you begin?"

Paige heard the question clearly but paused. She started to cackle sotto voce—I know what you want to hear, you unctuous bastard—that I loathe fat people and would implement all kinds of restrictions, Bloomberg-type stuff, antigluttony laws designed to humiliate folks who can't control their impulses. Fat taxes and whatnot.

You want good radio, Mel, so you brought in a skinny-bitch food writer.

Mel continued, "I assume there would be some radical changes to the supply chain in the wake of COVID."

"Mel, that is so hard to say, there's just so much work. COVID has, I think, opened people's eyes to a lot of things. Not just how food is delivered, but the quality of the soil and all of the rather fragile inputs needed to ensure people are well fed and that food justice prevails in every part of the country."

"One idea, then, the first thing. Maybe it would be to grant some form of vouchers for people to use at farmers markets."

"I would start, I think, with the schools. I would look to drastically reduce the sugars and processed ingredients. There's just no reason on God's green earth why school children should be in the vise grip of American corporate food interests. None." Paige was sweating, thinking hard, wanting to go.

"And your kids, what did you pack them for lunch today?

"I packed them crap Mel. Bologna with Cheez Whiz on white. Chips, a soda, and a Snickers bar."

Had Paige not been getting Petra, the babysitter, to start coming in the mornings to plug the void left by Trevor's meanderings and temporary—or maybe permanent—displacement from the family, she would have known what was in her kids' lunch, although in truth she wasn't even sure whether Petra had packed them a lunch or just gave each of them a fiver to buy whatever was on offer that day in the cafeteria. And that was bound to be exactly the same fare, the venal hyperglutenized nuggets that she had spent the last fifteen minutes excoriating.

"My kids are actually staying with their grandparents upstate for a few days. And when they're up there, I frankly don't have a say in what my mom whips up for them. Heh-heh."

More tepid half-truths. The kids were *planning* to go upstate but not until the weekend. She could not reveal, on National Public Radio's 1,100 or so affiliate networks and to God knows how many listeners, that she, a prominent food writer and nutritional advocate on the cusp of real celebrity, did not actually know what her own children were having for lunch that day, so she marginally adjusted or bent the truth; prevaricated—yes, that was the word that made her feel comfortable, so elegant and swoopy, like a stealth strike—she prevaricated and let Mel know that her kids were in the purview of their grandparents. What was the big deal?

The big deal was that food politics was getting crazy, Like Kardashian-Jenner crazy, a big-butted freak show with a red and blue divide and a nation split between the burgeoning population of the victims of readily available, nutrient-dense bricks and brickettes (Paige hesitated to call it food, since really this was simply an adulterated delivery mechanism for calories and was so many iterations removed from its source that it was more material than food) and the superconscious "others," the vegans and gluten avoiders and local food fanatics who attended the gatherings and festivals that celebrated their self-anointed specialness.

Who had the problem? You could make the argument that making large quantities of mechanized protein available to the masses was a way of inexpensively feeding the population, even if subsidized corn was synthesized to fill and augment and flavor just about everything from burgers to lemonade to bagged vegetables and that chickens and cows were not really animals anymore but units of production like so many left shoes produced in the old USSR, the image of all those carcasses swaying and stun hammers rattling off the brains of those sad-eyed *E. coli*–infected cows impossible to let go of. This was what pissed her off when she would do her research at the fast-food places—God forbid she would even touch a salad there—not that fat and sick people were mindlessly feeding at the trough of big food—but that there was such a disconnect between everything. It was just a sanitized mess papered over by pastoral imagery and spoon-fed like mush into the blobbed and stretched tummies of plus-sized Americans.

"Paige?" Mel seemed slightly agitated, and she had indeed drifted off. Why the hell hadn't she just said all this to Mel? And then she did. When she was done with her rant, Mel knew the episode was good box office.

"Wow. That was, if I may say so, about as frank an appraisal of American habits as I've heard on this program in a long time."

Mel. Hirsute Mel. Mercurial Mel. Brazen Mel. Caustic Mel. Pixilated Mel. Mel as an infinite regression, kicking back in the club chair. Mel, man of a billion, no—a bazillion opinions, maker of men and women. Abrasive Mel. Candid Mel. Mel, shaper of ideas. Mel, the hair on the back of his head absurdly long, still black as coal, coarse strands like a sadistic dentist. What was his back like? Nappy forest, no doubt. Paige abhorred back hair, just so weird, not like an animal, but suggestive of an animal. Blecch! Thick fingered too, a nightmare of a proctologist. In a sense that was who he was. Reaching in from the outside and poking and prodding. Paige felt him up there; she was twisted like in those women's laxative commercials: *Girl, you're having an off day.* That was it too, the whole country having an off day. They outnumbered the non-off days. Nothing was working right at the moment, but she could breathe in, that ujjayi breath that was so important. Ka'anuba Tempo breath. The breath the trainers kept touting. So good for the digestive system, purging the lymphatic system. Sooooo good. In through the nose and out through the nose, but then at some point it switched. Out through the mouth. Which was it? Out through the nose or through the mouth? What about Sondra? Was she still around? How long was this segment? Maybe they weren't live.

"It's my nature, Mel. I'm not a kid anymore. As a mother, you look at things differently. There's this notion of legacy attached to everything. You want affirmation too. It's not just you going"—and here she was about to say "tits to the wind" but remembered that this was public media and there was the sobriety factor, the need for supple badinage, not ribald prison talk—"all crazy out there, a kid fresh out of school looking to make a mark. People are watching you from every corner and rendering instant opinions. And it's not just us folk in the media." Arrgghhh, *just us folk*. What the fuck was that? Sounded like some Obama campaign jargon—2008 called and it wants its slogan back. Jesse Jackson might be the only person in America who could say "folk" and not make a person cringe.

"I would like to think that my writing might reach beyond the narrow world of foodies and, like Julia or M. F. K. Fisher, resonate"—eww!!, bad choice again—"with some kid in vocational school who wants to strike out on her own. But that in itself is vanity, wouldn't you say, Mel?"

"I wouldn't necessarily put it that way. Ambition perhaps, but not vanity."

"That's flattering, Mel. Really. I appreciate that."

It had been midmorning when Paige went into the studio, and even though there were no windows, it was darker now. Maybe the clouds worked over midtown where the studios were, but they were so penned in by the new residential towers—the silver buildings, ultra tall and thin, with only two or three and sometimes even a single (!) apartment per floor; it was becoming fashionable for corrupt foreign regimes to park capital behind shell corporations that invested in Manhattan condos—that darkness was not weather dependent anymore. And the thought of that—the ever-widening gap between her and "the others," people so cashed up that millions were a basic unit that came in tens or hundreds versus her pathetic castaway bunch of 401(k)s and IRAs that she forever had planned to link up into one mega-account, the reality being that all the dribs and drabs added together would have been about $100,000, so why bother? To live, really live, you needed to generate enough to live on comfortably tax-free and risk-free, which in the present would have been about two or three million, she figured. And that would assume your house was paid for, a whole different matter as they had bought the Tarrytown house for $849,000, with $275,000 down and a mortgage and tax bill that was almost $4,000 a month. Trevor was transferring money and she was scrambling until the last second, even having to liquidate a 401(k) from her old teaching job, which after penalties and federal and state withholding was barely worth the trouble, $18,000 becoming about $11,000 in the blink of an eye, about a month's worth of expenses.

"But Mel, it does make you wonder whether there is any future at all for the middle class here in New York.

Have you noticed how desolate it's getting in parts of Midtown, even with huge residential towers everywhere? And the effects of COVID are still here. People are going out, but we're still not back to the roaring teens. A food writer won't stand much of a chance pretty soon."

"That's a fair point. There's always Staten Island. Maybe the city's administration could be persuaded to put a subway line out there someday. I hear even parts of the Bronx are catching fire. Where do you see yourself in five years? Still in the New York metropolitan area, or do you have designs on the West Coast?"

What Paige knew about the West Coast was confined to the recent trips she had made to the Bay Area and to Napa, and some not so flattering field reports from Trevor, but his judgment could not be trusted these days. Her take was that it was completely different, and it was a question of picking your poison. New York was clannish, full of fiefdoms and roadblocks. California welcomed ideas and innovations but was crowded to the point of insanity, and full of paranoia and fatuous douches who promised to call and never did, or worse, gave you the "California blow-off," telling you to call them after they came back from Cabo in six months. She had never heard this in New York; even a billionaire would call you back, tell you to your face to shove it or abruptly hang up, but they did it, had the integrity to act. Out there it was too easy to get back in the car and put on your Coldplay download and sip your shit Starbucks drink while you blew through the merge light onto the freeway and put your mascara on. In New York you put your big-girl pants on and your snow boots and jammed your full-figured holiday-food ass into a car on the 6 down to Union Square for that meeting. Work-life balance had not yet become a thing in New York, even though there were more people working from home of course. And there was the commoditization of skills that was rampant in California, everyone and everything in the vise grip of some budget problem or pension scandal that undermined every fucking thing that happened in a city. San Diego was legendary for this, every public penny scrutinized like it was the last one ever minted, the bored retirees and officious ex-military types self-righteous and fanatical about any public entity spending money on anything unless it directly inured to their benefit, in which case it was their unalienable right to collect and brilliant policy. Trevor commented how San Diego was beautiful on the outside and morally and ethically bereft on the inside, a squishy middle filled with tepid politicians with retrograde attitudes about pretty much everything. Sometimes it seemed the place was just a vessel. You had groups who were *in* San Diego—the God's waiting room folks, the marines, the triathletes, the surfers—but no one was *of* San Diego, unless you counted the ocean, which in truth was the essence of San Diego. Trevor noted how the sheer mass of stucco, houses you could purchase in any color as long as it was salmon, could, on the wrong day, bring on a soporific effect, leaving you with no ideas and no plan.

But she was not there. In fact she was in the white-hot seat, the most riveting, sardonically on-point program being broadcast live in the New York metropolitan area. Radios and computers across the boroughs, from Canarsie to Spuyten Duyvil to Albemarle Terrace to Alphabet City, were carrying her session with Mel. Granted, not everyone was listening with intent, but she was a food writer, not a sad veteran back from Iraq or Afghanistan or Liberia with yet another harrowing tale about human suffering—my God, how public radio was so unrelenting about this—but a bona fide entertainer, breaking through the dismal gray postholiday city fog with ideas about health and eating and how to conquer the farmers market.

Don't pick your nose, don't pick your nose, Paige thought, watching Mel as he brought his hirsute knuckle within an inch of his nose, which upon close inspection—Paige had close-range vision like a jeweler's loupe—had several coarse black hairs coming out of it. Thankfully Mel just scratched. Olivia or whatever the editor girl was named in the booth gave the throat-slash signal—a little harsh there, girlfriend, especially for someone wearing a sweater set, but then Paige realized that she was what, twenty-five or twenty-eight at the most, and she probably had a winged and horned angel tattooed somewhere discreet and that it was part of the high-low thing that seemed to be everywhere, hidden tattoos. But that could change too; Paige wondered, If she had to get one, where would it go? What percentage of moms in their forties who went to Barnard got freshly inked? But that's what was wrong, framing it that way. Just get drunk and go. Fucking do it, Paige.

- 21 -

Trevor swore he could tell the difference between the brand-name stuff and the generics. Before he left North County San Diego, Trevor watched an old film with a turgid Max Steiner score. The intro foreshadowed some goofball murder, a mustached guy drawing a pistol in a nightclub and a little *pop-pop-pop* like a kids' air rifle and some starlet collapsing in the arms of her earnest lover-to-be. Steiner wrote mawkishly and predictably, but his scores told a story. But Steiner only made him think about another guy with a similar name, a philanthropist who made it in generic drugs, one of the first to get production offshore, first in Bayamón and then, when that got too expensive, in Bangladesh. And he looked the other way when there were reports coming out that some of the shortcuts in production included low-level toxins, not quite enough for the FDA to register, but enough that new symptoms started occurring. The commercials, the ones with the velvet-toned announcer warning of stroke, impaired vision, internal bleeding, cancer, and even death, sprung from the generics and the parade of fun new problems they introduced. But Steiner or Schwartz or Seligman or whatever his name was, was now immortalized in innumerable plaques and banners and signage commemorating his generosity, and his foundation spewed out cash for community organizations. Trevor had taken a ten-milligram Adderall—not some fake bullshit generic, but real branded Adderall, and he was doing all right on it, getting shit done, changing the flats on his bikes, throwing out tax returns older than five years (was it five for state and ten for federal, or vice versa?), remembering to let that little hose drain at the bottom of the washing machine when he went back to Tarrytown for some clothes. Paige bitched about the funky smell, but God forbid she should bend down and pull out the little rubber hose once a month. The washer just needed some love, a little love, that's all. He feared he would run out of the brand name and be stuck with a generic that was probably mixed in Bangladesh and cut with God knows what. What was the point of drugs if they were always taking shortcuts, fucking with the efficacy, the purity?

Convenient, he thought, how folks were suckers for weak people doing bad things and taking on a new identity. War criminals in Ecuador were just farmers. It wasn't their idea to exterminate anyone during the war; they were just in the wrong place at the wrong time. College football coaches fabricating identities, sleeping with coeds, and going on the nightly news in Norman or College Station and mewling about how much they'd hurt their family? Trevor wanted Hugo to be like those philanthropists, concerned with legacy. Trevor was starting to understand that just as parents were not raising children, but future adults, the process was inverted when it came to the last several decades of life, meta–reverse childhood. Trevor wanted for Hugo what he feared he would not have for himself.

Trevor couldn't break from tradition because he had no traditions. That was good to know. Bitter tonic, but good to know. His tradition was not to be traditional, or at least not to adhere to other folks' notion of convention. He seethed at organizations of all sorts. Anything with the word "community" in it rankled him: church, garden, spirit, association. The social contract sucked. His political stance was apolitical. He liked the ring of individual freedom part, which was Tea Party dogma but sounded grounded, American. Paige snapped at him when he had Fox on: "Why are you watching that garbage?" But it was what made the country so appealing, being left alone, homesteading, pioneering, the whole saga of moving and having rights.

He was back at the Avalon or Archstone; how was it that he could not remember the apartment building where he lived? When someone asked him, "Trevor, where are you living now?" he could honestly not distinguish between these two monolithic producers of efficient rental spaces whose impoverished attempts at facilitating gemütlichkeit façades rang hollow, and he had to think hard before he could answer. There was a numbing sameness to it all, the orthogonal landscaping, choked with hostas and low spruce, the Rain Bird sprinkler heads and dour Salvadoran landscapers sulking and slinking down in their battered little blue Nissan pickup trucks, held together with duct tape and refurbished parts. They snuck off furtively at lunch to wire money and re-up their phone cards at the storefront next to the laundromat, looking as always for cops. Trevor began to see these apartment buildings as the engine for sustaining illegal labor, and what he thought of as the "axis of landscaping evil," illegal labor, poison, and water, nothing that anyone needed to use, and if you counted the shadow health care system of the emergency room visits when a worker got injured, it was a secret wrapped in an enigma. Everyone wanted their grass cut and their hedges clipped on the cheap, but no one wanted to pay payroll taxes and health care. America, if you thought about it, was groomed by a massive shadow subsidy emanating from the axis of landscaping evil.

Not that it mattered now, when he was about to go in for some SER therapy—somatic-emotional release—something that he thought he was long overdue for, especially with his saggy adrenals, which were starting to make him wonder if he was a candidate for hormone replacement therapy, visions of having a ripped physique at age seventy starting to intrigue him, but tempered by the fact that it didn't look so hot when your head was mismatched with your body.

It was relevant because he was staring across the table at her, at Cat herself. Bored, he had driven the Acura to Brooklyn, through some heinous one-lane stuff on the BQE, which gave him time to look carefully at the old warehouse and loft buildings, once just vacant hulks, but now prized for period details and long-span interiors that worked with the resurgent interest in bottling and brewing and crafting. At Pomander Walk the partners started buying vacant warehouses in Elmhurst and Sunnyside and Red Hook for $60 a square foot that were worth $1,100 today, just another way that cash begot cash, lots of people having the ideas, some people having the cash, but not too many having both.

And he wondered why Cat was such an underachiever, having the raw means of exchange, the looks, the slinky body, the slightly oversize gray-green eyes that kept you transfixed with glimmer and wit and sparkle. How was it that she had so little self-esteem that she had three baby daddies and at forty-plus was still a barista sending her kids to a dodgy PS in Bushwick instead of via black car to Dalton or Collegiate while she dashed to spin and Jivamukti? Rather, she was sitting with him, or rather she was texting and he was staring at her.

"You look amazing," Trevor said.

"Thaaaanks," she said, without looking up. Trevor glanced around the place, Wythe Fish and Smoke, and saw that about two-thirds of the women were glued to their phones. More fodder for the theorists about how men were becoming expendable. Women were getting to the point where virtual reality was more enticing than actual reality. It was, Trevor thought, an inversion of porn, women surfing various media formats for emotional connections the way that men scanned the universe for titillation.

"I look okay, except I'm sick of these." She clasped her breasts from beneath and pushed them up. "I want some volume and I want some height. Maybe I'm ready to marry a superrich guy—ha—but I suppose that means I have to get a D-cup, but then I'm too smart for that. Who wants to be old with oversize saggy tits like Brando telling Maria Schneider she'll be playing soccer with 'em one day. And then there are the tats. They'll fade, and at least there's a narrative there—context, something relevant. A boob is a sac. They have to be in harmony with the rest of your vessel. I think that if you have a boob job and you get old and they are still there shouting out to the world and the rest of you has withered, no kind of definition, then that is a sad day."

Trevor sat with that, as they say, until that point, seeing Cat as self-preening and self-involved, but at that moment, those words made his opinion shift, a fissure in their relationship, which admittedly was nothing more than what she doled out to the rest of the crew at Red Hook, pulling her pants down to show them a raspberry just below her hip, calling everyone a *puta* or a bitch, smacking kisses here and there, and her specialty, clasping a guys bicep and holding it a beat too long, as if to say there's more where that came from.

Trevor watched Cat, so economical in her movement, her name so fitting, weirdly so, her integuments more lissome and supple than a person should be allowed to have. He wanted to possess her, at least some part of her, but there was nothing in the transactional sense that he could offer in return. But she was there, a temporary companion. Why? he wondered.

"Thanks for hanging out," Trevor had said. "I'm so between things right now, it's good just to kick back away from all the, you know, daily stuff." He tripped and fumbled badly as he said it, knowing too well these last months had been a personal journey but not the type that could be documented in a lavish men's magazine, a sun-burnished fortyish Westerner on a sojourn through the Urals or the Indonesian archipelago searching for meaning and sera extruded from rare shellfish that might, just might, hold the key to Alzheimer's. No, this was a desperate last four months, begging at his degenerating father's door, groping in the dark for something, the proverbial white light that he tried to see during his SER sessions but never could quite conjure. Where was the damn light? The Jews had it all parsed out, Neshama for the brain and Ruach for the heart, and another one for the liver, somehow all connecting and reconnecting during the week to align with God. Light for different days, and how the hell did he retain all this detritus? "Trevor, you have such a brilliant memory," that was the party line, but memory was nothing if you couldn't apply it for commercial gain. He would have been far better off as an idiot savant like Rick Nugent, who kept a printout of forward LIBOR curves in his notebook that he conspicuously unfolded during the pipeline meetings every Monday morning. Since a pickup of even a couple of basis points on a $3.5 billion debt portfolio meant a lot of cash in the partners' pockets, an obsession over swap rates got Nugent face time. So there was Nugent, every Monday wearing those ridiculous Gucci loafers with the brass horse bits (the blue suede boots were for Fridays), preposterous footwear for a Monday morning in the grim bowels of finance at 1370 Eighth Avenue, and his carefully selected all-American color palette, never much straying from the blues, grays, and reds (did he fancy himself presidential material?), solid as an anchor in a calm port. And Harshvardhan or Liu or one of the other interns would trundle in with the master sheet of assets that were mostly in Manhattan, but some sprinkled around the rest of the country. There were always two or three on the chopping block, underperforming, and unworthy of additional capital infusion, Sam Alterman's compact face turning to grizzle as soon as they were brought up. One of these was the Red

Hook complex where Red Hook Roasters was located; in fact, that was how Trevor found out about it in the first place.

"One goddamn tenant? Is that the end of it?" Alterman wondered aloud to a panel of blank stares every Monday morning. "Who's the genius—and that genius, by the way ought to be someone at this table—who told me about how hot Red Hook was becoming and that there would be a tsunami of leasing—I recall that the word 'tsunami' was in fact used in this context—behind this shitty coffee tenant? What are we throwing off here? Three-quarters of a percent?"

Trevor traced the beginning of his decline to that meeting. He of course had been the guy, the guy in the field who had gone out with Evan Paschman to Brooklyn on one of those March days when winter had subsided enough so that the city trees tightly harnessed in their little wire and rubber loop sets could think about budding, Paschman piloting his Audi A6 one-handed through the perimeter boulevards in Brooklyn, yelling and staring at his phone on the console—why did he have to look at the phone while he was driving Trevor wondered—a magician and impresario.

The two of them, Manhattan guys in tailored clothing (no Brooklynite in 2021 would be caught dead in poplin and khakis unless it was some kind of Pabst Blue Ribbon–fueled casual-irony-Friday -type of thing) got out of the Audi, checked the street signs to see that there was a window to safely park (you could never be exactly sure) on Tuesdays and alternate Thursdays between 11:00 a.m. and 2:00 p.m. Paschman picked up the phone and kept talking but was craning his neck staring at the signs, afraid of a tow. Trevor was self-conscious, tempted to pull his shirt out of his pants and scuff his shoes, wanting to be like one of those Nigerian rough boys with a muzzled hyena in Pieter Hugo's photo essays but feeling very tight-assed in Red Hook. And Paschman, who, from the cozy confines of the Audi, still redolent with Eau de New Car, could cite street names and building owners and rezoning docket information as breezily as an eight-year-old talking Pokémon, was, outside his bubble, an embarrassment.

Paschman knew all about these guys. In New York, there were two flavors, maybe three, but two main flavors of real estate guys (and it was mostly men in commercial, women making inroads though): the street fighters, mostly commercial real estate brokers, and everyone else, that is to say, everyone who did not have to sell for a living. But the best sales guys were the ones who, as Paschman liked to say, just "hit it boom!" "You think about it, this business, and you're dead. Who works on commission? Nobody works on commission, except us and maybe some schmucks selling boats in the Bayou. I gotta get up every day like it's going to be my last."

That's why the kit had to be airtight, or at least spendy. Paschman wore brands, gaudy brands, head to toe. Gucci like Nugent, Maui Jim, Hermès, it was a dog's dinner of horse bits, interlocked monograms, flouncy silk, and insubstantial leather soles meant more for Biarritz than Red Hook. But that was how Paschman rolled, his plangent ululations making a mockery of the tribal outfit, Ronald McDonald in hipster heaven. And if Trevor was honest, the guy somehow pulled off the ensembles, wearing the proverbial clothes, not the other way around. Taken individually, any one element would have been too vulgar to consider for the average guy, but the bravado and self-belief evinced by Evan Paschman at every waking moment were enough to make his armor submit.

It was this will, the chi or whatever you called it, that Trevor kept bumping up against, other folks seeming to possess a life force that propelled them forward, while Trevor's manifested as torpor, lethargy, and indifference. It was his life's challenge to cobble together those sad-sack forces and reinterpret them. He was convinced of his bad genetics, a paucity of correctly combined proteins and a hair-trigger nervous system that overreacted to everything from food to noise. Mosquitoes swarmed to Trevor when others were clinking their volutes, unaware that there were even bugs in the air. And then there was the inflammation, the overproduction of cortisol, his body's fight-or-flight mode on continuous high alert.

"Dude, you've got to see this chick who is the manager or something inside. I fucking swear I came out here once from a meeting on Third Avenue just to stare at her ass." And upon entering the great repurposed marine supply warehouse that had become Red Hook Roasters, Trevor saw it too, a flash of haunch in pumice-colored yoga pants with a low waistband embroidered with flowers. It wasn't showy per se, but it was the first thing Trevor saw, drawn by Cat's fortunate genetics.

"See what I mean, dude? I'd buy this building just for that," Paschman said, scrolling through his messages while Trevor ordered.

160 Van Brunt. The Van was super cool; how could he go wrong. He let Paschman drive back to Manhattan in the Audi, figuring he'd have to tackle the Red Hook subway-access problem head-on so he could give a personal account of it when he pitched the building to senior management, preempting the kind of prickly question Nugent would try to trip him up on, the subtext always being what a boots-on-the-ground guy he was, smelling the earth and getting his hands dirty while everyone else was just doing a flyby. Trevor decided he would include the bus and subway trip times, rush hour and non–rush hour, in his due diligence report. But there was some lingering doubt, Trevor having been just old enough to follow the Walentas story and Dumbo, which was the neighborhood of the future and always was to-be for about thirty years. War, the market, the Fed, Europe, China, all that exogenous stuff that could hit, and when it did, the axiom was that the outer—oops, "other" boroughs now, in more PC terms—would suffer first.

But it was on Van Brunt Street, and an ex–boat supply warehouse to boot, the salt-spattered charm of the sea and the charisma of the early Dutch reimagined with all the trappings, the verdigris steel exposed structure, the reclaimed-timber framing (was it structural? Trevor wondered), the polished and weathered stark beauty of the concrete floor, a practical application when it was built but now a feature coveted by the creative class. Trevor was an avatar, the one guy at Pomander Walk ahead of the curve, always reading—*Wired*, *Curbed*, *HBR*, *Cabinet*, *Monocle*, the *Economist*, *Granta*, *WWD*— just to stay on trend. You couldn't slack off like the guys on the train doing half the crossword and nodding off or the holdouts who still drank two or three Buds playing whist or canasta or some dumbass card game in the forty-three minutes or so it took to get to Rye or Valhalla. Finance, even if it was real estate finance, not nearly as esoteric as derivatives or equities or debt or commodities or FX, was still finance and changing continually, often affected by forces from other parts of the world and other industries.

"Deep dive" was Nugent's favorite phrase, so overused it provoked a smirk bordering on a chortle, not just for Trevor but for others around the conference room table as well, the notion that a bunch of cubicle jockeys had the *bandwidth* (yikes!) to attain mastery of any particular topic or subject, with its requisite ten thousand–hour study requirement striking everyone as ridiculous. Saying "bandwidth" for the thirty-second time in two weeks was, in itself, damning, betraying the sort of callow and insipid mind-set that infected much of the corporate world, but it was at the same time a precondition for success therein. Pomander Walk was an aspirational firm, profitable but not in the pantheon of uber firms, the ones with limitless capital, "patient" money, in the vernacular, able to invest hundreds of millions into the billions and ride out one or two down cycles until the market turned, and it always turned. "How do you get rich in New York real estate?" Alterman was fond of asking and answering himself: "Live into your eighties."

But Pomander Walk ran primarily on sweat. As margins got squeezed, finance had begun to resemble medical training, subjecting interns and even veteran employees to eighty-hour weeks, all-nighters, and not so subtle hazing and verbal abuse. Post-COVID was even worse. At home you were expected to be available at all hours. Even in a WFH environment, you could hardly go to the can without falling behind on some *mission-critical* task. And the vast majority of those involved memoranda, the old-fashioned kind, banged out on interoffice SOP forms, denoting cc and bcc, subject matter, and to and from on company-approved forms that suggested the quaint word "stenographer" every time Trevor went to type. Truth be told it was *harder* to make money from home, so folks were going into the office even on their flex days. This was Sam Alterman speaking, your captain from the cockpit. At seventy-two—and granted, he was a young seventy-two, preternaturally tan and fit from either tennis or squash depending on the season (Trevor had harbored a secret yearning to get an invite to Buzz's own court at his summer house on Ponus Ridge Road in New Canaan)—his habits were still old school. Pomander Walk was mainly about feeding investors information that implied the writer had things under control. "Don't confuse activity with productivity," an Alterman mantra, was on Trevor's mind when he fed the Pomander Walk beast. It was better to defuse things right away, and Trevor also learned to clearly identify the *conclusion* of an internal memorandum up front, sparing the reader—in most cases Alterman—the agony of reading a bunch of preamble that consisted of facts, sometimes well documented, other times hastily contrived for the occasion.

Banks, commercial banks, came and went in New York, a lot of foreign lenders—HypoBank, Soc G, Vereinsbank, Allied, Barclays—and a lot of them chasing the condo dollars, which had followed a trail from the Upper East and West Sides to Midtown, then to Times Square and the Far West Side, and inexorably on to Williamsburg and Dumbo and Red Hook. During the bubbles, the underwriting got slacker, the project being king and the dollars fungible. Bankers got paid by lending, by making the money work or, more recently, as the recession waned, by gambling. As the market heated up, the metrics got easier. Back in the day, you underwrote to a 20 percent margin, making sure you had a belt and suspenders, that is to say, contingencies on your contingency. Everyone bonded, the general contractor and the subs, in case things went belly-up. Now it was more like a casino game, double your money or go home, having had fun. It had gotten so crazy that stuff wasn't getting built because guys made so much holding the dirt, or the FAR—the buildable potential of the site—in the case of old buildings waiting to be redeveloped for a year or two, that it was stupid to even think of building. The developer, if their timing was off, could easily be the dope, the last guy looking for a chair to sit in.

Trevor saw that Cat was again sizing herself up, glancing at her reflection in the floor- to- ceiling glass in the front of Red Hook Roasters. In Argentina, a sagging ass was a national obsession; one's life, it seemed, could be measured in the physics of the backside. Trevor, of course, had hypothecated the size of Cat's breasts by analyzing their behavior in various scenarios, impeded by different fabrics and supported by different armature. He settled on them being orange-size, neither here nor there in the breast world, smallish but suiting her frame. She had been grazing her phone intermittently while he replayed a version—and to be sure, it was only one version—of how he got to be sitting there, across from her, in the building he had recommended that Sam Alterman and the other equity partners in the principals' fund at Pomander Walk buy based on the fact that there was a very alluring and enigmatic barista/server/impresario working in the coffee-roasting operation there; and because the building had not attracted a single other tenant until recently, when it was too late for him, his reputation at the firm was wrecked.

"Don't go there," he said.

"Go where?"

"Past the tipping point. Call it the Saperstein line."

"The what?"

"The Saperstein line. Jacqueline Saperstein, that lady-turned-freak who was all the *Post* wrote about for about two years back in the midnineties. She went down a very long and dark rat hole, one procedure after the next. You reach that inflection point where you're natural one day, and the next day, a victim of Dr. Whoever."

"Oh, God. Yeah, I do remember that a bit. Wasn't much of a *New York Post* girl in my twenties. Lot of sports and stocks. A guy's paper, don't you think?"

"One way to look at it. It's garbage now. At least I think it's a waste of time. Treading in murky water, you know."

"Yep."

"So?"

"So?"

"Who's the lucky guy these days? Or guys? Or girls? Or both?" Cat looked away, then at her phone, scrolling a bit, caressing the phone in her left hand and then flipping it over, gently, like an egg.

"Phttt. As if. Nobody. Well, maybe just a little bit of someone. Who are you to ask anyway? That's pretty bold of you."

"Just trying to do the right thing. I'm a seeker—what do you call those crazies, Truthers?"

"Ha! Trevor from Westchester, a cultist."

"C'mon, give me some color. I just got back from California. They're crazy and boring at the same time. I'm looking around out there, checking out the businesses, and I keep thinking that my team, at least the team I have in mind—me, you, my sister Phoebe, could knock it out of the park in that building."

"Two Forty-Five?"

"Two Forty-Five b. Don't forget the *b*. The doctor who built it in 1928 was very proud of the *b*, which was for his daughter Beatrice. No logic to the letter, just a bribe, probably some of it wound up in Walker's pocket, hizzoner at the time."

"Dang. Cool. You know a lot of shit about New York, but..."

"But what, Cat? We're never going to be together, so just let it rip. I'm a Truther now."

"Honestly?"

"Please."

"Ugh. Well, for one, I don't see you as a detail guy. Coffee is for fanatics. Nel drip pour-over? Measure coffee to the gram, get the grind perfect, small circular motions with the Hario, all wrist, no drip-through. Keep the level where it is, neither rising nor falling. Wet the filter, heat the vessel. Keep your eye on the other four and keep the rotation going just so. Talk to the customers, not too much eye contact, smile quickly and move on, no full engagement. Your clothes? Your gear? That apron that looks slapped on is perfection, hits the shoulder blade just so, showing just enough ink to tease. I don't need to measure the coffee for my pour-overs on a scale anymore. Once you do it several hundred times, you can do it by feel, but until then you need to get the scale out and measure the grams. Grams and fines, you gotta get the science down before the art takes over."

Wythe Fish and Smoke was pretty empty, nothing like its neighbor Red Hook Roasters, which had a steady trickle of business all day, with intermittent crushes from nine to ten and two to three when the hipster mind, engaged in some WordPress heroics or working through some vexing kerning issues on a new Futura-derivative font needed a boost. How did a joint like Fish and Smoke amortize its improvements? It was luxe, but comfortable, channeling the old appurtenances and feeling of the classic New York appetizing restaurants and reimagining the details with modern flair. The small marble hexagonal tiles used for backsplashes in delicatessens and dairy restaurants all over New York took on a gray patina over the years, sometimes looking dirty. The same with the mirrors in the old surviving places, which became speckled with oxidation. The designers of Fish and Smoke had done brilliantly, fastidiously evoking the modern fish and smoke house and catering to Brooklyn's ascendant beard and waxed-apron crowd as perfectly as could be, Trevor reasoned, ticking through the line-item expenses.

This was the new theater after all, presenting luxe materials in a shibui package, unobtrusive beauty. The gypsum-green shimmer of the glass tile backsplash played off the zinc bar, the smoked fish beckoning like violet and ocher jewels. Fish raised to fetishistic perfection. Trevor found it hard to believe that amortization, the hard cold calculus of earning a return on investment, was at the heart of this place too. Unless it was cash, and it could have very well been financed by the rackets, like a lot of restaurants in New York, the answer to the question the suits always asked when they were out at yet another fancy new place: "How'd they finance this?" It was natural to think that drug or prostitution or cartel money couldn't buy sophistication, but that was preposterous. No consultants asked where the money was coming from. Shit, whole apartments and buildings traded under the noses of the biggest law firms and brokers and accountants in the city and no one asked questions. Offshore money? Israel? Iran? Kazakhstan? Arms dealers and bandits and corporate cheats and every stripe of rogue player on the planet.

"Okay, I'm going to beg to differ. There is a lot you don't know about me. In fact there is probably almost nothing you know about me. For one thing, I play the viola."

"Huh? Okay, like the violin? Cool."

"Yes and no. Looks like a violin but tuned a fifth lower. And a real viola, a meaty powerful viola, is a lot bigger than a violin."

"Sounds cool," Cat said. Trevor sat back and pretended to add a little sugar into his cup, but just kind of sprinkled it around the rim.

"Yep. It's a misfit too, quiet and weirdly midrange. It is not a bright, happy instrument, but it's spectacular—essential—for chamber music." Trevor understood that Cat wasn't interested in chamber music, that most people were not interested in chamber music, except perhaps the people who played and taught it and an ever-shrinking audience of people with blue hair. That was the thing, at chamber music concerts, if you sat toward the rear of the hall, the audience in front was a gleaming sea of blue and silver, tarpon tethered to velvet seats. But maybe Cat could be part of the new breed, a younger hipper audience discovering the joy of classical music. That was what the new wave of conductors wanted: more free-form entertainment, more of a festival experience. Maybe he could paint a portrait of the music that was abstract and sexy enough to sell it to Cat.

She turned away, looking over the crowd now that it was 11:45 and the early lunch crowd started to trickle in. She was always drawn to the ritual, especially in New

York restaurants that had that "it" factor, every meal like opening night in the theater , the hostesses staging things at the front of the house, scanning the seat charts, and scrolling through the reservations—so busy and pretty and self-preening! Funny how Trevor had brought up an instrument—not that she cared a whit about the violin or viola or whatever it was that he was talking about—but the word "instrument" had fluttered through her mind when she saw the hostess station at Wythe Fish and Smoke. The insouciance of the hostesses, so studious and focused, deftly parrying the leering advances of the suited Manhattan business bros slumming it in Brooklyn. A half a decade on from Weinstein and Epstein and Lauer and Rose and a bit after the spray-painted fat man who occupied DC for a while and the vibe was still there.

Trevor was prattling on about classical music, about guys with names out of a musty closet, Hindemith and Primrose and Tertis, and about weird collections—"repositories," Trevor kept saying, which sounded to her like "suppositories," and truthfully if he kept on this way she was about to shove something up his ass, and she was really curious about, almost startled by, why she was spending time with him. A girl—no, a woman (she had to remind herself that north of forty, you had to self-refer as a woman)—with her looks and ability to banter and flirt could—no, should—by rights be with a younger, richer, hipper crowd, or at least a more exciting group, bikers or Euro guys or those frat types who worked at the investment banks. But there was something about Trevor, his particularness, that was alluring to her. Luc was cooler, but everything seemed predictable and scripted about him. Unlike Trevor, he was unable to process conflict or change or grasp why anyone would want to use a mechanical pencil that used 1.18 mm leads when they could buy a package of perfectly good pencils, mechanical or conventional hexagonal cedar number 2s, at Office Depot for $9.95. Without people like Trevor, the market for 1.18 mm mechanical pencils would be left for dead.

Trevor was such a fellow, mining the long tail for just about everything. Who the fuck even played the viola, let alone was obsessed with its archives, talking about planning to see something called the PIVA, the Primrose International Viola Archive in, of all places, Provo, Utah, on the Brigham Young campus?

"And who would have ever thought that a Mormon university would house something like those archives?" Trevor said. "Surprising because there is something maudlin—dare I say Old World Jew—about the viola. That haunting gypsy-like C string, its lowest, that allegedly makes people cry because of its haunting sonority, you hear it in Bruch and the Bach sonatas, which, even though they were transcribed for viola from the cello, have that sadness coming through. Mormons seem sunny and cheerful to me. I wonder what they think about having the world's largest repository of viola music in Provo. Or if they think about it at all."

"Jeez, Trevor. You're right. When you're right, you're right." If Cat had had a cigarette, she would have inhaled deeply, turned her face thirty degrees, and blew out a long plume of smoke. But all she could do was sip her mint tea. "Got to take it all in, huh. Bet I can make you squirm."

"Huh?"

"You can do it just with questions. According to research—the *New York Times*, of all places—you and I could fall in love just by asking each other thirty-five questions. Crazy days."

"Okay, I'm game," Trevor said.

"Not today, my friend. Just something to think about. Everyone's treading water. Bantering, flirting. Course, some folks act on their impulses. Nothing wrong with that either. Are you an observer, Trevor, or an actor? What would you say?"

He pulled a portable pen from his pocket and began to fidget, easing the clicker—silent—up and down. He bared his teeth. Cat started telling him about this guy Luc she was sort of seeing. She said the guy was a bartender upstate, but she was trying to get him to move to Brooklyn, start some kind of apothecary or aromatics company, and that she liked him in theory, but she was already starting to get bored. That was the death knell, as soon as a woman started to talk freely about you as an object, you were out of the picture.

The images of Cat's romance flickered for Trevor like a little flip book. He played it slowly, then quickly, first one frame at a time so that the images stuck, the timing and the details arrayed like dried flowers in a keepsake book, there for memories when he was about to die. Cat, her lithe frame at angles with her ass just so, her hip bones splayed, the small of her back concave enough to hold a shot or two of tequila. Then he played it quickly, his heart beating in rhythm with the surge in adrenaline provided by the Adderall—what a splendid surge of good feeling!—absolutely banging stuff, dreams with a hip-hop soundtrack.

That he could travel from viola to hip-hop, from meandering around California and the mind-numbing reality of the Archstone or the Avalon, or wherever it was that he was staying, back to the lurid screenplay that started to delaminate his domestic life, was in the end the best thing about him, he decided. He scribbled some neatly formed notes, keeping the writing small and legible, in his five-by-three-and-a-half-inch notebook, which in turn he kept in a leather sheath he bought from a Bulgarian Etsy vendor. He had one of his best mechanical pencils with him. He had, it seemed, like a billion of them, spanning almost the entire range of lead widths, so important was it to match his mood with the width and firmness of the lead. If he felt precise and sharp, he could size down to a .7 mm (the .5 mm and—gasp—.3 mm widths simply too narrow and fragile for his hammer-fisted grip), but he really felt comfortable in the bigger ranges, all the way up to those massive 5.6 mm leads, which were usually referred to as "artist's sketching tools" in the catalogues.

Trevor looked at sketching and jotting notes as one of his singular holdout pleasures. It was so Brooklyn, so 160 Van Brunt, so not Evan Paschman, writing a feuilleton. Paschman wouldn't have a fucking clue what a feuilleton was, but that was not strictly fair, since not a lot of people did. But it suited the time and the place perfectly, an occasional dispatch from an exotic locale, in this case a part of Brooklyn not conveniently served by subway.

And, as if he had conjured Lucifer himself, Trevor saw Paschman walk up to the service area at Wythe Fish and Smoke to place an order. Cat had her back turned to Paschman, and Trevor had been mostly looking down, so it wasn't likely the broker had seen him, but it surely would be just moments until he saw the two of them and invited himself over. With a flourish, Trevor ambushed Cat: "You want to move to California with me? I think you'd love it."

"Huh?" She had been glancing at her phone again, Trevor so unaware, like Krazy Kat needing to get hit in the head with a brick by Ignatz. "Wow, that's quite an offer—thank you." The "thank you" had that sing-songy air of boredom that beautiful women used to great effect to deflect unwanted overtures. It had such a dispiriting air of finality, of disinterest, of phlegmatic attention wandering, that Trevor had the notion of excusing himself to go take a leak and sneaking out.

"May I join you?" Evan slid into the booth next to Cat—they were at a four top—and Trevor noticed he was out of uniform, wearing a pair of $300 selvage jeans that looked like he had just bought them at Spindrift down the street, especially since he had one of his also $300 work shirts on with cuff links. Cuff links and selvage jeans! Pure hubris. And he smiled, baring his high-gloss caps, the grease dripping from the corners of his lips as he put his smallish hand on Cat's back and let it linger there for a beat or two longer than it should have for a casual greeting.

Cat fluffed her hair and recrossed her legs. Was it the variable reinforcement, not Paschman, that had Cat's attention at the moment? Trevor observed the next sucker in the queue for her ever-expanding network. And wasn't that the essence of it? An orbit of flirtation that fueled something. There she was, chatting up a guy who spent time in the cologne aisle, who wore jeans with decorative rear pockets, who called his friends "bro" in earnest, and for all Trevor's self-anointed hipness, he was being outflanked. Paschman, like Rick Nugent, and to some extent his own father, had that big-wave mentality. When he was in San Diego he saw bumper stickers that read "Eddie Would Go," and he learned that it referred to a surfer who bought it in a big wave. But that was the gist of it, go big or go home, like they said in Colorado. Did every state have a motto like this, a reference to big waves and big mountains that beckoned you or taunted you depending on your orientation? Maybe he was more fit for a state like Delaware, which probably should have a motto like "Save taxes or go home." Anyway, that was the idea of the smaller, colder states until he thought about Vermont and all the skiing, and hell, he'd be a misfit there too.

Paschman had his arm behind Cat on the banquette, and Trevor noticed it kept moving a bit toward her, to the point where he was "accidentally" grazing her shoulders once in a while. Based on eye contact and signaling—body positioning, the angle of deflection of her hips toward her subject, the degree to which her lips, moistened now, Trevor noticed, were apart, the frequency with which she stroked her hair—Trevor knew that Cat was inviting Paschman into her orbit. Trevor was a second-order date now, a derivative, marginalized.

"Yes," she said, "peekytoc crab tortillas! I've had them there." Paschman was connecting with her about restaurants and foodie stuff, and that pissed Trevor off because he was the foodie; that was his thing, having practically gone to culinary school listening to Paige detail her trips and research. He was the one who actually read some of Mhyrvold's giant tome and Larousse and was up on sous vide and emulsions and Michelin stars and regional Japanese and Chinese and for God's sake everything that was real about cooking. Any douche bag with an AmEx could go to a restaurant, so what, really, was the big fucking deal?

It was so, what was it—yes! Like college. It was exactly like being back at Cornell, the face-time scene in front of Willard Straight Hall that Trevor watched every day but was never actually part of. People of both sexes whom he talked to all around the other parts of campus were stone-faced when he approached them in front of the Straight. It was a performance. He never got this until he was twenty years out of school. He was not an actor. He was a stage manager. No, not even a stage manager. He was an assistant, a guy with a weird title, something like "key grip," which was, well, who knew what the key grip did. But Cat and Evan Paschman were having face time.

Wythe Fish and Smoke was at full throttle, the wait staff in their cuffed jeans and starched aprons spinning thick white china plates with artisanal smoked fish and house-cured radishes and condiments to effervescent hipsters. Trevor noted all this in his notebook, printing carefully with a Blackwing Volumes Lake Tahoe edition whose point needed to be sharpened. He also noted that with the gentrification of some of the remotest parts of Brooklyn, a certain chapter in New York City's history, the picaresque and tawdry mash-up of rogues and outlaws and misfits and cretins and scoundrels who stole and cheated and pillaged and prevaricated their way through the chthonic mess of the city's underbelly, was coming to a close. Something called "Billionaire's Row" was emerging on Fifty-Seventh Street, absurdly tall silver towers that obscured the orthogonal grace of the northward aerial view of Central Park. Trevor was no NIMBY shithead like the kind he saw out in San Diego, a whole lot of people masquerading their fear of the other with mahalo bumper stickers and fenced and vegetated privacy barricades that obviated the need to speak to one's neighbors. No, he liked growth—some kind of growth, sensible growth, ecumenical growth. But then, who was he kidding, there were no answers. It was the hundred-dollar bill theory, the idea that if you *gave* away sacks of Benjamins, there would be an outcry from some segments of the public. Free money would make lazy folks even lazier. The bills had germs. It was a regressive form of wealth transfer. It would foster drug use. At least in New York there was a frankness about partisan politics. It was clear who people liked and didn't like.

And Trevor didn't like this guy Evan Paschman, but he marveled at him. The unctuous, uninformed patter that was repulsive and weirdly compelling. Cat kind of liked it, but he was seeing now that she was an attention whore. She had wriggled closer to him in the booth. He was going to pay, that was clear, a clever barter on her part. Trevor was a putz for clinging to some retarded old notion that women were somehow empowered by paying for themselves. That dated him, that early emancipation stuff from the seventies in the wake of a softer and more man-friendly take on feminism from the Camille Paglia types. Equality was so out, millennials embracing old values like chivalry alongside the hookup culture. He was lost.

He was married, technically still, but he was thinking he could be right back in kindergarten for all he knew about the world at that moment.

"Look at this guy here," Paschman said, pointing at Trevor. "Can't pull the trigger on that building. Only got one life, buddy, and you better live it like a tiger." At this point he had his arm resting fully on Cat, and Trevor was almost shocked that she hadn't pulled away. It was his lunch, his money, his time, but she had made herself fully available to this guy. "It would be a shame if you lost it, buddy. Another broker showed it to the Ornstein twins. Those guys move fast when they like something. A kosher taqueria is what I hear. They'll print money."

"Can't vent commercial ovens there," Trevor said weakly. "The one thing you can do is noncooking effluent, a dry cleaner or in my case a coffee roaster, which is technically not food preparation, according to my zoning consultant." Cat looked at him like he had just shot her dog. He was the negative guy now, Paschman the booster, the visionary. Where was the justice here? Trevor thought he was the early adopter, the guy on the leading edge, versatile enough to mix finance with technology, seeing what was new in the world. He was a traveler—at least to the West Coast—looking at the culinary world. Paschman was rooted to New York, to the singular principle of making a buck. Everything Paschman did, from eating the same English muffin with the same jam to rotating his Hermès ties, to the same gym routine and restaurant rotation, was vectored to making a buck.

"You can vent cooking if you have a scrubber."

"A scrubber?"

"A special filtration system that gets rid of the nasty particulates. You need a special permit, but that's what the Ornsteins do. They aren't a pretty bunch—and sure not big on social skills—but they close. Surprised your guy didn't tell you that."

Cat was done now. "Gents, love to chat but I've got an appointment for my amino booster." Trevor and Paschman both looked up as Cat slid out of the booth, ready to snake through the bustle of Wythe Fish and Smoke onto Van Brunt and toward the Belgian block charm of Coffey Street, where her naturopath's office was. Anticipating the question from the men (and it was weird, they were both staring at her with the same frothy expectation, as would a dog waiting for his morning bone, two breathless vessels, wanting more out of her— men were always after her for something more than she wanted to give), she said, "I'm getting a booster shot."

As Cat walked away, Paschman's phone growled with bass and started to buzz and flop around on the Carrera marble table like a small trout. "Gotta grab this," he said, run-walking out of the restaurant to the Audi, leaving Trevor to pick up the tab, $134.62 before tip, for all of them.

- 22 -

"Who the fuck was Helmut Zacharias?" Eileen was exasperated with Hugo. Every day was getting crazier. Living with a spouse with Alzheimer's was her reality. She was living it now. At first it was a little bit charming, the quirky reference here, a harmless non sequitur there, but this was the new reality. Damned if she didn't think about that train coming when she got together with someone older. It was okay, though; she had resources, knew how to socialize. She'd be fine.

"Helmut Zacharias"—and here Eileen heard the German accent coming through, getting more pronounced as Hugo reverted back to the womb—"was a Cherman violinist who played jazz. Almost everybody thinks there was only a single jazz violinist, Stéphane Grappelli, but this is not so. Zacharias played in all the cabarets, and all over Europe." Hugo knew enough to know that even though he was fading, his wife—and it was stranger and stranger to him that he had this thing called a wife—was not now, nor ever was, interested in jazz esoterica. He was playing on the edges of the fringes on the periphery of a garden that he tended with a bizarre admixture of strange music and ideas. He liked sports still, but as dance, soccer as choreography. The colors of the jersey were different, so sometimes he would pick a color, a red the Brits called claret or a dark yellow they called amber, to root for. One team, Hull, had black and amber stripes to mimic its tiger mascot. He noted the veracity of the team in this respect, so much more accurate than the crass American football Bengals, who, though tigers themselves, sported a fakey-orange-and-black color scheme. True orange would limit a tiger's ability to be stealthy, would it not? But maybe that was just betraying his Eurocentric mind-set, which was still with him after what, a few generations in America, just like that vestigial accent that he couldn't shake, trying Americanisms occasionally that to his ear sounded like fingernails on the blackboard. Trevor used them, words like "dude" and "man" and even "bro," in jest, and to Hugo it sounded like another language. And the music, don't even start. Crazy how when just at the green flash part of his life he could stomach a tiny bit of the Rolling Stones, the whole country had shifted into some genre that he thought was broadly called "hip-hop," but he couldn't be sure if this was just another name for "rap" or what defined the stuff exactly. It was easier to punt the ball, soccer or football, take your choice. As a player, he loathed the goalkeeper punt—"a pass to nowhere," he liked to mutter under his breath as Schoenwald or Strauss, the goalkeepers for Hakoah on the tour, would put their laces through the ball and send it skyward, only to be headed back toward their own goal or left to bounce for contested possession. Hugo and the little winger Gruenbaum finally prevailed on Schoenwald to throw the ball out to the wing to retain possession, and this tactic was highly successful, usually the beginning of a multiple-pass sequence for Hakoah. The soccer arrivistes liked to talk about Cruyff and Rinus Michels inventing modern football, but Hugo knew this was claptrap. Hakoah circa 1925 invented modern football, with interchangeable positions, overlapping and passing into space.

"Hugo? Are you listening, Hugo? We'll be late for your appointment."

"Conlon Nancarrow too. Very interesting man. Met him at the Hilton one day. It was a roast for another composer, that fellow who wore a vest every day. He was fond of the player piano, that Nancarrow. Charming man, but a bit strange."

Eileen had Rufus swaddled and was cooing in his direction. Such a fine little dog, expressive and obedient. Rufus was napping more, scooching up close to Hugo when he catnapped, the two of them snoring contrapuntally sometimes. She had taken to therapeutic shopping, and what better place than LA? When did it become hoarding? That was starting to get to her. It was all orderly, that was for sure. And all the stuff had its place. Her rule now was FIFO, like the accounting rule, first in, first out; every new purchase needed an offsetting compensatory response to donate or discard. That was the mantra gleaned from that excellent book on tidying. (Who'da thunk that tidying could be an entire philosophy?) Get everything out and touch it. The stuff gave her *Gezelligheid*, a word her Dutch friend Birgit told her meant "coziness," and she felt it when she made a purchase or opened a box or went back to curate—that was the word—her collections. Only when the drawers started groaning did she begin an intervention, laying everything out in the KonMari way, inspecting every item to see if there was a tactile connection—a love of the object. But touching everything worked, stuff on the bubble given its walking papers. You needed to stage dramatic and sweeping interventions to ensure that you were surrounded by only the things you loved. Hugo was loving lists lately. She found pocket notebooks everywhere stuffed with facts—lists of bridges and streets in neighborhoods in Brooklyn and the Bronx. There was also a master list of sorts—random things that he had an affinity for. The big list was a start-and-stop affair, growing with each new attempt. Eileen picked up one of the more brightly colored notebooks and opened it:

Cyril Power

Gustave Baumann

regista

centrocamposta
mediano=cash register=Phoebe
trequarista=somebody good
mezzapunta
centrale=Trevor
diatonic harmony
my first Bolex
The Miraculous Mandarin
diatonic=white key
Freitag bag color palette denoting hierarchy of desirability for truck tarp acquisitions
pentatonic=black key
Milton Babbitt= non-tonality
Morton Feldman
N. Main Street
E.7th Street
Figueroa Avenue Bridge (1937)
Wyckoff Avenue
Explorers Club (1904)
Prospect Unity Club (1927?)
Erno Schwarz
Max Hoffman
Favoriten
coffee tree—five years to mature
"selling" doesn't sell
Mandlebrot seahorse=infinity in reverse!
rhubarb
senna

carline thistle root
cassia
elixir of wormwood
interstitial Los Angeles
sombrero
nutmeg
dummy
croquetta
rainbow
soursop
dragon fruit
star fruit
star anise
Star Jones
Lew Wasserman
anonas
ice skating on Paine Lake
calyx
cove
Icelandic dulse
Lydian mode espoused by George Russell—more compatible with tonality than the major scale
service tan
oxidized green
brown-black
black-blue
steel blue
verdigris

dust yellow
snakeheads in the LA River
Thai snapper in seaweed and embers (ate at Faith & Flower in LA—delicious!)
Michelins
winespas
Kingston Blacks
Ribston Pippin
Bushwacker
Capitol Cider
Upcider
Wassail
The Northman
Santa Cruz
Santa Rosa
Anacapa
San Miguel
Santa Barbara
Canarsie
Yellow Bar Hassock
Ruffle Bar
Big Egg Marsh
Throgs Neck to Silver Lake
Henry Cowell
Lou Harrison
Karl Weigl
legato
staccato

pizzicato
rubato
503
507
137
Was 1913 the official start of the twentieth century?
1904
the revival of the fisher—not a cat!
Ken Bellard
Captain Dewey Hiccomb's *Honeycatcher* (1904)
Hull City (1904)
New York City Subway (1904)
Astor Piazzola
Regina Carter
Helmut Zacharias
Excelsior Case Goods
hemp fiber
Harris Tweed serial numbers: 574467, 00954065, 784862, 116784, 103880, 01435034, 63473, 00624523; you can date these
fuyu persimmon
Grove Dictionary
Le Labourer
Leica 111c
viola
Blackwing 602
Winged Foot
Original Six

baritone sax
FC Beachside
Richard Wilbur
Zim
Thordahl
Maersk
MsC
Baldwin's
Seaside
Compo
Beacon's
Fleming
Geocaching
Cove
Jamestown
Glinka viola sonata
Columbus Renegades/royal blue and tan
Portland Explorers/forest green and gold
Las Vegas Ramblers/red and silver
Seattle Emeralds/pine green and silver
Hartford Whalers/batten board gray and marine blue
Salt Lake Rovers/parchment brown and matte silver
Double bell euphonium
pocket trumpet
pocket violin
Blickensderfer mfg.—first portable typewriter
Duncan Watts—"Everything Is Obvious"

Alden chromexcel brogues
figs
Abbada dates
Trevorawi dates
Khadrawy dates
Heuer Jarama
Heuer Temporada
Heuer Verona
Heuer Barrel Carrera in "tropical" variation
Heuer 2446 (perfect bi-compax)
Omega soccer timer
1980s Rolex GMTs especially worn by busboys in moderately priced Italian restaurants on the Upper West Side
sepia prints
DIN 1451
Bullet pencils with knurled eraser caps
wax cloth jackets
blanket-lined denim jackets
Hudson's Bay blankets
hemp and cotton-blend shirts
Casamigos reposado tequila
Farnum Hill cider
Reef Points cider—bone-dry
heavy cotton twill herringbone
Eberhard Faber
Hindemith
Pelikan

Julius Knipl
Jean Shepherd
Randy Horton
WM formation
Willie McCovey
Jerry Koosman
Ken Holtzman
Rudi Ball
Ernst Fuchs
Keith Magnuson
Bob Nevin
The California School
pomegranate seeds detached from the tenacious membrane
blood orange juice
car manuals from 1966/7
small tactical flashlights
Leica 8x20 monovid
weathered chambray
mid-weight wool socks
fennel toothpaste
red and blue editor's pencils
Marzocco two group head commercial espresso machines
crema
leaded Japanese animal figure paperweights (owls, dogs, etc.)
cream-colored German sedans from the 1960s

underground steam escaping from Consolidated Edison manholes

Mucu type RN-B comic paper notebooks in brown and gray

Heuer watch cases and dials circa 1972–1979: Montreal, barrel-style Carrera, Monaco, and Cortina

Brown-dial watches from the 1970s (remind me of Ken Bellard in a diving suit)

Fume watch dials (greige?)

psychogeography

Smilodons

Ives's strange marching band-inspired tunes

Lou Harrison concerto for violin and percussion

Lou Reed/Edgar Allan Poe retrospective at BAM

Dvorak string quintets

upcycled inner-tube products like briefcases, belts, and wallets

musical notation in composers' own hand

Sybil Andrews

Ukiyo printmaking

The Grosvenor School

Mara des Bois strawberries

varicolored Heath ceramic dinner plates

mil-spec hardware used on civilian clothing

updated fashion military shirts

Guayabera shirts (but not on me)

Ramos fizz with real egg white

freight companies: MSC, Triton, Zim, Werner, James B. Hunt

five-on-three advantage

passing with the outside of the boot

repeating three elements for design impact

proportions of early motorcycles

hectare

high schools with Native American mascots

Gershwin and Paulette Goddard

the concept of "fortepiano"

viola parts that resemble music

viola jokes

that Ajax winger, number 7, Eddy Hamel from New York, who made mazy runs with his head down—killed by Nazis

patatas with cashew cream and three-chili sauce

Il Bombonaro in Old San Juan—tiled floors, clear glass, and heavy flatware

espresso ristretto and an almond cookie at precisely the right moment of the day

Northland wood hockey sticks

hockey stick lies—still relevant in the modern game?

Andrés Iniesta

Unitas 6498

37 mm and 38 mm vintage watches

redheads with just enough freckling

Katuk leaf—4.9 grams of protein per half cup

Paulette Goddard sunning with George and Ira

Case Study Coffee
Water Avenue Coffee
Oblique Coffee Roasters
Gorilla Coffee
Handsome Coffee
Good Coffee
Cellar Door Coffee
Cove Coffee
Coven Coffee
Baldwin Beach Coffee
Tim Horton
Jim Neilson
Bobby Rousseau
Lou Fontinato
Ed Joyal "The Entertainer"
Mike Bossy
Börje Salming
Ric Seiling
Phil Goyette
Vic Hadfield
Gil Perreault
Bela Guttman
Eusébio
Rick Barry
Dan Issel
Randy Smith
Compo Beach Coffee
Paia Coffee

Albina Press
Top Pot Donut under the shadow of the monorail
cable stay bridges
Glinka unfinished viola sonata
Primrose
Tertis
Borisovsky
Trampler
Imai
optimal sizing for a viola—seventeen inches?
Visvim military coats
1.18 mm pencils
Lactae Hevea
Dainite
foam earplugs
Hamilton Avenue Bridge
145th Street Bridge
Fennel toothpaste
Marvis toothpaste
feral cats hunting
fishers in New York City
watermelon juice
steel-cut oatmeal, soaked, with organic maple yogurt, raw honey, and cinnamon
Tat soi
short overlapping wingbacks
Neeskens
Krol

Rep
Van de Kerkhof x 2
Rensenbrink
Bozsik
Budai
Hidegkuti
Cubillas
Randy Horton
Gullit
Tigana
Kogane
Marigold petals
Tepache
Red Russian kale
Horst-Voeller four-on-the-floor sedan in gray and off-white
Honoapi'ilani vest pocket park
Allen Street median
Cutler and Gross keyhole acetate sunglasses with green lenses
Luigi Nervi
Frog Hollow dried apricots
Napa market
Stiff brown duck canvas
rebar
walking upstream toward the Times Square shuttle
the M104
the 10 as it crests in Santa Monica

parks in New York demarcated by green that are completely paved over

Banshu weaving

roller hockey at Tompkins Square Park

roller hockey at Kihei next to the Pacific Ocean

roller hockey at West 83rd Street

roller hockey at East 67th Street

tailor shop on West 83rd street with antiquated-looking, sun-faded clothing

defunct record stores on and near Broadway

video production shops on 9th Avenue before the advent of digital

neighborhoods in Manhattan between real neighborhoods

4th Avenue

Bond Street (almost edible)

Park between 66th and 67th Streets and 1st and 2nd Avenues

skin care products with real grapefruit oil

downy hair that women have

rhubarb

cafés with clean design based on rustic wood, glass, and matte finish metal

American Radiator Building (Raymond Hood)

St. Johns bridge

Bryant Park at five p.m. on a summer Friday

Sashiko fabric

fresh journals and magazines with articles full of promise

shorts that hit at the correct place on the leg

old wool soccer shirts with collars that smelled and stretched

those old leather balls that weren't round and took on huge amounts of water

new soccer stadiums for the new U.S. league—Columbus, LA, Denver, Kansas City, New York, Cincinnati, Nashville

sea turtles

seahorses

funny-looking rays that float down to the aquarium divers and act like dogs

commuter clocks at Grand Central

The Paramount Building

Van Basten

Rijkaard

The "Gag" line

Schoenberg's quartets

137 Sullivan Street

Arlet apples the size of softballs from Samascott Orchards

*Cabine*t magazine FC

Prospect Unity Club soccer

Chinatown FC

FC Silverlake

Randolph P3 sunglasses

birds in Hawaii that are not crows but serve the same function; really just dressed-up crows

birds in Hawaii that are like small cardinals with striking white gray and red coloration

great bookstores in good cities that you come upon serendipitously

clandestine social clubs in Gravenhurst

Why don't you ever meet anyone who is from Gravenhurst

architectural follies at the top of skyscrapers from the golden age

starched and crisp-looking ballroom linens in the best hotels

insouciant and bitter union food service workers at fancy ballroom events

German-Jewish uncles who were completely inert at age fifty and dead at sixty-five

Bandy

Mario Lemieux

Marx toy guns

jeans from the seventies

guys playing basketball in the dead-of-summer heat on the hottest courts in the city wearing jeans and dress shoes

snorkeling in a crystal-clear cove

survivalists

sycophantic audience members at talk show studio tapings in New York and Los Angeles

bootstrap operations of variety shows in the 1960s
boat club members who get drunk and speed home
making films when directors had control
stores selling colossal amounts of bric-a-brac and noting that there is a "40% off" sale going on
Henry Kissinger sounded exactly like most of my family
list of people in the world who have read every word of every Robert Caro biography
If a great chef took road kill and made tacos, would anyone be able to tell?
cashmere makes bad sock material
The more austere the restaurant, the better looking the women become
five-on-three power plays
indirect free kicks inside the box
VAR
the way the ball bites on natural grass
Kapital bandanas in gold and brown tones
La Brea Tar Pits bronze Smilodon sculpture
Smilodon iconography in the middle of Hancock Park
Ed Sullivan
small to mid-sized cities with their own TV stations that you see when you're driving into town
omelet bars in chain hotels that can make a really good egg-white omelet
portmanteau

the last person in America who referred to dark-skinned people as "colored"

Chinoiserie

the idea of genetically recreating a woolly mammoth

the revival of dialogue-driven entertainment led by cable television

David Byrne

the decline of goalkeeper caps

button-down shirts: twin dilemma of tuck-in or -out and number of buttons to leave open

parables that are not obvious to the casual reader

strawberry and mint

fresh guava juice

kangaroo leather soccer boots

Gregory Ain pencil renderings

Erich Mendelsohn

soccer federation logos with graphics of old-style balls

one-handed operating folding knives

Bi-compax 7733 chronographs

Wild discrepancy in price between branded and unbranded sunglasses

Hevea brasiliensis

coconut kefir made in small batches

surf semiotics

fruit- and nut-studded baked goods from local bakeries in college towns

Juki sewing machines

Dubya Green Density
Ear of the Devil
Kalura
fleshy trout back
Sindelar
Spiegler
Champion Reverse Weave
burlap
Ventile
hemp
box and twine company signs from the 1920s
painted advertising on buildings
clear seawater pooling over brown sugar sand
quince, grapefruit, and kumquat lemonade
kumquats picked off a tree
Fuyu persimmon granita
bronze sidewalk medallion of the Chanin Building
pattern of footpaths in Madison Square Park
east–west Central Park walking options
Pain Quotidien walnut loafs
High Line before it was a park
smelling salt water from a golf course
convergence of farm, beach, and road in Sagaponack
Lineage: Hakoah/Magnificent Magyars/Ajax/Barcelona
cafés that are exactly the right size and admit the proper amount of light for the space
barista culture

shrubs (fruit and vinegar syrups)
avocado toast at that place in Healdsburg
fasteners—snaps, hooks, latches, screws, grommets, clasps, buttons
caricatures
spotted hyenas
burrata with roasted artichokes
roasted chickpeas with cumin
Western meadowlark
Scrub Jay
Kingfisher
Common Raven
transitional sections of Harold in Italy
Great American Songbook second tier
peppermint breath spray
Oriosa chronographs
confluence of barbed wire and heavy cotton twill
orthogonal grapevine plantings on undulating hillsides
tawny color palette—tan, wheat, brown, umber—of the California Central Coast
fava bean hummus with harissa and pillowy pita
3.0 CSI
250 SL
190 SL
356 Carrera 1956 1500
Ferrari GT California
Tombow Mono 4Bs

Baby pineapples
Napping on Metro North trains

Eileen surprised herself by actually reading each entry, some printed, some in cursive. It was as airy as prose, succinct and meaningful. Old thoughts, new thoughts, clever thoughts, stale thoughts, raunchy thoughts. The expression "it's all good" came to mind. Her kids used it, a California thing. Maybe it was all good. Her practice was good, a steady stream of moles, warts, fissures, augmentations, precancer treatments (shockingly reimbursed, for the most part, by Medicare, even with her vastly inflated charges), and modifications of the eyelid, brow, and, of course, lips. So good, this dermatology thing, a real career coup, although not without grief from her father, who wanted to know why he paid for eight years of private schooling so his daughter could lance boils off people's asses.

That kind of moral relativism was so maudlin, silly. Old-school. Lancing boils was work, honest work, work that required training. The aesthetic life. LA was a vast aesthetic marketplace, an avatar for the world. And it wasn't alone. You had Venezuela, a mostly poor country, but with a 1 percent class that made it the world's per capita leader for plastic surgery. Argentina was focused on butt lifts, fighting the droop, the inevitable sinking of the stern. That wasn't her turf, and truth be told, she had a hard time following when Ben and Vartan, the plastic surgeons from suite 301, started talking about their patients. Behind the prettiness and the silhouettes of perfectly formed people, there was the sawing and manipulation of gristle and bone that for Eileen took her profession a step too far.

She heard Rufus scurrying away. He liked to hunt for stuff in the backyard. Not a pure terrier, but enough to like getting his nose dirty. She kept boxes of sanitary wipes around for his nose and paws. She went to her vanity, everything so pretty. There were orthogonal rows of cosmetics. She liked things working back to front, tall bottles of cleansers in the back, toners next, foundation-type stuff next, and the paints up front. She was a freak about putting things back, not understanding how some women just kept buying new cosmetics and making higher and higher piles, like miniature Fresh Kills waste dumps. It wasn't hoarding if you knew where everything was, if you had a system. She wasn't going for the makeup right this moment, but another collection. The great thing about being a doctor was that there were always meds around. The pills were so tiny and crispy and colorful. And fast acting. What else was there to do on a glorious day in Los Angeles?

- 23 -

It was one thing to be reading those little slogans all the time: "Do one thing every day that scares you," like the one on the Lululemon yoga bags that came with the tiny $120 pants that rolled into a fist-size dollop of Lycra that when you looked at it should cost about $4. It was another to act out on it. Laird Hamilton was another avatar of the scary life, certainly one who could walk the walk. Trevor was mesmerized by one particular video of Hamilton shooting the Malibu Pier. There is a lead-up that looks fake of the surfer paddling at high speed hovering near the crest of a giant wave, a feat that in itself seemed surreal until the massive brown trusses of the pier come into focus and I'll be damned but the maniac picks a line that goes *between* the columns. Trevor, who feared taking a skateboard down a slight embankment, was stunned not so much by the audacity of the stunt but by the desire to do it, what impelled a man to wake up in the morning, have some avocado toast (avocados and raw coconut apparently being Hamilton's fuel of choice), and decide this was the day to put in and cheat death.

He had the score with him. Phoebe went out to Fairway for something, and he had a chance to pull it out. He still was amazed that there was so little security, that a rare Mozart score, albeit one that was still being studied for its veracity, was left out in full view of the public—tethered to its display by nothing more than a bull clip and a plastic sheath—and he was still trembling almost two hours later as he leafed through the brittle pages, referring back over and over to the faceplate (was that what you called the first page; it seemed an apt word but was probably wrong) with Mozart's gossamer signature, even his name bearing an ethereal lilt. The notation was precise, varicolored, a stream of sepia, black and half tone, evincing the full range of shading that only a quill pen and ink could provide. For the most part, there was an elision between the note and its base—the line or double or triple line employed to group semi- and demi- and hemi-quavers together to provide visual logic to the performer for rapidly played notes.

The backstory, according to Henry Lovett, the Bard musicologist who wrote the notes displayed next to the score, with the pamphlet raised up on its own little Lucite stand, crisply rendered in twelve-point Avenir type (how lovingly these small printers attended to these things, seemingly thumbing their noses at the consensus that printed matter was dying), was that the titular "Pichelberger Octet" was part of the Walsegg commission, the rogue amateur musician being fond of playing a parlor game with his guests that involved transcribing other composers' works in his own hand and having them guess the true provenance of the work. Walsegg had commissioned the *Requiem* from Mozart, one of the great pieces of self-fulfilling artistic prophecy, the composer dying himself before its completion. The octet was likely inspired by the K. 612 aria, "Per questa bella mano," dated March 8, 1791, for the bass singer Franz Gerl and the principal bassist of Shikaneder's theater, Friedrich Pichelberger. The aria, structured as a true virtuoso duo, and the bass instrument having to deal with arpeggios, double stops, and rapid scales, was thought to have made Walsegg think that an unusual scoring of two of each of the violin family would make for great entertainment.

The veracity of the score was another matter. Lovett suggested that it would have immediately followed the aria, making it K. 613 and bumping everything later up one K. number. Unlike the *Requiem*, there were not different hands and ink colors marking the score. Mozart's telltale elisions were there, and the structure and bright D major tone were reminiscent of the K. 593 string quintet. The *Kleine Nachtmusik*, K. 525, simply doubled the bass and cello parts, but, according to Lovett, Pichelberger's facility with the K. 612 convinced Mozart to take on the octet for some cash, especially since his wife had grown increasingly fond of spa retreats. Lovett's dossier ran sixty pages or so and provided almost a measure-by-measure analysis of the score, from the writing to the thematic material to the scoring. They were selling copies for $20, with an honor box, and Trevor had dutifully put the $20 in before he purloined the score itself.

He had no idea what the score was worth, whether he could sell it—presumably there was a market in Europe, although for something so rare and unusual, it would be almost impossible to dispose of it. It was only time that was his friend. He could hide it and produce it after a reasonable period had elapsed—a year or so—and claim that he found it at a market or lying on a table at Starbucks or in the trash somewhere (God knows, crazier things had happened in New York over the years). He also was dying to tell his sister, but how could he? She would think he had lost it, or worse, would rat him out.

Trevor had a freshly sharpened Blackwing 602 in his pocket. He pulled off the metal cap and unfolded his Pallares pocket knife, stroking the white horn scales before opening the main blade, soothed by the little thwack, something so Swiss and calibrated that it made him flutter for a second, before he put the blade of the penknife to the firm cedar of the Blackwing—that was certainly one measure of a really good pencil, that the wood casing was up to the cut and thrust of a decent penknife. Why sharpen again? He was thinking about this as he shaped the point, making two long flat cuts on either side, and then rotating the pencil to access the sides of the point. This was the delicate part of the operation, where too much pressure or too deep a cut would snap it and make you start over. But using a knife expertly in the service of sharpening a pencil was more efficient and less wasteful than using a sharpener, a fact that was noted in the war years. The cedar was crisp and aromatic, and the pencil was formed and reformed. Trevor wanted to jet out of the apartment into the damp March air, a transitional time in New York, good walking weather because it wasn't hot. It was raining on and off, the sidewalks carrying that spring sheen, the light formed by shady grays, and the towers of the grande dame buildings, the Eldorado, the Majestic, the Beresford, asserting themselves even in the dun light.

In the moment of the crime, the seconds it took to snatch the score, he had a predictable surge of adrenaline, his hands moving at speed, but his brain slowing in the manner of a flip book. Ignatz the mouse came to mind. He felt absurdly clumsy but was deft, almost offhandedly sliding—yes, that was it, the score had slid—the stiff papers into the maw of his canvas mason bag. The sleepy guard hadn't bothered to check it, in fact the guard was scrolling down his phone—and why on earth was the guard downstairs when the score was upstairs? This was one of those rare New York moments, a breach in security, miscalculating that some weird guy, a sort of middle-aged drifter/grifter, would have the cojones to snag a titular Mozart score on a damp March day, risking that his bag would be searched on the way out by a certain Nestor Cruz, rent-a-cop from the esteemed Albrighton Security Services Group, or "ASSG," as it was abbreviated on the shoulder patch.

So few people had come to see the score, on the second floor of the townhouse on West Eighty-Sixth Street owned by Bard College, that the exhibit and the security around it were on autopilot, as if a Mozart score had been planted next to the Central Park bridle path. Trevor had not preplanned the action, simply coming in with Phoebe, who was a champ at ferreting out these little New York things, haunting the tiny-typeface capsule reviews in the *New Yorker* and *Time Out* and the *Voice*, and even *City Beat* and local neighborhood papers that had that strange admixture of bad feature writing and ads for naturopaths and chiropractors. "Bus stop literature" was what Trevor called it, detritus that served a function, always at the ready if you were bored so senseless that you would want to read an article about the local community board and its involvement with whatever contentious development was getting the locals all riled up.

That cultivating instinct that his father and sister possessed came to him with coffee. The hiss and whirr and clanking of the process, the bittersweet aroma, the palette of light and neutral and dark browns, were deep mysteries, not unlike trying to pry the weird shrunken brownstone at 245B West Eighty-Third Street from its current owner.

Trevor heard the old brass latch squeaking with Phoebe's key and the rustling of grocery bags. He scrambled to stack the brittle papers of the score—there were about twelve pages , he hadn't counted—and stuff them into his man bag before Phoebe had a chance to see them. She'd take him for what he was—insane, at least temporarily. And he knew that. That made it okay, that he was on top of it. No one could say that as a rule—as a person—he was insane or crazy, just that he was rolling with it. Roll with the changes. He hummed it. Good driving song: just rolling, getting it done.

"Give me a hand, please," Phoebe said, backing into the apartment, the romaine and celery peeking out over the top of the bag. "I hate late winter for produce. This is the time of the year I wish we lived in California. Lucky bastards are picking the *variety* of local blood oranges they want. Nothing local is here, unless you're counting some of the storage apples, and I can tell you, they are on their last legs."

"Yeah, the fruit is great. Except the apples. Try to get an Arlet or a Greening or a Golden Russet out there."

"Big deal, it's a one-month season. After late October, it's over here too."

"Ahh, but what a month." Trevor dipped into his mental register, checking his West Coast notes. He had roamed the farmers markets out there, loved the one in Leucadia in back of a homely little grammar school. The closer you got to the ocean, the crappier the schools looked, as if to say you can spend the day outdoors in the salt air, so any old Butler building will do. What he recalled about his grade school experience was being indoors for what seemed like an eternity. There was a vast stretch of learning—rote learning, not this loosey-goosey, wavy-gravy assortment of art and yoga and self-realization that passed for school these days, but kick-ass, boot-camp math and sentence structure and physical science. Sitting there like a sandbag until the teacher signaled for a short break, the cookies and milk procured by one of the lucky students who actually got to stretch their legs down the corridor to fetch an old-fashioned milk crate with small wax containers, one to a student along with two chocolate ice box cookies. Rarely, and it was an extraordinary day when it did happen, the usual white milk was replaced by miraculous brown containers of chocolate milk. The infusion of chocolate syrup was an elixir that had shocking transformative power for a nine-year-old suffocating in an airless classroom with asbestos flooring and ceiling tiles. Two ice box cookies and no more. A culture of, if not quite deprivation, then parsimony, just enough. Today, a vast crate of Costco cookies would be wheeled in, one box to a customer—why not have twenty or thirty?

Maybe it was this deprivation, or sense of it, that impelled him to grab the Mozart score. It wasn't like he was cheating death or the taxpayers or his children, just himself. The score called out to him. He was befriending it, in a way. The Bard team would miss it, but they had many more—hundreds, maybe thousands of others to deconstruct with the virulent brand of academic obscurantism reserved for musical scores. Allusions to cadence, tonality, rhythmic interplay. That aria, the K. 612 "Per questa bella mano," just a song, but with the double bass obligato. The double bass deemed essential for the piece, a sure tip of the hat that the octet was for real.

One thing Trevor noted was that the double basses were not doubled simply for an "oompah" effect but alternated between melody and supporting parts. Mozart had created an octet knitted together by four string duos. He was dying to hear the piece performed, but for now could only stare at the score. His interest further rationalized the fact that he stole it. Or did he? The score had beckoned him. No amount of staring at it on the pedestal could match being able to see it in the comfort of his—well, his sister's—apartment. He had not stolen it in reality but had made it his pet. He wanted to take it out of his pack and show Phoebe.

"What did you think of that exhibit?" Phoebe asked. "Bard does a nice little job with that building. I take it for granted. It's like you live here and walk down Eighty Sixth Street a couple of times a day, and there's the dry cleaner and the pet barber and the nouvelle donut place and the dentist. But then there are these amazing little cultural gems tucked in here and there."

"Yes—they're almost too perfect. It's like we're super curated and endowed and don't drag the grime from the bus stop on our oriental carpets. But it's funny, because then they have these sleepy-eyed rent-a-cops guarding some very cool and, I assume, very valuable treasures."

"Ya know, I was thinking about that. You've got a Mozart score—okay, it's still getting authenticated—and how much could that be worth? I mean, the output has been frozen for a very long time, maybe a hundred years, and then this shows up. And it's not even a fragment or one of those Süssmayr bastardized scores with different-colored inks and stuff, but a complete score, and an octet no less."

"Well, if it's Mozart, it's worth a crap load, I'll give you that. But you can go years without it being accepted as authentic. Like the dealers somewhere right in the neighborhood who bought that dictionary that they claim was annotated by Shakespeare. It's his handwriting, the timing is right, and the fact pattern lines up, but there are scholars on the other side. Climate change, O.J., vaccines—you can make the pro and anti case for anything. You did notice the scoring for the octet."

"I didn't really look. I assumed it was a double string quartet."

"Uh-uh. Two of each food group—*two* double basses."

"Wow. How many of those are around?"

"Exactly. This one is a rare bird." At that Trevor sensed that his choice of pronoun was strange, "this" connoting that the score was possibly close by, where "that" would have safely established that they had left it at Bard.

- 23 -

"You're sounding very proprietary about that score? Did you slip it in your bag?" Phoebe laughed and fired up a slender vape stick. It hissed as she sucked in and then passed it to her brother.

"If you insist," Trevor said. He took a long hit. It wasn't harsh, but sweet and toothy. In the circumstances it was, as they say, hitting the spot. "I haven't tried vaping all that much, but it's ok." Phoebe reached for it back, but Trevor pulled it to his lips again and pressed the little button, drew his breath in, and held it. Better. "I might have to borrow this from you." He wondered about the competing effects of Adderall and pot. Weird that he would mix them when he thought about it. It was later in the day and the Adderall would be ramping down, starting to leave his bloodstream. For a guy who played it fairly safe in college, just a tiny bit of coke here and there, as opposed to the nightly snorting some of his roommates did, he was embracing the lifestyle now. Midlife, needing cash, needing an exit strategy. It had been years since he looked at those pathetic analyses that the financial planners did, showing in vivid graphics—a sea of red—the vast gulf between your projected retirement savings and what you needed to sustain your current lifestyle. WTF, if there was ever a chart designed to make you want to commit ritual seppuku right then and there, that was the graphic. Triple or quadruple your income, save 20 percent off the top. College, car, house, insurance, needy nieces and nephews, sports fees, vacation, eating out, utilities that seemed to double every month. Even at Pomander Walk, a company that had a reputation as a big paying firm, you felt the squeeze. Westchester taxes were oppressive, his house starting at twelve grand when they bought it and edging up to $19,000 now. Basically, the first forty grand you earned went to pay your real estate taxes alone! His first job out of school he was making $26,000. He had to beat that now to pay one of his bills.

As opposed to when he was younger and might have felt his heart beating quicker and wondering whether the weed was laced with something—you never knew about the procurement chain, the dealers needing to extend their supply—and starting to squirm and even getting a little panicky, this was the new Trevor, embracing just enough recklessness, the VC guys would maybe have called it "minimum viable recklessness," and he let himself kick back and become just foggy and giddy enough to not give a shit.

"I did feel proprietary about that score. Like Mozart wrote it for me. I'm always the one looking for tweaks. Like with my alt-dot-pro sports teams. Remember those?"

"Vaguely. Not really. You always had lists in your notebooks. Lists and lists and lists."

"Yes. I always had better ideas for teams. Better cities, better colors, better nicknames. I had a palette, still remember the colors: oxidized green, service tan, brown/black, steel blue, and dust yellow. I thought those were all great colors for NFL teams. And then there was a whole list of colors I got from the VW Type Thirty-Four Karmann Ghia: cast yellow and chrome blue were the coolest."

"Trevor, sometimes you are just downright weird. Is this the pot talking now?"

"Phht. There is nothing to do with a day except to live it. Richard Wilbur."

"You mean live it strangely?"

"It's a question of cultivation. What attracted me to Paige, aside from the obvious. We were on a date at Fairway, where you just were, and she was groping the citrus fruit. It was October and kind of warm but drizzling, like today a little bit. The kind of day that you only get in New York where everything is grayed out, a tryout for winter. You know the kind of weather I'm talking about, where you keep ducking in and out of stores and coffee shops and let yourself eat that ridiculous coffee cake they used to sell only at that spot on Seventy-Ninth Street. Must be some kind of cult or cabal with Hungarian expats who left with the king's secret cake recipes. You've had that, I assume. Anyway, Paige is in Fairway with her glasses on, picking through the bins with the best of the old ladies. The Oro Blanco grapefruit had to be just so, heavy for their size with smooth skin. They could not yield too much to the touch.

Anyway, back to Mozart. The idea that there is a Mozart score with two double basses that intermittently carry the melody—can you imagine that, practically a singular occurrence in the entirety of important chamber music literature—and I'm not counting the composers who get three paragraphs in Grove's—it's miraculous? Not to be a hater, but this should be a massive story, not some more bullshit about Simon Cowell or Carrie Underwood or the Yankees or Beyoncé or all the other *Post* nonsense. It's fucking MOZART!!

- 24 -

"There's always a last thing. A last place. Last dinner. Last purchase. Last bit of lint extracted from one's belly button. Last pet of the dog. Last sweep of the kitchen. Last spider seen. Last drink. Last book read. Shit, that's a toughie." Cat was leaning forward, taut as usual in gray and black skull-patterned yoga pants. Luc noticed that in the last month or so she had transitioned from jeans to yoga pants.

"I'm stiff here," she said, pointing to her lower back and the top of her butt. From his point of view there was nothing there but infinity, a heart, an apple. He stared. "Looks fine to me."

"C'mon, I'm serious. Give me a hand." He held her hips and worked his thumbs into her sacrum. They were both quiet. He approached the job as a masseur would, all business, the power of visualization, true healing. There were moments like this, interstitial moments of intimacy that hovered briefly between the detritus. The bills were there, always. So too the rent. And the imperative of jobs, not a single job, but a few at a time. The bartending was just a weekend thing now, this side business that Cat got him into, bitters and concentrates and elixirs, had moved beyond Kickstarter (387 percent funded out of a $14,000 goal!) and into a steady stream of inquiries. Not just the bar crowd, but the chefs were asking for the rhubarb root, chinotto, and cinchona bark extracts. Siobhan Gerber, who wrote the Recondite Food column for the *Times*, wrote him up as the "upstate bartender with an air of mystery, decamping from points north with apothecary bottles of jewel-toned shrubs and potions that were showing up in creative menus below 23rd Street." Heady stuff for a punk bartender.

"Thank you, much better," Cat said, whirling around. "I have to head in for my shift. Gonna give notice today finally. I think we are going to go big with this thing. I already have some feelers out in LA. There's a whole culinary thing going on downtown. They're even more incestuous than New York. If one gal's doing it, everyone wants in."

"Star fuckers," Luc said.

"Ha! Jealous?"

"Not for long. I see us in the Hollywood Hills in a year. That Julius Shulman place, hovering over the twinkling lights."

"Easy, partner. I'll take a cute two-bedroom cottage in Silver Lake."

"Throggs Neck to Silver Lake. The story of one girl. Two bedrooms, though—where are the kids going to stay?"

"Outsource. I dunno. With their dads." She was kidding, of course, but saw that Luc started to roll his eyes. Not again with the substandard mom crap. She was kidding! "Uh—I saw that look. I love my kids. You know how I work by now I hope."

Feckless, Luc thought. He hadn't heard that word in... maybe he had never heard that word but knew what it meant. His uncle Rick the banker, who went to Bowdoin and read for fun, probably taught him that. His father was a Local 2 guy, always dirty and bone tired. Local 2 guys had it tough upstate in the seventies, the gas crisis, then a recession, and then wild high interest rates like the U.S. was some kind of Central American country or something. It occurred to him that Cat was feckless. If that was the case, he was an accomplice to fecklessness.

She had made something out of this idea of a shrub and bitter business. They moved it from the little corner they rented to the back of the same building owned by Red Hook Roasters, and almost to his disbelief, he was negotiating to open a tiny tasting room on Coffey Street. Kinderhook Tasting Room. He toyed with Samascott but wanted to run with the Dutch revival feeling. He tried to tell Cat that the speakeasy thing was played out and that no one wanted secret cocktails anymore; they just wanted to walk into a well-lit space and have the bartender be friendly and mix them something good. After COVID, folks just wanted to get out of the house. Didn't necessarily have to be something so over-the-top new—like the date, oolong, nutmeg, and leather (!) cocktail that he had the other night—but bracingly fresh. For one of the first times since they had known each other, she agreed, sort of, saying that light was a good thing only until a point with a cocktail space, and then you wanted the interior ambience to take over, not to compete with the outside.

There was endless demand for booze served in a small room with industrial stools and salvaged wood and iron furniture. At least that was the story Luc served up to his uncle Rick Nugent, who was happy to oblige, a closet alcoholic who wanted to be a regular somewhere. The bonuses from Pomander Walk just kept piling up, and as he explained to Luc, you can only look at so many fund statements.

"Boy, that is rich," Cat said when she found out that Luc's uncle was in to the tune of $350,000. "Weird too. For the last year I've had a guy breathing heavy into my ear about being his partner in a coffee bar, and then this thing happens so organically. I am going to say something that might make you cringe, so cover your ears—it's like we got accidentally pregnant."

An upstate stalwart with a '78 two-tone blue-and-white Ford pickup, a Lab, a one-bedroom ranch house with knotty pine paneling and a mottled yellow linoleum floor five miles outside New Paltz center, and an attitude toward city life that bordered on disdain, Luc had come around to seeing Brooklyn in a whole new light.

"It's weird. It's like there's a halo or a rainbow over the place now. There's a murmur. I've heard the stories about the squealing subway cars, dangerous shadows, homeless people dragging rags. The smells. Now it's like Pabst Blue Ribbon opened a theme park. So fun and orderly."

"Ya—and in Manhattan they have like picnic tables in Times Square now. Check this out." She shoved her iPad in front of him.

Kinderhook Tasting Room is a newcomer on Coffey Street, tantalizing the neighborhood with "shrubs"—acid- and fruit-based infusions—bitters, and concentrated extracts. Another light beam shot from the urban-ag movement, Kinderhook's owners, Luc Lattimore an upstate transplant from New Paltz, and Catherine Gjertsen, have departed slightly from the salvaged wood and patinated metal aesthetic that is beginning to become jejune in the neighborhood, by dabbling in West Coast architectural photography from the Case House era. The outside is unmarked except for three tiny apples etched in intaglio into the metal door—purportedly an Arlet, a Golden Russet, and a Ribston Pippin—held in esteem by the proprietors, who met upstate at the fabled Mohonk Mountain House, where Nugent still tends bar once a week. Red Hook–based architects Spy + Merkle, known for incorporating nature-

focused erotic elements into their retail designs, have created a bar from zinc and driftwood with that invites patrons to engage in a cheeky parlor game. A half wall to the right of the bar reveals the "shrubbery" where steel vats and beakers that look purloined from the HBO's The Knick are attended to by earnest and efficient craftspeople attending to varicolored herbs, berries, and aromatics.

But caprice and erotic whimsy are beside the point at KTR. The liberally tattooed mixologists roam the room wheeling vintage cocktail trolleys. Drinks are made table or bar side, and the process is the show: muddling, infusing, stirring, measuring, and shaking with the precision of chem lab assistants, servers deliver spectacular drinks. The revelation of the discrete components of a drink, particularly in the luminous Night Shiver— kaffir lime and blackberry shrub, jackfruit meringue, and bitter chocolate rum— fully justify the lofty prices. Small plates are also being served in conjunction with nearby friends Wythe Fish and Smoke. On a recent Thursday evening, the room held court to traders and the local maker community in convivial, cross-cultural banter, fueled by KT's coterie of cocktail impresarios.

Kinderhook Tasting Room; 235 Coffey Street; Mon–Thursday, 5 p.m.–midnight, Friday and Saturday until 2 a.m.; 718.333.6137. Cocktails $22–$38; small plates $9–$35

"Wow—I love it. What is it?"

"It's our aspirational capsule review. Everyone does it. You like?"

"Uh- huh—seems like it was written by your friend Trevor's wife, Paige whatshername."

"I can write, baby. And I read enough of her stuff that you just get into the style. I am so vibing this thing. I sort of feel like I love you, but maybe I'm confusing it with just being so fucking excited about this."

"Personally, I'd like to skip right to the opening-night part. Friends and family. What the hell is jackfruit by the way?"

"It's yummy. Like slimy sweet guava. You like slimy sweet, n'est-ce pas?"

"Jeezus. That is gross." He swatted at her ass, but she freewheeled away. "Ha ha—too slow."

He had to admit the fake review was good, not far from his concept, in fact very close, making him think his and Cat's conceptual alignment was a good omen. He was absorbed in the culture of his new venture. Upstate he was a bartender, pulling premade mixes from underneath the bar and dumping them into speed-rack glasses filled with bottom-shelf liquors. There was something sad about the low-end brands, the Walmart of the booze world, the turpentine-sour funk of the vodka and bad tequila and stale fruit juices that went into shitty cocktails that folks still drank upstate, even at a grande dame resort hotel like the Mohonk.

Up there he was the antihipster, joking with Monty, the other bartender, about the dudes most likely to order a Pabst Blue Ribbon, which the hotel hadn't stocked since probably 1967. He couldn't go full beard and Filson in Brooklyn like he did upstate, needing to change his look to nonironic, so he clipped his own hair with the number two attachment, and shaved cleanly except for short dagger-shaped sideburns. Cat liked to see his face, she said, and he realized that so did he. He had worn a beard for so long that he had forgotten about his upper lip and chin, which he thought was reasonably angular and honest looking.

He was transforming. Or was it that Cat Gjertsen was changing him, in that insidious way that some magazines coached: "Make your man this, make your man that." At the checkout line at the Super Nine in New Paltz, he'd pick up the titles and chuckle, looking at the Photoshopped cellulite—did Britney really gain 150 pounds? Maybe she did, how would he know? And the advice was the best. This was America, at least a big part of it, dispensing love advice in a store selling stuff—careful not to use the word "food"—that made you fat and angry. Reading through the articles, he saw that he could be one of those guys, a "source" known by first name only—Randy, Jason, or Jawaan. The fake sources always had a panracial vibe and eclectic career mix—a finance guy, a guitar maker, and a vet assistant. He wanted to be the musician.

"Good luck with Evan," Cat said, bouncing toward the bus.

- 25 -

"Looks like about twenty nautical miles," said Hugo, studying a U.S. Coast Guard map that came from God knows where, but it was an original foldout map like the kind that was virtually left for dead, along with vinyl and the slide rule and other glorious artifacts making an analog comeback. That was part of the reason he was such a champion of things like pencils and and mechanical watches, things that evoked slowness and reflection.

Trevor hadn't checked—hadn't cared about how long the boat ride was from Ventura Harbor to Santa Cruz Island. After taking the score, he thought getting out of town was the thing to do, although there was scarcely a murmur, let alone any news item about a purloined titular Mozart score from the Bard Gallery on West Eighty-Sixth Street. He had sat in his boxer shorts—technically boxer briefs—in front of Phoebe's new giant flat screen—over five feet diagonally—and surfed the news channels.

Nothing. Lots about rental e-bikes in the city and another coyote that had wandered down the West Side Highway and made its way into Central Park, shocking the early morning dog walkers. But nothing, not even on WNYE, which loved that kind of stuff. He even had the temerity to walk back into the space to the scene of the crime. That's what Hitchcock would have had Jimmy Stewart do. So obvious, so nefarious. There had to be security cameras. But then he remembered the Internet was down at Phoebe's place the day they went to the museum. He had grabbed the score during an outage, pure luck.

Back in California, Trevor had an idea to take Hugo on an outing. Something nature based. They had never connected through nature, an émigré urbanite still traumatized by water after crossing the ocean as a toddler. Hugo connected the water with wind, cold, diesel exhaust, nausea, disorientation. The gulls darting in and out, the black-blue-gray monotony. The lack of a reference point. No soccer.

"C'mon, Dad. I think we both could use this. A novelty. It's a short ride." Trevor was expecting pushback, or more likely a flat out no.

"Very good. Very good. I would like that. When can vee go?" *Vee.* The accent still clinging.

Hugo was there, intrepid in his overdesigned windcheater and heavy fisherman's sweater that coiled around his neck to the bottom of his feathery beard, something new in his old age. He looked like he was going to Antarctica, not to one of the Channel Islands off the coast of Southern California in October. Trevor had opted to go the other way—shorts and a Patagonia fleece top stowed in his bag with lunch and the Mozart score.

Just thinking about the score made him shiver. It was too hot, too soon to pitch to some dealer in Europe, if he was desperate enough to go that route. Crazy thing was that he was quasi-homeless and the thing was becoming an albatross. He couldn't leave it at the Archstone—or was it the Avalon?—and certainly didn't want to bring it to Tarrytown. He thought about a safety deposit box but had seen too many episodes where the feds come in behind the branch manager for the big bust. It hadn't made the news, but any dealer would connect the dots soon enough. He thought about ditching it somewhere and coming back for it. Wouldn't it be funny if he left the score on Santa Cruz Island? Safe except for the island foxes, little buggers foraging at the campsite. He double wrapped the score—fragile, papery wafers, and put it in an archival plastic sheath. In a year he'd call his friend Rolf in Berlin. Give him a cut—couldn't trace it to a German guy who had never been in New York. That's where the dealers were. A plan, at last a plan.

Hugo also had a bag, strangely large for a day trip. As he boarded, the bag was so heavy that he swayed back and forth with the motion of the dock. Probably had soup in a steel thermos and a couple of hardback books from the Studio City public library. Trevor had packed enough lunch for both of them, but Hugo wanted his own stuff. They were on the top deck and it was getting warm, the sun becoming direct versus diffused. The port had a mix of real fishing trawlers, densely packed with netting and buoys crusted with shells and reeking of ocean funk. Bits of Steinbeck lived in the old California ports still.

"Piece of cake, I think," Hugo said.

"What?"

"This crossing. I brought ginger candies—you should have one now. But I don't get seasick."

"How would you know? You haven't been on a boat in eighty years."

"How do you know? I've been on a boat."

"When?"

"On the set, that's when."

"I mean a boat in the water."

"Now you're getting picky."

Trevor popped two ginger candies into his mouth, maybe one too many, the thick paste clinging to the inside of his teeth like mortar and making him worried that his chewing would loosen a molar or two. He didn't have dental insurance (why wasn't your mouth considered part of your body?), and a dental emergency would be the last thing he needed away from home. Home, though, was a moving target these days, the Archstone or Avalon really just a motel, and an increasingly unaffordable one at that. He was burning through the last of his JetBlue miles going back and forth to California; this was the last trip before he'd have to come out of pocket, and the last bits of his Pomander Walk severance were vanishing like popcorn in a gale.

The boat passed the buoy at starboard—red right returning—and sea lions barked at the ship. They were funny creatures, somewhat doglike, with old-man temperaments. Sharks could make you crabby, Trevor supposed. The ship was a flat-bottom rig, steel hulled, with impressive I beams delineating the passenger areas. The captain sat high in the center surrounded by a Loran system and flatscreen monitors. You could trace your journey in real time, the depth of the ocean a touchscreen away. Trevor fixed on the distant point of Anacapa Island, the smallest of the five islands in the Channel Islands National Park. In his experience, he didn't get seasick if he could fix on a distant point.

Hugo continued to look at the map, and Trevor worried his dad would get sick. "Why don't you look up from that for a couple of minutes, get your bearings a bit?" Hugo looked up, surveyed the ocean, and looked down again. "I am feeling fine," he said.

Trevor stood up, went down the steel ladder to the lower deck, thought about a snack, and decided to keep his stomach empty. Didn't want to risk a Technicolor heave if it came to that. The bounce of the boat picked up, and they were hitting swells. The sky was clear, and it was still a bit hot. Leaning over, he could catch the sea spray, spreading clear BBs across the gray heave of the water. The ocean here was chthonic gray, opaque and dense. Anacapa was on the left, Santa Cruz straight ahead. The motor seemed a bit undersized for the boat, more puttering than cruising.

"Did we stop?" Trevor asked.

"Yes. Again," Hugo said. "We are getting our money's worth on this ride." Trevor saw that his father was taking the chop like a champ, nonplussed, even reading his yellow *Financial Times* like he was on the 5:46 to Westport. Trevor thought that the vestibular system was supposed to get worse with age—his certainly had, to the point where he wouldn't ride the silly Dragon Coaster at Playland with the kids—but Hugo seemed immune.

"Poor chap," Hugo said, seeing the bulk of a fat seasick man who had stripped down to his red T-shirt and in a desperate play for relief had soaked himself with bottled water. He was on his side, the heft of his hairy belly unsheathed from the T-shirt and torqued over the bench, his spit-soaked mustache dripping. "Ecch," Trevor said, starting to struggle himself with his equilibrium. "Ginger candy, Dad?"

"No, thank you very much," Hugo said, not looking up from his newspaper.

The boat finally bumped into the small dock at Scorpion Anchorage. On dry land Trevor's head felt like it was still sloshing back and forth. There was a mandatory ranger's lecture about Santa Cruz Island: no services, no food, one boat back in the afternoon. Carry in—carry out. Don't go near the cliffs. Nothing about burying newly discovered chamber music masterworks. Trevor checked his pack, made sure the food and water were far from the envelope that contained the score. He had been checking it over and over on the boat, relieved that Hugo was absorbed. He couldn't help checking and double checking the package, assuring himself that it wasn't getting wet, wondering how much the thing was worth, if anything. Funny thing was that the further away he took the score from a huge city, the more its value seemed to diminish. In New York it was a museum object, in LA a little less desirable, then to Ventura, where it started to feel like a curiosity, nothing more. He remembered the cartoon show *Top Cat* from his childhood, based on the Bowery Boys. Always a caper with a crappy ending. Hugo liked to watch the show with him once in a while, chuckling at the funny mid-Atlantic accent that Top Cat, the boss, affected. Here, on a windswept island, uninhabited save for a legacy farmhouse inhabited by an older couple who had let a massive fig tree fruit into oblivion, the score seemed to be nothing more than faded ink on fragile paper.

"Do you feel up to walking a bit?" Trevor asked. Half of the passengers, the older ones and the ones with children in the group, decamped for the placid section of beach framed by the pier and a cliff so steep that it darkened the shore, even with the sun being practically straight overhead. Two glossy purple-hued ravens dove and flipped over, flying upside down, the only time Trevor had ever seen a bird perform that maneuver. Ravens were a western bird, only crows back east. Very similar but very different creatures. The ravens he could now see were a lot bigger—chestier—with a much larger head, almost pentagonal in shape, and a far more massive bill. They also had a bit of ruffling at the tip of the head. As athletes, there was no comparison. The ravens were phenomenal acrobats and, unlike crows, were able to soar. Crows just flapped everywhere. One of the ravens landed on a picnic table where people had left their backpacks and started to pry around, pecking the edge. To Trevor's amazement, it took the zipper in its beak and started to yank it. It couldn't quite get enough leverage, but it was a damn good try.

The two of them crept along the gravel path leading to the trailhead. Having gotten this far, Trevor, with his spinning head and sea legs, was nauseous and disoriented. What seemed like a good idea on dry land in Studio City, with the temperature at an Astrodome-like seventy-two and cotton candy clouds, was now sweaty reality. After a relatively balmy start in Ventura Harbor, the day was blustery and borderline cold on Santa Cruz Island, and they were still at sea level and buffeted by the cliffs. Up higher, the winds were sure to pick up to nearly gale force. Hiking was always underestimated. It was rarely walking. You were usually going up or down, and there were obstacles. The trailheads left poor options for a nonagenarian: steep climbs up railroad trestles. But Hugo was still up to it. In the sixties he had started doing a fitness routine with the a Romanian named Florin. It was equal parts yoga, Pilates, and boot camp. Florin was a stunt man with a mop top of whitish-yellow curls who did a couple of films with Hugo, and he had spent time in a German holding camp, where he developed the routine. Hugo had done it five times a week, fifty-two weeks a year, for thirty years. One hundred yards in, Trevor was the one panting. And he was in shirtsleeves, while his old man was still wearing the fisherman's sweater and Gore-Tex parka. Trevor had taken an Adderall, but a lower-dose one than usual. Thank God they came in different colors. He was sweaty and his heart was beating pretty quickly. He tried to subtly slow the pace, but Hugo kept going along at a fast clip. In fact he was starting to speed up—going uphill!

"Geez, Dad, you're looking pretty fit."

"I'm always fit. Ven have you known me not to be fit?"

"I suppose you're right. I'm just impressed, that's all. You look like you're going to cover the whole thirty-five miles of this island. "

"I could if it wasn't so windy." The wind came in short powerful gusts, kicking up loose dirt that was somewhere between sand and gravel—grandel, maybe. Trevor had on a pair of trendy shades that he'd paid an ungodly sum for—$350 or so—at a boutique in Costa Mesa. They were almost round and did not provide enough cover when the wind whipped the grandel around. Again, Hugo was prepared, with glasses that had leather cups on the sides. "Good move with those explorer glasses, Dad. Wish I had a pair of those."

"Vee can trade. It's not so bad for me."

"Thanks—that's really great of you, but you'll see, the grit will get into your eyes."

From the perspective of the ravens—who clearly were surveying the island visitors as much as, if not more than, the other way around, the two were an odd pair, one dressed for a day at the beach, the other for a polar cruise. The older of the two was moving at a quick, propulsive clip, while the younger one hung back, feeling behind him for his pack every minute or so like he was a suicide bomber. They got to the top of the cliff. Trevor saw dun- and buff-colored grasses, tan dirt, licorice seas. It was like the Hebrides, he imagined. Who'da thunk it so close to the 101 highway. Ranchers liked the island because who would steal a sheep out here?

There was no real cover, just low brush here and there. Hugo seemed preternaturally alert, his moist eyes flexing behind his explorer's glasses. He was also an innate observer, the director's keen eye parsing the scene for flaws and inconsistencies. If Trevor got the notion to bury the score somewhere, he'd have to excuse himself to pee. It was a strange impulse to begin with, taking a music score out to an island. It was a half gesture, a partial admission of guilt.

It was hot without wind, cold with it. Gulls dipped in and out of the coves. One sailboat was about, gliding despite the chop of the whitecaps. Who was on this boat? It was so solitary, it made Trevor wonder: a couple? A salty ex-navy guy? A party boat? It was not a day for the casual sailor. The serenity of a boat was a luxury. Time itself was the great luxury nowadays, replacing money. Drifting on a sailboat in the shadow of the Channel Islands on a weekday was something Trevor could not quite fathom, an extrusion of time and place that was practically obscene.

"Lunch, Dad?" Trevor shouted into the gust, the wind making it hard to hear for both men.

"What? Vat? Vat did you say?" Hugo was shouting into the air.

Trevor got closer: "ARE YOU HUNGRY?"

"Why not? Sure, I could eat something." The question on question. The fractured syntax. A foreigner still. Or perhaps the foreigner was returning in old age, an arc.

Trevor led them to a little detour off the path where there was a spray of larger rocks. Hugo sat down on the ground and finally unzipped his parka a bit.

"Aren't you hot in that thing? And that sweater? Looks like you could cook a pizza inside there."

"Ha! Wait 'til you get old like me. It is always cold!"

A gust came up that was so strong it dragged Trevor's pack a foot or so along the gravel. For a moment he had forgotten the treasure inside, the goods. He yanked back the pack. It tumbled over again. He anchored it with his foot. Hugo was clutching his travel bag like it contained all his worldly possessions. The wide-eyed toddler on the boat in a sea of weary adults. Trevor unzipped the pack and pulled out some snacks. There was a wedge of stinky cheese that tasted like morels and pepper that went amazingly well with those cranberry- and date-studded crackers that, while not exactly gluten-free, were promised to have been processed in a nongluten environment. Supermarket pastoral was a great tool, providing backstory on every morsel of food that you consumed. It had gotten to the point where Trevor was leery of buying anything without provenance. And it had to be written by the producers and farmers themselves, not outsourced to Korea. He could sniff out the crappy prose and fractured syntax.

There were almonds, of course, oily Marconas flecked with kosher salt and rosemary, and simple organic raw ones. The nonorganic ones were surely sprayed into oblivion; they all used too much water. What else? Yes, the grass-fed beef sticks, expensive at $3.95 per stick, equating to a whopping $60 bucks or so per pound! Note to self: grass-fed specialty beef products must be very profitable. Must look into that if the coffee dream fizzles. There was the bag of baby carrots, purple and gold and orange. Very fetching, very fibrous. Crackers with grains and no gluten. Those delicious ones from Costco that were so popular the store had taken to stacking them near the register. They must be selling a hundred thousand boxes per week per store. And for dessert there were fig cookies and dates.

Figs and dates. Nobody liked these fruits, or professed to like them. You could ask a hundred people and one or two would say they liked figs or dates. But they were kind of everywhere, in cookies, jams, and packaged dried and fresh, so Trevor concluded there were legions who secretly liked figs and dates and for strange reasons were reluctant to admit it publicly.

Trevor pulled out the cheese and wrestled his Pallares folding knife from his jeans pocket. Needing a surface to slice on, Trevor carefully pulled out the score in its plastic sheath. Putting a bandana between the envelope and the cheese, he tried to make a clean pass, but the cheese stuck to the surface of the knife, so he had to make two passes. He cut a couple of hunks and put them on crackers for Hugo. Again, his bag blew away a foot or two. He reached out with his foot and hooked it into the strap of his pack. He fished out the Marconas, little beige ovals in a sealed store package. He held the almonds in his left hand, and he plunged the big blade of the knife in with enough force that it went through the bag and pierced his left hand between his thumb and forefinger. It was so clean that for a moment there was no blood, but the knife went in deep enough to hit a nerve.

"Shit. Goddamn it!"

Hugo looked up and asked if Trevor was okay. Trevor was staring at the point of impact, waiting for the blood or some signifier that was commensurate with the piercing pain. What he hadn't expected was even more painful: he had dropped the sheath in pain, and it blew partly down the slope, caught an updraft, and flew about thirty feet away. The sequence was balletic and unfurled in slow motion, the blue-green plastic cartwheeling and tumbling like the ravens. Trevor could see it nestled against a clump of island grasses, in reach no doubt, but he had to get a better look.

Hugo asked about getting to the ranger station. Maybe they could stitch it. "It's not that, it's my stuff. The envelope! I have to get it." Trevor hustled over to where he had a better view of the bramble and the envelope. It was stuck there in full view, the blue-green plastic of the envelope he bought at Staples looking like an egregious interloper among the baked-out shades of dun on the cliff. It was very close, but the downward curve of the cliff was an issue. Between the slippery dirt and the shape of the cliff, there was no way to retrieve the score without risking a tumble into Santa Barbara Channel.

He got onto his belly and started to wriggle down, testing to see if there was any purchase on the dirt, if he could inch his way down. It was only thirty feet or so, the length of a decent size living room. He could do this.

"Vat are you doing?" Hugo was baffled. "You are going to kill yourself."

"Shit." Trevor hadn't heard his father but was shocked at how easily he slid. No way he could get near enough to grab it. There were a couple of bushes there, but they had the structure of a tumbleweed. He was aware of being part of a still-life tableau, literally feeling as if he still had life as well as in the artistic sense of arranged objects, in this case with a jarring man-made interloper among the natural landscape. Dalí came to mind, a surreal tableau, a man with outstretched hand grasping at air, a mysterious object shape-shifting into the atmosphere. Hugo was watching. He had removed his explorer's shades with the cups that had shielded him so well from the elements. The wind brought on tearing and a rheumy effect, the droplets falling on his windburned skin, which flamed a vivid red-olive in the sun.

"Please, Trevor, I think you should let it be. Whatever it is, it can't be that important. Papers, that's all." Trevor stared at the folder. So close. Truly irreplaceable. Maybe Bard had scanned it for posterity. Hopefully they did. He could not have it on his head that he was reckless and stupid enough to use an original Mozart score as a cheese platter in the windiest part of California. On a cliff. My God. Being a corporate fuckup was one thing. Drowning Mozart was another.

The intervals of wind were getting more frequent and powerful, small cyclones that whipped dirt and debris in crazy circles. The power seemed to come from underneath, from the dirt itself. Trevor sat back down, nothing to do, the array of lunch tidbits nestled in the lip of his pack, which he had secured with a rock. Hugo came over and ate some more. Very relaxed. Trevor wondered what was in that big duffel he was toting around.

"You planning to camp here, Dad?"

"Not a chance. Never camped a day in my life. Sleeping outside is for emergencies."

"But why did you bring such a big bag? Looks like you're running away from home. You're only about fifty miles away."

"I like to carry things, that's all. A book or two. Papers. Stuff. By the way, I guess there are no bathrooms here."

"Down at the campground, wherever that is. I think you're okay to find one in nature."

"Excuse me then." Hugo ambled off, with his bag, into what was essentially a forest of reedy grass, six feet high.

Trevor was stunned by the postcard beauty, the single sailboat looking like a tiny toy lingering just offshore. It must have anchored. What were they doing on that boat? Unfathomable leisure. Maybe the score would release and fly toward them, and they would retrieve it and bring it to the attention of a local music teacher who would run it up the flagpole until it found its way to Gustavo Dudamel's office in Disney Hall—and what an office that must be—who would connect the dots and get it back to the little Bard adjunct on West Eighty-Sixth Street where it began its journey. It was a preposterous long shot, but stranger things had happened. There was also the possibility that it would float back to the shore in Ventura and get picked up by a local. Lots of characters there, mowing the sand with their metal detectors for coins and lost engagement rings. They'd probably pawn it, and the broker would figure it out—now those were guys who could handle a hot music score!

"So, wish them well, your papers," Hugo said. "I better start heading back. I'll be slower going back than coming here."

Trevor crept to the edge one more time. Maybe there was something he missed, some angle, or a long branch that he could use as an aid to grab it. Nothing. Same steep curve heading into the rocky cove. Same squirrelly dirt. He pulled a pale blue bandana out of his pocket and fashioned it into a triangle, knotting it behind his head like a pirate. It was time to give up the ghost.

* * *

The ride back was less dramatic since the ferry was going with the current. It was a little choppy, but the boat kept up a steady rhythm. The dolphins were out, chasing and leaping and smiling. Hugo was standing and holding the steel rail. He finally shed his heavy parka but still looked nautical in his ropey sweater.

"What's next for you?" he asked Trevor, who had been catching the breeze, finally shedding the sea leg torpor and queasiness that had gripped him for most of the day.

"I don't know, Dad. I just don't know. I'm thinking about moving to California, but the kids are in New York, and Paige doesn't seem interested in moving out here. I can't take much more of this life as a vagabond, that's for sure."

"And that idea. The coffee idea. What ever happened to that?"

"Dead. The Satmars bought the building. That's what the broker told me, anyway. Not sure that I trust that guy though. Who knows? But with my situation, no cash flow and all, running here and there, it's just too crazy. You need to be—ahem—grounded to get something like that going. No distractions."

"Well, that's a pity." Hugo pulled out a folded piece of paper. He passed it to Trevor. "Here is a little memento of our trip."

Trevor opened it up. It had two numbers:
34.04842810874061
119.57410767674446

He didn't get it at first. Weird, long numbers. Was Hugo slipping further, randomly dispensing numbers without any logic or connection to anything? It finally set in that these were coordinates, latitude and longitude. It was Hugo's way of remembering the day.

"Thanks, Dad. It was a really nice day. Little bit of a bumpy start, but it was a long time coming, spending time with you like this."

Hugo smiled. "You are a good son and I love you. Take the paper back with you to the island. There is something there...maybe it's valuable. Sometimes it pays to be an emigre. People give you things. But then everything you have is a rental, like it was for the people who gave it to you in the first place. Maybe not your family, that's a different story. And without good coffee, what is the point?"

Made in the USA
Middletown, DE
26 February 2022